DANGEROUS
Love

Just then, the first limousine pulled up, and with little fanfare, Mary Grace Whittaker Bartlow exited the car, looking like a replica of Jacqueline Kennedy in her widow's attire. She paused only momentarily while her daughter and son stepped out of the limousine after her. They proceeded quickly toward the church.

Moments later, a Lincoln Town Car drove up, bearing Jack Billingsly, Richard Bartlow's attorney, and Alicia Carrel, the woman, according to the press, for whom Richard had left his family. Alicia was forty-six, tall, slender, with huge brown eyes. She had been a nobody from the south side of Chicago until she met Richard Bartlow. Her affair with him had made them both nationally famous.

Finally a taxi stopped at the curb, and out stepped Michelle Windsong, the twenty-five-year-old who reportedly had caused Richard Bartlow's heart attack after strenuous lovemaking. The crowd of reporters hushed as they got their first look at Michelle. She wore a simple white dress that skimmed the delicate curves of her slender body, and there was not a smidgen of makeup on her face.

Michelle was the last of the women who had come to mourn the death of Richard Bartlow.

CATHERINE LANIGAN

DANGEROUS Love

MIRA BOOKS

MIRA

ISBN 1-55166-163-2

DANGEROUS LOVE

Copyright © 1996 by Catherine Lanigan.

Printed in U.S.A.

It takes a band of angels to create a miracle.
My love and thanks to: Charlotte Breeze,
Kimberley Cameron, Dianne Moggy,
Amy Moore and Ilana Glaun,
the best miracle workers this side of heaven.

PROLOGUE

Chicago, Illinois
November 2, 1994

With Minicamera in hand, Barry Allen, a twenty-two-year-old recent graduate of Loyola University, stood on the steps of Our Lady of Sorrows Church waiting for what he knew would be the biggest break in his three-month-old news-reporting career. He was covering the Richard Bartlow funeral.

Barry had arrived at the church at three in the morning to stake his claim for this prime camera position. It had been announced yesterday at an earlier press conference given by Bartlow's attorney, Jack Billingsly, that no cameras would be allowed in the church. Fortunately, Barry was also a sketch artist, and after covering a courtroom trial last month, he'd proven his prowess at getting emotions on paper.

Barry worked for a fledgling cable television company, but he already had his sights set on a reporting job at WBBM-TV, the local CBS affiliate. As the hours clicked by and dawn approached, Barry was glad he'd come early. The press was out in droves for this one. He saw the stringers for *People*, *USA Today* and *US* magazine. He saw Pete O'Malley, a writer for *Chicago* magazine. The big boys were there from the *Chicago Tribune* and the *Chicago Sun Times*. Television vans from every news station in the city pulled next to the curb. Elke Sanderborg, the news reporter for Barry's rival cable station, "Chicago News", walked right up to him.

"How's it goin', Barry?" she asked sweetly, tossing her straight jet-black-dyed hair over her shoulder. Elke had made headlines herself by suing her network for discriminating against her because she was a white female instead of Hispanic. She'd dyed her naturally snow white hair black to prove the point. The suit was dropped, but Elke kept the hair so that no one would forget.

Barry knew better than to give anything away to Elke. She was a spider. She lured the toughest interviews into her web and trapped them, making them squirm and getting her story. Barry had seen her in action when he'd worked at her station as an intern while still in college. She had liked him then. He was just another harmless college slug.

"Don't even think of taking my spot, Elke," he warned.

"But, sugar, all the good spots are gone." She peered over the shoulders of taller, male journalists. She probably couldn't even see the street from her vantage point.

Barry frowned. "Too bad. Next time, get here at three like I did."

Elke dropped her saccharine smile. "Point taken." She looked around at the ever-growing crowd of journalists. "Isn't this unfucking believable? Just goes to show you that everybody loves an asshole once he's dead."

Barry clucked his tongue. "Richard Bartlow is a saint. Haven't you heard?"

"Oh, the *Time* piece," she said, referring to the feature article *Time* magazine had printed that week, with Richard Bartlow's face on the cover.

The morning sun rose brilliantly over the lake. Elke pulled out her Chanel sunglasses and put them on. "I saw it. So what? So the guy wanted to build houses in Arizona and give them away. Suddenly, everybody is acting like he's the Second Coming. Sorry, once an asshole, always an asshole."

Though Barry knew little of Richard Bartlow and had never met the man, he felt he should come to his defense on the principle of gender affiliation. "There are over three hundred of those houses, Elke. He proved that people don't have to live like rats. And—" Barry took a deep breath of the crisp morning air "—he single-handedly forced the entire home-building industry to take a long hard look at itself. Not to mention a few commissioners, a few senators . . ."

"Greed and graft will always be with us, Barry."

"I, for one, would stand in line all night to buy a hundred-thousand-dollar house for fifty grand." He bowed theatrically to her. "You, of course, do not work for peon wages. How *is* the high-rise condo life?" he taunted her.

"Peachy." She knitted her eyebrows, pretending to avoid the sun. Elke seldom passed along personal information. Especially facts about where she lived. Barry enjoyed watching her squirm as she realized her private life wasn't all that private.

"So, is that the tack you're taking with this story, Elke? Richard Bartlow, asshole, left his wife and two children for another woman. Nice Catholic girl, Mary Grace Whittaker, loses her home, has to ask her parents for help. Bartlow swindles his investors out of twenty million dollars trying to save his own ass in a real estate deal back in 1987. He ditches his girlfriend and goes to Sedona when this city gets too hot for him. Then he has a heart attack while making it with his twenty-five-year-old live-in girlfriend. To give this circus all three rings, Bartlow's will includes his ex-wife, his ex-live-in lover and his current live-in."

Elke clapped her gloved hands together lightly. "My, my, Barry, but you do surprise me. You *have* done your homework. Let me ask you, do you think that's true about the girl in Arizona?"

Barry shrugged his shoulders. "I only know what I read in the papers."

Elke wagged her finger at him. "Shame on you, Barry. Haven't you learned not to believe everything you read?"

"Don't tell me you're after the truth? I thought you wanted a story." His smile was cocky. "There's a difference."

Elke glared at him through her designer sunglasses. "I've been out here about fifteen years longer than you have, kid. I only call them the way I see them."

"So, how do you know Richard Bartlow is an asshole?"

"Personal experience," she replied as the sound of the Chicago Police motorcycle sirens announced that the motorcade was not far away. "I wasn't as lucky as you to get a job working on a cable station when I graduated from college. My first job was for Richard Bartlow."

Barry could not hide his genuine surprise. "No shit?"

"It lasted all of two months. I made a mistake on some reports I was typing. He personally trounced to my desk, called me a stupid bitch and told me I was fired."

"Jesus, Elke."

"It took me months to find another job. I had no money. Got evicted and had to live with a very scuzzy ex-boyfriend. But my next job was with the network. I haven't been fired since. And I never will."

Barry was in awe. No wonder she'd fought so hard to keep her job when the station had tried to oust her.

Just then, the first limousine pulled up, and with little fanfare, Mary Grace Whittaker Bartlow exited the car looking like a replica of Jacqueline Kennedy in her widow's attire. Heavily veiled and dressed in a black designer wool suit, black gloves and black shoes, she paused only momentarily while her daughter, twenty-five-year-old Penelope, stepped out of the limousine.

Penelope wore a black spandex minidress, black spike heels and a huge silver crucifix hanging irreverently down her nearly backless dress. She twirled a long fringed black silk shawl around her shoulders, pretending to ward off the morning chill. Penelope smiled for the cameras, paying special attention to the male cameramen. She ogled them and crouched in sexy poses while glancing out of the corner of her eye to see if her mother was watching.

"Hey, Penny!" Barry shouted to her. "Over here!"

Penelope turned toward the sound of his voice.

Barry smiled winningly at her. Sure enough, Penelope gave him a seductive smile just as he knew she would. When he pointed his Minicam at her, she bent down and gave him a deep-cleavage shot. Barry laughed as he watched her gyrate for his camera. He could tell she knew she looked hot. Very, very hot.

Barry smiled. "Thanks!"

"You're real cute, honey! What's your name?" she shouted back at him.

Just then, Lawrence Bartlow, the twenty-one-year-old only son of Richard Bartlow, walked up behind his sister and grabbed her elbow.

Lawrence was wearing a black off-the-rack suit, purple and black Nikes and sunglasses. Barry thought he looked like a pimp. The most startling thing about Lawrence, though, was that he'd shaved his head when he'd heard his father had died—at least that was what the rumor mill reported. Barry wondered if he'd pierced his ear himself and if it was his mother's or sister's dainty crucifix earring he wore.

"C'mon," Lawrence whispered to his sister. "Let's go."

Penelope ignored her brother, her eyes locked on Barry.

Barry frowned as he watched Lawrence's anger broil to a raging heat, but he kept his camera leveled on Penelope. Lawrence grabbed Penelope's arm forcefully. She winced and yanked her arm out of his grasp, and his nails scraped her skin. The camera missed none of the encounter.

Barry didn't know how he'd use this footage, but this stuff was too good to miss.

Penelope turned her attention back to Barry. "I asked you once real nice. Now, are you gonna tell me your name or what?"

"It's Barry!" he called out to her.

Lawrence shoved his balled fists into his pants' pockets. Barry could tell Lawrence wanted to hit somebody. Badly. All he needed was an excuse. As Lawrence's eyes darted over the crowd, Barry could see he was looking for someone to oblige him.

Minicams whirled and flashbulbs exploded in Mary Grace's face, but she held her head high as she walked past the journalists and photographers. For a moment, the press was content just to take pictures.

Mary Grace was only three steps from the church door when the journalists began asking questions. Even to Barry, they sounded like a gaggle of geese.

"When did you learn about your ex-husband's death?"

"How did you feel when you learned he died when he was in bed with his girlfriend?"

"Is there any indication there is enough money in his estate to pay back his investors of seven years ago?"

"How did you feel when you heard that Alicia Carrel was going to be here today, Mrs. Bartlow?"

Barry watched as she kept her ladylike cool. With every poised tilt of her chin, every turn of her head, she made certain each person there knew she was no low-life river rat. She was Mary Grace Whittaker. Her grandfather had built this church as a donation to the parish. Her ancestors went back to the Van Pattens in New York. The blood in her veins was blue, not red. Barry knew from his research that Mary Grace would always act the lady. He was glad she didn't let him down.

Looking like a black bouquet, a collection of microphones were shoved in Mary Grace's face. She gave the reporters all a look of disdain as they asked typical inane questions. Even Barry sometimes shook his head at the levels to which his job forced him to sink.

Mary Grace's smile was perfectly sweet as her eyes flashed them all a "go to hell" look. Then she pushed her way past the throng of reporters into the church.

Barry returned his attention to Penelope who was visibly angry that her mother had stolen the limelight. She was bending over so low he thought her breasts would pop over the edge of her dress. He turned his camera back to Penelope.

"Got it!" he shouted, giving her a sign with his thumb.

Lawrence glared at Barry.

Barry froze. It was as if he could read Lawrence's mind. He was everything Lawrence was not. Barry had a job and ambitions. Barry was the kind of guy Lawrence's father would have wanted his son to be. He peered deeply into Lawrence's bloodshot eyes.

Then Lawrence Bartlow sniffed.

Shit! Barry thought. He's on coke. And it was his guess he needed another fix.

Lawrence tried to grab Penelope's arm.

"Let me play with Barry s'more," Penelope said.

"Sure, sis." Lawrence started to turn away then pulled his angry fist out of his pockets.

Barry didn't see the punch coming. He was nailed flat.

His head hit the sidewalk and the pain dazed him for a moment. He raised himself on his elbows and looked up at the other journalists around him. They gasped. He gasped back.

Suddenly, Barry knew what it was like to be the object of scrutiny, the prey of the press. Every Minicam that had been focused on Mary Grace whirled toward the commotion behind them. Flashbulbs ignited in Barry's face. Another round of excitement had begun.

Barry just shook his head. He'd known when the story broke that this Bartlow funeral was going to spark some fireworks. He just hadn't thought he'd be in the middle of it all.

Lawrence grabbed Barry's Minicam out of his hand and smashed it on the pavement.

Barry heard the director from WBBM-TV ask his cameraman, who was sitting on top of the van, "Did you get that?"

As Barry watched helplessly, the cameraman gave his boss a thumbs-up sign and kept on taping.

He could also see that Elke was torn between helping him and getting the story. The story won out. She shoved her microphone in Lawrence's face hoping to get his anger on tape. She succeeded.

"You keep the fuck away from my sister, you ass-hole," he growled. "Or I'll fucking break more than your camera next time!"

Lawrence started to lunge toward Barry again. Barry's legs were shaking as he tried to stand, and he fell back to the pavement. He put up his arms to fend off a further assault. Damn! Barry thought. This job is too dangerous!

Penelope was trying to pull Lawrence off Barry and swat away the cameramen who were filming the various parts of her exposed body as she bent over and yanked on Lawrence's arm.

Lawrence wrenched his arm away from her. "Leave me alone, bitch!"

"I thought you were defending my honor," Penelope complained.

Barry watched as Mary Grace fought her way back to her children through the sea of reporters just as stubbornly as she'd battled her way into the church. She tossed Penelope's shawl over her daughter's derriere, righted her on her tottering high heels and shoved her toward the church. Then she quickly got Lawrence away from Barry.

Barry could feel his lower lip swelling. Jesus Christ! he realized. I'm bleeding! When he looked up, he was surprised to see empathy in Mary Grace Bartlow's eyes.

"I'm so sorry," she whispered quickly, then turned toward Lawrence.

Barry couldn't hear what she said to her son, but he immediately took off into the church.

"Who do you work for, young man?" she asked Barry.

Barry dabbed at the blood on his lip. "Cable Now."

The cameramen clicked away, catching every movement and word. He could tell Mary Grace knew she was being watched. She said nothing more and left Barry on the ground to fend for himself. Barry stared blankly at her as she disappeared into the church without further encounters.

Just then, a Lincoln Town Car drove up bearing Jack Billingsly and Alicia Carrel, the woman, according to the press, for whom Richard had left his family.

In unison, the Minicameras turned away from Barry.

"I'm old news already?" Barry asked Elke who put out her hand to help him off the ground.

"Afraid so," she replied with a chuckle. "C'mon. You don't want to miss this, do you?"

"Not on your life," he said, grabbing a portable tape recorder from his coat pocket.

"Too bad about your camera," Elke said with that halfhearted tone that told him she knew she had the edge on him now. But Barry had a small still camera he could use to piece together the story. He was a journalist, dammit. And a good one. He always came prepared.

Barry had researched Alicia Carrel's background just as thoroughly as he had Mary Grace's. What he hadn't been prepared for, though, was how beautiful she was in person. Alicia was forty-six, tall, slender, with huge brown eyes and precision-cut short black hair. The press loved her because she was photogenic—an underdog struggling career woman who enjoyed bantering with them as much as they loved writing about her. Alicia had been a nobody from the south side of Chicago until she met Richard Bartlow. Her affair with him made them both nationally famous.

Barry was surprised that Jack Billingsly was escorting Alicia since Jack was Richard's attorney and a life-long friend to Mary Grace Whittaker and her family. He'd always professed great loyalty to the Whittakers.

Barry wrangled his way toward the advancing Alicia and Jack. "I'm surprised you aren't with Mrs. Bartlow, Mr. Billingsly. You've known Richard Bartlow all his life and..."

Jack was clearly not happy about the situation. "Richard wanted it this way."

Barry's eyebrows shot up in surprise. "Richard Bartlow requested that you be his lover's—"

Jack shot Barry a damning look. Alicia bristled.

"Excuse me, Miss Carrel's escort?"

"Yes." Jack kept walking toward the church.

Barry was shocked by this piece of information. "Richard knew he was dying." He said it more as a statement than a question.

"No comment." Jack whisked Alicia into the church.

Before Barry had a chance to think, a taxi pulled up and out stepped Michelle Windsong, the twenty-five-year old who reportedly caused Richard Bartlow's heart attack with her strenuous lovemaking. Barry wasn't about to miss the story of the year. He readied his voice-activated tape recorder and checked his Minolta. He had plenty of film.

The crowd was hushed as they got their first look at Michelle. She was nothing like what Barry expected. For a moment, his fingers remained suspended over his camera buttons. It was as if he didn't dare breathe. He realized the rest of the journalists were staring at Michelle in much the same way.

Barry lowered his camera. He'd never seen anyone so beautiful in all his life.

A cool breeze lifted a lock of nearly waist-long wheat-colored hair. She wore a simple white dress that looked homemade and which skimmed the delicate curves of her slender body. Her shoes were inexpensive white pumps, and Barry could tell she was unused to walking in heels. There was not a smidge of makeup on her face, yet her cheeks appeared blushed like a newly ripened peach. Her skin was flawless and, though Barry knew she was from Arizona, she looked as if she'd never seen the sun. Her lips were neither too full nor thin, but perfectly balanced with her strong, high cheekbones and unlined oval forehead.

It was her eyes that were startling and held men and women at bay. They were crystal blue, the irises ringed with indigo that accentuated the whites of her eyes. She had exquisitely long dark lashes and perfectly winged dark eyebrows. When she looked at Barry, he felt she was looking straight to his soul.

In her long, billowing white cotton dress that hid her ankles and most of her shoes, she seemed to glide above the earth. As the sun moved out from behind a cloud and cast a shaft of light around her, she looked like an angel.

Barry thought she was walking into hell.

He glanced at Elke. Even she'd been taken aback. But she recovered in time to ask, "Miss Windsong, do you have any comment about the death of Richard Bartlow?"

"Is it true you were engaged in sex when he had his heart attack?" another reporter asked.

The flashbulbs blinded Michelle like klieg lights. She put her hand up to her face to ward off the reporters. At that second, Barry's eyes met hers. There was a pleading in them that seemed to come from within. He could tell she felt as if she were being sucked into a whirlwind.

"Please, the light hurts my eyes," she said, but no one listened as another dozen flashbulbs snapped. "I came here to give you the truth."

Barry almost laughed aloud. The truth? Who was she kidding? He wondered if she knew it was all right for her to keep silent. Though Barry was young, he'd learned quickly that the media industry was not interested in truth. The media only wanted a story, and today Michelle Windsong was a story. He wondered how much he knew of her was a lie. How much had the press distorted?

Michelle obviously thought reporters should know the truth. He wanted to tell her not to waste her time. But he was too late. She had no intention of remaining quiet.

"It's true that Richard and I had just made love . . ."

"My God!" a woman reporter exclaimed. "Are you aware there's been talk of having you arrested for manslaughter?"

Barry jabbed the brash female reporter in the ribs. She snarled at him and he shrugged his shoulders affably.

Michelle appeared to be instantly upset. Fear crossed her eyes. "It wasn't like that. Not like you've been writing. I had gone to the kitchen—"

"Miss Windsong, do you feel it is your place to intrude upon Mr. Bartlow's family at a time like this?"

"Richard requested that I be here."

"Then he *did* know he was dying?" Barry asked.

Michelle looked at Barry. She closed her eyes to press back the first tears Barry had seen that day. "Yes."

Barry stuck his arm out and halted his friend from WGN News who was about to ask another question. "I think it's time you went inside," he said to Michelle.

Barry offered his arm and she took it. He walked her into the church, to the first row of pews where an usher tried to take her arm.

"I'm with him," she said to the usher still clinging tightly to Barry's arm. "You don't mind, do you?" she asked him.

"Not at all," Barry replied. He couldn't believe his good luck at being seated with the principals of the story he was covering. Things like this just didn't happen to him.

The usher showed them to their seats, which were across the aisle from Jack Billingsly and Alicia Carrel. They were five pews back from Richard's ex-wife and his children.

Michelle's eyes scanned the altar and the fresco painted on the domed ceiling overhead. "I've never been in a church before," she whispered to Barry.

"You're kidding."

"No."

"Well, what do you think?"

"It's nothing like the spiritual places I've visited in Sedona where the red rocks soar to meet the azure blue skies and you can hear the sound of ancient Indian ghosts still whispering their prayers."

"God..." Barry had never heard anyone talk like this before.

"I remember the Hopi rites of passage I helped to conduct with my young Indian friends in the kivas under the earth. I know all about the Earth Mother and spirits that live in the trees and the wind. My parents taught me to worship one God and never any man. I know how the planes of heaven look just before falling asleep. I met my guardian angel when I was very young and I talk to it whenever I am afraid."

"Why are you telling me all this?"

She focused her luminous blue eyes on him, and Barry felt as if he'd been rocked to his core.

"Because you will tell the truth about me. About Richard. You are different from the rest of them."

"I am?"

"Yes." She looked away from him to the altar. "I know this church is thought to be a special place of peace, understanding and love. I had expected it to be like the sacred places I know in Arizona, but it's not."

Barry solemnly nodded his head. "I think I know what you mean."

Michelle looked up to see Penelope glaring at her with eyes filled with venom. Michelle drew in her breath and her hand flew to her heart.

"What's the matter?" Barry asked.

"That one . . . Penelope . . . she is sending me so much hatred. I have seen Richard's pictures of her, Lawrence and Mary Grace. However, Penelope looked like a child in the photographs." She shook her head. "I was not prepared for this evil-looking woman who wishes me so much ill."

Michelle hugged herself. "I feel an icy chill all over my body, as if someone is walking on my grave far in the future."

Barry was starting to get spooked by Michelle's odd way of talking. "Is it that bad?"

She gave him a knowing smile and touched his hand. "You will discover that I am psychic. Few in the world understand my gift. Even Richard did not believe me . . . until the end."

"Jesus." Barry shivered.

Suddenly, Michelle put her hand on Barry's arm to still his conversation. "Did you hear that?"

"No. What?"

"I thought I heard the sound of a woman's laughter. It's as if it were all around me. Can't you hear it? It's filled with hatred and bitterness." She wrapped her arms around herself. "I feel as if my blood has turned to ice." She closed her eyes.

When Michelle opened them again, she said, "It is Mary Grace's laughter I hear."

Barry's eyes shot to Mary Grace who was staring at Michelle with a stunned look on her face.

He had wondered if Mary Grace had ever seen Richard's girlfriend before. He knew now she hadn't. This coming face-to-face with Michelle Windsong was obviously a shock for her.

Barry wondered if Mary Grace was thinking the same thing he was—that Michelle in the flesh was not the wanton whore, the voodoo witch who had seduced her husband by forcing him to drink a mind-altering potion. Michelle Windsong was a mere child, an innocent and harmless waif, who didn't look to be Richard's type at all.

Barry watched as Mary Grace turned to look at Alicia. He saw her eyes scan every detail of the suit Alicia was wearing. Even Barry knew that Alicia was the best-dressed woman in the church. He didn't miss both the admiration and jealousy in Mary Grace's eyes.

Barry noticed the way Alicia clutched Jack's sleeve, as if he were a life preserver and she was drowning in a tempest. He looked back at Mary Grace. There was no mistaking the evil looks she was sending Alicia. Barry watched as Alicia returned some of her own.

The duel was on, Barry thought. He could tell from the hard set of Alicia's face that she was frustrated. It was his bet that she wasn't quite the Hester Prynne everyone had painted her. He wondered if Alicia had really stolen Richard from Mary Grace or if there was another story yet to be told. Somehow he suspected there was, and as every reporter knew, truth was always more bizarre than fiction.

Barry marveled at Alicia's ability to maintain a cool facade while being barraged by dirty looks from all of the Whittakers' friends. His hat was off to her. She was stronger than most women.

According to the newspapers, Alicia's business was struggling. But Alicia had flare. She was creative and confident. She had a way of making a dress bought from an outlet store look great. It was that same panache she applied to her advertising business. Barry was betting Alicia would find a way out of her financial woes and soon.

Barry didn't miss the way Mary Grace's eyes dropped regretfully to the ten-year-old suit she wore. He guessed it had been a long time since she had had enough money to buy something new. Probably not since her divorce from Richard.

The rigid, tight set to her pursed lips told him his deduction was right on. There was no mystery about Richard's bankruptcy at the time of his divorce from Mary Grace; he'd left his wife and children nearly destitute. One of Chicago's richest men had lost it all. The story had been in all the newspapers.

He remembered that Mary Grace had been quoted at the time as saying, "Richard was a sorry excuse for a husband or a father. I hope he rots in hell."

A hush fell over the church as the casket was rolled down the aisle to the altar. The priest sprinkled the casket with holy water and infused the air around it with the smoke of burning incense.

Barry noticed there was not a single flower on the casket. His eyes went to all three of Richard's women. Each of their faces was granite. There would be no flowers for Richard Bartlow.

THE WIFE

1

Mary Grace Whittaker Bartlow bowed her head serenely as the priest began the requiem mass. She was amazed at the inner calm she felt. All her life she had admired Jacqueline Kennedy's poise, dignity and calm during her husband's funeral. Then years later, when the truth of his infidelity came out, Mary Grace wondered if Jackie's poise wasn't perhaps due to the fact that she didn't give a damn that John was dead.

Mary Grace decided that apathy was responsible for her own lack of emotion at Richard's funeral. She refused to believe she was in shock. When Jack Billingsly had called to tell her of Richard's death, he had expressed his concern that she was in shock, suggesting that she see a doctor. She'd blasted him for the advice. To be in shock would have meant that she still cared about Richard. Mary Grace would rather have been tarred and feathered than let anyone know she'd actually felt any kind of emotion for Richard Bartlow except anger, disgust and loathing.

She thought back to Jack's telephone call three days earlier and the flurry of emotions the news of Richard's death had caused. All of them negative.

Mary Grace had just come home from meeting with a new client. In truth, Cynthia Folsum was a very old friend who'd hired Mary Grace as the interior designer for her new lake house in New Buffalo, Michigan, as a favor. Mary Grace had found it difficult to stomach

Cynthia's superior attitude when they were seniors at Woodlands Academy in Lake Forest. She found it even more difficult now.

Mary Grace's mother, Caroline, had insisted Mary Grace attend the all-women's boarding school because it was a Sacred Heart school and all the Kennedy women, including Rose herself, had attended Sacred Heart schools. Caroline's obsession with the Kennedys and anything that smacked of the Hyannis Port and Bostonian life-style spilled over into the Whittaker household. The fact that Mary Grace was a dead ringer for Jackie Kennedy didn't help.

Caroline had gone to great pains to dress Mary Grace in knockoff Chanel suits, pillbox hats and A-line cashmere coats. Caroline would drag a resistant Mary Grace through Marshall Field's and Carson Pirie Scott and Company to find "the right" pastel wool Easter suit. Mary Grace had hated all those outfits because her pre-puberty body looked more like a pale pink block of Bazooka bubble gum than the narrow-hipped figure it took to be chic. It wasn't until three years after Jack Kennedy's death that Mary Grace's body slimmed down and curved out. But by that time, the Jackie look was fading, though many Chicagoans would try to keep it alive for another thirty years. Cynthia Folsum was one of those women.

Mary Grace frowned as she looked at the blocked-out pages in her daytimer, reminding her she would be spending a great deal of time with Cynthia Folsum. Mary Grace had taken the assignment. She needed the money.

"It's all Richard's fault," Mary Grace said to herself for the hundredth time. "If Richard hadn't divorced me, I never would have had to work for a living. Never would have had to grovel to my parents for money to eat." She slammed her daytimer shut.

Just then, the phone rang. It was Jack Billingsly, her lifelong friend and hers and Richard's attorney when they were married. Now he was Richard's attorney. Though Mary Grace had been pleasant to him when she'd seen him around town, she'd never forgiven him for the defection.

"Mary Grace, how are you?"

She wanted to blast him with a ton of truth. Not very ducky, she wanted to say. I'm in debt up to my ears. I hate living in this seedy, godforsaken structure that my blue-collar neighbors call a house. My children have more problems than Oprah can deal with in a month's worth of let-me-help-you-see-the-light television broadcasts.

"Fine," she answered tersely.

"That's good." Having never cultivated the art of small talk that most attorneys used to keep their clients calm during a crisis, Jack always blurted out the truth. "Richard's dead," he said.

Mary Grace was speechless for a moment then asked, "Who shot him?"

"Why would you think he's been murdered?"

"Go ahead and tell me the truth, Jack. Somebody's irate husband beat me to the punch and robbed me of the one pleasure I've dreamed of in this life . . . shooting Richard myself."

"I'm sorry to hear you're torn apart over his death," Jack said sarcastically. "He died of a heart attack."

It suddenly hit Mary Grace that this conversation was for real. She wasn't dreaming it. Richard was dead. Slowly, she sank into a chair. "You're not joking."

"No, I'm not," Jack said, regaining his legalistic hauteur.

Mary Grace felt her mouth go dry. Her hands were shaking so badly she needed both of them to cradle the receiver. "How . . . tell me everything, Jack."

"He's in Scottsdale, as you know. Or was . . ." Jack blundered over the details.

"Yes, yes. Living with that whore, Michelle Windsong," she answered impatiently.

"I received a call from his attorney friend, Dennis Maitland."

"I've never heard of him," Mary Grace countered. She felt as if she were living in a surrealistic play. This was Richard's life Jack was talking about, and there were all these people involved in Richard's life whom she didn't know. Why were *they* there at his passing and she was not? Richard was part of her life. He had been the biggest part of her life. For a long, long time, he'd been her only life. Strangers had shared his bed and now his death.

It didn't matter that she hated the very air Richard breathed—her world had been set off-kilter by this news. She had never thought that Richard would die before her. She'd always thought he would be there, even if it was simply for the sake of hating.

"They played golf together. I don't even know if Richard had given him any business, since I still handle most of Richard's legal affairs. Which brings me to the fact that you are requested to be present at the reading of Richard's will."

"You've got to be kidding."

"Why? You are his ex-wife and the mother of his children."

"Richard has mentioned me in his will?"

"I can tell you that he has, but that's all. I'm not allowed to say to what extent. Only that you are requested to be present."

"I don't suppose you'll tell me who else will be there?" she asked.

"No. But I will tell you that it was one of Richard's requests that I escort Alicia Carrel to the funeral."

Mary Grace's hands were like ice, and she supposed that was why she could see that they were trembling but she couldn't feel them. "Would you repeat that?" She felt her anger build.

Jack sighed audibly into the receiver. "Mary Grace, please. This whole situation is awkward enough for me, as it is. Couldn't you let up a bit?"

"Why should I? My family's attorney, best friend to me for over twenty years and my father's racquetball partner, tells me he is escorting my dead husband's mistress to my dead husband's funeral and you want *me* to lighten up? Are you nuts? You know, J—Jack," she began. Her anger was causing her tongue to trip over itself. Sputtered words, her marriage counselor had told her during her divorce from Richard, was a sign of uncontrollable anger. She was caught between her desire to express herself and her learned behavior that prevented such outbursts.

"Uh-oh. Here it comes," Jack said.

"I'd just like to know why it is that everyone always takes Richard's side. Why is it that everyone treats me like I have the plague? Why is it that you aren't taking *me* to the goddamn funeral?"

"Because you give everyone such a shit-hard time, Mary Grace."

She stopped cold. Jack had said that before, hadn't he? Was it when she and Richard had divorced? Or was it later when she'd tried to take Richard to court for failure to pay child support? Maybe Jack was just on Richard's side, period, and that was how he wanted to be counted. Jack was on the red team. She was on the blue. Jack was the enemy just as much as Richard was the team's leader. "Fine," she said through clenched teeth.

"Look, Mary Grace. I'm sorry."

"No, you're not."

"I am. Really. I know this has been a shock to you. Maybe you should see a doctor."

"Screw you, Jack!" She started to hang up the phone.

Jack was screaming into the receiver. "Mary Grace! Don't hang up on me! Please! Mary Grace! Are you there?"

She tried to calm herself, taking a deep breath. She couldn't help wondering if Jackie Kennedy had hung up on one of the Kennedy brothers when they were giving excuses for her husband. Jackie would be gracious. Well, so would she. "What is it, Jack?" she asked pleasantly.

"Please don't be like that, Mary Grace. I want to help. I know there have been some harsh words between you and me because I remained Richard's lawyer, but I want you to know that I've always thought the world of you and your family."

"Thank you, Jack," Mary Grace replied. "I'm sorry for my behavior. It's just that this is . . . well, I guess it is a shock to me." She put her forehead in her hand and stared down at the threadbare carpet. "I never thought it would turn out like this. Any of it. My life. Richard's death." Emotion choked off her words. She felt the first threat of tears sting her eyes. She fought them stubbornly. Mary Grace didn't like tears, they were an embarrassment. "How did he die, Jack?" she finally asked.

Jack hesitated a split second too long.

Mary Grace's antennae were on alert. She sat up ramrod-straight in the chair. "How did he die, Jack?" she demanded.

"He was in bed when it happened," Jack answered.

Mary Grace's imagination spun a picture at warp speed. "He was in bed with *her*, wasn't he, Jack? In bed screwing his teenage whore?"

Jack nearly groaned. "Michelle is not a teenager. She's twenty-five."

"Same thing."

"She had just left. Dennis told me they were to play golf that morning. He met Michelle as she was coming out of the condo. She made some comment that Richard didn't have much energy left for golf."

"Jesus, Mary and Joseph! She screwed him to death!" Mary Grace shrieked.

"He had a heart attack," Jack reiterated.

"The media will not see it that way, Jack. I promise you. You just wait and see what they do with this story. I'll be made a laughingstock again," she moaned.

"Nothing like that is going to happen, Mary Grace. How Richard died has no bearing on you and your life, whatsoever. You are being overly sensitive."

It was the first time that day Mary Grace had laughed. In fact, she hadn't laughed that loudly and deeply in weeks, even months. "Jack, for an attorney, you are so naive."

"Perhaps," Jack replied with a defensive tone in his voice. "In light of the fact that in recent weeks Richard has become nearly a hero to every American who has ever bought a house, I think the press will treat him respectfully. So far, that has been the case."

"I hope to God you are right, Jack," she said adamantly.

Mary Grace happened to glance down at the magazine rack next to the chair. She spied the copy of *Time* magazine she'd bought at the drugstore with Richard's photograph on the front cover. *It's just like Richard to die on me right when I'm getting back on my feet,* she thought. She had been living for the day her design business would take off and she'd be successful. She wanted to become as famous as he was so she could shove her success and fame in his face the way he'd been doing to her.

Yes, it was just like Richard to make the world think he was some goddamn hero. The savior of millions of people who wanted to own their own homes, but who couldn't because the price of residential building had become exorbitant over the past ten years. Richard had found his niche, all right, she thought ruefully. He always liked to think he ranked right up there with Lord Krishna, but Mary Grace knew better. Richard never made a move without an angle. He made certain he'd benefit somehow, usually in a major way. *I wouldn't put it past that bastard to die just to piss me off!* she said silently.

She didn't dare voice her anger to Jack, who would probably call the paramedics to come get her. Jack was a paid employee of Richard's—he didn't know the real Richard. No one knew Richard the way she did.

"What was that you said, Jack?" she asked. She was so lost in her own thoughts she hadn't heard his last word.

"I said that I need to speak with both Lawrence and Penny. If I don't get hold of them this afternoon, would you have them call me?"

"Penelope should be at her apartment by now. Hopefully, she was at work today. Lawrence has a tendency to turn up at her place more often than he does here. But if I see him or hear from Penelope, I'll tell them to call."

"I'd appreciate it. The funeral will be in four days at Our Lady of Sorrows Church. I'm leaving tonight for Scottsdale and I'll be flying back with the body day after tomorrow."

"I'm assuming there won't be an open casket," she said.

"How did you know?"

"Richard always said he thought viewing the body was a manipulative tactic devised by Catholic priests to frighten the living into donating more money to the Church, as if the money would save them from death."

"He told me the same thing," Jack replied.

"It's just as well. I don't want to see him," she said more to herself than to the attorney. "Thanks for calling, Jack. I'll see you at the funeral." She hung up.

Mary Grace stepped out of her nine-year-old black Joan and David pumps, dropped her ten-year-old black snakeskin and alligator purse on the chair and walked from the small foyer/living room/dining room into the kitchen/breakfast nook/family room. The shabby little two-story house she rented off Cicero Avenue, directly beneath the flight path of every plane headed for Midway Airport, had always felt compressed to her. Today, it was suffocating.

The house had been built during World War II when only the worst building materials were used domestically. Every corner that could be cut was. The result was a square box structure that sold for twenty-five hundred dollars. In today's market, Mary Grace doubted it would bring that much.

The roof shingles should have been replaced a couple decades ago. The exterior hadn't been painted since the mid-sixties; she knew that because that was the only time this particular shade of avocado green was popular. The furnace worked only when the temperature hovered around freezing—once it plummeted below the single digits, it chugged away, but the house was never warm. The bathroom was a wrecking crew's dream. The floor peeled up and the wallpaper peeled down. The ceiling tiles had rotted, but only in the corners, giving the ceiling a hexagonal design. She had regrouted the black and lavender tiles. She tried to tell herself there was something campy about the pseudo–Art Deco color scheme in the bath, but her inner voice shouted back that everything, *everything* in this house was ugly.

When they'd been married she and Richard lived in a sprawling two-story mansion in Winnetka, only two blocks from Lake Michigan off Sheridan Road. But it had been nearly eight years since she'd lived that lifestyle. Why was she still not used to her new life?

She surveyed the kitchen. The sink was piled high with dirty dishes, and the countertops were filled with cans of soup, tuna, vegetables and boxed macaroni cheese, the staples of her diet for many years now. She would have put away the groceries, only there was no room in the two cabinets in her dingy, dinky kitchen.

She washed out a copper-bottom pan, opened a can of chicken noodle soup and poured it in. She turned on the gas heat of the thirty-year-old stove and sighed heavily.

"So much for making dinner," she said to herself as she began to straighten up the kitchen.

It probably wouldn't have been difficult living in this house, she thought, if she had been brought up in a blue-collar neighborhood with a steelworker for a father and a mother who was a waitress. Unfortunately, Mary Grace had been brought up in the heart of the Chicago Gold Coast. All her life her friends had always sought her counsel when it came to decorating and home furnishings, because Mary Grace had what they strove vainly to achieve and never did. She had good taste.

Mary Grace was sixteen when she realized her eye for line, depth, color, balance and design was a gift. She had been blessed by God with talent, just as were poets, composers and artists. It all began when she had volunteered as set designer for the Woodlands Academy production of *Bells are Ringing*.

For weeks, Mary Grace pored through her mother's decorating magazines and the home furnishing section of the *Chicago Tribune*. When those sources didn't give her everything she needed, she visited the Chicago Library and discovered *Architectural Digest* and books filled with the home interiors of royalty and movie stars.

She went back to her school and began putting together her personal vision of what a young woman's apartment would look like in New York. She borrowed furniture from her mother's attic and wicker pieces from her neighbors' porches. She scavenged garage sales around Winnetka and found lamps, draperies, tables and a cracked porcelain-footed bathtub for fifteen dollars. She learned how to use a staple gun to reupholster chair seats and hang draperies. She taught herself to hand-stencil prop walls. She arranged cloth flowers she'd made long past midnight one night when she was supposed to be studying American history and algebra. Mary Grace was consumed with blending her fabric colors with paint colors, having discovered she had an eye for tone, light and shadow. She nearly drove the play's director crazy with her incessant need to make the set perfect.

When opening night arrived, the audience lambasted the overly dramatic acting and poor direction, but they all applauded the sets. Caroline told Mary Grace her very own friends had asked if Mary Grace had used a professional's help. None of them could believe that a high school girl could have such good taste and such an exacting eye. They couldn't do better themselves, they told Caroline.

That night had been Mary Grace's triumph.

Now, as she looked around her little house at the odd juxtaposition of fine reproduction furniture, oil paintings and elegantly upholstered sofa and chairs against a structure the landlord refused to repair, she realized that it had taken her thirty years to achieve that kind of triumph again.

Just this week, Mary Grace had won an award as best new designer for the room she decorated at the Junior League showcase home in Lake Forest. Accolades rang in her ears, just as they had when she was sixteen. She had worked hard for that award. The competition was incredibly tough this year, and though she believed she deserved it, she'd never thought she would win. Many of the other designers had husbands in the wholesale or design business who helped their wives. Mary Grace had been forced to be twice as creative and innovative on half the money and half the resources.

For seven years, Mary Grace had dreamed of making her mark in her career. She'd scrimped, saved, done without, planned and visualized the day when she would show Richard that she was just as capable as he at earning a living. Every time she'd skipped a meal to pay for night classes, she'd told herself it was worth it to see the look on Richard's face when she'd beat him at his own game. For years she had cultivated a thirst for victory. And now she'd won the award.

It was ironic that she'd learned about Richard's death today of all days, the day she had intended to telephone him in Scottsdale. She'd planned just how she would tell him about the award. The *Chicago Tribune* had taken color photographs of the house for the newspaper, and a fantastic shot of herself was planned for the front page of the Home section. Once the article was out, she'd intended to buy thirty copies and send him one every day for thirty days. For an entire month, she'd wanted him to realize what he'd given up when he'd divorced her.

Now that Richard was dead, there would be no phone call and no thirty copies of the *Tribune*. His death had deprived her of her victory, and for that she hated him all over again.

Mary Grace finally found room for the cans of soup and the rest of the groceries under the sink with the cleanser and steel-wool pads. She scrubbed the scratched stainless-steel sink and wiped it out with a dry towel, hoping it would gleam. Instead, it sat dully in the middle of the white and gold-speckled Formica countertop, gaping at her like a vacant eye. She folded the blue linen towel she'd bought on a shopping spree at William Sonoma's in Lake Forest at least a decade ago and laid it next to the ugly sink.

She smiled at the towel. "Just goes to show, quality endures."

She went down the short hall past the black-and-lavender-tiled bath, past her son Lawrence's room— where he sometimes slept and sometimes did not—to her own bedroom. It was a ten-by-ten cubicle in which she'd crammed her four-poster mahogany rice bed she'd gotten in the divorce from Richard and a nightstand, turned sideways against the bed. It was impossible to open the drawers of the nightstand, but she needed it to hold the Waterford crystal lamp and her box of over-the-counter generic-brand sleeping pills.

She crawled onto the bed and flopped back against three rows of down-filled pillows covered in a fading Jay Wang chintz she'd bought a year before the divorce.

She crooked her arm and pressed it against her eyes. She felt as if she were a thousand years old. She was tired. Tired of change—and today her world had changed again.

Richard had died.

2

New York City
June 1966

Mary Grace awoke early the morning of her departure for Paris. She was sharing a suite with her parents, Caroline and James Whittaker III—her mother always insisted they stay at the Waldorf when they went to New York to see plays or to shop. This was Mary Grace's fourth visit to the Waldorf. She knew the hotel and the surrounding area well.

The first time she'd visited New York she'd been only twelve. The hotel on Park Avenue between Forty-ninth Street and Fiftieth was built in 1931 and was a sedate version of her favorite Art Deco style. On that trip, Mary Grace had learned that the hotel had been moved from its earlier site, between Thirty-third and Thirty-fourth Streets, where the Empire State Building now stood. Two Astor mansions had stood on that site from 1857 to 1893, until a feud developed between Mrs. Astor and her nephew, William Waldorf Astor. William moved to Europe and from there supervised the construction of a thirteen-story hotel on his New York site called the Waldorf. Mrs. Astor, not to be outdone, built a connecting seventeen-story hotel on her site and called it the Astoria. The hyphenated hotel became the place to be seen and was frequented by "The Four Hundred," the city's elite.

Mary Grace loved the story of the Astors and their outrageous, flamboyant ways of dealing with each other and life. Because her own father was the owner of a large commercial-construction company in Chicago, as a child, Mary Grace had liked to think of her family as being in the same league with the Astors.

Caroline told Mary Grace that she was related to the very old Van Patten family, one of the first settlers of New York when it was still called New Amsterdam. She told Mary Grace that in America, they were as close to royalty as one could get. "The blood in your veins is blue, Mary Grace. You are an American blue blood. You remember that and always act like a lady. It is your responsibility to never do anything to mar the Van Patten name." Mary Grace noticed that her mother never mentioned anything about the sanctity of the Whittaker name.

Caroline took Mary Grace to the Palm Room at the Waldorf-Astoria where they met some of the elderly female members of the Van Patten family for tea. Mary Grace was only twelve at the time, but she was quick to note the turned-down corners of her great-aunt Beatrice's mouth when Mary Grace did not hold her teacup properly. She saw the glint of disdain in her aunt Regina's eyes when Mary Grace crossed her legs instead of keeping her feet flat on the floor. And she did not miss the clucks of their tongues when Caroline tried to explain to her distant relatives why she and James lived in "the West" instead of in New York where it was "civilized." To hear her elderly aunts talk, it sounded as if Chicago was inhabited by twenties' gangster mobs, spraying bullets as they drove the streets. Mary Grace wanted desperately to come to her mother's aid and set the old biddies right, but Caroline sharply reprimanded her in front of them when she tried to interrupt, causing her to blush with embarrassment. Mary Grace didn't know who she hated more at that moment, her mother or her snotty aunts.

When Beatrice and Regina left, Mary Grace couldn't help wondering what was so good about being a Van Patten. As she watched them walk out onto the street where their chauffeurs opened the doors to black Cadillac limousines, she decided their attitude was warranted. They had the best of everything and they lived in the crème de la crème of cities . . . New York.

It was on that first visit to New York that Mary Grace became enthralled with architecture and interior design. Though she paid little attention to the Louis Sullivan buildings and the Frank Lloyd Wright structures that elevated her native Chicago from the mediocrity of most Midwestern cities, she believed New York was without parallel. With every breath of New York air she inhaled, and every morsel of history she digested, Mary Grace's life changed.

From that time on, when her girlfriends, Cynthia Folsum and Kathryn Norwood, pored over the newest issues of *Seventeen* magazine, *Glamour* and *Movie Screen* magazine, Mary Grace would be dissecting the elements of design in *House Beautiful* and *Home and Garden* magazine. When her girlfriends talked about what they would wear to dinner in the city with their parents or to Mass that weekend where they were sure to see many boys, Mary Grace turned a deaf ear to their conversations. She had little interest in dress design, line or form. She didn't care that her hat, bag and gloves didn't match. Nor did she care if hemlines rose or fell.

She left the shopping to her mother who always bought boxy jacketed dress-suits that would match the shoes she already owned. As long as she had plenty of baggy sweaters to cover up the fact that she'd developed rather fully by the age of fourteen.

Few of the girls who attended Woodlands Academy dated before the age of sixteen—by parental decree. The summer of 1963, there were boys from Wilmette, Kenilworth and her own neighborhood in Winnetka who asked fifteen-year-old Mary Grace out for movies or a hamburger. But she turned them all down, saying that she was still too young to date.

She liked flirting with the boys and she basked in the attention they paid her. She liked the fact that when she gave them her telephone number, they would almost always call, and she enjoyed talking on the phone for long expanses of otherwise boring time. One boy, Robert Gerry, sent her poems he said he'd written himself, until she found the same poems in her *Poets of the Romantic Period* textbook.

Boys were fine as long as she didn't have to deal with them on an ongoing basis. She didn't like feeling pressured by them. Some of them talked openly about sex with her, as if *she* knew something they didn't. She felt awkward, ignorant and even frightened, and she knew she definitely wasn't ready for this part of adult life, even though her body seemed to be leading her into the arena with a will of its own. She almost wished she could stay fifteen forever.

As she looked out over Park Avenue from the huge picture window in the sitting room of her suite at the Waldorf-Astoria, Mary Grace was glad she had grown up and graduated from boarding school. She was about to embark on the greatest adventure of her life. She was going to Europe without her parents.

The door on the right side of the sitting area opened and her father walked out into the sun-filled room. Ever since she was a little girl, Mary Grace referred to her father as James the Third, she liked pretending he was a king and she was a princess.

James the Third was wearing a summer robe of brown silk with black-satin lapels over his chocolate brown monogrammed pajamas. The room behind him where her mother was still asleep was dark. Mary Grace had often heard her mother say that one of the main reasons she loved good hotels was that she could sleep till noon because the windows were covered with heavy draperies. Mary Grace always laughed to herself when her mother said that, because Caroline wore a powder blue satin sleeping mask to bed nearly every night, and to Mary Grace's knowledge, Caroline had not risen before eleven since Mary Grace had gone to boarding school four years ago.

James the Third was a tall, slender man with dark brown hair that had just begun to gray. His eyes were round and wide and the color of an Illinois prairie sky. His jawline was strong and assertive, and though his lips were a trifle too thin, Mary Grace thought he had that kind of aristocratic nose and high cheekbones that spelled *old money*. Which was probably why Mary Grace's mother had fallen in love with him.

"Good morning, princess," her father said in that cool, even voice he seldom ever raised. Mary Grace could only remember one time when her father had spoken harshly in anger and that had been well deserved: eight years ago, James had caught an employee embezzling money from him. Mary Grace had learned every cussword in the book that night.

"'Mornin', Daddy." She smiled as she offered her forehead for him to kiss.

"Did you sleep well?" he asked as he poured himself a cup of coffee from the serving tray the waiter had brought to the room promptly at seven o'clock, just as James had requested the night before. He picked up the *New York Times* and unfolded it.

"Not a wink."

"I didn't think you would. It isn't every day a young lady goes off to Europe for the first time."

"Unchaperoned," Mary Grace added proudly, but her father seemed not to be listening.

James sat in a tan-and-black-striped club chair next to the window. He put down the paper and looked at his daughter. He still couldn't believe she had grown up so quickly. It seemed like only last night that he'd missed her first-grade school play. He supposed that all fathers felt like this when they realized, only too late, that their life with their child was over.

There had never been enough time for him to get to know Mary Grace. She was a quiet girl, almost neurotically withdrawn during those clumsy preteen years. She had developed a woman's figure, yet she played with her dolls, had tea parties and lived in a fantasy world until she was fourteen, even fifteen. He couldn't remember a single conversation he'd ever had with her on an intimate, father-daughter level. James had grown up with one brother, Gregory, who now lived in San Francisco with his wife and three sons. They'd always engaged in male activities. He'd hoped when Mary Grace was born that she might turn out to be a tomboy, but he'd had no such luck.

Mary Grace was all girl, who liked pretty things, never even wanting to learn to ride a bike, and who was perfectly content to shop with her mother or read in her room. James hadn't the slightest idea what interests she had, other than the ludicrous notion that she wanted to be an architect.

James had told Mary Grace that his firm employed some of the best architects in the country and that he knew talent when he saw it. He told her she was wasting her time trying to break into a man's world, but she wouldn't listen. He had overheard her telling her girlfriends that her main interest on this trip was to see European architecture.

Sometimes he almost wished she were more like her friends, Cynthia and Kathryn, who only cared about finding the right husband. He couldn't help wondering if Mary Grace only pretended to be uninterested in boys when she was around him and Caroline. Maybe she was a hell-raiser. Maybe she was one of those kids he'd heard his friends talk about; the kind who one day was perfectly normal and the next they took off to "find themselves" on a surfboard in California. That very thing had happened to Ken and Ann Dickerson last summer. Their valedictorian daughter had met a half-wit art-school dropout at UCLA and now she was living in a hovel in Venice, California, selling suntan lotion at a surf shop.

James knew the kind of embarrassment Ken and Ann had faced from their friends. Not only would he be unable to handle the pity he would see in all their faces, should something like that happen with Mary Grace, but because of the ridicule, he'd lose half his clientele. Mary Grace's behavior could ruin his career.

He took a deep breath. What was he thinking? His daughter would never do anything to jeopardize his business. Mary Grace's saving feature was that she was such an odd duck.

Although she was eighteen and still a teenager in his eyes, he had agreed to allow her to go to Europe only because she was traveling with her two friends, Cynthia and Kathryn, whose parents he knew well. While the girls were in Paris, they would be staying with Charles Henderson and his wife, Véronique. James had known Charles for thirty years, there wasn't a more conservative traditionalist on the continent. The girls would be in good hands.

His eyes were stern as he looked at Mary Grace. "Unchaperoned, yes. But not without rules," he said, a warning tone in his voice.

"Daddy, I'm not going to do anything . . ."

"See that you don't," he said primly. Then he softened his approach. "Mary Grace, you are eighteen years old and that is the age of consent."

"What does that mean? Exactly?"

"It doesn't mean you can do anything you want. It *does* mean you can marry without my approval."

Mary Grace rolled her eyes. "That would be stupid! I'm not going to do that."

"I know you aren't." God, how he hated talking to her. He was probably the most successful residential and commercial builder in Chicago, and he felt as if he were tripping over his goddamn tongue every time he tried to have a conversation with his own daughter. He knew perfectly well she wasn't the least bit interested in boys. What he was trying to say was that he didn't want any wild antics, such as skinny-dipping in the Tivoli Fountain like Mark Chase's daughter did two summers ago.

Everybody knew because pictures made it back to the local papers. Shit! Raising children, daughters especially, was a hard nut in life. Why couldn't he have been blessed with a son, instead?

"What I'm trying to say, Mary Grace, is that I hope you will not do anything to . . . well, er, embarrass your mother or me while you are in Europe." He hoped she'd take his words as a warning.

Mary Grace watched her father squirm in the chair as he tried to choose his words perfectly, but only ended up bungling the whole thing. She knew exactly what he was getting at. Nearly every one of her parents' friends' children had done something outrageous over the past three years that made James the Third and Caroline very nervous. She could tell by the beads of sweat on her father's perfectly shaven upper lip that he was scared to death she would do something equally rebellious.

The fact that she, eighteen-year-old Mary Grace, perfect Catholic virgin and a for-the-moment keeper of the Whittaker family reputation, had power over her father had never crossed her mind. It was a revelation.

"I will do nothing of the sort, Daddy," she said quickly with an assuring smile.

He exhaled deeply. "Thank God."

Mary Grace was shocked that James the Third had actually been worried about her actions now that she'd been released from the academy. Her mouth gaped, but she instantly closed it.

"Don't you trust me, Daddy?"

His eyes shot to her face.

Then she saw it. Distrust riddled the edges of his eyes and clung to his quivering lower lip. Just how much power *did* she have?

"Of course I do, Mary Grace. You have never done anything to make me think otherwise. You have been...I mean, you are a model daughter."

Yes, she thought. But you don't *like* me, do you, Daddy?

James continued. "You have worked very hard to maintain your status on the honor roll at Woodlands Academy. You have been accepted at both St. Mary's College in South Bend and Barrett College. Your mother has made no secret that she prefers Barrett College for you—it's run by the Sacred Heart nuns and it's close to home."

"Daddy, South Bend is only an hour and a half away. I can take the South Shore train, you know."

"I realize that, but I rather like the idea of your being close, as well. But we can talk about that when you return from Europe."

"I want to go to St. Mary's, Daddy. You'd better prepare yourself for that." It was the most assertive statement Mary Grace had ever made. She wasn't about to go to Barrett College when, at St. Mary's, she had the chance to be across the street from Notre Dame, where she could take graduate classes and attend special seminars, lectures and workshops on weekends. Mary Grace did not want to be "close to home." In fact, she wanted to go to school as far away as possible, but her father refused to pay for an East Coast school. And James the Third was terrified of any college in California, so she never mentioned that she thought Stanford University was the ultimate.

Mary Grace had seen Stanford's campus when she and her parents had gone to San Francisco four years before to visit her uncle Gregory and his family. They had driven two hours down the coast to Monterey and then to Palo Alto for her father's business meeting at Stanford University. She had loved every old building, every face she saw, and mostly, she had loved San Francisco. Just like in the song, she had left a good-size chunk of her heart in that beautiful city.

James cleared his throat in that authoritative manner he only seemed to use when Mary Grace was around. "We'll talk about it when you return," he said emphatically.

"I want to talk about it now."

Just then, Caroline walked into the room, stretching and yawning. "Talk about what?" she asked, pulling the edges of her pink-and-white hand-painted Odette Barca peignoir over her small, perfectly rounded breasts.

Mary Grace frowned. She lowered her head. Why couldn't she have inherited her mother's graceful shape instead of her grandmother Whittaker's Victorian hourglass body? Caroline extended her long swanlike neck toward James as she kissed him. Then she laid her temple against his as they both turned to Mary Grace, smiles spread across their lips.

Mary Grace felt as if she were facing a firing squad. The fact that her parents would be paying for her college education meant they could rule her life. They could choose where she went. They could keep telling her how to live, how to dress, what to think, what friends to keep and who to marry, and she had no way to stop them. She was as dependent on them now as she had been when she was an infant. They thought so much alike, it was difficult to tell where James ended and Caroline started. They were an unmovable force.

It took every ounce of courage Mary Grace had to press the issue with her parents. "We were talking about college," she finally said.

Caroline looked at James the Third. "You didn't tell her?"

"Uh, no," he replied sheepishly.

"Tell me what?" Mary Grace felt the hairs rise on the back of her neck.

"That I sent your preregistration payment to Barrett College this week."

"You did *what?*" Mary Grace was out of the chair like a shot. She felt her blood surge to the top of her head and her face explode into crimson. Her hands were shaking as she gaped at her parents. "I don't want to go there!" She wanted to shout at them, scream at them. She wanted to take the pretty blue-and-white china vase on the tea table and fling it out the picture window. She wanted to take control of her life, but she was actually losing control.

"Mary Grace, sit down!" James the Third commanded.

Caroline gasped, clearly horrified at Mary Grace's display of anger. "Your father has spent a small fortune on your education so far. He'll probably have to spend another fortune on your college tuition for four years. The least you can do, young lady, is be appreciative."

"I am appreciative," Mary Grace said, feeling her father's glaring eyes on her as she sank timidly into the chair. "It's just that I wanted to choose for myself . . ."

"College is an enormous decision to make, dear," her mother explained. "We didn't want you to feel pressured, like so many other children seem to be these days. Then, if you made the wrong decision, you would blame yourself and that would cause more pressure."

As Caroline continued talking, Mary Grace couldn't help thinking that her mother had not only chosen Barrett College, but that she would probably choose her courses, as well. What else was Caroline planning for her life? Was she going to pick her husband? The number of children she'd have? Her house? Her neighborhood?

Suddenly, it occurred to Mary Grace that her mother might have *already* planned a great many things. How could she stop her? More important, she wondered *when* could she stop her? This year? When she was twenty-five? Forty-five?

"And so you see, Mary Grace, we are only doing this for your own good."

God! How she hated that excuse! Parents always said that when the truth was, they just wanted to control their children. They were power freaks. It wasn't until now Mary Grace realized how *often* her mother had said those words to her over the years. Why hadn't she paid attention before? Or if she had, why hadn't she confronted her mother?

Mary Grace paused as she looked at the beautiful faces of her parents. They were like one of those golden couples on the cover of *Town and Country* magazine. For the first time, she realized their smiles looked as if they'd been simulated by a cartoonist. Their eyes were bright and happy, but devoid of any depth. She realized she was nothing more to them than one of the precious Ming porcelains they collected.

She didn't stand a chance against them, at least for the moment. Her only option was surrender.

"Barrett College will be fine," Mary Grace said flatly. It was all she could do to keep her anger in check. She wanted to blast them with the sound of her voice, like Joshua blasting his trumpet. The only problem was, these two weren't about to crumble or even take a single step back. She had no doubt they'd already devised a backup plan and a backup to the backup plan. Sometimes there was wisdom in default.

"We thought you would see it our way, dear," Caroline said with a supercilious smile.

Mary Grace couldn't help thinking that, on the morning of her departure for Europe, she had crossed a distance more vast than the Atlantic Ocean in discovering the kind of people her parents really were. That morning, she shed her childish self and stepped into an adult's skin.

It was with new eyes that she looked out at her own life. In the space of a tiny suspended moment, Mary Grace's world had shifted. Her parents had changed before her eyes. She had never been quite so disappointed.

3

Mary Grace tried not to think about her future as she rode in a taxi with her parents through midtown Manhattan on her way to New York Harbor where she would board the luxury liner, the *Queen Elizabeth*. She had wanted to fly out of O'Hare airport to La Guardia and then on to Paris. But Caroline had insisted that Mary Grace and her friends take the famous ocean liner to Europe because the Cunard Steam Ship Line had announced plans to retire the *Queen Elizabeth*. Caroline talked often of the many ocean voyages she'd made to Europe on the *Queen Elizabeth*. And of her mother, Grace Van Patten, who had sailed on the *Normandie* in 1935 when it broke the transatlantic record of crossing the Atlantic Ocean in four days, three hours and two minutes.

Caroline had convinced Cynthia and Kathryn's parents that this ocean voyage would be not only an experience of a lifetime, but the proper launch for the girls' Grand Tour to Europe. Mary Grace wondered if Cynthia's parents cared the least bit about Grand Tours and Eastern Seaboard traditions. Kathryn's parents were not as wealthy as Cynthia's family and all they had complained about was the cost. Finally, Caroline had agreed to pay for part of Kathryn's voyage.

Now that Mary Grace was seeing her mother with new eyes, she realized how incredibly manipulative she was. Caroline was subtle in the execution of her plans, her wants and her priorities. That summer, a lot of Mary Grace's friends from school and church were going to Europe. However, she and her two friends were the only ones taking an ocean liner.

No wonder life was so difficult. Every time she wanted to do anything like the rest of her friends, her mother stepped in and changed it somehow. It was as if Mary Grace didn't have a mind of her own. She was amazed she'd gotten accepted to any college, considering how little she'd used her brain!

Mary Grace cradled her chin in the palm of her white-cotton-gloved hand and watched the buildings stream past her. God! She wished she could be let loose in this city for just a day. She wanted to see more than the Van Patten houses and the family haunts. She wanted to visit some of the more adventurous areas and every tourist trap she'd ever heard about or seen in a movie. She wanted to explore the places tourists didn't go anymore, but once had at the turn of the century. She loved the romantic Victorian era and the even more glamorous Edwardian period.

Mary Grace knew that Caroline would never allow her to venture out by herself in New York. She thought it odd that her mother would let her go to Europe on her own when she wouldn't let her explore this city. But Mary Grace knew her mother was controlling her European trip: every hotel room had been prebooked and she had a list of good restaurants in each city. In Paris, they would be staying with her parents' friends, the Hendersons, and in Rome, her mother had even made a reservation at Pasta Luigi's off the Via Condotti for June fifteenth. She had a list of shops to visit, sights to see, museums to view and monuments to photograph. Caroline had even given her friends' phone numbers in every major city she would visit. The girls would be gone one month, and in that time, Caroline would know where Mary Grace was every morning and every night.

Going to Europe would be as safe as flipping burgers on the backyard charcoal grill, she thought ruefully as the taxi turned down Forty-second Street toward the docks.

When they pulled up to the pier, Mary Grace's frown turned to a huge smile. The scene was as loud and festive as a Hollywood set. The *Queen Elizabeth* was stately and grand, and the railings were lined with tourists waving and calling out to loved ones onshore. The steam whistle blew and people both on the ground and the ship howled, laughed and shouted. Streamers fell through the air and handfuls of confetti rained down on Mary Grace as the taxi driver pulled her bags out of the trunk of the car.

While James led the way to the loading area, Mary Grace was awestruck at the scene around her. For the first time, she felt a thrill race through her as the enormity of her undertaking hit. It was probable that her grandmother had stood on this very same pier in 1935. Her mother had sailed from this port in 1937 and again in 1955, 1958 and 1962. Mary Grace understood now what Caroline meant about carrying on with tradition. She felt guilty for not realizing how fortunate she was to belong to a family that *had* traditions. She was a Whittaker and a Van Patten, and she had blue blood in her veins. She was sailing to Europe on one of the last voyages of the majestic *Queen Elizabeth*. She was a fortunate girl, indeed.

She turned to her mother and embraced her. "Mother, thank you for this trip." She pulled back and let her joy fill her eyes. "I'm the luckiest girl in the world to have a mother like you."

Caroline's elegant head tipped with a terse nod as she pursed her quivering lips. Mary Grace knew her mother thought emotional displays were not proper, especially in public. "I hope you have a wonderful trip, dear."

"Thanks, Mom."

James signaled his wife and daughter to join him with the purser. "Here's your passport, Mary Grace. I've taken care of all your paperwork. This man will take us to your stateroom. He tells me that the other girls are already on board."

"I thought Cynthia's parents were supposed to meet you here, Daddy," Mary Grace said.

"So did I. Well, there's nothing I can do about it now. I'll give their hotel a call later and verify our dinner plans tonight." James put his hand on Mary Grace's shoulder and gently pushed her toward the gangplank where the steward was to lead them to the stateroom.

As they boarded the ship, Mary Grace became more caught up in the festival atmosphere. She hadn't been on the main deck five minutes, when a man carrying a bottle of French champagne bumped into her and, rather than excusing himself, grabbed her by the shoulders and kissed her soundly on the mouth.

"Bon voyage to us all!" he said sloppily, then blew a kiss to Caroline and raced up the stairs to the upper deck.

James the Third cast his royal scowl at his retreating back. "I'm going to report that man to the head steward's office," he said to their steward.

"I'll be happy to do that for you, sir," the young man said.

Mary Grace saw the look of disdain on the guide's face. It was bad enough her father was a killjoy, but now the steward knew it. And by the time they set sail, half the crew would hear the story. From the brochure, Mary Grace knew there were over five hundred and eighty crew members on the *Queen Elizabeth*. She hoped her father didn't plan to stay on board any longer than necessary.

"Daddy, he didn't mean anything by it. He was drunk and just having a good time, that's all."

"I will not allow a stranger to molest my daughter."

"Geez, Daddy! He just kissed me. It was no big deal."

"It's a big deal when I say it's a big deal," James growled angrily.

Caroline gave Mary Grace her famous knock-it-off-before-you-make-it-worse look.

When they reached the upper deck, the steward opened the door to a luxurious, frightfully expensive suite with two walls of windows looking out on the Hudson River. The room was decorated in light blue and gold. There were two double beds, two chairs, a table and a television set. One set of dark blue American Tourister luggage sat at the end of one of the beds. Mary Grace knew in an instant those belonged to Cynthia. A second set of inexpensive suitcases belonging to Kathryn had been placed at the end of the other bed.

"Your luggage will be up within the hour, Miss Whittaker," the steward said, handing her the cabin key.

"Thank you," she replied. He pointed out the amenities of her cabin, then left.

James pulled an envelope from his pocket and handed it to her. "This contains enough money for all your tips both going to Europe and on the voyage back. Do not tip the steward, your dinner waiters or the stateroom maid until the end of each trip."

Mary Grace didn't know the first thing about tipping. "Thanks, Daddy. I don't think my spending money would have covered all this, too."

"That brings up another subject. If for any reason you do run short of cash, just go to an American Express office and we'll wire you some more. All I ask is that you don't go overboard with the spending."

"I never have before."

"There's always a first time," he said with a warning echo in his voice.

Caroline smiled at Mary Grace. "Your father and I understand that this voyage is a strain for Kathryn's parents. We want you to be mindful of their financial position when you go shopping and sightseeing. We felt that if we took care of the tips, Kathryn wouldn't feel embarrassed about not having enough money. We want you girls to have a good time."

"Thanks, Mom." Mary Grace wondered how it was that Caroline could make her feel guilty for having a friend who was not wealthy. It was a subtle dig at Mary Grace's judgment and choice of companions, but it was there all the same.

Just then they heard the sound of a xylophone, announcing that all visitors must go ashore. Mary Grace hugged her parents and thanked them again. She walked with them back to the gangplank where they exited the ship.

Caroline and James stood on the dock. Mary Grace watched as Caroline turned to James and whispered something in his ear. He laughed, put his arm around her and they walked away. Mary Grace waved frantically to her parents and tried to call to them, to make them turn and wave just once more, but they were absorbed with each other.

The ship hadn't left yet, but Caroline and James had already forgotten about their daughter.

Mary Grace's arm dropped slowly like a flag being brought in for the night. She went up to the top deck where most of the passengers had gathered to throw streamers. She knew she would find her girlfriends smack in the middle of the party. And she did.

The drunken man from earlier was kissing Cynthia. Or rather Cynthia was kissing the man. He was still carrying his champagne bottle.

Kathryn was tossing streamers at the other passengers who were laughing and shaking hands with everyone around them. Kathryn seemed oblivious to Cynthia and her kissing frenzy with the drunken man.

The tugboats were leading the ocean liner away from the dock, into the river, then farther out to New York Bay where they would then sail into the Atlantic Ocean.

Mary Grace walked up to Cynthia. "Hello, Cynthia. I see you're kissing my new boyfriend."

"What?" Cynthia instantly broke away from the stunned man.

He teetered backward on his heels, his grin wide. He blinked at Mary Grace. "It's you! The girl of my dreams!" He came toward her with open arms, his lips puckered for a kiss.

Mary Grace ducked.

He embraced the air and almost fell flat on his face. He stumbled a foot and a half before getting his bearings and turning back toward Cynthia. "I was wrong! You're the girl of my dreams." He lurched for her just as Mary Grace put her arm out and stopped him.

Cynthia looked at her friend. "You were kissing him, too?"

"No, he kissed me. In front of my parents."

Cynthia glared at the man. "Wow! You must be really drunk."

He shrugged his shoulders. "Don't look at me like that . . . girl of my dreams . . ."

Mary Grace frowned. "I think you're in dreamland, all right, fella. What's your name?"

"Greg McGraw," he said, opening his eyes wide. The late-afternoon sun glinted off the water and shone in Greg's face. He had emerald green eyes rimmed with thick black lashes that matched his black hair. In this light, Mary Grace could see there were no lines in his face and he still had that soft youthful roundness to his cheeks. She guessed he wasn't more than two or three years older than they were. It was quite possible he wasn't even legal age, yet. He was tall, about six foot, with broad shoulders and a narrow torso. He looked a lot like her father, and she guessed he played tennis or racquetball, because his arms appeared quite developed beneath his short-sleeved knit shirt.

"And what is your cabin number, Greg McGraw?"

"I don't remember."

"That figures."

"What's yours?" He asked.

"One fifty-one," she answered quickly, then wished she hadn't told him. "Look, you need to get some sleep and sober up. I've got things to do, myself."

"Okay," he said, saluting her. He turned on his heel, nearly fell down, but somehow managed to keep upright. He half walked and half stumbled away.

Mary Grace laughed as Greg left. Cynthia was scowling at her. "I thought he was cute."

"He's drunk."

"But you gotta admit, he's really cute."

Mary Grace rolled her eyes as she grabbed Cynthia's arm and went over to Kathryn, who was talking to a sweet-looking elderly woman and her husband. She looked up as her two friends approached.

"Kathryn, we're going down to the cabin to divvy up the closets and drawer space. If you want any for yourself, you'd better come with us."

Kathryn turned anxiously to the elderly couple and shook their hands. Then she quickly followed Mary Grace and Cynthia along the outside deck to the staircase. "You two are not going to believe who is on this ship."

Cynthia waved her hand dismissively at Kathryn. "If it isn't Paul McCartney, I'm not interested."

"If one of the Beatles was on this ship, we would have read about it," Kathryn retorted. "I realize all you care about is rock stars, Cynthia."

"That's not true. I care very deeply about movie stars, too. Life does not begin and end with Mick Jagger."

"Oh, for God's sake," Kathryn growled. "Forget I said anything."

Mary Grace grabbed the handrail as she started down the staircase. "If Cynthia isn't interested in your news, Kathryn, I am. Who is it?"

Kathryn passed Cynthia on the stairs to walk beside Mary Grace. She whispered in her friend's ear. "The entire Yale sculling team."

Mary Grace's face was unresponsive. "So?"

"Yalies? You're not excited about Yale men?"

"Should I be?"

"Jesus! Mary Grace, sometimes you are as ... No! More annoying than the kissing bandit back there."

Kathryn jabbed her thumb to indicate Cynthia, who was smirking.

Mary Grace shook her head. "You're sounding like Yvette Mimieux again, Kathryn." For three years, Mary Grace had accused Kathryn of imitating the young starlet—everything from her breathy manner of speaking, to the bleached-blond Rapunzel hairstyle she wore, to the cinched waist, full-skirted, tight-bodiced shirtwaist dresses she preferred. Now she feared Kathryn was trying to imitate one of the characters the actress had played in a movie.

"She's a wonderful person."

"You've never met her!" Mary Grace argued.

"I can think of worse things than being married to a Yale man," Kathryn bantered back.

"You aren't making any sense at all, Kathryn. Just because a boy goes to Yale doesn't mean he's a good person."

"It means that more than likely his daddy is rich," Cynthia chimed in. "I'm with Kathryn. There could be worse things."

By the time they reached their cabin and Mary Grace had unlocked the door, she was convinced she was traveling with two idiots. It was going to be a long voyage. "Am I going to have to listen to this all the way to Southampton?"

"No, not at all," Cynthia assured her. "If you aren't interested, that means there's more for us to pick from."

Mary Grace entered the beautiful stateroom. "You make it sound like you're picking grapefruits at the supermarket."

Cynthia laughed. "It's not that easy. I wish it was."

"Hey!" Kathryn exclaimed as she rushed over to the round table between the two chairs. Sitting on top was a huge bouquet of red roses, rabbit fern and baby's breath. "There must be three dozen roses here."

"Who's it from?" Mary Grace asked, looking for the card.

Cynthia pounced on the small white envelope. "My God! They're from Greg McGraw. The card says, 'To all my dream girls. Luv, Greg.'"

Mary Grace groaned as she peered at the card over Cynthia's shoulder. "I hate it when people write love as l-u-v. It's so..."

"Un-groovy?" Kathryn suggested with a laugh.

"Yeah. Very un-groovy."

Cynthia frowned. "You know what your problem is, Mary Grace? You need to cool it."

"Yeah, cool it," Kathryn said, looking at Greg's card. "I think we're going to have the time of our lives on this trip. Isn't that what we're supposed to do?"

"Yes, it is," Mary Grace said. "It's just that I don't see how a couple dozen roses from some drunk guy is a sign that our trip is going well."

Cynthia smoothed a hand over the back of her perfectly teased blond "flip" hairdo, lifted her chin haughtily and stared down her nose at Mary Grace. "That is because, Mary Grace, you have no vision."

4

The Yale sculling crew was not traveling as guests aboard the *Queen Elizabeth*, but rather as members of the galley staff. They were waiters in the main dining room.

Cynthia was depressed for over an hour when she discovered the truth at dinner their first night at sea.

"I can't tell you how royally pissed I am about this, Kathryn!"

"It's not like I got the wrong story intentionally, Cynthia," Kathryn said defensively.

"Are you sure about that?" Cynthia challenged, eyes glaring.

Mary Grace had to intercede between her two friends, a common role for her. She often wondered why they spent time together, when on the surface it looked as if they didn't even like each other. Cynthia acted pompous and haughty with everyone, and because Kathryn's family was not as wealthy as the Folsums, her prejudices were beginning to show.

"Must you always pick on Kathryn?" Mary Grace asked Cynthia as she shot the elegant blonde a withering look.

"I'm not," Cynthia sniffed.

"You certainly are," Mary Grace retorted sharply. "In fact, you pick on her twice as much as you do me. Why is that, Cynthia? What are you afraid of? That she might take away one of your potential boyfriends? One you haven't even met yet?"

"*Moi*? Afraid?" Cynthia laughed airily, but Mary Grace detected the faint edge of tension in her voice. "I've never been afraid of anything in my life. After all, what's there to be afraid of, really?"

Kathryn looked down at the row of silver forks next to her gold rimmed plate. "Without her daddy, she's just as poor as I am."

Mary Grace expelled a frustrated sigh. "You are *not* poor, Kathryn."

"To her I am." Kathryn raised her head and leveled her eyes at Cynthia. They glistened with cold truth.

Cynthia didn't flinch. She kept her hands folded in her lap. "I'll never be poor," she said flatly. She picked up her water goblet. "I have an inheritance all my own. A trust fund. I'll never be poor."

She kept her gaze even with Mary Grace's stare, but Mary Grace wasn't fooled for a minute. Cynthia was lying about something, but she wasn't sure what it was. Kathryn, though, seemed to buy it.

"That's lovely!" Kathryn said. "I'm happy for you. I wouldn't want anyone to have to live like I do."

Mary Grace turned to her. "What's so terrible about how you live?"

Kathryn looked at the forks again. There were tears in her eyes. She gazed across the dining room that was filling up with beautifully dressed rich people. Mary Grace knew that her friend loved all this elegance, this life-style. Though the Norwoods had enough money to send her to Woodlands Academy, they never went on a vacation and Mary Grace never saw them dressed like these people. They had both worked in order to send Kathryn to boarding school. They would have to work even harder to send her to college next year, but they were determined to give her the best future they could.

Mary Grace knew her friend felt guilty taking so much from them. She felt guilty that she was still dependent on them. Sometimes, she talked about finding a boy to marry, like Yvette Mimieux did in that movie. Then her parents wouldn't have to worry about her and pay for her schooling. She loved her parents and she wanted them to spend their money on themselves. But they seldom did.

Kathryn gave Mary Grace a piercing look. "How do you think you'd feel if your best friend's parents had to foot the bill for your trip?"

Cynthia gasped and threw her hand over her mouth. Her eyes were wide as saucers. "They didn't!"

Mary Grace dropped her gaze and her shoulders slumped. "I wouldn't like it at all."

"Neither do I," Kathryn said coolly.

"Then why did you come?"

"My parents were embarrassed, but they wanted this trip for me. It's an opportunity they said they'll never have. They intend to pay your father back."

"Oh, shit!" Cynthia was still in shock.

"Would you shut up?" Mary Grace said sharply.

Cynthia shook her head. "I will not. I had no idea this was going on, Kathryn." She put her hand on Kathryn's shoulder condescendingly.

Kathryn shook it off. "Don't you start with the pity crap, either, or so help me, I'll . . ."

"You'll do what?" Cynthia challenged self-righteously.

Kathryn's beautifully full lips formed into an uplifted crescent. "I *will* take your boyfriends."

Mary Grace and Cynthia had often stated that Kathryn was probably the most beautiful senior at Woodlands Academy. These past six months she had matured and become even more beautiful. Whereas Cynthia needed her elegant, chic North Michigan Avenue boutique wardrobe to make the most of her cosmopolitan looks, Kathryn needed nothing. She was a natural beauty. Her skin was flawless, with not a freckle or zit in sight. Her hair was naturally pale blond, though she sometimes lightened it even more with lemon juice and Sun In. And her figure was perfect. She was tall, over five foot nine inches, with long, lean legs, slim hips, a small waist and perfectly shaped breasts. Of everything, Mary Grace envied Kathryn her figure. She knew Cynthia envied her fine facial bones and features.

Kathryn had the ability to walk into a room and make every man and woman look at her. She had an attitude of confidence that neither Mary Grace nor Cynthia shared. It was Kathryn's mesmerizing beauty that balanced the trio.

Mary Grace looked at Cynthia, her eyebrow cocked. "She can do it, too."

Cynthia backed down. "All right, already. Truce."

Kathryn was the first to laugh, sounding like crystal prisms clapping each other. She tipped her beautiful head, tossing her shoulder-length blond curls.

"That's better!" Mary Grace, the peacemaker, sighed.

Just then, they were joined by the elderly couple whom Kathryn had befriended earlier that afternoon as they set sail.

"Mr. and Mrs. Sheldon Rose," Kathryn introduced, "this is Cynthia Fulsom and Mary Grace Whittaker of Winnetka, Illinois."

They all shook hands and exchanged greetings as the head waiter came to their table. Dressed in a black tuxedo, he was tall, dark-haired, brown-eyed and not a day over thirty.

"My name is Ian Welsh and I will be your waiter for this voyage," he said in a thick British accent.

Cynthia eyed Ian like a jeweler scrutinizing a diamond. Mary Grace wanted to smack her. She was pleased when Ian pretended not to notice Cynthia's appalling behavior.

"My assistant is Richard Bartlow," Ian continued as a young blond blue-eyed man, also dressed in a black tuxedo, approached the table with a tray filled with butter, bread and glasses of ice water. "This is Richard's maiden voyage on our ship, but not his first attempt at serving." Ian's tone was pompous and typically British. "We are pleased to have his assistance in the dining room. If you need anything at all, please ask myself or Richard. We are at your beck and call." He cast a glance at Kathryn as he said this.

The server, Richard, busied himself with setting out the tumblers of ice water and distributing rolls and butter patties with silver tongs, then quickly went back to the kitchen while Ian took the dinner orders.

Now that the elderly couple were seated, the conversation was pleasant but strained. Cynthia spent most of her time canvasing the dining room for potential dates, though she seemed to find none except the waiters. Mary Grace was sure she'd never dated a blue-collar worker in her life, and she didn't intend to start now. She had her sights aimed high.

While Cynthia became more and more discouraged with her perusal of the available men in the dining room, Mary Grace turned her interest to Mr. and Mrs. Rose.

"Where in New York do you live, Mrs. Rose?" she asked.

"Park Avenue. Eight seventy-five Park Avenue," Mrs. Rose said it as if Mary Grace was supposed to know what the address meant. She seemed disappointed when Mary Grace didn't make the connection. "We live right under the princess."

"Lee Radziwell? You live in her building?"

"That's right, dear," Mrs. Rose replied, clearly satisfied she'd made the impression she'd hoped.

Mary Grace now had both Kathryn's and Cynthia's attention. They were giving her the how-did-you-know-*that* look. "Why, her penthouse was just photographed for *House Beautiful!* I just love what her decorator did. That view out that expanse of windows is breathtaking, isn't it? Have you seen her place?"

Mrs. Rose looked thrilled to be asked the question. "Actually, dear. I have. Of course, I peeked in when the workmen were laying the floors. I haven't been formally invited up . . . yet," she said as if expecting an invitation at any moment.

Mary Grace thought Mrs. Sheldon Rose was a crack-up. "May I ask, Mrs. Rose, how was it you knew about the Yale sculling team being on the ship?"

Mrs. Rose wrinkled her nose like a bunny. She seemed tickled that someone was interested in what she knew. "I asked around, dear. When you get to be my age, people think we're invisible. I hear all sorts of things from strangers. They tell me their innermost thoughts and secrets. Sometimes they actually want my advice. I guess that's because I've lived so long they think I should be wise. But I'm not."

Mr. Rose patted her hand affectionately. "Now, that's not true, dear. I think you're very wise." He looked at Mary Grace with milky blue eyes. "She's eighty-two. I'm eighty-four. We've been married since I was nineteen.

We've raised six children. Two died in the war. Four survive. She's seen me through bankruptcy twice and the deaths of every one of my family except our last four children. I haven't been bored for a single minute with this woman. I think she is very wise."

Mary Grace felt a tug at her sentimental strings. "What a beautiful, wonderful thing to say, Mr. Rose. I only hope someday someone says that to me," she told him as the server returned to the table and placed salads in front of each of them.

When he tried to serve Mary Grace, his arm grazed her right breast. She looked up to meet his glance.

"Excuse me, miss," he said.

Mary Grace frowned at the good-looking young man with the thick crop of golden hair. God! He was being fresh, but in order to put him in his place, she'd have to draw a great deal of attention to herself. She knew her cheeks were blazing red with both anger and frustration. She wanted to slap him!

He was smiling at her. His teeth were perfectly straight and glistening white. She noticed that he had a suntan and shockingly brilliant blue eyes. He was so handsome he nearly took her breath away, but she was too angry at him to think of anything else.

Richard Bartlow left the table and returned to the kitchen for the guests' ice tea.

Ian Welsh grabbed his arm. "I saw that, Bartlow," he said with a superior tone.

"What are you talking about?"

"Do you want to get the boot? Then keep harassing the guests. They'll file a complaint and you'll be gone, but good."

Richard lifted a tray with glasses of ice tea. "You've got me all wrong, Ian. I know very well who Miss Mary Grace Whittaker is. Her father, James Whittaker, is one of the most influential businessmen in Chicago."

"I've never heard of him."

"That's because you're not from my neck of the woods. I know these midwestern girls. Don't worry about me. I can take care of myself."

"Just see that you don't get caught fraternizing with the guests, Richard."

"Don't give me any of your limey shit. You don't give a damn about me. All you care about is your own ass because the head steward will call you down for my mistakes."

Ian winced. "Yes, he will."

"Look, you can't tell me that half the guys working here aren't looking out for themselves. Why, I've even seen you pay just a bit too much attention to that divorcée from Dallas. I'm not doing anything you wouldn't do, Ian."

"I'm older and so are the women."

"But it's the same goddamn game. I'm younger than you are and so is my stomping ground." Richard flashed a charming, though insincere smile. "I know exactly what I'm doing. Why do you think I requested your station? From the minute I saw the guest roster, I knew I wanted to meet Miss Mary Grace Whittaker." Richard poked his forefinger into Ian's chest for emphasis. "James Whittaker is my ticket to ride."

Ian glared at him. "Just make sure nobody sees you."

"No problem, friend. No problem at all." Richard went back to the dining room.

* * *

"Mary Grace is going to be the next Frank Lloyd Wright," Cynthia announced proudly to the Roses over dinner.

"An architect? That *is* a lofty ambition," Mr. Rose said.

Mary Grace remembered her confrontation with her parents earlier that day. "Yeah, well, I've discovered I might have set my sights too high."

"What?" Cynthia's back went ramrod-straight with shock.

"Huh?" Kathryn leaned forward, her eyes riveted on Mary Grace's solemn face. "What's going on, Mary Grace? What haven't you told us?"

Mary Grace was stunned at the burning she felt at the back of her eyes. What were tears doing there? she wondered. She was in a formal setting with her two best friends and two total strangers, and her life was being discussed as though it were part of the menu. "Nothing."

"Bull roar," Cynthia replied. Clearly, she wasn't going to back down until she knew the story. "You are my friend, Mary Grace. Friends should know everything. How can I help you if you don't tell me what's happening?"

"You can't help this," Mary Grace said, picking at her salad.

Mrs. Rose patted Mary Grace's hand. "You needn't tell your friends in our presence. You have plenty of time to share your feelings with them after dinner."

Mary Grace smiled wanly at the older woman. "Your husband was right. You are wise."

The server returned and removed the salad plates and handed them to a busboy, whom he introduced as Stephen Galesburg. Stephen, who looked to be in his early twenties, was much shorter than Richard Bartlow, with brown hair, brown eyes, a very strong jawline and a stocky physique. Stephen placed the used dishes on a huge tray and took them to the kitchen. A second busboy brought out the entrées.

Ian Welsh returned to the table and served the entrées himself. He turned each plate so that the meat portion was facing the guest. He snapped his fingers at Richard and ordered him to pour coffee and refill the ice teas. He snapped his fingers at Stephen and told him to bring more rolls and butter. Ian's manner was crisp yet friendly toward the guests, but Mary Grace couldn't help noticing that his attitude toward Richard and Stephen was condescending, almost patronizing. She realized that for Ian, his current occupation was his life's career. He'd been trained in the old British school. Richard and Stephen, on the other hand, were definitely American, and though they were efficient in their jobs, she knew this was only a temporary position for them.

Richard walked past Mary Grace's chair, filled her water glass, refreshed the rolls and butter, and though his arm passed very close to her shoulder, he never touched her again. She was beginning to think the whole thing had been an accident, after all. Richard was only doing his job.

The food was divine and, according to Mr. and Mrs. Rose, the wine selections were not only adequate but surprisingly diverse.

By the time dessert was served, Mary Grace was feeling the pressure of Cynthia's anxiety to know what turn of events had taken place in Mary Grace's life. The three girls declined dessert and coffee and asked Mr. and Mrs.

Rose to excuse them. Mrs. Rose explained that she liked to linger over her dessert and coffee and that they might take as much as another hour in the dining room. They were most happy to excuse the girls.

Cynthia practically dragged Mary Grace out of the dining room, hurrying them up the carpeted stairway to the upper deck then down the highly polished wood deck to the front of the ship. Metal and plastic chairs had been stacked against the wall at sunset. They took three chaise longues and sat under the stars.

Huge voluminous clouds that looked as if they were backlit drifted across the indigo sky. Mary Grace thought she'd never seen so many stars. The wind in her hair felt cleansing as she closed her eyes, indulging herself in the sensation of being suspended between earth and sky.

She took a deep breath and exhaled before she told them. "My parents are sending me to Barrett College."

"I thought you wanted to go to St. Mary's," Kathryn said.

"I do, but they won't allow it. They said it was too far away. They want me to stay close to home."

Kathryn would be happy going to any college, Mary Grace knew, as long as it didn't put her parents in the poorhouse. She'd been accepted at Mundelein College in Mundelein where they lived, and she had no problem with commuting to school every day.

"It's the kiss of death," Mary Grace said. "It's bad enough I couldn't go to Stanford University or someplace where I can actually study architecture. If I went to St. Mary's, I'd be close to Notre Dame, I could take extra classes there sometimes."

"Not to mention all the men," Cynthia said lightheartedly.

Mary Grace was too depressed to berate Cynthia for her shallow outlook. "My life is over."

"Your life isn't over," Cynthia tried to cheer her up. "It's just temporarily derailed."

"You don't understand what's going on. My parents are going to rule everything in my life. If I thought it was bad before, now they've really got their hooks into me. And what can I do? I can't pay for my education myself!"

"I know what you mean." Cynthia sank her chin into her palm and glumly looked out at the infinite expanse of dark sea.

"You know, when you think about it, our choices aren't so terrific," Kathryn said. "I can bust my butt going to school to get a teaching degree or be a nurse, then you work for a year, maybe two. But really, your folks are always after you to find a guy, get married and have kids. My mother never talks about anything else. It's always, 'Who's taking you to the dance this weekend, Kathryn? Are his parents Catholic? What parish do they belong to? Is he going to college? Does he have a job?' I hear that every day."

Mary Grace turned to her. "No kidding? They do that?"

"Yeah."

Mary Grace had known Kathryn for more than five years and she'd never known this about her life.

"My mother says that because I'm pretty, I should nab a good one. That's how she says it, too. Like I was out fishing or something."

"Well, hell!" Cynthia chimed in. "Isn't that what we *are* doing? Fishing, hunting. It's all the same. I figure if that's what we're doing, we might as well go well armed."

Mary Grace shook her head. "What are you talking about?"

"The folks at home won't rest until we're married and out of their hair. That's how I read this situation. Frankly, I can't wait to get the hell out of Dodge. I intend to aim high, straight and use an elephant gun to bag my man. I'm going after a millionaire at least. Maybe a count or an Italian duke."

Mary Grace was shocked. "You're serious?"

"Damn right I am. I've figured it all out. First, you pick out the one you want—check his family background, financials, read up on him in the newspapers and magazines. The higher the profile, the harder they fall. I figure what I've got going for me is youth, smarts and a passably great face. I'm not Kathryn gorgeous, but I can hold my own. Then, after I pick out the guy, I throw myself at him. Get his attention. Once I have his attention, I pull back—even back off. Stay mysterious. Just when he's about to give up, I throw myself at him again. Now, he's enticed. Then, I disappear. He can't find me. He goes nuts trying to find me. Finally, I throw myself at him again and demand that he marry me. He pops the question and bingo! We live happily ever after."

Mary Grace couldn't believe her friend was serious. "You've been seeing too many movies."

"You're nuts," Kathryn said.

"Nuts?" Cynthia shook her head. "I don't think so. Hell, with your looks, Kathryn, I guarantee you could hook the richest man in America. You'd be set for life."

"What about love?" Mary Grace asked. "Where does love fit into all this?"

"You're the one who's nuts. This is real life, Mary Grace. Love is for saps. I can't believe you're even suggesting such a thing. You, Miss Architect USA. You don't even care about boys . . . men."

Mary Grace looked out at the lonely sea. "I always thought there was no sense in worrying about it. I always thought he'd just be there for me. I'd look up one day and God would put my husband in my path."

Cynthia howled. She laughed so hard she choked. Kathryn giggled at first. Then she chuckled. Then she laughed out loud.

"I've heard some funny stories, Mary Grace, but that's a riot," Kathryn said.

"Everybody knows it's hard as hell to find the right husband," Cynthia said. "Kathryn is going to do all right. I never worried about her. She's been practicing since she was fourteen how to get a man. He won't be a millionaire, but she'll find a husband, all right. I'll get my millionaire, you can count on that. But shit, Mary Grace, you scare the hell out of me! I figured you'd be the career woman out of the three of us. You're the one who's supposed to have brains."

"I *do* have brains. Plenty of them," Mary Grace said defensively. "Besides, I'm not getting married for a long time. I've got four years of college ahead of me, even if it is at Barrett."

Kathryn touched Mary Grace's shoulder. "It won't be so bad, Mary Grace. I'll be commuting to school and I'll get to see you more often this way."

"I thought you were trying to cheer her up, Kathryn," Cynthia said.

"She is," Mary Grace said, patting Kathryn's hand. She inhaled the sea air. "I don't care what you say, I'm holding out for love. Just like that nice Mr. and Mrs. Rose. They've been married all these years and look how he pays so much attention to her. He treats her like a . . . princess. That's the way it should be."

They were all silent for a long time, watching the stars slide by as the ship streaked through the black night waters.

On the observation deck suspended above the prow of the boat and under the navigation bridge, Richard Bartlow stood at a railing watching the three pretty girls from Chicago. This was his favorite place on the ship, especially this late at night when he could feel the power of the ship as it sliced through the mighty Atlantic Ocean.

He never dreamed he'd be so fortunate as to be on the same voyage as the three girls from table sixty-two. With the wind rolling over his face, he'd caught only bits and snatches of their conversation, but he'd heard enough.

This was his fourth run to Europe as a waiter. He'd been working his way through college now for over four years waiting tables. Richard loved to travel and the only way he could see the world was to work his way there. On this trip, he'd made friends with a lot of the crew members. All except Ian, his head waiter, but he figured that was because he'd tried to romance Ian's girlfriend, one of the secretaries in the purser's office. Richard had only dated Chris to find out what kind of crowd was booked on this trip. Once he discovered that Ian was interested in Chris, he'd backed off.

There was only one person on this voyage *he* was interested in. Richard had done a bit of research, a practice he'd been taught in English literature and American history classes at Yale. The Whittakers were loaded.

He gazed down at the girls stretched out under the stars, looking as if they didn't have a care in the world.

That was the kind of attitude and mind-set that wealth gave a person, he thought.

Mary Grace wasn't as pretty as the tall one, Kathryn, but she did have fascinating breasts he'd wanted to fondle the minute he'd laid eyes on them. Besides, it wasn't Mary Grace's body he was after; it was her father's business connections and money he wanted.

Yes, Mary Grace was the one he intended to make fall in love with him.

5

Mary Grace slathered a thick coat of suntan lotion on her arms, legs, upper chest and abdomen. She placed a white terry-cloth beach towel over the lounge chair, put her sunglasses on and stretched out to enjoy a peaceful afternoon away from her friends.

Mary Grace had always been a loner. Now she knew why. People and their habits made her crazy. Thinking back to earlier that morning with her cabin mates only made her more appreciative of her time alone.

Kathryn had risen at dawn and insisted on doing her calisthenics in the room while she and Cynthia tried to sleep. It took Kathryn over forty-five minutes to complete a thousand leg lifts and two hundred waist twists. Now Mary Grace knew why Kathryn had such a perfect body—she worked at it.

When Cynthia had gotten up, she had to have a cup of coffee immediately and nobody got it to her fast enough. She made a pest of herself calling the room steward to have coffee brought to her. The steward had brought cream. Cynthia wanted milk. When he returned with the milk, she complained that the coffee wasn't hot enough. Finally, he told her that an early breakfast buffet was being served on the sun deck. She could get hot coffee with milk there faster than he could bring it to her.

Cynthia was not happy. She had to put on her makeup, which took her nearly an hour before she felt she was presentable.

While Cynthia hogged the bathroom, Mary Grace had picked up her paperback copy of *The Carpetbaggers*. She'd hidden the racy novel at the bottom of her train case so that her mother wouldn't find it. She knew her mother would have thrown a fit if she knew she was reading "smut." Mary Grace thought of the book as the beginning of her independence from her.

When Cynthia had announced she was almost ready to go to breakfast, Kathryn returned from her morning walk around the deck. She was wearing a pair of white shorts and a madras-plaid hooded windbreaker. Her cheeks were rosy from the exertion and there was a light film of perspiration on her forehead. She wore not even a smidge of mascara and she'd never looked more beautiful.

"Come on, you guys! It's a beautiful day out there. I can't wait to try out the pool." She flopped down on the bed next to Mary Grace.

Mary Grace pulled the sheet up to her chin, self-consciously.

"I was talking to one of the stewards," Kathryn continued. "He told me that last winter they completely overhauled the ship. They've never had the pool before, all the plumbing is new and so is the air-conditioning. If we'd have taken this trip last summer, we might have gotten a room without a bathroom! Can you imagine that?"

Cynthia walked out of the bathroom and said, "I never would have made it to Southampton alive! I'm a bathroom person."

"No joke," Mary Grace said, reaching to the end of the bed for her white seersucker robe that matched the baby-doll pajamas she wore. She slipped out of bed and into the robe before either of her friends could see her body.

"Sorry," Cynthia said, standing aside so that Mary Grace could pass her into the bathroom. "I have my own bath at home and the maid always cleans up for me. Just tell me when I'm hogging it. I'm not doing it on purpose. It's just habit."

The memory of that morning began to fade as Mary Grace lay on the sun deck feeling the warm rays of the sun caress her body. "Hmmph. Habit," she said to herself. She turned her face from the sun. "A bad habit."

"I'm not sure I can find one of those, but I'll look," a male voice said.

"What?" Startled, she yanked off her sunglasses.

"I asked if you cared for a drink," someone said, bending down toward Mary Grace.

With the sun in her eyes she couldn't see him. She put her sunglasses back on and she cocked her head to the side so that her face was shielded by his shadow.

It was Richard Bartlow. He was wearing a white shirt and black pants. The sun danced in his hair like golden fireflies, and his eyes were as blue as the sky and sea, yet more clear and inviting. But it was his smile that dazzled her most of all.

Suddenly, she was intensely aware that she was wearing her first two-piece bathing suit. It wasn't really a bikini, but the two skimpy patches of black gingham check fit her full chest snugly. The bottoms were cut just below her navel with cutesy red strawberries embroidered on the side of each hip. As usual, Mary Grace had not found the kind of bathing suit that made her feel comfortable. That year, she had itsy-bitsy teenie-weenie bikinis to choose from or countrified gingham checks that covered her body as well as she could expect. Still, she had hoped to find something sophisticated. Even though she knew they were going to Europe where half the women sunbathed without any top at all, Mary Grace still couldn't bring herself to flaunt her breasts.

"I don't care for anything," she said tersely, wishing he would go away.

"I can get you a piña colada," he offered, still smiling charmingly.

"I'm not legal," she said.

"You can say that again."

"What?" This time when she took off her glasses, she looked him in the eyes. She was convinced that he was referring to her breasts. Most boys usually made some crack about her body within seconds of meeting her. She hated it.

Richard was looking into her eyes. His gaze didn't waver. "Sorry. I shouldn't have said that. It's just that I've been working this ship for several seasons and I'm not used to seeing anyone my age."

Mary Grace wasn't sure if it was the casual, friendly tone of his voice or the way he stood purposefully blocking the sun for her so that she could see him that caused her to drop her guard. "You're a lot older than I am."

"I just turned twenty-one in January."

"See? I told you! I was eighteen last September."

"Yikes!" He slapped the side of his face with his hand. She could see his gold-and-blue-stone college ring as it flashed in the sun. "I did think you were closer to my age."

"I'm not *that* much younger," she said with a flirtatious smile.

"True. These are international waters. Do you want a drink? Mai Tai? Singapore Sling? You name it."

"No, thanks, I don't drink."

"Ah! Not only a beautiful woman, but a wise one, too." Richard pretended to tip an invisible hat to her before he walked away.

Mary Grace watched as he went from lounge chair to lounge chair, taking orders for drinks, then filling them. She pretended not to notice that each time he delivered a trayful of drinks, he passed by her, no matter how far around the pool he had to go.

She rolled over onto her stomach so that he couldn't see her face. She tried to read her smutty book, but the paragraphs didn't interest her one-tenth as much as Richard did.

She liked the way he walked, with his shoulders square and the gentle sway of his narrow hips. He planted his feet assuredly on the deck as if he possessed the ship and the sea beneath. There was an aura of mastery about him that she'd only seen in older men like her father. Richard was different from Ian, who knew his domain was the dining room.

Whatever space he occupied, Richard made it into his own territory. There was nothing predatory about his manner, but rather he was presumptive in attitude. The immense sun deck was manned by half a dozen waiters who moved timidly within the confines of their station. Richard crossed lines and barriers; he went where he saw he was needed.

She watched how he made idle chatter with the older passengers and told them jokes that made them laugh. She noticed that he paid particular attention to the fattest, oldest and ugliest women. He told them how pretty they looked in their beach coverups. He brought them extra towels and let them know when they were getting too much sun. He helped an elderly man with a portable transistor radio. He took photographs of couples sitting poolside with the cameras they handed him.

Though the other pool waiters were half as busy, when the passengers needed assistance or another drink, they called for Richard by name.

They had been at sea only twenty-four hours and already Mary Grace could tell Richard was king of his domain.

By the end of the afternoon, Mary Grace had used over half her bottle of suntan lotion. She had turned over every thirty minutes, as her mother had always instructed her, and she hadn't read a single word of her book. The bartender was closing down the sun-deck bar as the passengers left to change clothes for cocktails and the early dinner seating. The waiters picked up the empty glasses and used beach towels, throwing them into huge royal-blue canvas hampers.

Mary Grace was the last to leave the deck. She stuck her arms through her white terry-cloth coverup. She had acquired a perfectly even tan. She slid her feet into her sandals, thinking that Cynthia's earlier suggestion they all get manicures and pedicures might not be such a bad idea.

Richard walked toward her. He was the only waiter left on the deck.

"So, beautiful lady, will I see you at dinner tonight?"

"Of course," she said, thinking how odd it was that an ordinary question and an equally ordinary response could elicit this rush of excitement through her body.

Mary Grace didn't trust these unfamiliar feelings. She looked at him. "Can I ask you something?"

"Sure," he said, flashing her that open, friendly smile.

"I watched you today. How you treat the passengers. How nice you were to everyone. Some of them were pretty demanding."

"That's true. They can be very demanding sometimes."

"But you're not tired in the least."

"No. Should I be?"

She shrugged. "You must like your work, then."

"I suppose I do."

She shielded her eyes with her hand as the sun descended in a huge orange orb. "You don't strike me as the waiter type."

"That's interesting. Because I'm not just a waiter, Mary Grace Whittaker. I'm a lot more than that." He leaned down so that his face was very close to hers. His eyes were piercing.

She wondered what it would be like to feel his lips on hers. Mary Grace had been kissed on dates in high school, but never anything serious. She'd once had to fight off a linebacker from New Trier High School, but all he'd done was grope her a little and he hadn't kissed her... not really.

At this moment, gazing into Richard Bartlow's intense blue eyes, Mary Grace felt she'd never done anything so intimate in her life. She'd heard her father say once that "Life spins on a dime." She felt herself spinning as she peered deeply into Richard's eyes.

"I...I didn't think so," she finally said when she found her voice again. "Who are you?"

"I'm a recent graduate of Yale. I was on the sculling team last year. I wanted to see Europe one more time before I start graduate school."

"Oh," she said weakly. He was taking her into the territory where he was king. She could feel herself surrendering to his will as he told her of his plans and goals. He was sure of himself and his future. His energy was so focused she felt as if she were being run over by a freight train. Richard knew where he was going and Mary Grace knew instantly that he was going to make his dreams come true.

"Once I get my master's in business, I'm moving to California where the building market is hot."

"Building?"

"Yes. I intend to build houses, churches, hospitals, skyscrapers . . . anything they let me build."

"I . . . I don't believe this!"

"Believe what?" he asked.

"I've always dreamed of being an architect."

Richard was stunned. "You're kidding? I never met a girl who even knew how to spell it, much less study it."

"This is weird." She shook her head.

Richard sat down on the end of the chaise longue next to Mary Grace, having obviously forgotten he was supposed to be getting ready to work the dinner shift.

"This is just incredible, Mary Grace. I talk to my friends and family at home about building and they think I'm nuts. Nobody there knows what I'm saying. And the trouble is, I get so excited just thinking about subdivisions with my name on the street signs that I either bore everyone to tears or drive them crazy. But I can't help it."

"I know just what you mean, Richard," she said enthusiastically. "My girlfriends always want to discuss movies or rock stars or fashions, and I want to go look at plumbing fixtures."

Excitement sparkled in his eyes. "This is just great, Mary Grace. Too great!" Exuberantly, he kissed her cheek. "It's as if we were meant to meet! Kismet!"

"You think we were fated?"

He jumped off the chaise and held out his hand to help her up. "I'm convinced of it. How many times have you taken this voyage?"

"Never."

"See? That's what I'm talking about. This is my fourth trip. I've never met anyone I was attracted to. No one who shared the same dreams as I do."

"And we have a lot in common?"

He smiled charmingly and shook his head. "Lady, I think we're gonna surprise each other." He took her hands in both of his. "Look, I've got to get ready for the dinner shift." He laughed. "I don't want to get thrown overboard this far from land. So, how about meeting me at midnight on the observation deck."

He dropped her hands and started walking backward away from her. "Promise you'll meet me?"

She nodded, smiling. "Okay. Midnight."

He dashed away. Just as he got to the staircase, he turned and waved to her. Then he vanished down the darkening stairway.

Mary Grace was still breathless from being in Richard's presence. She hadn't the slightest idea she'd just been baited and hooked.

6

Mary Grace met Richard every night at midnight on the observation deck. They kept their romance a secret, even from her girlfriends. By their second day at sea, Cynthia was spending time with Greg McGraw, now sober but still spending too much money at the ship's florist on Cynthia. Kathryn kept herself busy by getting her first facial, massage, pedicure and manicure. She went to the ship's beauty shop and had her legs waxed, her eyebrows shaped and her hair professionally bleached and conditioned. She swam a hundred and fifty laps in the pool every day in addition to her regular exercise routine. She shopped in the ship's boutiques, and at dinner she told the other girls how fast her days sped by.

Mary Grace was terrified Richard would lose his job over her, so she made a special effort not to let her eyes meet his when he served her dinner each night. She went to the pool every day and handed him notes she'd written to him. He answered her back on the same sheets of paper, delivering his notes when he brought her ice tea.

The thing that Mary Grace liked most about Richard was that he was genuinely interested in what she had to say. When they were finally alone at midnight, they would look at the stars and talk about their plans for their lives. Richard told her he wanted to build houses and shopping centers. He despised the ugly slapdash ranch houses being built around the nation, he believed it was possible to build houses with character and grace at affordable prices. He told her that everyone in the industry said it couldn't be done. He said it was his destiny to prove them wrong.

"I'm going to be famous someday, Mary Grace. You wait and see. People all over America are going to know who Richard Bartlow is. I'm going to break all the rules these pompous asses think are so damn sacrosanct."

"I believe you will," she said.

"You do?"

"Yes. And one of those pompous asses is my father. I can't wait to see the look on his face when you make headlines and I tell him I know you."

Richard stopped short and looked at her closely. "Whittaker. You're not James Whittaker's daughter?"

"I call him James the Third."

"Shit." He raked his hand through his thick blond hair. "This is too much."

Mary Grace didn't like the dread she saw in Richard's eyes. She was afraid that now he knew the truth about her family their relationship would change somehow. "Don't hold it against me," she said lightly but feeling a sick, heavy tug at the pit of her stomach.

"I read about him in *Newsweek* two years ago. What a stroke of genius it was to convert that warehouse district on the south side of Chicago into a mall. And then I read about his idea to build a shopping mall straight up in a skyscraper. You think he'll pull that one off?"

"I'm sure he will." Mary Grace realized that suddenly Richard was more interested in knowing about her father and his projects than he was in her. She felt diminished by the change in conversation. She was having a good time with Richard, but she hadn't realized he and his opinions were becoming important to her.

Richard took her hand and kissed it, then lifted it to his cheek. With his other hand he smoothed a lock of windblown hair from her face. "You look almost ethereal in moonlight," he said softly. He lowered his face to hers.

She knew he was going to kiss her. All this time together and he hadn't kissed her yet, she thought. She'd waited for this moment for three days. She'd dreamed about it every night and visualized it every afternoon while she sat by the pool. Now that she knew it would happen, she felt timid and awkward. She was suddenly afraid.

She shivered.

"Are you cold, Mary Grace?" Richard asked huskily as he moved his lips closer to hers.

"Yes . . . no," she answered, wondering if she should walk away. Once he kissed her, their relationship was going to change again. They were friends now. Comrades in dreams, she liked to think of themselves. But he was going to take her on another kind of discovery. She thought she wanted to know what it was like to be kissed by such a handsome and compelling man, yet she couldn't help wondering if he and the kiss would be too much for her. What if he overwhelmed her? What if his power was greater than hers? What if she disappointed him? What if he disappointed her?

His lips touched hers tenderly at first, testing her response. He moved her hand from his cheek to the nape of his neck and left it there. He slipped his hand around the back of her waist and slowly, deftly pressed her body against his.

His lips were strong and commanding, just as she hoped they would be. He smelled like the sun and cologne and he tasted like mint toothpaste. His lips captured her mouth in a possessive kiss. His tongue prodded her lips apart, then plunged into the interior of her mouth.

Mary Grace had never been French-kissed, though Cynthia and Kathryn had told her all about it. She remembered the rule the nuns had taught them never to let a boy kiss you longer than two seconds. Now she knew why.

She felt as though her blood had turned to lava as it surged through her body. Tingling chills spread across her breasts, and for the first time in her life, she ached to have them touched and caressed. The touch of his tongue against hers sent a new wave of goose bumps over her back and abdomen. She felt the pit of her loins ache. She sank her fingers into his nape, forcing his mouth to slant over hers again and again.

She pressed her body against his without guidance. She wanted him to know how their bodies melded together. She wanted to feel his chest against her breasts and discover the kind of secrets he could show her.

He slipped his hand down to the base of her spine and pressed her abdomen against his very hard, very large erection. His breathing quickened. "We should slow down, Mary Grace," he said between kisses.

"Richard . . ."

He slid his hands to the sides of her waist and onto her hips and cupped her buttocks, pressing her into him.

Richard was sweating.

Mary Grace pressed her breasts against him again. "Richard, please," she moaned as he plunged his tongue into her mouth once more. "Touch me. Please . . ."

"I don't . . ." He shook his head, then threw it back and pressed her pelvis into his erection. "Oh, G . . . od," he groaned deeply.

Mary Grace didn't know what had come over her. She was engulfed in a torrent of passion she hadn't known existed. She was breathing as fast as he was. Perspiration crowned her head. She wanted to touch, kiss and lick every part of him. All the inhibitions she'd experienced her whole life were shattered in an instant. She moved her hands to her neck and unbuttoned the front of her shirtwaist dress. She slipped the sleeveless bodice to her waist and unhooked her bra.

She wanted him to see her breasts, see what had prevented her from ever loving herself.

Richard gasped as the moonlight struck her creamy, dewy skin. He took her breasts in his hands. "I've never seen anyone so beautiful ... so magnificently beautiful ..."

He caressed and massaged. He rubbed her nipples between his forefinger and thumb and nearly made Mary Grace's knees buckle. She moaned with the sounds of surrender.

He kissed her breasts. He took the nipples into his mouth and suckled them. He stroked her with his hands and kneaded the flesh until he heard a tiny yelp escape from her lips.

"Mary Grace, you're the most beautiful woman in the world. You've got to know that."

"Richard ... just don't stop touching me." She was gasping for breath. She never knew it was possible for a man to make her feel so important, so appreciated. In eighteen years she'd never felt like this. She wondered if it was possible to feel like this for the rest of her life.

"My God, I could make love to you every day and every night for eternity," he said.

Mary Grace knew then that she would find a way to make Richard marry her. She forgot about college degrees and architecture school. She forgot about buildings, houses, trusses, gables, roof pitches and vaulted ceilings. She knew now why women gave up their dreams for a man. She wanted nothing except to ride this pitch of excitement each day of her life.

She hiked up her skirt and urged him to put his hand between her legs. Mary Grace was shocked at her own boldness. She didn't know what had come over her and she didn't care. There was no time for thinking any longer. It was time to feel.

Richard slipped his fingers between her wet lips and found her bud. She slid back and forth against his fingers and she could feel herself getting wetter with each stroke.

"Richard . . ." She put her mouth on his shoulder and bit his flesh as she climaxed on his hand.

He groaned and withdrew his hand as she slowed her rhythmic gyrations. He pulled her pelvis closer and rubbed, putting his mouth over hers as he ejaculated.

She swallowed his cry of passion, then held his head to her breast as Richard leaned into her, exhausted.

"God, Mary Grace. I've never done anything like that in my life," he said.

"But, you're so much older and so much . . ."

"Look, I'm no angel. But I promise you, no one has ever done this to me." He looked down at the wet stain his semen had left on his khaki pants. Then he lifted his face to hers and smiled.

Moonlight caught in his blond hair and danced in the soft, watery lights in his eyes. "Richard, I've never, ever done anything like this. And I *have* been an angel."

He chuckled lightly as he touched her cheek. "You're crying, Mary Grace." He folded her into his arms so that her bare breasts pressed against his shirt. "Please don't cry." He hugged her tightly. "Did I . . . hurt you?"

"Oh, no, Richard. Nothing like that. It was just that . . . you were so kind to me . . ." All she could think about was that he'd told her she was beautiful. Magnificently beautiful.

"I wasn't kind at all," he said firmly. "I was being damn selfish, if you'll know the truth."

"You were?"

"Seeing you in the moonlight like this, Mary Grace, you could drive any man crazy. I took advantage of you. But I'm not sorry in the least. I'm glad I did what I did. I wanted you and that was all there was to it."

Mary Grace's mouth went dry. "Was that all?"

Richard pulled away and looked into her eyes. "Right now, my thoughts are all messed up. I had a very particular plan for my life, Mary Grace. I know just where I'm going and how I'm going to get there. I can't be sidetracked."

She shook her head. "I'm not doing that."

"The hell you aren't, standing there looking like a goddess in the moonlight. You make me want to take you all over again. I swear to God, Mary Grace, you are a temptress. I can't . . . I won't give up everything I've worked for because . . . because of you."

He started pulling up the bodice of her dress.

"I can do that," she said slowly, rehooking her bra and placing her left arm through the armhole. She watched how he looked at her body as she moved her arms. His eyes were big as saucers, and as she looked down at his crotch, she could tell he was getting hard all over again. Mary Grace Whittaker realized she had power. She had enormous sexual power over Richard Bartlow. He could protest all he wanted, but she was the one calling the shots. She had never realized how incredibly exhilarating this kind of power could be.

"Like I was saying, Mary Grace, I have my plans." Richard watched as she buttoned the bodice of her dress.

"I heard you, Richard," she said sweetly. "Plans. I have my plans, too."

He cleared his throat. "Good, then we understand each other."

"I think I understand very well," Mary Grace said evenly, enjoying turning the tables on him. She believed he thought she was going to throw herself at him. Instead, she did as Cynthia had explained to her and Kathryn: back away when you want to intrigue them. She finished buttoning her dress. She looked up at him and kissed him soundly on the mouth. "I have to go, Richard. It's getting very late. I don't want you to get into trouble."

"No—"

She interrupted him. "Sleep well," she said and walked away.

She was nearly out of sight when she heard him call, "Mary Grace! Wait! Will I see you tomorrow?"

She didn't answer. Instead, she just disappeared into the night.

Mary Grace unlocked the door to her cabin. The lights were out. She started to tiptoe into the room when suddenly the lamp was switched on.

Kathryn and Cynthia sat on the double bed, still in their dinner dresses, arms folded across their chests. They were scowling.

"Okay. Where have you been?" Cynthia demanded.

"We looked all over this ship for you. We thought maybe you fell overboard," Kathryn scolded.

"Geez, if I'd wanted parental supervision on this trip, I would have invited Caroline and James the Third."

Cynthia's scrutinizing gaze made Mary Grace uncomfortable.

"You're a mess. Who is he?" Cynthia wanted to know.

"Who?"

"The guy who's been mauling you for the past three nights."

"It was only tonight. So, don't get in a dither," Mary Grace said, hoping to shock both her girlfriends.

"Aaaaaahhhhh! She's seeing a man!" Kathryn shrieked.

"I don't believe it!" Cynthia said firmly. "Saint Mary the Virgin Grace would *never* let a lowly man touch her."

Mary Grace should have been mortified, but she wasn't. She should have felt guilty for sinning against the Church, but she didn't fear the fires of hell in the least. It was odd how one night in Richard Bartlow's arms had so easily caused her to throw her morals overboard. Perhaps she was discovering who Mary Grace really was for the first time in her life. Perhaps she'd always thought half those rules the nuns had taught her were silly and impractical. What did celibate nuns and priests know about sex, anyway?

Mary Grace crossed her arms smugly and sat on the bed opposite her friends.

"Are you still a virgin?" Cynthia asked anxiously.

"Of course, but I wouldn't care if I wasn't."

"Oh, God! We've lost her!" Kathryn shrieked again.

"You have not. I'm just the same as I always was," Mary Grace said, then stopped herself. "Actually, that's not true. I'll never be the same again."

"I know. It's like that, isn't it?" Cynthia asked knowledgeably.

Kathryn whirled to face Cynthia. "Did you and Greg...?"

Cynthia shook her head. "Be serious. I can't investigate his background until we get to London. I'll decide then."

"Who's the guy?" Kathryn asked Mary Grace.

"Richard Bartlow."

"The *waiter*?" Kathryn and Cynthia were aghast.

Mary Grace nodded proudly. "I did just as you said, Cynthia. I threw myself at him, then backed off."

"Oh, God." Cynthia's shoulders slumped. "You're supposed to use that method with a millionaire. A regular guy can lose his mind. What if he goes crazy on you or something? You'll be the cause of his demise!"

"Richard and I are going to be just fine. We have exactly the same goals and dreams. He wants to be a builder and I want to be an architect. We talk so easily to each other. We're a perfect match. I'm going to marry him."

"The hell you are!" Cynthia jumped to her feet and rammed her fists on her hips. "Now, look here, Mary Grace Whittaker, this is *not* how you play the game. Some poor schmuck like Richard Bartlow or Greg McGraw may be cute and fun for a week at sea, but marriage... that's another matter. Your parents would go ape!"

"You really think so?" Mary Grace hadn't considered that.

Kathryn peered closely at Mary Grace. Then she looked at Cynthia. "I don't like that mischievous look in her eye, Cynthia."

"Look, Mary Grace. Don't be making rash statements like this, okay? You have a lot to learn about this guy. Give me a chance to check him out. Let's see who he really is before you decide to get married. Is that a deal?"

"You're going to find out about Greg when we get to London?"

"Yes."

"Good. Then you can check on Richard at the same time. Then, after that's done, I can let Richard know he's going to marry me."

"Wait a minute. You mean Richard hasn't proposed to you?" Cynthia asked.

"Not yet, but he will," Mary Grace said confidently.

Cynthia flopped back on the bed. She looked at Kathryn. "It's okay. She's still a virgin and he hasn't proposed. I guess Mary Grace was right, after all. Nothing has changed at all."

Mary Grace smiled at her friends, who seemed so happy about that trivial piece of information. They hadn't seen Richard's face when he looked at her. They didn't know the kind of power she had over him.

Richard would marry her, all right. And soon.

7

Richard placed his hands on either side of Mary Grace's face, pulling her toward him for a long-awaited kiss. The minute his lips touched hers, his body reacted. His tenderness became eagerness as his lips hungrily took her mouth. He sank his fingers into her silky blond hair, holding her head in his grip so that he could control the kiss. He felt his desire spiral out of his loins like a tornado, sucking him in, then spinning him with a force so strong he nearly blacked out.

Never before had he counted the minutes to be with a girl. He couldn't sleep or eat. He thought he'd go insane every afternoon watching her read by the pool in her bathing suit that only made him dream about what she'd look like in a real bikini.

He wanted her like he'd never wanted anyone in his life. He almost felt overpowered by her.

Richard realized that he wanted her with the kind of all-consuming passion he'd always reserved for his career. He knew that his passions had been born in him early in life. For as long as he could remember, Richard had dreamed of nothing else but getting the hell out of Gary, Indiana.

Richard's father, Bud Bartlow, had worked the blast furnace for the United States Steel Corporation since the day after his high school graduation in 1943. Bud married Janet Elm, a waitress at the truck stop on U.S. 20, a week after graduation when she discovered that their one-night stand had resulted in a pregnancy. They lived in an apartment over an auto-body shop until Richard was four years old. Not until they moved into a two-bedroom brick bungalow in a blue-collar neighborhood on the west side of Gary did Richard realize there was more to the world than welding fenders, patching tires and spray-painting cars.

Richard's childhood was a haze of unhappy people in unhappy jobs, living in houses and places they hated. When Richard was in junior high school, he discovered that his father was the most educated man in his family, his mother's family and among their friends. Richard despised their narrow minds and their lack of ambition to seek anything for themselves beyond the city limits of Gary, Indiana.

Though Richard played high school football, basketball and baseball, and excelled in all three sports, his vision was much broader than the football scholarship at Indiana University his father urged him to accept. Richard's dreams for himself involved a lot more than simply graduating as a football jock.

He worked hard to maintain his grades and stay involved in high school clubs that would help promote his college career and even his life beyond college.

When he was a sophomore in high school, he sneaked into a special "career night" for seniors only. The sports-oriented lectures were heavily attended, but Richard chose the lectures where there were plenty of empty seats. He was one of four boys and one girl who listened to a fascinating and mesmerizing talk on marketing by an instructor at Ball State University.

Jim Wheat was a short man with a loud voice and enough energy to fuel the next Sputnik. He paced the floor and flung his arms from side to side, extolling the benefits of keen marketing strategies in the business world.

Richard was hooked.

Wheat explained that once a person chose a field of business—and it didn't matter what the field was—the difference between success and failure was marketing. He told them how to identify a market, search demographics and cross-pollinate sales, promotions and networks, using every source available to sell the product.

Richard remained after the lecture to talk to the instructor. Wheat told him that he got his education at Yale. Though he had studied social sciences, he was friends with several professors who held extracurricular workshops to explain new theories about economics, marketing and global trade.

"The world is changing quickly," he told Richard. "Space travel is going to be big and so is everything with it."

"But how do I find my place in the world?" Richard asked sincerely.

"Tell me, what is the number-one thing in your life you really hate? Hate with a passion?"

"That's easy, my house. My neighborhood. My parents hate it. I hate it."

"Why?"

"Because the house is a rat hole. It's just a couple of square boxes made out of crap lumber and it looks like all the other crumbling rat holes up and down the street."

Wheat looked up at Richard, who was at least a foot and a half taller, raised his arm and clamped it on the boy's shoulder. "You've just identified your passion in life."

"What?"

"Change it. Change the whole damn thing. Build new houses that are not dark and crappy. Build places where people are happy to live. Make them light and full of sunshine. Make the rooms bigger or even smaller. Change the ceiling. Make them round not square. Let your imagination flow. Let your mind go to its farthest limits. In fact, don't let anything limit you, Richard. Look beyond every rule you've been taught. Do you see what I mean?"

"I'm beginning to," Richard said enthusiastically. "I'd love to come to Ball State and learn from you."

"Me? If all goes well for me, I won't be there by the time you're ready. This is just a stepping stone for me. I've already started a corporate consulting business. I'm working on my Ph.D. and I should have it next year. Someday, I'll be world-famous. There's no stopping my ideas. I plan to show the Fortune 500 how to run their corporations. When they get in trouble, I'll bail them out. Everyone is going to remember me when I die."

Richard had never heard anyone talk like Jim Wheat. He only ever heard how bad the world was. He listened to his prejudiced father blame all his personal woes on the blacks or the Republicans or the Russians. According to Bud Bartlow, it was impossible to break out of the steel mill. Impossible to break out of his unsatisfying marriage. Even a trip to Hawaii was impossible because his money went to Richard's clothing bills, food bills and school supplies. Hawaii was as far away to him as the moon.

Richard literally threw out his entire memory bank that night and reprogrammed it with Jim Wheat's words. He solicited a promise from Wheat to stay in touch—if he was ever near Gary again, Richard wanted to hear him talk. Wheat shook his hand and promised to help him in any way he could.

Richard did not tell his father that he had applied to Yale for a football scholarship. He wrote to Professor Daniel Greenburg, Jim Wheat's instructor, and told him about his dream to study under him at Yale.

He didn't hear back from Professor Greenburg until a month before his graduation, when he received his acceptance to Yale. Greenburg informed Richard that he had recommended him for a scholarship and that he was pleased he'd been accepted. Scholarships to Yale were few, and though Richard's grades were not as high as some of the other applicants, it was Richard's *desire* that had landed him the scholarship. Greenburg suggested that Richard enter the school of art and architecture since he planned to become a residential builder.

The one stipulation was that not only was he required to play football, but he was expected to try out for one of the other teams for spring training. His choices were tennis, golf and sculling.

Bud Bartlow nearly went through the roof when he discovered that his son could not be talked out of attending a "sissy" school like Yale.

Richard stood his ground. He explained to his father that he was not going to college to play sports, but to build a foundation for his future.

Bud thought his kid was nuts. Richard knew that for years Bud had dreamed of attending all the Indiana University football games, sure his son would bring home a victory. He talked about putting an IU sticker in the back window of his brand-new Buick. He'd already told the sportswriter at the *Gary Post Tribune* that he would provide the paper with extra photographs of all the football games and give personal interviews.

Now Richard was telling him he was going to Yale.

Bud put his hands on either side of his forty-two-inch beer belly and glared down the end of his bulbous nose.

"Everbody knows Yale don't win football games. Hell! Them sportscasters don't even announce their scores back here."

"They do, too," Richard said. "And I'm going to be the best quarterback they ever saw."

"Bullshit! Them sissy coaches don't know shit."

"I don't care, Dad," Richard replied adamantly. "Professor Greenburg personally recommended me to the recruiting board because I wrote to him three years ago."

Bud Bartlow screwed up his ruddy red face. "That guy a Jew?"

"Forget it." Richard waved away his father's incessant biases. "I'm going to Yale."

"Fine. Then you can pay for your own goddamn train ticket and your supplies and any other goddamn thing you want!"

"Fine! I will!"

And for the next four years he did exactly that.

Richard loved every leaf of ivy on Connecticut Hall, every roar of the crowd in the Yale Bowl and every one of his classes in city planning, art history, sculpture and painting. By the time he graduated, he discovered that, not only did he love American Colonial architecture, but he understood the Greek, Roman and Egyptian principles of design and function upon which it was based. And he knew his education wouldn't be complete until he experienced those fine Roman buildings and Greek temples firsthand.

Attending Yale wasn't the hardship his father had hoped it would be. Nearly forty percent of the students

were on scholarship or loan. They all worked someplace on campus. Richard's first job was as a waiter in
one of the upperclassmen's dining rooms located in a
residential "college."

Being a waiter taught Richard that getting to meet the
rich and powerful was as easy as serving soup. For the
first few months, he kept his distance from the upperclassmen, whose names he'd gotten from his roommate, David Weston, who worked in the registrar's
office.

David was on a scholarship and was enrolled in the
law school, but Richard thought he'd never in his life met
a person with a more larcenous mind. Together, they
stole student files and Xeroxed personal and financial
information. By the end of the first six weeks, Richard
and David had a lead on exactly who the monied students were. They researched family trees of the not-so-
rich but politically or socially powerful students. David explained that power was not always to be found in
money. There were old families in America whose name
on a board, a ballot or a city-planning commission could
direct the flow of millions of dollars.

By the second semester of his freshman year, Richard's affable and charming personality had won him the
influential friends he coveted. It wasn't until his football career kicked off in his sophomore year that he won
the respect of the last diehard Eastern Old Guard seniors and graduate students.

Richard found he not only liked the limelight, he
craved it. He liked being called "king" and he intended
to focus his efforts to ensure that he always remain a
king.

His only disappointment in college was women. Because his father was a nobody, content to work in the

mills and live in Gary, Indiana, all his life, Richard carried his father's identity with him. He discovered that it was a curse not to be born a Vanderbilt, a Morgan or a descendant of the American Revolutionary War. In the tightly controlled and contrived world of matchmaking among the American aristocracy, Richard was not king, but merely a servant.

No matter how well he dressed, how polished his manners, or how erudite his conversation, Richard flunked women.

The pretty, fine-boned girls—with delicate hands that touched their expensively maintained pageboy hairstyles, and with cashmere sweaters not wool, and silk blouses not cotton—knew without researching his family background that Richard was not one of them.

They were different, he thought, these pedigreed women who would never be required to work a day in their lives, unless they pursued a career for the intellectual stimulation. As he walked the streets of New Haven, Connecticut, on weekends and saw the Vassar girls from not-so-far-away Poughkeepsie, New York, driving through town and campus in bottle-green convertible MGs and shiny new red Mustangs, he realized they might as well be from the moon. To them, Richard was invisible.

They were nothing like the friendly—though naive—girls back home. Richard had lost his virginity when he was sixteen, after scoring his first touchdown. Susie Lisle was a cheerleader on the Varsity cheerleading squad. She was short, stocky, cute and had big boobs. She'd flirted with Richard for weeks between classes, letting him know she was interested. Once he made the big touchdown, he was a hot item. Susie rushed him. They screwed in the back of her father's old jalopy, but Richard didn't care about the condition of the car. He only cared that Susie was now his girl.

Unfortunately, he was so focused on his schoolwork, team workouts and football games that he didn't have much time for Susie. By the time basketball season rolled around, Susie had found a boy who was more preoccupied with Susie than he was with athletics.

No, he thought, the Vassar girls were far from friendly. They were haughty and cold as ice. How it was possible that a good-looking, red-blooded all-American football star like himself could go all the way through college without getting laid was beyond him. And it pissed him off.

He supposed that was when he learned to hate women.

Because he worked and took required classes during the summers, Richard never went back to Gary, Indiana. He never saw Susie again. And he never returned to see his family. Neither of his parents drove to New Haven for any of Richard's college events, or even for his graduation.

When his father had a heart attack and died on the floor of the blast-furnace room, Richard was still feeling rejected and bitter. Though his mother pleaded with him to come home to comfort her and even promised to send him a train ticket, which she could ill afford, he refused. He sent a twenty-dollar funeral wreath to the man who thought he was a "sissy," and he never thought about his father again.

Looking back was not a thing Richard did well. He only had eyes for the future.

As he stood on the upper deck of the *Queen Elizabeth* in the moonlight with Mary Grace Whittaker,

Richard could see his future as clearly as the bright stars above. He was going to make love to Mary Grace Whittaker. He was going to make her fall in love with him before she had a chance to go off to college and find some well-bred prelaw Ivy Leaguer. He was going to make sure she thought he was the Ivy Leaguer of her dreams.

There was not a doubt in Richard's mind that Mary Grace was the girl for him. She had more sex appeal in her little finger than both her girlfriends combined. That first night at dinner when he'd served her salad and seen those glorious tits, his hands had itched to touch them. Then, when she'd bared herself for him, he *knew* he'd died and gone to heaven. A rich girl, with an influential daddy in Richard's chosen field and big tits, to boot!

Richard was right when he'd told Mary Grace their meeting was Kismet.

8

The ship docked in Southampton early in the morning. Only a buffet breakfast was served, leaving most of the kitchen staff free by nine o'clock. None of the passengers were allowed to disembark until ten o'clock.

Richard knew he had only one hour to set the course of his life.

He sent a message to Mary Grace by way of her room steward, who was on his way to the luxury cabins to gather envelopes containing the staff tips.

Mary Grace read Richard's note, then turned excitedly to Cynthia. "He wants to meet me in ten minutes."

"Just cool your jets, Mary Grace. This shipboard-romance thing was fun while it lasted, but don't get carried away. You don't see me running after Greg, do you?"

Mary Grace waved off Cynthia's warning. "I'm not going to get carried away. It's broad daylight and we have to leave the ship in less than an hour. What can happen in an hour?"

"Sometimes you are so dumb, Mary Grace, you scare me," Cynthia said.

Kathryn frowned. "Oh, leave her alone, Cynthia. She's a big girl." Then she wagged her finger at Mary Grace. "Don't go thinking he's Prince Charming. Just remember, we're in England now. There *are* princes here. Maybe you'll find a real one!"

Cynthia rolled her eyes.

"Ugh! You two give even worse advice than my parents."

Richard was waiting for Mary Grace on the observation deck, under the staircase where no one could see him. Because the first passengers hadn't started to disembark, there were few people about the community areas. Still, he had to be careful.

"Mary Grace," he called as he saw her approach.

She smiled widely and rushed into his open arms. He kissed her ravenously and she kissed him back.

"The trouble with kissing you, Mary Grace," he said, "is that once I start . . . I don't want to stop."

"And we have to stop?" she teased.

"Yes, we do." He took her arms from around his neck, then placed her hand on his erection. "See? That's why we have to stop."

"Oh, my God!" she replied, wide-eyed. Then she smiled and laughed.

"It's not funny," he said. "Besides, that's not what I wanted to say."

"What did you want to say, Richard?" She pressed her full breasts into his chest, pushing them against the hard wall of muscle.

"Will you marry me?"

"What?"

"Will you marry me?" Richard was amazed how incredibly easy those words were when you knew you wanted to say them. And he wanted to say them more than he'd ever wanted anything in his life.

"Why, Richard, you haven't even told me that you love me."

"I love you, Mary Grace," he said, thinking how incredibly hard *those* words were, even when you didn't mean them.

"And I love you, Richard."

"You're kidding?" For some reason, her words stunned him. He didn't understand how or why, but they did.

"No. I love you. Just as you love me."

"Good. Then you'll marry me?"

Mary Grace looked at the serious set to his face and the determination that gleamed in his eyes. She didn't know what love should look like, but she supposed that at a time like this it was important that the man be serious and determined.

The fact that Richard wanted her pleased Mary Grace enormously. She'd discovered that besides being loved, she needed to be wanted. Caroline and James the Third loved her, she supposed, in their own fashion, but she'd never felt they wanted her. During her childhood years, she'd been sent off to more summer camps than she cared to remember. And the second she was old enough to attend boarding school, they'd enrolled her in Woodlands Academy. Mary Grace had never quite understood why they wanted her close by, yet didn't want her under the same roof.

Thank God, Richard was nothing like her parents, she thought. Richard wanted her. All of her. Forever. She couldn't have been happier. "I'll marry you, Richard."

His face exploded with joy. He picked her up and whirled her around and around. "You will? You're not just playing games with me? You'll really, really marry me?"

"I'll really, really marry you."

He laughed and hugged her close. He lifted her again and kissed her. "You've made me the happiest man on earth."

"You've made me happy, too, Richard," she said, knowing her heart was smiling, too.

"I can't go with you to London," he said quickly. "I've been booked for the return sail to New York."

"Richard, no! We're going to have such a wonderful time."

"I know. But frankly, Mary Grace, I need the money..."

"Richard, I have plenty of money. Money is not the problem."

"Money is always the problem, Mary Grace." He put his hands on her shoulders and laid his forehead against hers so that their noses almost touched. "I've got it all figured out. Where will you be, say, around the fifteenth?"

Mary Grace started to laugh. Caroline's ridiculous schedule, which she'd intended to toss out the window on their way to London, was about to come in handy, after all. "I'll be in Rome at Pasta Luigi's, having the best pasta in the world," she said confidently.

"I've heard of it. I'll meet you there for dinner on the fifteenth."

"What? How are you going to manage that?"

"Don't ask questions. Just trust me. You be there and I'll be there."

Just then, they heard voices coming toward them. He kissed her quickly. "I gotta go before they catch me. Promise you'll be there?"

"I'll be there," she assured him.

He started up the stairs. "Tell me you love me again."

"I love you, Richard."

He flashed her a brilliant smile. "Don't forget. You're my girl now."

She put her arm on the railing and leaned her face against her hand, looking at him dreamily. "I'll remember," she whispered as he disappeared up the stairs.

In London, the girls photographed the Beefeaters with their Kodak Brownie cameras they'd received as graduation presents. They walked across Vauxhall Bridge and looked at their reflections in the muddy Thames. They went to the Tower of London, listened to Big Ben, rode on a double-decker bus, photographed Buckingham Palace and ate fish and chips until Kathryn said she'd throw up.

Once they agreed they had enough pictures to satisfy their parents that they'd "seen" London, they did what *they* wanted to do. They went in search of the Beatles, the Rolling Stones, The Kinks, The Yardbirds, Herman's Hermits and Petula Clark. They found cellar pubs filled with smoke and young kids listening to "the Mersey Sound." They bought miniskirts, ribbed turtlenecks, Edwardian baby-doll dresses and chunky shoes in Chelsea and Soho clothing shops owned by young designers who were not yet famous. They bought pots of Yardley lip slickers in every shade—from bubble-gum pink to frosted yellow—and slathered themselves with lavender-scented colognes.

Caroline had booked the girls at Claridge's Hotel, but once they discovered that only business types and middle-aged American tourists stayed there, they moved to a hostel closer to the action.

Cynthia loved the smoky pubs, the music and the dancing. She stayed out till dawn nearly every night, drinking beer, smoking Turkish cigarettes and kissing sweet-faced English band members. She never went to the same club twice, telling Mary Grace that someday these boys would be famous and she could say she'd kissed them all once.

Kathryn's long, lean legs looked incredibly smashing in the miniskirts she bought. No matter where they went, people snapped pictures of her, thinking she was a London model. Kathryn hammed it up for the cameras and affected a British accent. On the day before they departed for Paris, Kathryn met a twenty-six-year-old Englishman who claimed to be a professional photographer. He asked to take her pictures while Mary Grace and Cynthia were busy trying on low-riding, cotton bell-bottomed slacks, which the designer promised would be the coming trend.

Kathryn didn't even ask the man's name, though she gave him hers, when she agreed to cavort on the streets of Chelsea for his expensively lensed camera. She leaned against red telephone boxes, whirled around lampposts and put her arm around gap-toothed cabbies. She petted a collie being walked by an elderly matron and plunged her face into a bouquet of English violets. She wore a tan racing cap she'd borrowed from a passerby and stood barefoot on top of a bronze dog-head hitching post with an old man looking straight up her miniskirt.

The photographer handed her his card and told her he thought these pictures were the best he'd ever taken. He wrote down her address in America and asked where she would be the following week. She gave him their Paris address with the Hendersons and told him from there she was going to Rome, staying at the Hotel d'Inghilterra.

Blithely, she looked at Peter St. John's card, thanked him and walked off with her girlfriends, never giving him another thought.

In Paris, the girls were met by Charles and Véronique Henderson at the airport. Mary Grace took one look at Véronique's leopard-skin capri pants, black low-cut skintight blouse, gold high-heeled sandals and chunky gold jewelry and knew that, though the clothes were quite expensive, Caroline would have a fit if she knew this woman was planning to show her daughter the "smart" side of Paris.

Véronique was older than Caroline by a decade at least. She was thin, dark-haired and pale-skinned and absolutely beautiful. She had full, sensuous lips that looked stained by the dark purple shade of lipstick she wore. Her eyes were nearly black and so intense and captivating that Mary Grace had difficulty looking away from them.

Véronique radiated a presence that had little to do with her outrageous clothing. Mary Grace suspected she was the kind of person her mother referred to as having "charisma."

"Bonjour, mes petites!" Véronique exclaimed when they emerged from the gate, putting her long thin arms around all three of them. The smell of Chanel Number Five was asphyxiating.

Charles Henderson was his wife's antithesis. He was tall and thin, with a long, narrow deadpan face and thinning dull brown hair. He was dressed in an English wool navy blue summer suit, white shirt and navy blue tie. He was the picture of decorum.

"How do you do?" He asked each of the girls properly.

The Hendersons' apartment was located on the tiny Île de la Cité, one of Paris's most expensive neighborhoods. The valet brought their suitcases up from Charles's Renault, while Véronique showed the girls around the apartment. The ceilings were fourteen feet high and it seemed to Mary Grace that every inch was covered by intricate moldings, frescoes and oil paintings. What little furniture existed was antique, and the upholstered pieces were covered with white sheets and drop cloths.

At first, Mary Grace thought perhaps the apartment was under renovation. Then she realized that Véronique was a sculptress, artist and potter. The apartment was both her home and studio.

Their hostess asked the maid to bring tea, fruit, bread and cheese to the dining room for a light lunch. The room was long and narrow and bordered by three sets of French doors that opened onto a balcony overlooking the Seine. In the center of the ceiling was a huge copper and glass chandelier that Véronique explained her father had commissioned to be made during the Empire period. The chandelier itself was fashioned in the shape of a fleur-de-lis, each branch holding three more branches of dangling fleur-de-lis–shaped prisms. The large rectangular table was made of wood so distressed that Mary Grace nearly picked up a splinter when she placed her bare forearm next to the hand-painted plate. The silver was sterling and, according to Véronique, over a hundred years old. The wineglasses were made in Venice during the French Revolution. The wine decanters and teapots were equally as old and, though chipped and damaged, they were exquisite.

"My things are quite unique and very, very old," Véronique said in a thick French accent. "My ancestor made this table with his own hands over three hundred years ago. I have little that wasn't handmade. There is a feeling of connection with the divine when one is creating something by hand. I believe that we were all put here to be creators. I don't understand the modern fascination with machine-made items."

Mary Grace took a hunk of grapes from the fruit tray. Spreading a thin coat of Brie over a crusty piece of French bread, she listened with fascination as Véronique continued.

"Your parents, Mary Grace, asked that I show you Paris. We will spend only one day seeing the great monuments and cathedrals. It won't take long. You can spend weeks viewing the Louvre, but we don't have the luxury of time. There are other things I would like you to see."

"Really? Like what?" Mary Grace asked.

Kathryn smiled. "How about Dior?"

Cynthia kicked her under the table. Kathryn frowned.

Véronique laughed. "You are young. I forget this. Of course you should see Dior. It is an experience, to say the least. I guess I'm so used to being here, I don't think about what is important to young people. Sometimes I get absorbed by my mission."

Mary Grace looked at her quizzically. "I don't understand. Mission?"

"My life's path. I think it is important for each of us to make our lifetime purposeful. My path is to enrich the world with my sculpture."

Mary Grace tried not to pay attention to the arched eyebrows her friends shot each other. She was enthralled.

After their "repast," the girls were shown their room, which had been used for years to store Véronique's sculpture. Most of the pieces had been placed on wooden shelves that ringed the room. Heavy cream-colored silk draperies edged in gold silk bullion trim puddled on the polished parquet floor and framed a set of French doors that opened onto a small balcony. A white hand-painted armoire stood against the wall opposite the magnificently draped four-poster bed. The bed was big enough for six people and there were easily a dozen down pillows covered in salmon-colored crinkled silk, each trimmed with pearls, lace or gold tassels.

Next to the bedroom was a completely tiled bathroom with a footed porcelain tub, white porcelain toilet, bidet and pedestal sink. Véronique told them the fixtures were twenty-four-carat gold and had been commissioned by her grandfather in 1914. When the city had been occupied by the Nazis, Véronique helped her mother hide the faucets in the walls of their country house.

Hanging from the gold towel bars were the finest linen hand towels Mary Grace had ever seen. Some were monogrammed in fine silk threads. Others had organdy borders. Still others were patterned with delicate "drawn work" that created a cut-out design along the edges. The girls had never seen anything like it. Everything—the apartment, the furnishings, the sculptures, Véronique—amazed them.

Just before they all retired for the night, Véronique explained the tour of Paris she'd mapped out for them. She told the girls she had a great deal of work to do the following day, so they would be on their own.

Mary Grace, Cynthia and Kathryn assured her they would be just fine exploring the city.

From the top of the Eiffel Tower to the back of the *bâteaux mouches* that took passengers down the Seine, Mary Grace and her friends saw Paris. They snapped photographs of each other at the Arc de Triomphe, on the steps of Nôtre Dame Cathedral and on park benches at the Jardin de Luxembourg. They drank a Pernod at the Café des Deux Magots and bought sacks of roasted chestnuts on the street corners of the Left Bank. They investigated the Louvre, the Museum of the Luxembourg and the Cluny Museum and decided they needed another month to view the art alone.

They went to Les Halles, wandered among the vegetable and fruit stalls and consumed huge bowls of French onion soup covered with thick, stringy cheese. Mary Grace bought an armful of white gladiolus from a street vendor for Véronique, hoping that their drama and grandeur would please her. And they did.

In the evenings, the girls stood on their little balcony and watched the sunset and the lights come on across the city.

In Mary Grace's mind, there was no place like Paris. No matter what time of day or night, there was a suffused kind of lighting that made the entire city appear to be dusted with gold. It was magical and mysterious. It was dreamlike and heavenly. Mary Grace thought that it was perhaps due to the energy sent out from the hands, brains and hearts of all the artists, poets and sculptors. Paris was unique—of that there was no question.

Mary Grace had known little of the Hendersons from her father, and she was glad she hadn't asked. She knew James the Third didn't have the first inkling about his friend Charles's wife. James would never have understood someone as insightful and deeply wise as Véronique. He would have disapproved of her because she was so utterly unique.

Mary Grace had learned a lot from their hostess, and had it not been for the fact that Richard would be waiting for her in Rome, she thought she would like to remain in Paris forever.

For the rest of her life, Paris and Véronique would remain in the mists of her memory and she knew she could never think of one without the other.

9

Mary Grace and her friends arrived in Rome with their spirits flagging and their expectations low. After Paris, what was left? They intended to see the Colosseum where the lions ate the Christians and the Vatican where the Catholics had been ruling peoples' lives longer than the Romans had. Maybe a little shopping on the Via Condotti, but that would be all. Then they would wait for their departure back to Heathrow.

"What could possibly happen in Rome that could top Paris?" Cynthia asked as their taxi pulled to the curb in front of the Hotel d'Inghilterra.

Mary Grace was proud of herself for not once giving in to the temptation of telling her friends about Richard. Every night since she left him in Southampton, she fell asleep remembering the touch of his hand, the smell of his cologne and the feel of his kisses. Oh, God. His kisses. It was all she could do to keep still when she recalled the pressure of his lips against hers.

They were finally in Rome and she would be seeing him tonight. Then . . . she didn't know what would happen.

Their room was larger and more sparsely furnished than she'd imagined. But she loved it. It had such a European feel with its fireplace and simple wood mantel, wooden floors and high ceilings. There were two beds, neither of which looked wide enough for one person. They all agreed to take turns sleeping on the floor.

There was little of the opulence or sense of history that she'd felt at the Hendersons' apartment. However, she told herself, this was a public building and not a private home. The beds were covered with summer-weight cotton duvets and Italian cotton sheets. The armoire that stood between the two windows overlooking the cobblestone street was intricately carved and a fine example of nineteenth-century workmanship. It was a lovely—if somewhat functional—room.

The hotel itself was rife with historical fact. This was where Henry James had stayed on his first visit to Rome. Since it was only a short walk from the Piazza di Spagna, one of the oldest parts of the city and the most fashionable shopping district, Mary Grace knew they couldn't ask for a better location.

After unpacking and procuring a city map from the hotel *direttrice*, Mary Grace, Cynthia and Kathryn headed for "Lo Shopping" on the Via Condotti, Via Veneto and Via Sistina.

The Italian designers were wild compared to the serene and elegant fashions they had seen in Paris. Pucci slips, bras and panties were executed in hot fuchsia-colored silk. Rich chocolate browns were swirled around neon pistachio green on nighttime concoctions that Mary Grace knew would make her dizzy. They steered clear of the designer shops like Gucci, which were crammed with American tourists. Instead, they followed the Roman girls into shops where they found sensuously soft kid-leather purses, shoes and gloves at prices none of them could pass up.

There was nothing subdued about the energy they found in Rome. Here, the traffic moved twice as fast as in Paris or London. Mary Grace learned that Romans had been complaining about the traffic since ancient times when chariots raced recklessly through the city and ran over dogs, chickens and pedestrians.

They sat at a sidewalk café on the Piazza del Popolo having *granita de caffé* or espresso ice and looking at the Santa Maria del Popolo, a church built to consecrate Nero's burial ground.

"I'm exhausted," Cynthia said, rubbing her feet.

"I'm exhilarated," Kathryn replied, loading her ice coffee with more brown sugar.

"I must have spent a fortune," Cynthia complained.

Mary Grace laughed. "You mean, you spent your father's fortune. Do you even *have* any travelers' checks left?"

"Of course! Besides, I bought presents for my mother and father." She grinned at Mary Grace. "They won't say a thing when they see the bargains I snatched up for them. Have you ever in your life seen such shoes? They feel like marshmallows!" She rooted around in the leather tote she bought at Number 35 Via Veneto and pulled out the pair of leather loafers she'd bought for herself and slipped them on. "Mmm...I've found paradise."

"Tomorrow, let's go to the Vatican," Mary Grace said.

Cynthia waved her hand dismissively. "I wouldn't be caught dead in that place. I say we do the Roman thing."

"I want to shop some more," Kathryn said, gulping down the espresso.

Cynthia screwed up her nose at Kathryn. "What for? You've only bought one pair of shoes and a purse."

Kathryn tossed back a long blond curl. "I intend to put on every outrageously priced suede dress, skirt and boot in this city. I'm going to try on cashmere sweaters, knit miniskirts and those thigh-high white leather boots I saw back there on the Via del Corsa. I'm going to wear every piece of cloth, leather and silver . . . God! Did you see the silver engraved bracelets on the Via Condotti, Number 31-35, I think. What I wouldn't give for one of those."

. Mary Grace frowned. "But we should see the Sistine Chapel and St. Peter's Basilica and all these famous churches . . ."

"Why?" Cynthia asked.

"Because I told my parents we would."

"Mary Grace, are you always going to do everything your parents tell you to? Sometimes I wonder why you didn't just become a nun or something. You know, of all the girls at school, you're the only one who believed that crap the nuns told us. Don't you ever think for yourself? Just because we're in Rome, we don't *have* to do the Catholic thing. Frankly, I'm here to see all the ancient ruins. The Roman Forum, the Colosseum, the Senate where Caesar was murdered, the Temple of Jupiter, Aphrodite's Temple. Flesh, degradation, erotica . . . paganism. . . .*that's* what made Rome famous."

Mary Grace's eyes went round with shock. "I can't believe you're saying this to me. Surely you're interested in the Vatican . . ."

Cynthia shook her head. "Not in the least."

Mary Grace turned to Kathryn. "You want to see Michelangelo's and Raphael's paintings, don't you?"

"I'd rather lie naked in the sun on the Spanish Steps. Which I just may do." Kathryn smiled sweetly and finished her espresso. "I think I'll try a cappuccino next."

Mary Grace's jaw dropped. "Both of you are . . . are changing! And right before my eyes!"

Kathryn pulled out a pair of sunglasses she'd bought for five dollars from a street vendor. They were fantastically well-made of tortoiseshell and shiny brass fittings—bigger than the ones Jacqueline Kennedy always wore. "Good. I'm ready for a change. I'm not particularly happy with the girl I was back in Mundelein, Illinois. I think . . ." She leaned back in the folding chair, crossing her arms behind her head and lifting her face to the warm summer sun. "I want to stay in Rome forever."

"How can you say that? We just got here! You don't even know this place yet."

"I feel like I've come home." Kathryn rolled up her shorts to expose more of her thighs to the sun. "Have you noticed how these Roman girls dress? I've never seen such tight short skirts in my life. And I love those high-heeled sandals they wear with no backstrap. That flop, flop with each step is *so* sexy. No wonder these Roman guys are always pinching butts. The girls are more aggressive in their own way than the guys are."

Cynthia nodded. "I'm with you all the way, Kathryn. I feel like I want to immerse myself in this city. The last thing I want is to be reminded of home, church and my parents." She glared at Mary Grace.

"Sorry. I didn't know you felt this way. Now I do, okay?"

"Okay." Cynthia said.

Kathryn took off her sunglasses. Her face was already turning pink from the sun. "I have a suggestion. Since we all want to do very different things in very different ways, I suggest we split up. Mary Grace, you go to the Vatican and buy your rosaries and holy water. Cynthia, you check out the fleshpots of Rome. I figure that it doesn't cost anything to try on these clothes. As long as the shops will let me do that, that's where I'll be."

"What about dinner?" Mary Grace asked, intending to be at Pasta Luigi's that night to meet Richard.

"I say we find our own dinner. We go back to the hotel when we want."

"I love the idea," Cynthia said. "But you were the one who wanted to share cabs and split meals to save money. Are you sure you want to do this?"

Kathryn smiled. "So, I'll walk. Rome isn't as spread out as Chicago. And I'll eat later . . . on my way back to America. I'm not going to waste one minute of shopping time on anything silly like eating. Just keep those cappuccinos and *granita de caffés* coming!"

Mary Grace shook her head. "Have it your way, but twenty years from now, you'll be sorry you didn't see the Vatican when you had the chance." She rose and picked up her shopping bags.

Kathryn replaced her sunglasses. "What you fail to understand, my dear, is that twenty years from now, I'll be living in Rome. Yep. I'm going to find a way to live here."

Cynthia stood and put her hand on Mary Grace's shoulder. "Don't worry, this temporary brain malfunction is due to sun poisoning. She'll snap out of it in a day or two."

"Oh, shut up," Kathryn said, turning her face to the sun again.

Mary Grace looked at Cynthia. "I'm going to Pasta Luigi's tonight for dinner. Do you want to come with me?"

"Frankly, I don't give a damn about Pasta Luigi's. Probably because your mother told us to go there. No, I'm hoping to find a cute Roman guy on one of those little red scooters who is willing to show me some fleshpots."

Mary Grace rolled her eyes. She was glad now she hadn't told either of them about Richard's proposal and their rendezvous that night. Both her friends had lost their minds and they would think she had, too.

Mary Grace sat at a table at Pasta Luigi's for four and a half hours. There was no sign of Richard.

She checked the time with the headwaiter every thirty minutes to make certain her watch was accurate. She worried that she had gotten her dates mixed up. Opening her purse, she pulled out her palm-size Hallmark datebook and looked at the calendar. No. It was June fifteenth.

She was where she was supposed to be. Richard was not.

At a quarter to midnight, Mary Grace gave up her vigil, paid the bill for the two baskets of Italian bread and two cappuccinos she'd consumed and left the restaurant.

The night was incredibly balmy, with a half moon overhead that looked twice as big as the moon in Illinois. How symbolic, she thought. Even the moon was broken in two, just like her heart.

She'd never been in love before. She'd always thought those sad songs exaggerated the pain of a broken heart. But this was actual, physical pain.

She crossed the cobblestone street and rounded the corner, where she found a boy and girl about her age kissing in the moonlight as they stood next to the storefront glass window of a fashionable men's boutique. Earlier that day she'd been so smug thinking how Richard would kiss her under the Roman street lamps.

Tears filled her eyes as she tore her gaze from the young lovers and continued down the sidewalk. Since

Richard's first kiss, she'd been soaring through the universe, dancing among the stars, and now, suddenly, the earth had shot up to meet her. She felt crushed.

She couldn't help wondering if he'd ever planned to meet her. How many others had there been like her? Had he just wanted to add her to his list of gullible women? Richard was so handsome, there had probably been dozens. No, hundreds! Oh, he was very good at romancing. Very good. He'd fooled her so easily. Had the voyage been any longer, she knew she would have been very tempted to go all the way with him. When she'd been in Richard's arms, she hadn't cared about morals, mortal sins or hell. The sad truth was, when it came to Richard, she would have risked anything for him.

She continued walking toward the hotel, thinking about Richard.

"Mary Grace!" Richard's voice seemed to call out to her from a distance.

She kept walking.

"Mary Grace! Please, wait!"

She turned around and he was there. "Richard!" She ran toward him and opened her arms.

He grabbed her by the waist, lifting her off the ground. He kissed her. "Mary Grace! I thought I'd lost you! You weren't at the restaurant . . ."

"I thought I'd lost you...I waited and waited..." she said between tiny kisses he planted on her lips, cheeks, eyelids and forehead.

"There was a horrible rainstorm in New York. Lightning everywhere." He kissed her mouth ravenously, the way she loved. "The plane was delayed six hours. I got here as fast as I could."

"Oh, Richard. I love you so." She kissed him back.

"Did you miss me?" he asked, grinning from ear to ear.

"Incredibly."

"Oh, good."

His kisses ignited the passion her body remembered all too easily. He moaned, pulling her pelvis into his so she could feel his erection. He backed her up against a brick wall and leaned his body into hers, pressing his chest against her breasts.

"Mary Grace, you have the most fabulous body in the world. I can't wait to make you mine."

"Don't tempt me, Richard," she said, letting her eyes delve deeply into his crystal blue pools. She felt her soul falling down, down into his gaze as she closed her eyes and surrendered to his power.

"Tell me you love me again, sweetheart."

"I love you," she answered just as his hand slid up her rib cage and captured her full breast. He caressed it with slow circular motions that sent hot waves of desire across her abdomen and deeper to her loins. She opened her mouth more and moaned as his tongue took possession of hers. She ached to feel his bare hand on her breasts, her stomach, between her legs.

Richard was panting. He pulled away reluctantly. "Mary Grace, I have a surprise for you."

She was looking at his kiss-swollen lips, wondering why he was not still kissing her. They could talk later. She put her arms around his neck. "What did you say?"

"I've arranged everything," he said.

"What are you talking about?"

"I rented a Fiat. Red. We'll drive down to Naples tonight. Take the early-morning flight to Palermo and be in Taormina by eleven. There's a coliseum there that's four hundred years older than the one here in Rome.

From the top row of stone seats, you can see Mount Etna, which is still spewing lava. It's pretty spectacular against the night sky." He kissed her cheek and his eyes gleamed with happiness. "I want to see you in the moonlight in that coliseum. I wanted the most romantic place I could think of as a setting."

"For what?"

"I went to the embassy in New York and got us a license to be married in Sicily."

"What? Now? Tonight?"

"Well, tomorrow," he said. "What's the matter? Don't you want to marry me?"

"Well, yes. I just thought you meant ... like someday. I was thinking of a formal church wedding with my girlfriends as attendants."

"I was thinking about you and me. *Our* romance. Not what your parents want for you. When are you going to think about yourself and not what your parents want you to do?"

Mary Grace couldn't help remembering that her friends had accused her of the very same thing that afternoon. Had she always done that?

She knew she had. Her parents had planned out her entire life for her. And she had let them.

Here was Richard standing before her, offering his love and his life to her. She had a chance to stand on her own. Make her own decisions. She could change the course of her life with this single act. There was no question Richard's idea of a wedding was far more romantic than a church filled with nuns and priests and her parents' friends in Chicago. She could see it now. They would have a sit-down roast-beef dinner at the Hyatt. There would be mashed potatoes and green beans and champagne. Maybe an open bar. Everyone would tell her she looked lovely and they would go away with not a single memory that would make her wedding any different from the others they'd ever attended. The trouble was, there would be little Mary Grace would even remember.

Richard was offering her the memory of a lifetime.

"Do I have time to get some clothes from the hotel?"

"Yahoo!" Richard shouted, picking her up and whirling her around.

"Richard, put me down!" She laughed with him.

"I like doing that. It makes you think I'm strong. And besides, I like the way your body feels as it slides down my chest."

She laughed again and kissed him. "Are you sure you're in love with me or just sex-starved?"

"Both," he said as he took her hand and they walked toward her hotel.

Mary Grace had been right earlier that day when she'd thought they were changing. Suddenly, she realized she was making the greatest change of all, and it felt very, very good.

10

T he Hotel Cape de Taormina looked as if it had been carved out of the seaside cliff it dominated. Sitting majestically atop a rocky hill, the hotel faced a forty-foot sheer drop to the deep sapphire blue waters of the Mediterranean. The harbor below was host to more yachts than Cannes during its film festival each year at the end of July. Movie stars from all over the world, including Liz and Richard Burton, attended the Taormina awards night, each one coveting the solid gold apple award given to the film industry's finest performances.

All along this western coast of Sicily were smooth gravel beaches where Hungarian princesses and Swedish models sunbathed on white wooden chaises under yellow-and-white striped canvas umbrellas next to Polish dukes, Hollywood movie moguls, English stage actors and German industrial tycoons.

Mary Grace had never heard of Taormina, nor its film festival, and Richard explained that was because the elite and wealthy who frequented the place wanted to keep it a secret. He'd discovered it the summer before when he'd overheard passengers on the *Queen Elizabeth* talking about it at dinner. He and one of the other waiters had sought out the hotel as a lark. They realized they had stumbled into paradise.

"I've learned a great many things by eavesdropping," he said as they waited for the bellboy to deposit their luggage in their room.

"I'll just bet you have," she said, following him into the suite.

As she watched the bellboy put her suitcase on the luggage rack, she thought about Kathryn and Cynthia finding her note. She hoped they understood, but she knew they were probably cursing her right now for not letting them in on her secret.

If Richard hadn't shown up and she'd gone back to the Hotel d'Inghilterra alone, she wondered if she ever would have told them the truth. They would have been able to see her sadness, but she didn't think she could trust anyone, not even Kathryn or Cynthia, with this intimate information. No, she would have kept her life with Richard a secret. Even if he'd broken her heart.

Richard tipped the bellboy as he left.

Mary Grace tried to ignore the king-size bed covered in a pale blue linen duvet and skirted in a blue-and-white-striped dust ruffle. She walked to the French door that opened onto a small balcony. Leaning over the railing, she realized there was no earth beneath her, only the sea. "My God! Richard, come look at this. It's like being suspended in the air."

"Isn't it magnificent?" he asked, looking at her and taking her into his arms.

"The ultimate," she said and kissed him hungrily.

Richard broke away quickly. "Now, don't get me going. You have no idea how much I want to take you over to that bed and . . ."

"And what?" She loved teasing him. She knew he couldn't resist her. She liked this power she had over him, and she hoped she could keep it for a long, long time.

"You get changed while I make a call and see if our wedding is still on."

Mary Grace took out the white eyelet sundress she'd brought. She put on a tortoiseshell headband, to which she'd glued white silk daisies to match the embroidered daisies around the scoop neckline of the dress. She slipped her feet into white espadrilles, then applied peach-colored blush and peach-colored lip gloss.

Richard hung up the phone. She stood before him waiting for his approval.

But he said nothing about her appearance. Rushing past her into the bathroom, he jumped into the shower, washed his hair and shaved. He then dressed quickly in dark blue cotton-twill pants, white shirt and navy tie. On his feet, he wore Italian loafers and no socks.

They drove into the village and parked a few streets away from the little church where they were to be wed. They began to walk, hand in hand, toward the chapel.

It seemed that everywhere Mary Grace looked she saw flowers. Lining the streets were enormous clay pots with profusions of geraniums and brightly colored petunias and ferns. The store windows were underscored with flower boxes, and even the apartments above sprouted flowers on balconies, in windows and doorways. Hanging ferns, ivys and geraniums were suspended from most rooftops.

She loved the cobblestone streets and brick sidewalks. There were tourists everywhere—the cacophony of different languages being spoken was like music to her ears. She never wanted to go home, she wanted to stay in this enchanted land forever.

The chapel was small, dark and cool. Like everything else on this island, it looked as if it had been carved out of the hilly rock. The walls of the church were the natural walls of a grotto, to which stucco had been applied and then frescoes painted over. The altar was made of a huge stone, looking oddly pagan and sacrificial, she thought, and there were no more than thirty pews.

The priest was dressed in monk's robes, and as he walked toward them, Mary Grace started to tremble. What was she doing? She didn't know who Richard was at all. She hadn't even thought to ask if he was Catholic—though obviously he was since he seemed to know what he was doing. She looked at Richard. He seemed cool and confident as he shook hands with the priest, even conversing with him in Italian. What else was there about Richard she didn't know?

Richard handed the priest a sheaf of papers, including his and Mary Grace's passports.

"*Grazie,*" the priest said.

They followed the small, darkly tanned man to the altar where they stood in front of him. He smiled broadly.

"You will please excuse my English. I will say ceremony in Italian."

"Fine," Richard replied.

Mary Grace nodded and smiled.

The priest began reading from his prayer book. Between the Latin and Italian passages she didn't understand much except the look on Richard's face. He was beaming; he couldn't have looked happier. And that made her happy.

Richard had purchased a simple gold band, but because he'd had to guess the size, it was a bit too small. The ring was shiny and new, though, and she loved it. Someday they would have enough money to buy her a suitable diamond. Maybe next year, she thought.

Putting his hand on Richard's shoulder, the priest motioned for him to kiss her. He kissed her tenderly, then began laughing as he shook the priest's hand. Mary

Grace shook his hand, too, then they signed the proper papers—one set in English, to be filed with the state of Illinois, and one set in Italian, to be filed in Sicily.

Mary Grace signed her name to the first page as Richard watched. "I can't believe it," he said. "I thought you'd forget and sign your maiden name."

She shook her head and laughed. "I'm a Bartlow now and I always will be."

Richard kissed her again and thanked the priest.

The noonday sun was brilliant as they walked out of the grotto church. Mary Grace shielded her eyes with her hand. Her eyes watered and for a moment she couldn't see Richard. His form seemed to waver in front of her, and she was afraid that if she reached out to touch him, she would find nothing.

He took her hand. "C'mon. I'm starved. Let's get some pasta."

"Food?" she asked, still trying to focus. "You can think of food at a time like this?"

"I haven't eaten since yesterday morning. I could eat the rocks. Think of it as our wedding supper."

They walked past the square and down a block to a little restaurant that sat behind a tall wooden fence. A cluster of olive trees with branches folded overhead like laced fingers kept the stone-floor outdoor dining area cool and shaded.

They sat at a round table covered with a red checked cloth. Richard ordered a bottle of Chianti, salads, grilled redfish and huge bowls of spaghetti with meatless marinara sauce.

"The pasta is so light here, it's like eating gelatin," he said.

"Know what my grandfather always said to my grandmother when she tried to serve him Jell-O for dessert?" she asked him.

"No, what?" Richard said, picking up her hand and kissing her fingers.

"Eating Jell-O is like opening up your mouth and letting the moon shine in."

They laughed together. Mary Grace was surprised at how important it had suddenly become to be able to make Richard laugh. She hoped she could always do that. She wanted their life to be filled with laughter, fun and romance.

The pasta was just as Richard had described. He explained that real Italian pasta was so light because the flour in Italy was different from American flour. Even though there were Italian cooks in New York and Chicago who were just as adept at making pasta, one had to experience Italy to taste really good pasta.

"Then we'll come back here every year for our anniversary and eat really good pasta," she said between mouthfuls.

"Deal," he said, winking at her. "It's always going to be like this for us, isn't it, Mary Grace?"

"Oh, yes, Richard. It will if I have anything to say about it."

The loss of Mary Grace's virginity was aided by the fact that she'd consumed half a bottle of Chianti at lunch and part of a second bottle that Richard bought to take back to their room. It was not aided by Richard's adeptness in bed.

"It's going to hurt like hell, but there's no getting around it," he'd said unromantically.

Mary Grace winced and nearly cried out when it happened, but Richard covered her mouth with a kiss. If it hadn't been for the hours Richard had spent that night playing with her breasts, kissing, licking and sucking every inch of them, Mary Grace would have felt enormously slighted in her first experience with love-making.

She was determined to get better at it.

They made love on the balcony at three o'clock in the morning with Mount Etna streaking the sky with shooting spires of lava. They made love in the shower, in the bed and on the floor. They tried different positions and no matter what she did, Mary Grace couldn't get enough of Richard—nor did *he* ever seem to tire.

She thought it odd that his kisses had seemed so romantic, nearly spiritual, and yet lovemaking wasn't the same at all. It was exciting, but for some reason, no matter how many times or how many different ways they did it, she kept thinking there was more to it than this.

As dawn neared, Richard became sleepy. Finally, he put his head between her breasts and closed his eyes. Looking out the French doors, Mary Grace watched the first glimmer of the dawn's pink rays scamper across the horizon and skate across the blue Mediterranean. As her left hand rested on Richard's shoulder, a sunbeam struck her golden wedding band.

She was married. She'd had a ceremony performed by a Catholic priest, and they'd consummated the marriage no less than half a dozen times. They were as married as people got, she supposed. She had shared her love and her body with a stranger.

She wondered if it felt any different to marry someone you'd known for a long time. Marrying a stranger was exhilarating, she thought, but she couldn't help wondering if the excitement was from joy...or fear.

Mary Grace had never before done anything on the spur of the moment. But that was because she'd never *done* anything in her life. Even her girlfriends had noticed that. She didn't even pick out her own clothes— her mother did.

She guessed no one could accuse her of not thinking for herself anymore. She had met Richard on her own. She had decided to accept his proposal of her own free will and she had married him. She had marked the course of her life, and she intended to make it grand.

11

The night Mary Grace left for Taormina, Kathryn returned to the hotel to find Peter St. John waiting for her.
He told her that he'd submitted his photographs of her
to a friend at British *Harper's Bazaar.* They'd been so
well received, he wanted to sign her as a model. Peter
told her that the first assignment would be a spring collection to be shot on the Via Veneto in Rome. Kathryn
could hardly believe this was happening—just that afternoon, she'd wished she could stay in Rome and now
she could.

After Kathryn and Peter went out to celebrate and got
drunk, Kathryn returned to her hotel room to find
Cynthia just as drunk after a night on the town with a
cute Roman boy on a scooter. It was only when they
awoke the next morning that they discovered Mary
Grace had left them a note explaining she had gone to
Sicily to marry Richard.

"God! Is she crazy?" Kathryn asked. "She doesn't
even know this guy!"

Cynthia clucked her tongue. "That girl is something
else. She's declaring her independence from her parents."

"What do you think they'll do when they find out?"

Cynthia shrugged. "They'll go ape, of course."

As soon as they arrived back in the United States,
Mary Grace blurted out the truth to her parents, Rich-

ard by her side. Richard had told her for days that she should expect them to be surprised, but they were her parents and because they loved her, they would want her to be happy.

"Get in the cab, Mary Grace," James said, barely able to contain his anger. "We'll talk about this on the way to the Waldorf." He began pulling her by the arm.

Richard started after her, but James blocked his way. They stared at each other, eye to eye. "I don't know where the hell you think you're going, but it's not with us."

"She's my wife," Richard said confidently.

"Not for long she won't be," James growled, pushing Mary Grace into the cab behind her mother and getting in after them.

Mary Grace waved to a forlorn-looking Richard as they drove away.

Richard decided that the better part of wisdom was to let Mary Grace have the evening with her parents while he went back to his apartment and arranged to have his clothes shipped to Chicago.

Richard had very little in the apartment he shared with two friends who were working on their graduate degrees at New York City University. Other than his guitar, some self-help books, the last of his college textbooks he hadn't been able to sell, his toiletries and a modest wardrobe, Richard owned nothing.

Mary Grace had given him her address and phone number in Winnetka. He boxed up his jeans, madras shirts, high-top Keds, penny loafers and jackets and sent them to himself in Winnetka.

Richard sat on an electric blue Naugahyde beanbag chair and wrote a long letter of explanation about his marriage and move to Illinois to his roommates, along with a check for his third of the rent for that month. He left the forwarding address for his mail.

Then he telephoned Mary Grace at the Waldorf-Astoria Hotel.

"Hello, sweetheart. How are you doing?"

"Not so good," she said, sniffing.

"What are they doing to you, darling? Please don't cry. I don't want to hear you cry. Everything will be all right once they get used to the fact that we're married. They're in shock, honey. Once they get to know me, they'll like me."

"Do you really think so, Richard?" she asked.

"Of course. They'll see how much in love we are and how happy you are, and they'll come around."

"But what do we do in the meantime?"

"You fly home with them just as we planned. I'll take the bus—"

"Richard, I can buy you a plane ticket," she protested.

"Forget it. We'll need the money to find an apartment. Nothing fancy. Just something to get us by until I find a job. Which should take me about two and a half minutes in Chicago. My school record is impeccable. Honest. Everything is going to be great. You'll see. *They* will see."

"Oh, Richard. You make me feel so much better. I was beginning to think my life was over."

"It's only the beginning, baby. Only the beginning."

Richard hung up and was just about to leave the apartment when Bob Ribordy walked in.

Of his two roommates, Richard had known Bob the longest, both of them having graduated from Yale. Bob had worked his way through Yale, just as Richard had, but they hadn't known each other that well until the last semester of school, when they decided to get an apartment together in New York. Still, their relationship was not close; Richard liked to keep people at a distance.

"Hey, buddy! When did you get back?" Bob shoved his Foster Grant sunglasses onto the top of his head as he noticed the packed boxes. "What's going on?"

Richard looked down at the boxes that held everything he owned. "I got married."

Bob started laughing. Richard frowned. Bob laughed even harder, grabbing his sides as he folded into one of the beanbag chairs, the only furniture in the living room. "No joke?"

"No joke." Richard started filling a cheap leather valise with his bills, correspondence and the stack of résumés he'd had printed on good-quality paper, which he'd been sending out to corporations across America for the past four months with no results.

Bob stopped laughing. He laced his fingers and laid them across his chest. "So, who is she? Where did you meet her? What's her name?"

"It's all in the letter I wrote you." Richard motioned to the countertop in the minuscule galley kitchen. "I left a check."

"Oh. So, you're not going to tell me?" Bob's eyebrow arched.

Richard busied himself with shuffling through papers. "I'm in a hurry."

"I can see that." Bob expelled a heavy frustrated sigh. "You must have just met her, because when you left there was no girlfriend I knew about, unless you were holding out on me, which tells me you don't trust me and you don't think I'm your friend."

Richard rammed some more papers into the valise. God, he hated these pseudointellectual types! Bob was studying to be a psychologist and in the process he drove everybody nuts. Richard had his own agenda for his life and he didn't like anyone poking around in his private affairs. His father had always tried to do that, and it had pissed him off then. It still did. "I'm married. I'm moving to Chicago. Her name is Mary Grace Whittaker. That's all you need to know."

"Asshole," Bob said without his normal good-natured tone. "You're as closed off as a dead-end street. I was just being friendly."

Richard whirled. "No, you weren't. You were being nosy. You want a subject for your next class project? Go to Bellevue."

"Whew!" Bob shook his hand as if he'd burned it. "Sorrrry!"

Richard realized he was overreacting. "Look, I'm under a strain right now. I'm dead on my feet from the traveling back and forth across the damn ocean and Mary Grace's parents are giving us a hard time."

"I can imagine." Bob folded his arms across his chest again. "Want some advice?"

"No." Richard sat down. "But I have a feeling you're going to give it to me, anyway."

"You got that right. You met this girl and she knocked your socks off or you knocked hers off. I know you, Richard. You don't do anything spur of the moment. You're a thinker, a planner. Some might say a schemer."

"Thanks a lot, asshole."

Bob shrugged. "I call 'em as I see 'em. I can't see how you, of all people, would meet a girl and fall in love that fast."

"Hey! When Cupid strikes, he hits hard."

"She must be a knockout."

"She is. Christ, I've never seen a body like Mary Grace's. I didn't even know they made women like that."

Deep furrows creased Bob's forehead. "But what's she like?"

"Sweet. Fun. Do anything for me. Her interests are the same as mine. She wants to be an architect. And her father is loaded."

"Ah! I knew there was something more going on than just being bitten by the love bug."

"Shut up."

"So, you got everything you wanted, after all, didn't you?"

"Yep. I did. My life's going to be a cakewalk from now on."

"For her sake, I hope so," Bob said ruefully.

"What's that supposed to mean? I'll be good to her. Give her everything she needs and wants. I mean, how tough can that be? We'll be sensational together," Richard said firmly.

Bob smiled. "Okay, you've convinced me. She sounds wonderful." He stuck out his hand for Richard to shake. "I wish you both my best."

"Thanks," Richard said, shaking Bob's hand.

"See, Richard. That's wasn't so hard, after all."

"What?"

"Being human," Bob said, folding his arms over his chest once more and smiling smugly at Richard.

James booked the three of them on the first flight to Chicago the next day. He couldn't wait to get home and have his daughter's marriage annulled.

He went to see his priest, his bishop, and getting no satisfaction, he demanded a private meeting with the cardinal of Chicago. James was told that no matter how badly he wanted to end the marriage, even if he contacted the pope in Rome, the marriage could not be annulled because Mary Grace and Richard didn't want it to be.

When Richard got off the bus two days later, Mary Grace was waiting for him at the station. She flew into his arms. Now that they were together, her life would fall into place. She just knew it.

She told him she'd found an apartment. It was small, off Ontario Street in the city and close enough to most transportation so he could get around easily, no matter where he found a job.

Richard took one look at the plush pile carpet, the newly painted walls, the harvest gold appliances in the kitchen and the breathtaking view of the lake and rejected it.

"I can't afford this. Maybe in a year. Two years, possibly. I'll bet this place cost over three hundred a month."

"Four-fifty," she said sheepishly.

"Forget it. Find something for a hundred and fifty."

"*What?* Nobody lives in an apartment for a hundred and fifty dollars!"

"They do it every day, baby." He ran his forefinger along the side of her jaw to her chin. "So will we."

When Richard had told her that he had no money, Mary Grace had not understood he meant *no money.* She learned that he'd used what he'd earned on the *Queen Elizabeth* to arrange their wedding and to buy her ring. He'd paid for his bus ticket, leaving him five hundred dollars to pay the first month's rent and security deposit and to get them started off in life. He didn't have money for furniture, a television set, china, clothes or food, other than the cheapest and most basic items.

Mary Grace knew now why her parents kept telling her that "No one can live on love alone." She hated that they were right.

Mary Grace knew her father had tried everything to rid himself of Richard whom he was convinced was an opportunist. The entire affair smacked of exploitation, he said, only Mary Grace just didn't see it. Finally, James tried to reason with her.

He took her to Chez Pierre for lunch, hoping, no doubt, that the posh surroundings would show her what she would miss in her life. Renting a cheap motel room on a weekly basis was all she and Richard could afford. She didn't need her father to tell her it was demeaning.

The waiter poured ice water with lemons sliced so thin, they looked transparent into Mary Grace's water goblet.

"Daddy, I don't want to discuss this."

"Well, I do," he said while signaling the headwaiter. "Your rash decision has resulted in a poor choice of men."

"You don't even *know* Richard. Why don't you give him a chance? He's not some bum off the street. He graduated from Yale. I've seen his résumé, and frankly I think you could use someone like him in your firm. He's applied at Sloan and Winter," she added coyly, sipping her water.

The headwaiter had just arrived at the table. James was about to order a drink, when the mention of his fiercest competitor's name stopped him. "He *what?*"

"I suggested it."

"Mary Grace, what the hell are you doing?"

"Order your drink and I'll tell you." Mary Grace folded her hands in her lap. This was the second time in her life she felt powerful. The tiny network of veins in

James the Third's face had turned him beet red. She reminded herself to treat him gently—he wasn't accustomed to changes or surprises of any kind and she'd given him both . . . in spades.

James ordered a Scotch and soda. "And make it a double."

Mary Grace kept her expression neutral as she continued. "I'm getting you back for treating me like I haven't a brain in my head. That's what I'm doing. If you think Richard is such a poor choice for me, why would you care that he goes to work for your competitor? The reason is because you *do* think Richard might be an asset. I know you, Daddy. When did you call your SWAT team to investigate Richard?"

"From the Waldorf," he answered, taking a deep gulp of his Scotch.

"That's what I thought. And what did you find out?" she asked confidently, knowing how impeccable Richard's college record was. She'd seen his grade card and his letters of recommendation from his art history, city planning and architecture professors. In her mind, Richard had accomplished everything she wanted for herself.

"Where's he from, Mary Grace?"

"Huh?" The question caught her off guard. It was a simple question, but one she'd failed to ask Richard. Frankly, she hadn't cared where he was from. He was from heaven, she wanted to say. Weren't all angels? She and Richard had been too busy making love, looking for apartments, making love, planning how to deal with her parents, making love, job hunting and making love to ask stupid questions like "Where are you from?"

"Gary, Indiana. His father is dead—died in the steel mill where he'd worked all his life since his high school graduation. Did you know Richard refused to attend his own father's funeral? He hasn't seen his mother since he left for Yale. He had nine roommates in four years. I think that's a little excessive. And in each instance his roommates asked for a transfer. He doesn't smoke, drink and never tried marijuana, which I think is amazing for a college student. Even *that* makes me suspicious."

Mary Grace felt tears come to her eyes. "Why do you want to hurt me?"

"I don't want to hurt you. I want to protect you."

"No, you don't. You just want me live out the plans *you* made for me. I've upset those plans by marrying Richard. But nothing has changed all that much."

"Really? I think a great deal has changed. I think he's turned you against me and your mother. You never used to talk to us like this."

She looked off to the right where a young, well-dressed couple sat at a table holding hands. Mary Grace recognized them from her church. They had married last December. They both had trust funds to keep them from ever knowing what a hundred-and-fifty-dollar-a-month apartment looked like. "I'm just growing up, Daddy. That's all." She turned back to face him after beating back her tears. "In the fall, I'll still go to Barrett. I'll still be home for all the holidays—"

"Stop right there. What makes you think you'll be going to Barrett?"

"Well . . . I am." Suddenly, it hit her. "Aren't I?" Panic flicked through her like a strobe light. She felt her face go numb and her tongue seemed to swell in her mouth. "You're not taking away my college fund?"

"If you remain married to Richard I am."

"You're trying to bribe me." She said it as a statement because there was no question in her mind. She'd heard her father could be ruthless in business, but she'd never seen it. Until now. "But I want to be an architect, like you."

"You should have thought of that before you married Richard."

"And so, if I divorce Richard you'll send me to school."

"Any school you want."

"Any school I . . ."

He nodded. "Yes, your mother and I believe you pulled this stunt because you were angry with us for not letting you go to St. Mary's. We are willing to concede that we may have overstepped our boundaries on that point. It was just that your mother wanted you close to her. She cares a great deal about you. So do I."

Mary Grace couldn't help thinking he'd thrown that last part in as an afterthought. A wrap-up to his sales pitch. She wondered how many other girls went through trials like this. Did it happen to everyone at her age? And would she be wiser or just more brokenhearted for the experience? She felt her stomach lurch.

Mary Grace placed her hands on either side of her plate. She touched her salad fork with her ring finger. The gold was shiny, new and untested. "You haven't spent two minutes with Richard, yet you think my decision is unwise. Tell me specifically what it is about Richard you don't like. Apart from my rash decision, that is. Tell me why you think he's so incredibly wrong for me."

James finished off his Scotch. "Look around you, Mary Grace. These are the kind of people you've known all your life. We live like this. This is our world. It is affluent, it is buffered from the seedy side of life in order that we can accomplish greater things. We aren't nailed to a cross of making do. Over there is a doctor I know who is working on a cure for cancer at Northwestern. There's one of the best trial lawyers in America. There's a man who intends to run for the state senate. People like us make the world better, Mary Grace. We are privileged. It is our responsibility to marry within our ranks and continue to give back to the world more leaders and innovators. You can't do that when you're struggling to simply feed yourself." Leaning forward, he placed his hand over hers. "He's not one of us."

Mary Grace was surprised he didn't throw in a line about the "divine right of kings." He'd never sounded so pompous in his life. Slipping her hand out from under her father's touch, she looked him in the eye. "To hell with you. You make me . . ." She put her hand over her mouth and pushed herself away from the table. "Sick."

Mary Grace walked quickly to the elegant bathroom and vomited.

12

Mary Grace had been married two months when the doctor confirmed she was pregnant—two months pregnant. She thought it utterly romantic that she'd conceived Richard's child on her wedding night in the most beautiful place on earth. She felt special, as if the angels had blessed her.

Richard was still reeling over the fact that his father-in-law had tried to bribe Mary Grace into leaving him. Mary Grace had recounted everything about her luncheon with her father, repeating every word of his lecture. Richard intended to use each of those words to nail James Whittaker III's coffin shut.

When Mary Grace returned from the doctor's office, Richard didn't pay any attention to her. She began humming a song as she looked through the newspaper ads for cheap used furniture for their cheap apartment.

"Did you tell your father I got the job at Sloan and Winters?" Richard asked.

"I told him you were offered a job there."

"Why didn't you tell him the truth, that I started the middle of July?"

"I wanted to keep my options open," she answered, wishing they would stop talking about James the Third so she could give him the good news about the baby.

"Why?"

"I'm convinced he's going to offer you a job. Soon."

Richard rolled his eyes and turned away from her. "I don't know why I bother talking to you about my career. You have no concept of how these things work. The reason I went to work for Sloan and Winters is because I want to show your father that his biggest mistake was underestimating me and my abilities. When he finds out the truth, he's going to be pissed at you for lying to him *and* he's going to think I put you up to it. I wish you'd keep the hell out of my business."

"Richard! What an ugly thing to say to me," she said, thrusting out her lower lip in a pout. "You hurt my feelings." She hoped he would apologize for his outburst and comfort her. But he didn't.

Instead, he stood by the window sulking.

Mary Grace was beginning to feel more than a little slighted. He acted as though she'd tried to hurt his career intentionally. She was only looking out for their best interests, but Richard didn't see it that way.

"Richard, come sit by me, please." She patted the cushion of the hand-me-down avocado green sofa Cynthia's mother had given her.

"I don't feel like it."

"Richard, I have a reason why I did what I did, but I can't tell you about it with you all the way over there."

"It's a small room, Mary Grace. Try."

"Fine. Have it your way. I'm going to have your baby, Richard."

The silence howled around Mary Grace.

Finally, he asked, "Are you sure?"

"Yes. I went to the doctor today. That's where I was."

"I thought you went to the drugstore." He finally turned toward her.

His eyes were filled with panic, she saw, and his face was tight with fear. "I lied," she said. Mary Grace's happiness deflated like a balloon. Richard didn't want this child.

"And how is that going to make a difference with your father?"

"He can no longer try to get the marriage annulled or talk me into a divorce. Too many of his friends know about our marriage now. With a baby on the way, his first grandchild, he will come around."

Richard walked over to her and knelt at her feet. He put his hand on her knee. "You really think so?"

She touched his hair tenderly, pushing an errant lock off his forehead. "I think you will be shocked at how fast he will put his differences aside."

Mary Grace was right. She went to her parents' home in Wilmette without Richard and told them about her pregnancy during their cocktail hour, while they waited for friends to arrive for dinner.

Caroline nearly swallowed the olive in her martini. "So fast? You must have gotten pregnant on your wedding night."

Mary Grace smiled. "I did," she replied, relishing her triumph.

"Oh, God," Caroline said with distaste.

James the Third studied his Scotch and soda. "I hadn't really thought about the fact that I would be a grandfather. It was something I knew would happen to me . . . someday. But I don't know if I'm ready for this."

"It doesn't matter if you are or aren't. You'll be a grandfather in March—around the fifteenth, I'd say."

He looked at Mary Grace. "This does put a different light on things, doesn't it."

"I think so," she replied confidently.

Caroline looked at James. "I, for one, don't want my grandchild growing up in a hovel. I think we should buy them a house."

James drank his Scotch very slowly. "I agree. I've got those lots out in Lake Forest. We could build something for cost. It wouldn't be so bad. The schools are good. No crime." He laughed. "Hell, that's because it's so far out, no one wants to live there."

"But, Daddy, you bought all that land out there to develop."

"Sure, twenty years from now."

"Oh." Mary Grace hung her head.

"Tell Richard to come around to see me on Monday morning. I'll find something for him to do at the firm."

"I don't know if he'll do that, Daddy."

"Why the hell not?"

"He's working for your competition. He needed the job. He wanted me to have a home. Because you were so mean he had to take what he could get."

"Judas Priest! Do I have *any* control of my life, anymore?"

"It would seem not," Caroline answered.

"Well," James said with resignation, "tell Richard I'll give him a higher position with more pay."

"That would help, Daddy."

Caroline looked into her empty martini glass. "I suppose this means I should plan to have Richard over for dinner to meet our friends." She looked at her husband.

"Yes, dear. I think that's what you should do."

Mary Grace's pregnancy was a lark. After the initial weeks of morning sickness, she experienced nothing but good health, energy and enthusiasm for the road her life had taken. This turn of events was nothing short of glorious.

She spent her days designing the kind of house she'd always dreamed of for herself; a two-story traditional redbrick Greek Revival design with a double sweeping staircase leading from the foyer to the second floor. She told Richard she wanted to feel like a princess in her house, and she made all the appropriate decisions to ensure that feeling.

Richard told her she was crazy to put such an imposing foyer in a house with only twenty-five hundred square feet. He would rather have a larger family room or a library for himself. But Mary Grace wouldn't budge. She didn't want a house like everyone else's. She told him she would serve guests in the foyer if she had to, she wanted that European feel she'd experienced in Paris and Rome.

While the rest of Chicago designers were decorating houses with Early American furniture or garish contemporary steel, glass and psychedelic colors, Mary Grace chose white marble for the entry and beige carpeting for the rest of the house. The cabinets in the kitchen were dark cherry wood with brass hardware, and she outfitted the bathrooms with white porcelain fixtures and white tile. She intended to update the rooms over the years with wallpapers, paint and fabrics as the styles changed.

She went to the Merchandise Mart with her mother and found the designer showrooms overstuffed with harvest golds and avocado greens. Mary Grace preferred more subdued earth tones like white, taupe, beige and sandy pink for the essential upholstered pieces she needed. She put most of her money into one well-constructed tuxedo sofa for the living room done in a heavy taupe silk fabric. She chose two unpainted Queen Anne–designed chairs and lacquered them herself in white enamel. She found a large slab of pink quartz stone at the landscape company her father used and made it into the base of a coffee table, topping it with glass.

Because draperies were too expensive, Mary Grace bought cheap white sheets and hired a seamstress to border the side, top and bottom with black braiding. Then she tied them back from the windows with black silk cords and tassels. Someday she would be able to afford white lacquered plantation shutters on all the windows, she told herself.

She bought an inexpensive wooden table and four Windsor chairs for the kitchen and painted them a buff brown, leaving the legs of the table white. She found a white, black, brown and beige plaid cotton material, which she made into seat cushions, curtains, matching place mats and napkins.

As she became bigger, a king-size bed began to look more inviting, and she spent the largest part of her bedroom budget on the bed itself. She then bought a pair of used white distressed French nightstands at an auction in Wilmette that reminded her of Véronique. She hired the same seamstress to make a heavy damask buff-colored dust ruffle, as well as a duvet cover out of heavy black velvet with buff-colored silk-cord piping on the edges. The seamstress suggested she monogram all her linens, and when Mary Grace replied she didn't know how to embroider, the seamstress gave her lessons. Mary Grace was a fast learner. In the center of the black velvet duvet cover, Mary Grace stitched Richard's initials in the same buff silk thread she used to monogram their white sheets and pillowcases.

Mary Grace worked night and day during her pregnancy on her new home. She attended dried-flower arranging classes at the elite floral-design shop her mother used, and she learned to frame the botanical prints she found at an antique shop on Rush Street. She studied seed catalogs, landscape books and gardening magazines, and asked questions of every workman who labored on her house. She wanted to know everything. If she had to give up her college education for Richard, she intended to squeeze every morsel of knowledge out of her home-building experience.

It was her first attempt at home and interior design, proving to herself and her mother she had a keen eye for blending colors and balancing space. Caroline not only commended her for staying within the budget James had given her, but for stretching it as far as it would go.

Mary Grace was only nineteen years old when she and Richard moved into their new home. Two weeks later, on March 15, 1967, she gave birth to her daughter, Penelope, with less than six hours of labor and an easy delivery. When Mary Grace returned home from the hospital three days later, she couldn't imagine what all the fuss was that women made about being pregnant and giving birth.

Placing Penelope in the white crib Cynthia had given her at her baby shower, she told Richard she was the happiest woman alive.

Richard replied that he was happy she was happy.

For Richard, the best part of all was that James was footing the bill.

13

———▶◀———

Richard worked incessantly at first, then compulsively, and by the second year of his marriage to Mary Grace, he worked obsessively.

No matter how innovative his designs, or how aggressively he cut deals with the developers for land, with the suppliers for lumber, or with the local manufacturers for plumbing fixtures, Richard never felt accepted or appreciated by James Whittaker III.

Richard and James danced the self-destructive flame and moth duet. Richard had married Mary Grace for the prestige of the Whittaker association. Within his first year at the firm, his fame had soared like a rocket. Richard's bids for big construction projects were not only taken seriously but given special priority. The Whittaker name opened doors at city hall that would have not opened for a mere Bartlow. Richard met with high city officials who wanted the quality and thirty years of experience that the name Whittaker implied.

James employed fifteen architects, each specializing in different aspects and phases of construction. They built everything from shopping malls to stadiums to skyscrapers; commercial construction was the company's forte. The only sector the company experienced weakness in was residential home building and planning. Richard discovered that James had speculated on several large tracts of land in the western and northern suburbs, however, he hadn't yet formulated any plans for development.

Richard knew if he could make startling innovations and create a profit center for James in this area of the business, he would win the old man over to his side. He had found a niche for himself and he began to fill that void.

On his own time, Richard investigated the land itself by walking every foot of it. He went to the city planning commissions in each suburb and spoke with their officials. He researched demographics and planned highways, toll roads and interstates for proposed expansions. He spoke with downtown retailers about ideas for suburban stores, and he read the local weekly newspapers, paying particular attention to the voice of the people and editorial sections. Learning what the population of those areas liked about their suburb, he would know what would appeal to them in the future.

He interviewed local merchants, talked with homeowners and went to regional and national builders' conventions. He talked, listened and listened some more, absorbing information whenever and wherever he could.

Richard spent two years putting together a plan for an exclusive residential community, and he found that he'd never been happier. He was using every creative cell in his body and he felt as though he could take over the world. His life had never been better.

By the summer of 1968, Mary Grace wondered if she would ever be happy again. At seventeen months old, Penelope was a curious child who insisted on discovering life through her own experiences. She had already managed to fall down both sets of stairs while toddling out of her bedroom in the middle of the night. She had burned herself on every hot object in the house, from Mary Grace's hot rollers to a burning log in the fireplace, and she'd learned how to unhook the rubber bands on the cabinets her mother tried to close off to her. She'd also started climbing up on tables and chairs and had mastered how to push her high chair to the kitchen counter and climb on top of it to jump off.

Penelope was a daredevil and she loved it.

Being an only child, Mary Grace had had no concept of how much work babies could be. If Penelope had been a passive child, life might have been a little easier. However, even the pediatrician told Mary Grace that her daughter had been given a double dose of energy. From the first weeks of life, Penelope had slept only four hours a night. By the time she was seventeen months old, she was sleeping six blessed hours, but she did not nap during the day.

Richard refused to let Mary Grace hire a maid, on the grounds that she had nothing to do except care for a small child and clean the house. He resented the fact that she wanted to be kept as a princess. She snarled at him that he was no longer a prince.

By the end of August, 1968, Mary Grace thought the world was being torn apart by the seams. Bobby Kennedy had been killed in June; the National Guard had been called into the inner city in Detroit to prevent race riots, and the governor of Illinois had ordered the National Guard to stand by during the Democratic Convention in Chicago. Nothing, it seemed, could stop the bloodshed in the streets that summer.

Mary Grace wished she could make more of an impact on the world—like Cynthia, who was going to school at Berkeley in California. The world was changing, her friend had found a different drummer to lead her band.

Cynthia marched for the poor, marched for an end to the war and participated in sit-ins, lay-ins and love-ins. She wrote to Mary Grace often, telling her about the fascinating lectures she attended at school and the excitement on campus, and describing the incredibly intellectual men and women she'd met. Cynthia had been among the war protesters who stormed the Pentagon in October, 1967, when she'd met Norman Mailer just before he was jailed.

It had become "chic" to protest the war and, above all, Cynthia had always been "chic."

Mary Grace felt her life was not only tame, but dull compared to Cynthia and to Kathryn, who was living a glamorous life in Europe as a model. However, she provided the stability for their patchwork group, keeping each informed of the other's adventures and telling them both she missed them terribly. She didn't let them know, though, the truth about herself—that she was lonely.

Richard's life was in the city, meeting with architects, builders and politicians, trying to land the contracts on new city buildings and malls. Not only was he gone every day at six in the morning until after seven most nights, but he spent his weekends playing golf or tennis with potential clients or working on his two-year-long "dream project." The only time he sought Mary Grace's company was when her presence was required at a client dinner or during the odd evening meal at home at which time he would tell her about his triumphs during the day.

Except for sex once a week, Mary Grace felt she served no purpose in Richard's life other than to provide the stability of a marriage.

She didn't believe Richard was having an affair—only because she'd made enough discreet inquiries. Whenever she called his office or tracked him down at her father's club or on the golf course, Richard was always where he was supposed to be.

What Richard had done was worse than infidelity, she decided. He had closed her out of his life. She wondered if he ever thought about her or Penelope. He never called her during the day to find out how she was or what she was doing, the way her father did with her mother. Richard simply didn't give a damn.

It was while Richard was watching Arthur Ashe win the United States Open Tennis Championship on September 9, 1968, that Mary Grace realized her marriage was over. Walking into the family room, she shut off the television set.

Richard bolted out of his recliner. "Are you nuts? Arthur Ashe is about to make history! The first black male to win a major tennis tournament and you turn off the television." He snapped it back on.

"I'd like to make a little history of my own," she retorted.

Richard didn't look at her as he watched the color picture come back into view. "Can we talk about this later?"

"No, goddamn it!" she screamed, and not only shutting off the television but pulling the power knob off the set. She clutched it in her palm, holding it behind her back like a kid in a game.

"Give me that," he stormed.

"Richard, I want to talk."

"About what?" he asked angrily, putting his face in his hand and looking at her.

"Do you love me?"

"Oh, fuck. Not now!" He started out of the chair again.

"Yes, now. You never pay any attention to me, Richard. We don't have any time together. We don't even go to the movies together. And when we do go out, it's always with other people. Why is that, Richard?"

"You tell me." He began walking toward the kitchen.

"Where are you going? I'm trying to talk to you!"

"Christ, you sound like my mother. I just wanted a Pepsi."

While he rummaged in the refrigerator, she followed him into the kitchen. "I was thinking we could go back to Europe. Just the two of us. You haven't had a vacation since we got married. You're overworked. We could stay with Kathryn at her villa in Rome. She's asked me a dozen times to come for a visit. She's gone half the time—we'd have the place to ourselves." She smiled, hoping her suggestion would erase his frown.

He opened the Pepsi bottle and took a long slug. Then he looked at her. "I make eleven thousand dollars a year working my ass off for your father. Who, by the way, doesn't give a rat's ass if I live or die. But that's okay. I keep my job there because he tolerates me. The other guys in the office, they *know* I got my job because I'm married to you. I have to work twice as hard, twice as long and be twice as smart just to keep even, because everyone thinks I have this great advantage. Even though we don't have a mortgage to worry about, the cost of the upkeep on this place is a killer, Mary Grace. The heating bill alone wipes out a major chunk of my pay. I've got yours and Penelope's mouths to feed. And *you* want to go to Europe."

He finished off his Pepsi in one long gulp.

"Baby, you married the wrong guy. What you need is Onassis. If you hurry, you can catch him before he marries Jackie."

"I just want to go away with you." Mary Grace wrung her hands. "Alone. The two of us." She didn't know what to do. She wanted to bring Richard closer to her but she was only shoving him away.

"Are you sure that's *all* you want?" he challenged.

"What are you talking about?"

"This comes out of the blue, if you ask me. For my career, the timing couldn't be worse. You know very well that I'm making my presentation to your father and the rest of the architects tomorrow morning. I've spent nearly every extra minute since I signed on with your father on this project. This is *my* baby. And you want to go away to Europe and visit one of your girlfriends and her fag boyfriend or whatever the hell he is." His words hissed angrily through his gritted teeth. "If I didn't know any better, I'd say you were trying to sabotage my career. Is that what you're doing? Because if it is, it won't work!"

He stomped back into the family room. "Now give me that goddamn knob!"

"No!" she screamed. "I'm not finished."

"Well, I am!"

She backed away from him as he came toward her. She didn't like the menacing look in her husband's eyes. "Forget Europe. Forget about Kathryn."

Looming over her, he suddenly looked like a stranger. She didn't know who this angry, self-centered man was, he bore no resemblance to the boy she'd met on the ship.

He had practically worshiped the ground she walked on then. What had happened to him? What had happened to *her*?

"I love you, Richard. And I just wanted to spend some time with you."

He held out his hand for the knob. "And I just want to watch some television."

As she looked into his blue eyes that had once held her captive, she realized his soul had turned to ice.

She handed him the knob.

"Thank you," he said flatly, walking away from her.

Mary Grace almost wished they'd come to blows—then she could point her finger at him and accuse him of physically abusing her. But the blows he struck had damaged more than her skin; they'd struck her heart.

The following morning, Mary Grace got up after not having slept all night. She'd clung to her side of the king-size bed, crying and listening to Richard's deep breathing as he slept through her night of torment. Weighing her options, she found she didn't have many.

She imagined every scenario that filing for divorce would cause. Her parents would gloat over her decision, her mother wanting to know each and every wrong Richard had committed against her. Just the thought of Caroline's interrogation forced Mary Grace to rethink the whole idea of divorce.

James the Third's reaction would be worse because he would pull the granddaddy of all trips...Catholic guilt. If she divorced Richard, she would be ostracized, even excommunicated, from the Church. Since the only social life she had was with some of the young mothers in her church, Mary Grace knew she'd never be able to hold up her head again if she divorced. As much as

James had fought the marriage in the beginning, he would fight the divorce. He was a die-hard Catholic, and Catholics did *not* divorce. He'd told her that a hundred times when he'd wanted her to annul the marriage.

Richard knew her father as his co-worker and boss; he knew James as a model to emulate, whose level of successes he wanted to attain. James was his golf partner, tennis partner and father-in-law, and Mary Grace realized she was jealous that her husband of only two years knew her father better than she did.

Even though her mother had been sweet to her, showing her some of the finer points of cooking, housekeeping, laundry and baby care in the past two years, she still related to her mother on a child to parent basis. They weren't friends the way she was with Cynthia or Kathryn. Her relationship with her parents had not grown at all since her marriage—if anything, it had actually become more stilted.

Mary Grace was stuck in Lake Forest, miles away from Wilmette and the things she used to do. She was more like a hermit, sitting in her beautiful house, caring for her beautiful daughter, waiting for life to happen. Because she found it un-Catholic, unmotherly and un-American to blame a little baby for keeping her confined to her house, she decided to blame Richard.

Mary Grace needed affection, love and attention, and in that order, but she was getting none of it from Richard. It was odd, now that she thought about it, but she'd never gotten much of those things from her parents. She realized that all three of them were very much alike: they were self-absorbed. With plenty of time and energy to do what *they* wanted, none of them made a place in their lives for Mary Grace.

Moving silently across their room, she went to the hall linen closet where she kept her sewing basket and sewing machine. She took out a long needle with a large eye and a spool of heavy white thread, and chose a pair of sharp embroidery scissors.

She went back to the bedroom and began her work. Her stitches were crude but efficiency was all that mattered this morning. Mary Grace was not particularly interested in the execution of her task as she was in its speed. There wasn't much time—she had to hurry.

When the alarm went off, Richard went to slap his palm down on the snooze button, but he couldn't move his arms.

He felt as if he was caught in some kind of tight-fitting cocoon. With his arms plastered against his sides and his legs out straight and only his head showing, he was a prisoner in his sheets.

"What in the *hell* is going on?" Richard yelled as he struggled to wrest himself from the body-length straitjacket that bound him.

Mary Grace sat in a rocker beside the bed.

"I wanted your attention," she said with a smirk.

He struggled anew to get out of the sheets. "You are fucking nuts, woman! Crazy as a loon! You get me out of here or I'll—"

"What, Richard?" she screamed back at him. "Hit me? Kill me? Beat me to a pulp? I don't think so. I think from now on you'll have a greater respect for me. That's what I think."

He stopped thrashing and looked at her. "What do you want?"

"I want some attention . . . for starters."

"Okay," he said calmly. "You have that. What else?"

"I want you to tell me you love me."

Richard rolled his eyes. He couldn't believe this was happening to him. "I love you. Now, are you satisfied? Let me out of here."

She shook her head.

Looking at the clock he realized he was going to be late for work on the most important day of his life. "Do you have *any* idea what time it is? I've got that presentation this morning."

"Tell me you love me and *mean* it, Richard!"

He watched as Mary Grace brandished her embroidery scissors. What did she intend to do with them? Pluck out his eyes? Cut off his dick? What kind of sicko was he married to? And what had he done to set her off? If there was anything Richard knew, it was that Mary Grace was his meal ticket, now more than ever.

He was on the verge of making a name for himself in Chicago. If he could talk James into backing him on this project, his name would be golden for the rest of his life. This was his bid at the big time; he'd worked for nothing else since the day he'd joined the company. He *had* to make that meeting this morning, and he *had* to keep Mary Grace happy. He didn't like it, but he had to give her what she wanted.

"I love you, baby. You know I do." He said it just the way he'd said it on the boat and on their honeymoon. Maybe there was still hope. She'd believe him. "Really, Richard?" she asked, tears in her eyes.

"Really, baby." He glanced at the clock.

"I want to go away on a trip, Richard. I want us to get back to the way we used to be."

"I'll make you a deal. I can't afford Europe, even if we did stay with your friend. But I've got a friend who has a condo in Scottsdale. I'll take you there for a long weekend—four days is all I can take off. Provided..."

"Provided what?"

"Provided I get the deal this morning. This is the biggest day of my life, Mary Grace. You don't understand what this can mean to us."

She started crying for real. Jumping out of the rocking chair, she went to Richard and kissed him, hungrily like when they were on their honeymoon. He kissed her back.

"Now, cut me out of here, baby," he said.

Mary Grace snipped the stitches, yanking at the top sheet to free him. Richard leapt out of bed and grabbed her by the shoulders. Suddenly, he saw fear fill her eyes and she flinched.

He pulled her to his chest and held her tightly. "I promise I will never do anything again to make you that upset, Mary Grace. Please forgive me. It will never happen again."

He kissed her, more quickly than the last kiss, then dashed off to the bathroom to shower. He knew she was satisfied.

When he returned to the bedroom, he found his best suit, shirt and tie laid out on the bed beside his wallet, keys and briefcase. And as he dashed through the kitchen, Mary Grace handed him a cup of coffee with cream and sugar, just the way he liked it. She kissed him again and waved goodbye from the back door as he drove down the driveway and out to the street. That was a close call, he realized.

When Richard telephoned that afternoon and told her he'd won the bid, Mary Grace asked when she could book their reservations to Scottsdale. He explained that now that he would be the general on the job, he didn't have time to go to Scottsdale. James was depending on him, he said. However, he promised that as soon as the permits were pulled and the ground-breaking ceremony was behind them, he would take her away.

Mary Grace had no idea she would wait three years for her trip to Scottsdale.

14
→←

Lawrence Bartlow nearly killed his mother. As she lay in intensive care for three days after his difficult birth, Mary Grace was surprised she'd survived it. Two weeks prior to his premature delivery, she had developed toximia. In addition, her son became stuck in the birth canal for over twenty-two hours before the doctors performed a cesarean section. She was exhausted. When the doctor told Mary Grace her baby was a boy, she had asked to see him, but the nurse replied, "Not just yet, we have to fix his head."

Images of grotesque human distortions swam across her drugged mind. Imagining the worst, she didn't even bother to look at the baby. She closed her eyes and planned to leave her body. Forever.

Mary Grace didn't want to live. She had done everything in her power to make Richard pay attention to her and give her the affection she needed. But her husband wasn't interested in her needs or wants. He told her she was demanding and selfish. Worst of all, she believed him.

The night she went into labor with Lawrence, she'd begged him to get off the phone and take her to the hospital. She told him she was in pain, but he didn't believe her.

Richard was sitting in his recliner watching the Bears game and talking to Hal Anderson, one of the architects from the office. He was laughing and talking about a project they were working on, discussing how well everything was going. Mary Grace knew she wasn't interrupting anything important.

"Richard, I need to call the doctor. I'm in a lot of pain."

He waved her off.

A stab of pain racked her body, and she clutched her abdomen, sinking to the ottoman. "Richard! It hurts! Please, call the doctor!"

"Look, Hal. I gotta go. I'll call you back in a minute." He hung up and shot Mary Grace a disgusted look. "What kind of tricks are you up to this time? The baby isn't due for three weeks and . . ."

Suddenly, Mary Grace's face turned ashen.

"What is it?" he asked, sounding suddenly alarmed.

"I hurt," she whispered. "This isn't like the last time." She clutched her abdomen again.

"Okay. I'll call the doctor." He dialed the number and handed her the phone. "You talk to him. It's your baby."

If she'd had the energy, she would have given him a dirty look, but she felt as if she was dying. She could hardly speak as she described her symptoms to the doctor.

Paying no attention to her, Richard kept looking past her to watch the touchdown being made on television.

She hung up the phone. "He says to come to the hospital, immediately."

"What?"

"You heard me," she said, grabbing her abdomen again. This time, the pain was searing and she felt she might pass out.

"But I'll miss the game." Richard glared at her. "This is a false alarm. Guys tell me these stories all the time. The baby isn't due yet."

Mary Grace shook her head. "Get Penelope, and after you take me to the hospital, you can take her to my mother's. I'll call and make sure mother is home."

She listened to Richard grumble as he went upstairs to get their daughter, then placed the call to Caroline.

After a brief conversation with her mother, Mary Grace lay down on the sofa to wait for Richard to return.

A few minutes later, Penelope raced into the family room but stopped short when she saw her mother.

"Mommy!" Penelope screamed. "You've made a mess!" Mary Grace looked down to the pool of blood seeping into the sofa.

Penelope rushed to the kitchen, returning with a kitchen towel. "Daddy is going to be so mad. Hurry. Mommy, we have to clean it up!" Penelope sopped at the mixture of water and blood. "What is it?"

"Penelope, it's all right, sweetheart." Mary Grace grabbed her hand. "Don't worry about it. I have . . . to get to the . . . car." She tried to stand.

"But Daddy will *kill* you, Mommy, if he sees this mess!"

"Right now, darling, I don't care." Mary Grace pushed herself off the sofa. She felt as if her knees would buckle, but at least she was standing. "Take my hand."

Taking it, Penelope helped Mary Grace as best she could. They walked out through the laundry room which led to the garage. "Over there, darling, is my night case. I'll take that with me."

Penelope picked up the American Tourister train case Mary Grace had gotten as a high school graduation present and which she'd taken on her honeymoon. Except for her trip to the hospital to give birth to Penelope, Mary Grace—who'd always thought her life would

be filled with exploring exotic cities and architecture—
had gone nowhere. Once again, Mary Grace and the
case were going to hospital.

As she eased her pain-riddled body into the car and
Penelope hopped into the back seat, Mary Grace silently took back what she'd said when Penelope was
born. Birthing was all the horrible things she'd ever been
told—she just hadn't realized how lucky she'd been with
Penelope. This time, her luck had run out.

Lawrence Bartlow's christening was set for November twenty-sixth, the Sunday after Thanksgiving, in
order that both Cynthia and Kathryn could attend.
Mary Grace was thrilled when she received a fashionable note from Rome in which Kathryn stated she would
be in Chicago for a modeling shoot for *Vogue* and would
stay over for the christening. A scribbled missive from
Cynthia on handmade stationery informed Mary Grace
that she would fly in especially for the event.

Richard was surprised that Mary Grace's friends
would be attending the party, but he was more stunned
at James's reaction to Lawrence's birth. The man was
positively weepy over the fact that there was a boy in
the family.

"A boy! My God, I still can't believe it," James said to
Richard at the church while they waited for the priest.

Richard smiled thinly. "I'm glad you're so pleased,
James."

"Hell, I'd about given up when Penelope was born.
My brother, Gregory, he had the boys. I thought the
world of those boys. Still do. I don't know what Greg-
ory did, but he's got two incredible young men there.
Yes, he sure does. A doctor *and* a lawyer in the family.
Now, that's something to be proud of."

All Richard could think of was the cost of the education. Gregory must be ready for the poorhouse, he thought, putting one son through medical school and the other through law school. Lord, he hoped his son decided to become a builder like himself. He wondered how much of his fifteen thousand dollars a year he needed to put away to pay for Lawrence's college education. He didn't know how to save ten cents at the rate Mary Grace went through money.

It seemed it was always something: Penelope needed new clothes, the washer had to be fixed, or the car needed a new transmission. He worked his ass off and it was never enough. Mary Grace wanted new family room furniture. The cheap stuff she'd bought when they first married was falling apart, she said. It was time they bought quality goods.

One thing Richard knew: quality cost plenty.

Richard had chosen Jack Billingsly to be Lawrence's godfather. Jack was the same age as Richard and was one of three attorneys James employed. He had handled the legalities for the HeatherWood Subdivision Development Project in Buffalo Grove, and Richard was so pleased with Jack's precise work and honesty that he began asking Jack to play golf. They soon became friends.

Jack was a good-looking, bright, easygoing man who rarely moved quickly on any decision in his own life. He told Richard he was in no rush to marry. He had a particular kind of woman in mind for a life mate, but all the girls he'd known growing up in Wilmette weren't interested in the kind of life he wanted.

Jack wasn't drawn to the idea of a house in the suburbs or children. He wanted the kind of woman who was career-oriented, who wanted to travel, go to the theater and play golf with him. He wanted an intelligent woman, one who was a great conversationalist and who was politically erudite.

Though Jack's family was well-to-do, his parents had always worked hard—but they had fun, as well. Jack was the kind of person who never took anything for granted and didn't expect favors from anyone. He disliked the way most of the wealthy girls from Wilmette and Winnetka seemed to think that life "owed" them, simply because they existed. He found them shallow, selfish and lazy.

When Jack talked to his friend about it, Richard always nodded morosely and said, "I know what you mean."

But pretending not to notice Richard's sullen response, Jack kept looking for his own "dream girl."

Mary Grace had chosen Kathryn to be Lawrence's godmother. She had first suggested Cynthia, but Richard had rejected that suggestion instantly, stating he would not have a marijuana-smoking political-activist hippie responsible for the upbringing of his only son, should he drop dead on a building site.

The morning of the christening, Cynthia showed up at the church dressed in a chic black and beige Bob Mackie suit, with black shoes and black leather purse to match. Her hair was nearly white blond and flowed down her back like a waterfall. She was tanned berry brown and looked the picture of the California dream girl.

Richard's jaw dropped. "Cynthia?"

Cynthia smiled smugly at Richard and shook his hand. "I know you were expecting Patricia Hearst. Don't believe everything you read, nor everything I tell you, either!" Laughing heartily, she turned to Mary Grace and embraced her.

"Doll, you look wonderful," Cynthia exclaimed.

"I most certainly do not. I've gained ten, fifteen pounds."

"Liar," Cynthia said, taking a critical inventory of her friend. "I don't give a damn if you gained fifty, you'll always be beautiful to me." Cynthia hugged her.

"I wish I'd hear that from my husband," Mary Grace whispered.

"God, I missed you. I didn't realize how much until now." Mary Grace saw a tear at the corner of Cynthia's eye. "We'll talk later," Cynthia said.

Just then, Kathryn came through the church doors. She was thinner than Mary Grace remembered, but as startlingly beautiful as ever. Her hair was a blend of honey and wheat that spiraled to the middle of her back in soft curls. She wore an apricot, brown and rust-colored velvet patterned suit that smacked of Italian design, her shoes also distinctly Italian in their sexy cut. She carried a matching soft kid envelope purse.

She greeted Mary Grace and Cynthia with hugs, but there was a warmth missing in her embrace that Mary Grace noticed immediately.

"You're more beautiful than ever," Mary Grace gushed.

"You, too, *cara mia*." Kathryn smiled a posed smile. She turned to Cynthia. "I got your Christmas card."

Cynthia's eyes were laser sharp as she assessed her friend. "That was almost a year ago. What the hell's been going on with you? You used to call me all the time. I've sent you half a dozen letters and no answer. I'm surprised you showed up."

"I was busy," Kathryn said with a vacant sound to her voice that matched the dull look in her eyes. Mary Grace realized something was dreadfully wrong with her friend.

Cynthia took Kathryn's arm. "Busy, hell. You're avoiding me and you know it. I'm here now. And you will tell me what the fuck is going on."

Kathryn's eyes wandered around the room, landing on Richard, on Jack Billingsly, anywhere but on Cynthia. "Later. Where's the baby? I want to hold the baby." She looked anxiously around the church, finally locating Penelope and baby Lawrence with Caroline and James in the front pew. Kathryn went over to see them.

Mary Grace shot Cynthia an accusatory look. "What is going on with you two? And why don't I seem to know why a bomb is about to go off at my son's christening?"

Cynthia shook her head. "I didn't know she was this bad off. Otherwise, I wouldn't have come."

"You tell me what's going on, right now." Mary Grace glared at her, her look one of menacing determination.

"Okay, calm down. I'll tell you." Cynthia took a deep breath. "To put it succinctly, Kathryn was living with this Italian count. Or so he said. A playboy was all he was. Antonio raced cars in Monte Carlo, lived off Kathryn and while he was knocking her up, he was also knocking up another model, Martinique, or something like that. Anyway, Kathryn found them in bed together, freaked and tossed him out. She got an abortion, but the butcher botched the job and now she's not sure she can have children. The problem is, she's still in Rome seeing him with Martinique, and their love baby is due any day. The Italian press loves the story. They've made Kathryn into this weirdo because she's depressed all the time and won't model over there. Hence, her push to model here all of a sudden. I figure the story will break in the U.S. once she gets famous. That ought to take a minute and a half."

"I can't believe she didn't tell me. I'm her friend."

"Why would she tell you when you're her role model? She wanted what you have. A husband and kids. I think she wanted the idea of marriage more than she wanted Antonio. He wasn't her type. She needs to find the right guy and then it will all fall into place for her. But right now, she's pretty messed up."

"I can't imagine *anyone* wanting my life. If she only knew the truth..." Mary Grace watched Kathryn, who was holding Lawrence in her arms as if he were the most precious thing on earth.

Cynthia nodded. "I think it's time you gave her a dose of reality, doll."

Jack Billingsly was completely taken with Cynthia and Kathryn—Richard could tell by the way his friend's eyes followed them about the church. Jack was on his way toward Kathryn to introduce himself, when Richard grabbed his arm. "Put your eyes back in your head, buddy," Richard said. "She's a heartbreaker."

"I don't get that impression at all."

"They all are."

"All, Richard?"

"Yeah, all women are out to break your heart, your butt and your bank account." Richard's tone was dour. "Take Mary Grace, for instance. She was just as beautiful as her friends the day I met her. I almost didn't know which one I wanted. But Mary Grace was softer. She just looked more loving. Or so I thought. Now..."

"Now, Richard?" Jack's eyes were filled with wariness.

Richard stopped himself. He'd said more than he should. This man was James's friend, too, and Richard knew Jack was fond of Mary Grace, even though she wasn't the kind of woman he wanted for himself. He thought of Mary Grace as a little sister, and such relationships had a tendency to endure, Richard thought. It was dangerous for him to plant any seeds of doubt in Jack's mind about their relationship. Richard was still employed by James Whittaker III and until that situation changed, he had to play the game.

Richard wore his most charming smile. "Now, Mary Grace is a mother—twice. And now, she's not so glamorous. For me, she's perfect. For a guy like you, who's in the market for a cosmopolitan kind of babe, I'd think twice about Kathryn, who looks a bit too natural with my son. Notice that Cynthia hasn't even glanced at the baby yet. She's still chatting with Mary Grace."

Jack nodded. "I see what you mean. Kathryn wants—"

"Yep. The double B's. Burbs and babies."

Jack slapped Richard on the shoulder. "Thanks. You may have just saved my life."

Richard smiled again. "Don't mention it. What are friends for?" He was happy to share his insight on women with his friend. Women were predictable, and Richard knew he had a knack for understanding them.

That is, until his mother walked into the church.

15

Janet Bartlow had always abided by her son's wish that she not intrude in his life in Chicago. Richard had made a hasty trip to Gary, Indiana, to see his mother on his way to Chicago after he and Mary Grace arrived back from their marriage and honeymoon. He'd told Janet that he was going to make a new life for himself and that if she loved him, she wouldn't spoil it for him by making a nuisance of herself. Still despondent over Bud's death, she had agreed to leave him alone. She wanted Richard to be happy.

But now, six years later, Janet was learning to put her own life back in order, and she decided she didn't like being put on a shelf, forgotten and alone. She wanted more than the occasional phone conversation with Richard when he was at the office, where she couldn't disturb his family.

Janet had waited a long time to have grandchildren and she wanted to know them: they were her blood. It was common, blue-collar blood, but it was hers, all the same.

Because Richard was reluctant to tell his mother anything about his wife, his job or his life in Chicago, Janet learned to use devious methods to extract the truth. Whenever she telephoned Richard's office, she would ask casual questions of his secretary or his assistant. How was Richard doing? Was he really in a meeting or playing golf? Or was it tennis today? How was his wife doing? Questions like that led to a wealth of information, Janet found, especially when the secretary was busy and Janet made a pest of herself. The woman would tell her what she wanted to know just to get her off the phone.

Richard told Janet only the generalities of his life. He was married and had a daughter. It wasn't until she happened to phone the office on the day Lawrence was born that she discovered she was a grandmother for the second time. Janet knew that if he could, Richard would have kept Lawrence's birth from her.

But Janet knew Richard's Achilles' heel. He was ashamed of his parents and his very humble beginnings. She'd never understood *why* he felt this way, only that he did. And one of the reasons she was here today was to find out why Richard wanted her to disappear from his life.

Janet wore her best light blue polyester suit she'd bought at Sears last Easter. It was a spring color, but she didn't think anybody would notice. She would have liked to have matching shoes, but they cost over twenty dollars a pair and she didn't have that kind of money. She was working the night shift at the old truck stop on Highway 20, but she'd recently gotten a second part-time job working the breakfast crowd at Denny's. She was still paying off the house, Bud's funeral and a ninety-five-dollar-a-month car note on her Pacer, but she was doing okay. She was forty-eight years old and she wanted the same thing Richard wanted: respect.

Four years ago, Janet had learned that her son attended Our Lady of Sorrows Church. And when she discovered from Richard's secretary that Lawrence had been born, she knew the next step she would take.

Janet never said anything to Richard about the baby when she phoned him at work a few days after Lawrence's birth. She waited to see if he would announce the good news. Instead, he barely spoke, saying he was on his way to a meeting. He promised to call her, but as usual, he never did.

Janet waited another week, then telephoned the church offices at Our Lady of Sorrows. She asked if a date for the Bartlow christening had been set yet. The secretary gave her the information and Janet thanked her and hung up.

She knew that to make Richard realize she intended to become part of his life she would have to do all the work.

"Richard, there's a woman here..." Mary Grace nodded toward the back of the church where a brassy, middle-aged woman was standing.

Looking nonchalantly over his shoulder, Richard snapped his head in a double take. "Excuse me," he said curtly to Jack and Mary Grace. As he strode away, he could hear Mary Grace ask Jack, "Do you know who she is?"

Richard walked up the aisle as fast as he could to meet his mother. He couldn't believe this was happening. "What the hell are you doing here?"

"I want to see my grandson." Janet smiled as she spoke.

"You weren't invited."

"I'm well aware of that," she replied harshly. "But I have a right to be here."

"No, you don't," he argued. "You have made things very difficult for me."

"Why? I wanted to surprise you. Just tell them your mother is here. Use that brilliant mind you're so proud of, Richard."

"I can't do that," he said, shoving his shaking hands into his pockets.

"Why not?"

"I told them you moved to Nova Scotia. I told them you were dying of cancer."

Her tired blue eyes wrinkled as she narrowed them. "Tell them I had a miraculous recovery, Richard."

"Shit."

"Don't cuss in church," she reprimanded, as if he were six years old. "I *am* your mother and I *am* the baby's grandmother. I'm just as much a part of this family as you are. Now, *tell* them." Her eyes were hard as steel ingots.

Richard knew he was cornered. "How can I trust you not to tell Mary Grace the truth about the lie I've been telling her?"

"How can I trust *you*...ever? You're the one who has been lying. Not me."

He glared at her as anger surged through his body. Janet had no manners, no social graces and, obviously, no respect for him or his wishes. She wanted to destroy him and the life he'd built among the beautiful people, the jet-setters and the movers and shakers of Chicago. The only things she was concerned about were her own selfish, self-centered needs. God! How he hated the woman.

But the bottom line was, she had him by the balls.

"Fine," he said. He crooked his arm for her to take and plastered a charming smile on his face. He walked her to Mary Grace, who was standing with Cynthia and Jack.

"Darling!" Richard said to his wife. "The most amazing thing has happened. My mother has made a miraculous recovery and she's flown in from Nova Scotia for the baby's christening. Mary Grace, this is my mother, Janet Bartlow."

Mary Grace's eyes popped open. "Your...mother?"

Jack looked from Richard to his mother then back again. "Your mother?"

"Your mother," said Cynthia flatly, knowingly.

"How do you do?" Mary Grace extended her hand, giving Janet a warm smile.

"Very well," Janet replied formally.

Richard caught the tone of pretense in her voice immediately—Janet was up to something. She could be devious when she wanted to be, and he had a sick feeling that this was one of those times. He watched as his mother moved closer to Mary Grace, who was introducing her to Jack and Cynthia.

"That's a beautiful suit," Janet complimented Cynthia. "I wish I had nice clothes like that. But then, it takes a lot of money. Which I don't have much of, that's for sure." She chuckled.

Richard knew at that moment his mother was a snake. She was here to weasel her way into his life—not because she loved him, but because he was her ticket to the kind of life-style she wanted.

"Thank you very much," Cynthia replied.

Mary Grace took Janet's hand. "I know you'd like to see the baby, meet Penelope and my parents. We have so much catching up to do." She led her toward the front of the church.

"We sure do, honey," Richard heard Janet reply. She cast a damning look at him.

When Mary Grace was out of earshot, Cynthia looked at Richard. She couldn't hide her smirk. "You've got some shrapnel stuck to your cheek, Richard."

"Shrapnel?"

"From the bombshell that just dropped," she said and walked away.

The christening party was held at Richard and Mary Grace's house. There were over two hundred guests in attendance, most of them Richard's co-workers, clients and potential clients.

Mary Grace had decorated the house in autumn colors of gold, rust and brown. From her flower-arranging classes she'd learned how to dry her own yarrow, wheat, roses and German statice. She'd twisted grapevines into wreaths, then decorated them with pinecones, dried flowers and paraffin-preserved fall leaves, hanging them on every exterior door of the house. She made papier-mâché cornucopias and filled them with gourds and dried flowers. And she wrapped the banisters of her double stairway in grapevine garlands, adorning them with clove-studded oranges, lemons and limes. She'd begun all of these projects in the middle stages of her pregnancy, when the doctor had confined her to at least four hours of bed rest a day. Even Richard had to admit the house looked wonderful for the celebration of his son's birth.

Richard wanted to seek out some of the officials from the city planner's office he'd invited, but instead he found himself cornered by his mother.

Janet was babbling about the house. "I've never been in a house like this. It's a mansion."

"No, it's not. Far from it. In fact, I think it's too small, but I'd never tell Mary Grace that. That would just be *another* thing she wanted."

"She do the decorating?"

"Yes," he said, taking a drink of his wine spritzer.

"And pick out the furniture?"

"Yes." He groaned, bored with this conversation.

"Are those real?" Janet asked, pointing to the exquisitely matted and framed prints hanging on the wall in the dining room.

"No. They're cheap copies Mary Grace found at a garage sale or something disgusting like that. She framed them herself."

Janet's eyes widened in appreciation. "She knows what she's doing, don't she?"

"'Doesn't,' Mother," he corrected.

Janet paid no attention to him. "She make this?" she asked, picking up a spicy boiled shrimp and dunking it in a New Orleans–style sauce.

"She couldn't boil water when I married her. She's learned a few things." He looked at the shrimp tray, placed next to the petit prime-rib sandwiches and the vegetable tray with crab dip.

A large group of Richard's co-workers walked into the dining room.

"What a spread, Richard!" Hal Anderson said, picking up a tiny sandwich.

"I suppose you spent hours slaving away over all this food, huh?" Lynn Peters joked.

Richard smiled proudly. "I thought I'd never get out of the kitchen." He laughed and walked away from his mother, glad for the diversion. Janet was about to make him nuts.

* * *

Satisfied her guests didn't need her attention for the moment, Mary Grace went in search of Cynthia and Kathryn. She found them standing by the French doors in the family room, looking out to the backyard.

As she approached, Kathryn said wistfully, "I never knew how much I missed home."

Mary Grace handed her a cup of mulled wine from a tray nearby. "You have no idea how much *I* miss Rome," she said ruefully.

Looking at one another, they broke into both laughter and tears.

Cynthia rolled her eyes. "You two can be so sappy," she said, whisking a tear from the corner of her eye with her fingertip.

"God, those were the days, huh?" Mary Grace said.

"It doesn't look like you've got it too bad," Kathryn commented, then hung her head and turned away from them.

"Kathryn, Cynthia told me what happened."

"Did you, Cyn?" Kathryn looked at her over her shoulder.

"I thought she should know. She wondered why you latched on to the baby so quickly after arriving. It's not like you, Kathryn. You've never obsessed over kids before. You're taking on a bunch of guilt—"

Kathryn whirled. "Don't preach to me, Cyn. You just don't know." Tears started to stream down her cheeks and she brushed them away quickly.

"Come on, let's go outside," Mary Grace offered, opening the French doors.

The sun was high and it felt good on Mary Grace's face. Being with her friends on this warm November day, she couldn't help thinking of how her life had once been. But she wouldn't allow herself to dwell on her own problems today. Kathryn was in trouble, and she wanted to help—she just wasn't sure if she could.

"What hurts the most, Kathryn, losing him or the guilt you feel about the abortion?" Cynthia asked.

"Him. Definitely him. He told me he loved me. Even when he was boffing *her* he told me he loved me. What a shit he was. What an asshole! And I feel wretched about the baby. I . . . I think I'm guilty of murder or something."

"Bullshit!" Cynthia stuck her hands on her hips angrily. "That's just some more crap we learned in school. If you'd ever studied really ancient wisdom and mysticism, you'd know the soul doesn't enter the fetus until birth."

Mary Grace looked at Cynthia. "Is that true? Where did you learn that?"

Kathryn rolled her eyes. "Probably smoking dope with Rudolf."

"How many times have I told you that crap you read in the paper is just that . . . crap. I never smoked dope with Nureyev. I was there, true. I was everywhere, but I didn't do half the things the papers said I did. Or my mother said I did. I did participate in the be-in in San Francisco the winter before the big be-in in New York. I marched with Joan Baez and half of Hollywood. I made connections you wouldn't believe. I know guys who plan to run for the governor of California someday—I don't know if they'll win, but stranger things have happened. I've been to all the rock concerts and met half the rockers . . . Jefferson Airplane, the Mamas and the Papas, Otis Redding. Everybody. I dated half the guitarists in most of the bands. That was during my music period. Now I'm only dating movie executives. No directors or actors or artsy types, just the guys in the offices."

Kathryn rolled her eyes again. "And I thought *I* had problems."

Cynthia shrugged. "See? I've made you feel better already." She smiled.

Shaking her head, Mary Grace said, "You're something else, Cynthia. But how does Kathryn deal with the pain she's feeling?"

"Find another guy to love," Cynthia said. "Nothing cures an old love like a new love."

"Easier said than done," Kathryn replied. "I just feel like digging a hole and crawling inside."

"I know the feeling," Mary Grace said.

"You?" Kathryn's eyes filled with surprise.

Cynthia put her hand on Kathryn's arm. "We *all* feel that way sometimes. It's allowed, you know. But you have to fight back. Make him know that the *worst* mistake he ever made was letting you go. You want to come back to Chicago and model? Then be the biggest thing that ever hit the cover of *Vogue*. Work out twice as hard. Date the richest, best-looking guy in Chicago. Make him eat his heart out."

Kathryn brightened. "I like this idea."

"Revenge is always a great motivator. I use it myself..."

Kathryn nodded. "I think you may be right. It would do me good to come back here, for a while, anyway. I can stay with my parents. Save some money." She looked down at the cup of mulled wine. "Look, they don't know about the..."

Mary Grace's face filled with empathy. "They will never know. Promise."

"It would hurt them if they did. I don't think they'd stand in judgment. My parents aren't like that—"

"That's where you're lucky," Mary Grace interrupted.

"I know. But my mother would just worry. I don't want her to worry about me. I'll be all right. In time."

Cynthia hugged Kathryn then Mary Grace. "Let's make a pact," she said emphatically. "Right here, right now. That we will never lose touch with one another like we almost did. And that we do a better job of looking out for one another. This life is getting tough for all of us. Just think, if I hadn't come here today, you both would have thought all kinds of things about me. We need to stick together. Kathryn, you've got to get better at letter writing. And I promise to come back to Chicago more often to see you Mary Grace. Even if we can't get to Rome, we'll call you on your birthday. How's that?"

"Great idea!" Kathryn said.

"I love it!" Mary Grace agreed.

They stacked their left hands atop one another. "We're more than friends. We belong to each other."

"Hear, hear!" Kathryn and Mary Grace said in unison.

Janet poked, peeked and probed every room, cabinet, closet and cupboard in the house. Feeling like a spy, she took great care to make certain no one knew what she was really doing. She took note of the refurbished furniture, the handmade curtains in Penelope's room and all the other corners Mary Grace had cut because she was watching costs.

It didn't make any sense. According to Janet's standards, the house was incredible—she just wished now she'd spent more time reading *Good Housekeeping* and *House and Garden* instead of the *National Enquirer*. She didn't know crystal from glass, china from Melmac.

Richard told her he didn't make much money, but this party alone must have cost some bucks. Maybe Mary Grace did grow all her own flowers and dry them, but she still had to have spent five hundred bucks on the liquor alone for the christening.

That was five hundred bucks that could have been lining Janet's pocket.

Richard had turned his back on his mother when she'd asked him to come home from college when Bud had died. She didn't have a soul in the world to help her through her grief, but now that grief had turned to a hard rock that had imbedded itself permanently in her heart. Janet clung to her grudge, it comforted her when she felt lonely and it warmed her when she felt hopeless. She would make Richard pay for not helping her during her time of need. He was her son. He needed to learn a lesson.

Janet found Richard in the living room saying his farewells to a man and woman who were more beautifully dressed than anyone she'd ever known in Gary. As they walked out the door, she approached him.

"Richard, would you call me a cab?"

"What?"

"Call me a cab."

"To take you all the way to Gary? That'll cost over a hundred dollars."

"Really?" Janet smiled.

"I'd rather drive you myself," he said harshly.

"No, you wouldn't. You'd rather spend the money than spend the time with me. Your father was the same way."

"He never *had* any money to spend."

"That's right. And he didn't leave me much, either. Which is why I want you to give me the hundred bucks and I'll take a bus home."

Richard's jaw dropped open. "I can't believe you're saying this!"

"Of course you can. You owe me, Richard. Plenty. You wanted your precious little family to think you didn't even have a mother. How could you do that? When your father died, I realized you were an iceberg, but I told myself you were grieving. I made up excuses for you. Truth is, nothing moves you, does it?"

Shrugging his shoulders, he looked away from her. He refused to answer.

"You'll give me the money or I'll tell your wife and her snooty mother and fancy-pants pop that you lied to them." Janet crossed her arms giving him a challenging look. "I'll blow the whistle on you, Richard."

"You wouldn't dare. I'm your only son."

"And a son of a bitch you are, too."

A malicious smirk wrinkled Richard's handsome mouth. "You made me that way."

"It's a tough world." She wasn't budging until she got what she came for.

"I'll call a cab to take you to the train station here in Lake Forest. You can take the South Shore to Gary."

"That'll be just fine," Janet replied. "I'll wait here while you get my purse and jacket. I'll take the money in cash. No checks."

"Shit," Richard hissed through angrily clenched teeth.

Richard continued to pay his mother a hundred dollars a month over the years until her Pacer was paid off, and in return, Janet agreed not to make a pest of herself in his life. She didn't ask to see her grandchildren and she turned down most holiday-dinner invitations Mary Grace extended to her, claiming holidays meant extra work hours for someone like herself in the restaurant industry.

Mary Grace thought it odd that Janet never visited, and she tried to call her to tell her about Lawrence's first steps, his first words, his first day at kindergarten, but Janet kept herself at a distance.

By the end of the decade, Richard was paying his mother two hundred dollars a month. He resented every penny of it. However, Janet never blew the whistle on him.

At least the bitch kept her promises, Richard thought to himself every time he wrote out her monthly check.

16

—▶◀—

It was the worst of economic conditions to start a business, but Richard didn't believe in bad timing, he told Mary Grace. It was 1980 and Ronald Reagan was running his presidential campaign based on the financial woes of the country. Inflation was staggering out of sight, interest rates soared daily. The home-building business had ground to a halt but Richard was intent on being his own boss. He still believed that James didn't give him the respect he deserved.

"I have to strike out on my own," he said to Mary Grace late one October Saturday afternoon in the kitchen of their Lake Forest home. "He's never going to give me credit for all I've done for his company. I can work my ass off there for the rest of my life and I will never see *my* name on the front of the building."

Mary Grace put her finger to her mouth and motioned with her head toward the family room, where eight-year-old Lawrence was playing with his Star Wars figures. Penelope was in the dining room working on a book report for school on the new IBM Selectric typewriter. Between the sound effects Lawrence was making of light sabers clashing and space ships firing and the stream of watered-down cusswords Penelope invented each time she made a typing mistake, the noise level was enough to give Mary Grace a headache.

"You're just being stubborn about this," she argued while she made a chocolate mousse for yet another of his corporate dinners.

Richard munched on a carrot. He was trying to watch his weight, she knew. He'd just finished a killer golf game that afternoon but Mary Grace could tell his mind was not on sports these days.

"I'm being practical. Leaving the protective wing of James Whittaker III would be the best thing for me."

"I've said it before and I'll say it again—I'm against the idea, heart, mind and soul."

"That I know," he replied ruefully.

Mary Grace heated some water and sugar in a saucepan on the stove. "Richard, I haven't been living under a rock lately. I've been listening to what your clients have been saying at these dinners, and even *they* wouldn't start a new business now."

"I can do this. I know I can, and I don't like the fact that you aren't supporting me."

She pulled out the blender from under the cabinet and poured in the melted sugar, Kahlua, brandy, a bag of chocolate chips and cracked four eggs into the mixture before turning on the machine. It whirred so loudly she had to shout to be heard.

"You're dreaming, Richard. That's your problem. You believe if you think big, it will automatically happen. I think you should stay where you've got it good." She turned off the blender.

"You're just scared we might have to tighten our belts. God help us if that would happen, huh? Maybe you might even have to go to work."

Mary Grace didn't know how Richard knew she was frightened of the idea of going to work, but somehow he'd discovered her fear. "I'm a mother. I have the children to take care of," she said defensively as she began whipping cream in her Kitchen Aid industrial-size mixer.

"Penny is thirteen and Lawrence is eight. They aren't infants, you know."

She waved her hand at him dismissively. "I don't want to talk about this. And don't call her Penny. I hate that name. It sounds so . . . cheap." She folded the whipping cream into the chocolate mixture.

"She's the one who changed her name. Talk to her about it."

"You're her father. *You* talk to her," she retorted.

Just then, Penelope walked into the kitchen, slapping her typed pages against her thigh. "Talk to me about what?" she demanded as she leaned saucily against the kitchen counter. She was tall for her age, nearly five foot ten inches, and she had Richard's body with long lean legs and shapely rounded hips. Her body was nothing like Mary Grace's had been at thirteen, and she was thankful for that.

Penelope was beautiful in an arresting way that reminded Mary Grace more of Kathryn than herself. Penelope had high cheekbones and a high forehead, a narrow nose that wasn't too long, full sensuous lips and Richard's beautiful crystal blue eyes. If nothing else, Richard and Mary Grace had given their daughter the right mix of genes.

"Nothing," Richard said curtly. "We weren't really talking about you."

"Daddy, would you do me a favor and read my book report?"

"I can't. I have work to do. Maybe next time."

Penelope's eyes turned brutally cold. She stuck out her chin and squared her shoulders. "No big deal. I didn't need your help that much, anyway." She turned quickly, her long blond French braid nearly slapping Richard in the face.

Mary Grace watched as her daughter retreated running up the stairs just the way Mary Grace had run when her father had hurt her feelings and she didn't want anyone to see her tears.

She cast Richard a damning look. "Can't you spend ten minutes with her sometime before she goes off to college?"

"She's thirteen. She'll be here for five more years." He leaned over so that his face was close to her. "And must you always ride my ass about her?"

Mary Grace shook her head, thinking that it was important that she stay home with the children because she was the *only* caring parent they had. She supposed she should face the fact that Richard was an absentee father. He was never there for any of them—even when he was physically at home, he wasn't available emotionally.

Lawrence was playing in the family room when his father entered. The eight-year-old boy had carefully set up his *Star Wars* toys over half the room. In the corner by the French door to the patio was the Degobah System, the area of swampy land where Yoda lived. Near the television set was Cloud City, where Hans Solo had been frozen in carbonite. There were a dozen Storm Troopers scattered across the carpet.

Lawrence prided himself on his *Star Wars* toys; he had every single action figure from both *Star Wars* and *The Empire Strikes Back*. The figures had been acquired at great risk in Lawrence's estimation: sick with ear infections nearly every month of his life, Lawrence had received a new action figure or toy each time he'd had to go to the doctor for a penicillin injection.

Lawrence believed he was just as much a hero as Luke for living through such torture, identifying with the orphaned Luke in many ways. He believed he looked like him, with blond hair and blue eyes. He didn't have a robot or a friend, Chewbakka, but he had his sister, Penelope, and most of the time she was very friendly to him. She sort of looked out for him because she was older.

Penelope had told him she didn't like their father, either. She thought he was mean and hateful and so did Lawrence. After years of trying to get his attention in every way they could think, they'd both given up. They'd learned to ignore him the way he ignored them. And when their father was in a bad mood, they learned to stay out of his way.

Lawrence pretended not to hear how his father treated his sister earlier, but he knew Penelope was hurt. He'd seen the way her lips pressed together and then quivered just before she began to cry. Penelope was like his mother: they hated for anybody to see them cry.

Lawrence turned his back on his father when Richard walked into the room. He kept playing with his toys, hoping his father would decide to go to bed instead of coming in here and messing up his fun.

Richard sat in his recliner chair. The second his body hit the chair they both heard an awful crunching sound. "What the hell?"

Lawrence threw his hands to his cheeks and began crying. "Not my Land Speeder!" He was trembling as he turned to his mother, who had also entered the room. "Daddy broke my Land Speeder!"

"Oh, for Christ's sake." Richard reached under his hip and pulled out the crushed brown plastic toy.

"My *Land Speeder!*"

"Quit crying like a wimp. You're my son! Now shut up."

Lawrence grabbed the ruined toy and held it to his heart. Clamping his mouth shut, he put his head down like a bull ready to charge. Then suddenly he turned away from his father. Wiping his nose on his sleeve, he picked up his At-At and hoisted the leggy gray plastic toy under his arm. He scooped up his figures of Hans Solo, Luke Skywalker and Jabba the Hut, and walked around behind his father.

"Your toys don't belong in *my* chair to begin with," his father continued. "It's your own fault your toy got broken. You hear me, Lawrence? Your own fault."

"I hear you, Daddy." Lawrence's voice sounded low and deep like that of an old man. Then he raced out of the room with his toys and up the stairs to his bedroom. He slammed the door as loud as he could so that his father could hear how angry he was.

"That was just great, Richard. You've managed to hurt both their feelings in less than ten minutes. I think you ought to apologize."

Richard got up from his chair. "Forget it. I don't owe anybody anything." He stormed out of the room and upstairs.

Mary Grace watched Richard leave the family room, knowing he would go to his den and sulk. She didn't know what he did up there. Read. Look at *Playboy*. She hadn't the slightest idea.

Many times she'd been tempted to pick the lock and scour his desk for clues. But clues to what? To an affair she was certain he wasn't having? To Richard? What was there to figure out that she didn't already know? Richard felt trapped, and the idea frightened her to death.

It was always like this with them now; they seemed to fight about everything. And when he wasn't fighting with her, he was upsetting the children. Why couldn't he see that he was just as responsible for molding their characters as she was? Time and again she tried to talk to him about them, but he always changed the subject or left the room. He wanted nothing to do with his own children and Mary Grace felt sorry for them all.

The only thing Richard cared about these days was hounding her to get a job and help out with the bills. He wanted her to fire the cleaning woman who came twice a week, but Mary Grace didn't think she could survive without her help. He'd already taken away her credit cards—she'd gladly handed him her Marshall Field's and Carson's cards, thinking that would appease him. But that hadn't been enough. He closed her accounts at all her favorite design shops, the florist, the home-accessories boutique and at William Sonoma's, where she found wonderful gourmet gadgets to indulge her new pasttime: cooking.

Mary Grace had bought all the best cookbooks, from James Beard and Julia Childs to Wolfgang Puck. She purchased a microwave oven and a Cuisinart electronic slicer, dicer and shredder. She invested in Teflon-coated pans, so that nothing would ever stick again, wire whisks, meat mallets, garlic presses, pastry brushes in seven assorted sizes and a full set of stainless-steel gourmet ladles, spoon and spatulas. And with these marvelous utensils she turned out fantastic meals.

Mary Grace's expertise in the kitchen was reflected in the pounds she gained in the process. It was a vicious cycle: she cooked to stay busy and feel worthy, and she ate to fill the void she felt from her empty marriage. The fat repulsed Richard, which then made her feel even more worthless and so she continued to eat. She pretended the extra weight didn't bother her in the least; the truth was that it depressed the hell out of her.

She was a fat, unemployable, unwanted wife. Life couldn't be more miserable.

To increase her unhappiness, Cynthia moved back to Chicago, and she wanted to see Mary Grace. Cynthia told her that her parents had moved to Miami and now she felt the coast was clear to return to her favorite city. She persuaded Mary Grace to come into the city and meet her for lunch at the Drake. Mary Grace tried to beg off, but as usual, Cynthia's forceful personality prevailed.

Mary Grace got to the restaurant early. She wanted to be seated before Cynthia arrived, intending to hide beneath the table, the cloth and a napkin, if necessary. She didn't want her friend to see the shape she was in.

As Cynthia followed the maître d' to the table, Mary Grace noticed that every man in the room was watching her friend. At thirty-two, Cynthia had never looked as beautiful or as sophisticated. She wore a navy blue knit dress with gold buttons on the sleeves and matching gold and navy shoes that must have cost as much as the dress, Mary Grace thought. Her hair was perfectly cut and colored in a soft, modified "Farrah" style. Mary Grace recognized the cloud of Halston perfume that enveloped her.

"Doll!" Cynthia exclaimed with open arms and a warm hug as the maître d' left them. "You look like shit," she said, sitting down.

Mary Grace frowned. "Thanks a bunch."

Empathetically, she reached out her hand. "I had no idea it was this bad."

"Yeah. I've gained almost thirty-five pounds."

"Not that. Your marriage. I didn't know you were this unhappy."

Mary Grace felt tears spring to her eyes and fall over the edges of her chubby cheeks. "Do you know how humiliating it is for me to even be here with you? You look like an aerobics queen. How do you stay so thin? Never mind, don't answer that. You wouldn't understand my problems. Your life is so much easier than mine."

Cynthia leaned forward. "Nobody's life is perfect. Not mine, not Kathryn's and not yours. We just have to learn to make the best out of the hand we're dealt. Someday I'll tell you a *real* hard-luck story, but not today. It's your turn today."

The waiter arrived and asked if they wanted a drink.

Cynthia looked him dead in the eye. "Bring two glasses of very cold—and I do mean cold—Chablis. And keep them coming."

"I don't need any wine."

"Maybe not," Cynthia said, "but for now, it will help. Talk to me, Mary Grace."

Mary Grace poured out her heart. She told Cynthia about Richard's idea to leave her father's firm and that she was against the plan. She presented her case for why such a move wouldn't work and Cynthia listened. She told her that Richard wanted her to go to work, that he'd cut off all her money. He barely gave her enough to feed the children and keep the house up. He'd become a miser, obsessed with the cost of things and what she spent.

She told Cynthia that Richard barely touched her anymore. Ever since Lawrence was born, he had become more distant with each year. And the birth had been frightening for her—she never wanted to have any more children. She told Cynthia that she wasn't interested in sex because she might get pregnant. Since they were Catholic and didn't believe in birth control, their sex life wasn't important any longer.

"I guess Richard and I have never been close. I thought we were close when we first married, and maybe we were. Maybe everything really started falling apart when Penelope was born. I'm not sure. I just don't know how to get him back."

Cynthia chewed her bottom lip thoughtfully. "Look, doll. There are a lot of ways to make a man happy. It's plain to me you're not using any of them."

"Huh?"

"For one thing, you're hiding."

"I most certainly am not!"

"First you hid behind your marriage to Richard to keep from proving yourself in college. Then you hid behind Penelope's birth to avoid the prospect of going to work and having to perform there. Then you hid behind Lawrence's birth to keep yourself from having to go through that trauma again, providing a convenient excuse not to sleep with your husband."

"It's *not* an excuse!" Mary Grace said a bit too loudly and the diners at the next table turned to stare at her.

"And anyway, I don't want to talk about it," Mary Grace waved her hand dismissively.

Cynthia sat back in her chair and folded her arms across her chest. "How many times a week do you say *that* to Richard?"

"I . . . don't know. I never thought about it."

"Well, start today."

Mary Grace peered closely at Cynthia. "How come you're so smart about this kind of thing? You've never been married."

"Precisely the reason I *do* know so much. I've lived and dated with so many different men, I can pinpoint their types in less than fifteen minutes. I haven't been stuck with only one man and learned only one guy's behavior. Every person is different, but there are some things that apply to all men."

"Such as . . ."

"Don't tell him his ideas about *his* career, *his* life and the work that brings him *his* esteem are stupid. That's the first killer to a relationship. Second of all, go get your tubes tied if you don't want any more kids, but the best way to drive a man out the door is to cut him off in bed. Scream at him. Yell, rake his back with your nails, punch his lights out, but you better be ready to knock his socks off in bed when you're finished. You'll lose him if you don't. And lastly, don't let yourself go to pot."

"I *knew* you'd bring up the fat thing," Mary Grace said unhappily.

"What? This is some kind of sacred cow? Get real. This is Cyn here, doll. Have you ever seen his secretary?"

"Yes. She's fifteen years older than I am and happily married to a very wealthy man."

"Who cares? I'll bet she's killer gorgeous."

"Cheryl is very pretty for . . . a fifty-year-old," Mary Grace admitted.

Cynthia expelled an exasperated sigh. "For someone whom I KNOW is very smart, you sure are dumb. Age has nothing to do with anything these days, kid. I know women in L.A. who are twenty-five years older than their boyfriends and their boyfriends couldn't care less. You know what they like? Fun. And happy attitudes. Smarts. And sharing. If you think about it, you did all that when you first met Richard. You laughed with him, planned with him, dreamed about the future. You were going to be an architect. You never talked to him about children."

"I got pregnant on my honeymoon, for God's sake! And there's nothing I can do about it now."

Cynthia reached out to her. "You're right. There isn't. But you can do something about who you are."

Mary Grace probed Cynthia's face, but she found nothing but sincerity. She felt tears spring up again. "I have to make this work. My mother...my father are still waiting to say I told you so."

Cynthia squeezed her hand. "It's going to be okay, Mary Grace."

"Help me," she said in a choked whisper.

"I will. I promise."

Cynthia gave her a diet to follow that she'd discovered in Los Angeles. It was a low-fat, no-sugar, high-grain, vegetarian diet. Cynthia told her it would clean her out and put her in touch with her own energies.

Then she enrolled them both in an aerobics class in Winnetka, which was equidistant for both of them to travel.

Mary Grace went to Weight Watchers and learned how to measure, weigh and analyze food. She visited bookstores and found books on natural gardening and cooking. And she discovered Martha Stewart's column in her women's magazines and began growing her own herbs and drying them.

Now when she bought Saran Wrap, it was not to cover bowls of leftover mashed potatoes, but to wrap her body after she smeared her cellulite-covered hips and thighs with a smelly seaweed concoction Kathryn had sent her from Europe.

She drove Penelope to tennis lessons and gymnastics. She became den mother for Lawrence's Cub Scout troop and encouraged him to become a Boy Scout, even if he was the only boy there on initiation night without his father.

Hardest of all, she told Richard she agreed that it was time to leave her father's company and strike out on his own.

Richard called his new company Bartlow Building. Mary Grace thought the name sounded too plebeian, too ordinary, but Richard wanted to see his name on billboards. James the Third was irate with Richard for leaving and refused to speak to his son-in-law for months. He accused Richard of stealing his client list.

Richard denied the allegation, but Mary Grace saw him slip a thick manila folder into the center drawer of his desk one night and lock it. Then he locked the door to his den so that Mary Grace couldn't learn the truth.

17

Richard Bartlow kicked up a storm in Chicago when he started his own business, raising more roofs than any other home builder in the city's history. As the Reagan years swept the nation out of "stagflation" and into "sound economics," Richard surfed ahead of the wave and built vacation cottages at Lake Geneva, high-rise condos along the Harbor Country, Indiana's lakeshore, and "second summer homes" in lower Michigan. He became an investor in the luxury condominiums that were so popular in Vail, Aspen, Siesta Key, Florida, and at Lake Travis in Texas.

He discovered quickly that the commercial and residential markets dominated by James Whittaker III were impenetrable for him now that James's colleagues had branded him a traitor. So he built elsewhere. And he took advantage of tax shelters that allowed even a middle-income executive to afford a second home, even if it was just an apartment on Lake Michigan.

For the first time, Richard was wealthy. His personal income rose to over four hundred thousand. He bought himself a Piaget watch, a black Mercedes 500SL and Italian suits made of wool so fine the pleated pants hung like silk.

He joined the Chicago Yacht Club and told Mary Grace he was "investing" in a sailboat. He bought five- and ten-thousand-dollar corporate tables at all the charity functions Cynthia organized, ensuring that his bids on the silent-auction items were always the last and the highest. And he made certain all his friends and potential clients were around when he was doling out the cash.

These days, Mary Grace looked back on her family life when the children were small and realized that, though she'd complained, Richard had been home more then than he was now.

He flew regularly to Aspen and Vail to inspect his "investments," and to New York to meet with investors of his Florida projects. He drove his Mercedes to Michigan City, Indiana, and New Buffalo, Michigan, during the construction phase of those projects. Mary Grace knew better than to complain, even though this was bad, she thought, life with Richard could always get worse.

Richard Bartlow was born to be a high roller. Nobody performed the job more effectively.

In 1987, Penelope was twenty years old and attending Indiana University in Bloomington, Indiana. She was drop-dead gorgeous, played a tough game of tennis and smoked cigarettes and drank whiskey because her father loathed both vices.

Penelope had wanted to go out of state to school, but Richard would not allow her to go to East Coast Boston College the way she'd wanted.

"Every girl I met at those schools was a bitch. You can go to any college in the MidWest, provided the tuition is within reason. Or you can get a job."

King Richard had spoken, Penelope told her mother, using the royal moniker for Richard, just as Mary Grace had with James the Third.

Mary Grace did not want her daughter attending a religious college—four years at Woodlands Academy was enough. She wanted her to have a more rounded education. Mary Grace still envied Cynthia's California education.

Penelope could have gone to the University of Illinois, but early on she realized that King Richard would save over three thousand dollars a year if she went to an in-state school. Penelope picked Indiana, forcing her father to pay more for her tuition and room and board. For over three months they had argued about her decision nearly every night he was home, which added up to less than a two-week period. There had been a lot of yelling on Penelope's part, and at one point she'd demanded that he tell her he loved her.

Richard had slapped her across the face for insulting him.

Penelope hadn't batted an eye. She intended to get even with him someday. But as the years moved on, Penelope told her mother she hadn't given up hope of getting her father's attention.

Lawrence was fifteen and having a very difficult time dealing with hormones, acne, the lack of girlfriends in his life, school, his asshole father and his neurotic mother.

He hated sports because his father loved them and his sister was so good at them. He joined the debate team, but discovered that he couldn't debate any issues without becoming belligerent and angry. He was too much like his father, he thought.

He studied only enough to get by and keep the teachers off his butt. He lived in his room, where he stepped over piles of dirty clothes, dirty dishes and smelly wrappers from the Big Macs he consumed after school and on Saturdays. He watched cartoons, played Nintendo video games and otherwise withdrew from his family and life. And he never, ever told his overprotective mother he used his lunch money to buy weed and "X" from the buttoned-up yuppie high school senior, Matt Ressing, who lived next door.

Lawrence was five hundred points ahead of his all-time high score in "Space Invaders" when the phone rang. Picking it up at the same time as his mother, he realized it was his father calling from his car phone.

"I'm on my way to the airport," Richard said between bouts of static on the only communication link to his family he used these days.

"Where are you going this time, Richard?" she asked. Lawrence yawned.

"Florida. I'll be gone for a week. Maybe more."

"Richard . . ."

"What?"

"Nothing. I was thinking of the Field Museum ball, but that's next month."

Lawrence turned down the volume of the special effects on his game while he listened to his parents' conversation. He depressed the "gun" button and knocked off three more enemy planes.

"Things are really shaking up, Mary Grace."

"How's that, Richard?"

"Christ! Don't you ever listen to anything I tell you? There's been a stock-market crash, for God's sake! But that's not the worst thing. This repeal of the tax-shelter laws is going to put me out of business."

"You've said that kind of thing before."

"Well, this time it's happening. We're in deep shit," he said.

"I bought my gown for the ball today. I need you to put some more money in my account."

"*Again?* I just gave you five hundred dollars!"

"That's not *money.* Do you have any idea what a decent gown costs these days, Richard. Fifteen hundred. That's how much!"

"Are you fucking nuts? Take it back. I can't afford it."

"Bullshit. You are such a miser, Richard. You spend a fortune on yourself and nothing on me or the kids. For years, you've been playing this game of giving and taking away at your whim. You give me a full-time maid, not because you love me, but because Hal's wife has a maid. At the same time, you won't give me enough money to buy necessities like food for Lawrence and me."

"I thought you were on a diet." He laughed with a mean sharp edge.

"You give me that money or the check will bounce."

"Well, I guess it's going to bounce, Mary Grace. What do I have to do to get through to you that I'm in a bind? Did you fire the maid?"

This time she laughed. "Of course not."

"Shit," he groaned. "I can't afford a full-time maid anymore, Mary Grace. What the hell do you do all day, anyway? And don't give me that crap about the kids. Lawrence wouldn't know if we were alive or dead, he's so zoned out. I don't know what the hell's the matter with him these days."

Mary Grace hesitated before answering, "It's a phase."

"Bullshit. He's about as fucking weird as anybody I've ever seen. When I was his age, I had a job delivering papers and worked Saturday afternoons at the Western Auto."

"Lawrence is not you, Richard. Thank God," she retorted.

Lawrence zoomed around an enemy plane and hit it dead on. That one was for his mother coming to his defense. Maybe she wasn't so neurotic, after all, he thought.

"I don't need this shit, Mary Grace. Take the damn dress back. And tell Cynthia we won't be buying any more tickets to her charity balls. In fact, tell her I'll hire her to put on a charity ball for the Richard Bartlow Bankruptcy Fund." He laughed and hung up without saying goodbye.

Mary Grace heard the click. "Richard?" Then she heard a second click. She shook her head. "Lawrence."

She hung up the telephone. Going into the pantry, she took out an entire roll of plastic trash bags. Then she went upstairs to her son's bedroom and knocked on the door. "May I come in?"

"Yeah," he said dully.

Mary Grace opened the door and leaned against the doorjamb with her arms akimbo. "Now that you've taken up eavesdropping in addition to smoking pot, give me one good reason I should continue defending you."

"What . . . are you talking about, Mom?"

"You were listening in on the extension."

"No, I wasn't."

"Don't lie to me, Lawrence. I used to do the same thing when I was your age. Only I didn't lie to my mother about it."

"*You* smoked pot?"

She rolled her eyes. "I listened in on the phone," she said. She walked into the room, and started picking up Lawrence's dirty clothes and throwing them into one of the trash bags.

"Oh," he said, watching her vacantly. He had a puzzled look on his face.

Mary Grace continued picking up all the clothes. Then she stripped the bed of the linens, leaving the bare pillow on the bare mattress and rolled-up comforter at the bottom of his bed.

She tied a knot in the garbage bag and put it in the hall, then she took another bag and double-bagged it. She filled it with his clock radio, his collection of Transformer toys and every single Garfield figure, mug and toy he'd collected since he was eleven.

"What are you doing?" Lawrence finally asked as he watched her strip his room bare.

She took the pins out of the posters on his walls and rolled up the paper. "I'm showing you how your life is going to change, Lawrence."

"What?"

"From now on, you will not have any radio, stereo, television, Nintendo, Walkman, tape players or toys. No books, no pictures, no nothing."

"But Mom!"

"Every piece of clothing on this floor is no longer your property, Lawrence. If I finish cleaning and you are only left with the clothes on your back, too bad."

"Hey! Just because you're pissed off at Dad—"

She whirled and faced him. "Do *not* ever make the mistake of cussing in front of me again. This has nothing to do with your father. This has to do with you. Everything in this room goes! You'll get it all back at the end of the semester when I see your grades improve and you start rejoining the world again. I can't believe you, Lawrence! You, who are smoking dope and probably taking something else. Once I go through these pockets, I'm sure I'll figure it out. You may think I'm stupid, but I'm not, Lawrence. You're the one who is stupid. You sit up here spacing out with a bunch of mindless video games so you don't have to face the fact that you're unhappy. Well, tough! I'm unhappy, too. But you don't see me hiding away in my room."

Lawrence stared at her and she stared back.

She stood in the middle of her son's room with a black plastic bag in her hand, trembling from the tip of her toes to the top of her head. Suddenly, her body had started shaking uncontrollably.

"Mom..."

Her eyes seemed to bug out of her head. She was shaking so violently the headband in her hair fell out. Her eyes started rolling back in her head and she felt cold, freezing cold. It was as if reality had stuck its frozen finger in her mind.

"Mom! What is it?" Lawrence put his arms around her.

"I...I...I'm s-so...so...sorry...sorry," she stammered as she clung to her son. He was warm. His natural instinct was to help her, comfort her, love her. That's what Lawrence was doing, Mary Grace thought. He was loving her. This second reality of her life hit her equally as hard as the first. Lawrence loved her. Maybe Richard didn't give a damn about her, but her son loved her.

Mary Grace forced her mind and heart to take control and as she did, the trembling stopped.

"Mom, are you okay?" Lawrence's face was filled with fear.

"I...I'll be fine. Really. Maybe I should sit down." She felt as if her bones had turned to jelly.

She sat on the bed and Lawrence sat with her, holding her hand. "I just realized I am such a bad example for you. It came as quite a shock."

"You're not a bad example. You never smoked pot."

"I know. I didn't mean that. I meant that I've been hiding out here, just like Cynthia said. I thought I could escape the pain I see other people having to face. But in the process, I only made things worse. I created my own hell."

Her laugh came out in a high-pitched tone. "Don't think this lets you off the hook," she continued, feeling her inner strength return.

Hanging his head, Lawrence wouldn't look at her.

"What else have you tried besides the pot?"

"Just some 'X.'"

"What's that?"

"Ecstasy. It's a trip, all right, but later I get these really bad headaches."

Mary Grace rolled her eyes. "And I thought you had sinus headaches. What a laugh you must have had while I chased around trying to find you decongestants and aspirin."

Lawrence put his arm around his mother. "I wasn't laughing. I thought you loved me."

Bursting into tears, she held Lawrence in her arms and he cried with her. She stroked his blond hair and kissed his cheek. They shared their tears, promising each other they would try to make their own lives better.

And for now, she knew they both meant it.

18

Mary Grace took off her soaked sweatband as she drove up the driveway from her morning of aerobics, grocery shopping and errands. She couldn't understand it—she was dieting, jumping up and down to music she hated and she still hadn't lost an inch. She could feel the roll of fat just below her waist when she leaned across the seat to pick up her purse and Richard's freshly laundered shirts.

Richard would be home in three days from New York, and he would want clean clothes to pack for yet another trip to God only knew where. Frantically, she checked the shirts to make certain the laundry hadn't broken off a button or ripped a collar. Richard had flown into a rage the last time she had his shirts cleaned because the harsh bleaches and overly hot irons had ruined the buttons. Mary Grace hated living this way. She dreaded it when Richard was gone, but she was starting to also dread the time he spent with her. She wished she had listened to Cynthia years ago and gone back to school to get her degree.

Shutting the car door, she walked into the house. Maybe she should just get a job like Kathryn had suggested, she mused. Get her mind off her fat and her fathead husband.

The minute she unlocked the door, she knew Richard had come home early—she could smell his cologne.

"Richard?"

There was no answer. Then he came to the edge of the staircase and stared down at her from above.

"Richard, what are you doing home so early? I wasn't expecting you till Friday."

He frowned menacingly at her. "What in the hell do you have on, Mary Grace?"

His eyes were so frighteningly cold, she felt as if they'd frozen her thoughts. Momentarily, she forgot where she'd been that morning. She looked down at herself. She was wearing a lavender and purple leotard and tights with white and purple Nikes. "My new aerobics outfit. What do you think?"

"You've taken up aerobics? Now that's a laugh. What for?"

"To lose . . ." She started to reply, then noticed he was carrying a suitcase. It was not his usual black leather garment bag, but one of their very large Louis Vuitton suitcases, which Richard always called "steamer trunks" because they were so large and heavy to carry.

Mary Grace felt the hairs on the back of her neck stand on end. Her jaw tensed, and she felt her stomach lurch, then sink to the pit of her abdomen as if she'd just been stabbed.

She knew.

She knew by the vacant look in his eyes and by the nervous twitch in his jaw. Richard was leaving her for good.

Her mouth felt like a desert. Her tongue had swollen to a thousand times its size, making speech nearly impossible. This was not happening, she thought. Richard couldn't leave her. He could *never* leave her. Even if he didn't love her, which she had doubted for many years, he still needed her influence with society, her connections. Didn't he?

What had happened to tilt her world out of balance?

"Do you love someone else?" Mary Grace heard her own voice ask.

Richard laughed. Then he laughed louder and longer. "Christ! You are so fucking stupid, Mary Grace. If i. were just another woman, I could have had anybody I wanted so many times, you can't imagine. When are you going to get it through your head that I'm busted? Everything's gone—I have no job, no savings. Hell, I may not have my leased car at the end of the day. You've lived so long in your cozy little world of make-believe that you have no clue as to what is really going on out there."

"What are you talking about?"

He started down the stairs. "I have two friends in New York who committed suicide because of this crash. I could have done that. But no, I stayed around trying to make something happen, and in the process I lost what I had managed to put aside. You figure out how to pay your bills yourself, Mary Grace, 'cause I haven't got it."

"You *do* have another woman!" Mary Grace started to lunge at him, beat him, hurt him the way he was hurting her, but he held her off at arm's length.

"It doesn't matter. The point is, you and your father can't help me any longer. I'm off to greener pastures. This house is yours. Take the furniture and all the other shit you've bought over the years. I don't want it. I don't know why I didn't leave years ago."

Mary Grace could barely form her words. "Why didn't you?" She thought if she could break him down he would tell her he loved her.

"Stupidity. Lord knows I haven't been able to stomach the sight of you for a long time. I guess you figured that out when I quit making love to you."

"I'll...I'll lose the weight, Richard. Honest I will," she started to plead. Tears filled her eyes and her hands started shaking.

"You've said that for twenty years."

"But I will. Please, please don't leave me, Richard."

He just glared at her.

"What'll I do?"

"What do I care? Go ask Daddy, since you can't seem to figure out life on your own."

"Never!" She screamed as a lifetime of rage came spilling out of her mouth. "I will never ask them for a dime!"

He smirked and turned away, walking toward the door. "Better take everything he'll give you because you'll never see a penny out of me. I haven't got it."

"But what about the children?" she asked as a torrent of tears streamed down her cheeks.

"You can have them." His words were coldly brittle.

He opened the door and Mary Grace knew she might never see him again. She was desperate to keep him in the house. If she could just talk to him, beg him somehow to stay, they could work it out. She had to believe she could make him stay. "Please don't go, Richard. I love you. With all my heart, I love you."

"I don't care," he said, closing the door.

"No!" Mary Grace's shaking hands flew to her face. What would her parents say? What would her friends say? She would be an outcast, just like Caroline had always warned her. How would she care for herself? She'd never had a job, she wasn't trained for anything. She would be destitute and the worst part was ... she could no longer lie to herself and convince herself that Richard loved her.

Suddenly, her pride crumbled—she would do anything, say anything to make him stay. She raced out the front door and down the sidewalk as Richard backed his Mercedes out of the garage. She ran toward the car, still hoping to stop him.

"Richard! Wait! Listen to me!" she screamed as she threw herself at the passenger door. She tried to open it, but Richard hit the automatic-lock button. "Richard, stop!"

But he kept backing out of the driveway. Reaching the street, he put the car into Drive as Mary Grace ran around the front of the vehicle toward his side. He put his foot on the accelerator. Mary Grace reached for the door handle, but she was too slow.

Richard drove away and he never looked back.

THE OTHER WOMAN
— ▸ ◂ —

19

—▶ ◀—

Alicia Carrel was a scrapper. Born by natural means in a farmhouse near the Sangamon River in central Illinois to Alice Bennett Carrel, twenty-two, and Harold Carrel, forty-two, with her five-year-old sister, Clare, watching in awe and disgust, Alicia howled, wailed and screamed at the indignity of being born into the painfully austere and impecunious world of the Carrels.

In 1946, the small crop Harold had been able to wrest out of the rich land he'd inherited from his grandfather, Clyde Carrel, did not fill the larder with staples and canned beans, peas or corn for the winter. When Alicia was born on a sticky, blisteringly hot August 18, 1947 night, the Carrels had been undernourished for nearly a year. They looked forward to bringing in a good crop that would line the cupboards and their pockets so that they could stay alive for another year.

Although she was only twenty-two at the time of Alicia's birth, Alice looked over forty. Premature silver mingled with her dull, dark hair and continual exposure to the sun had lined the corners of her cornflower blue eyes. But it was despondency, hopelessness and joylessness that cut lines around her mouth and caused her shoulders to slump and her gait to shuffle. She felt as old as the ancient ground she hand-tilled to grow the family's vegetables, the only thing that would sustain for another harsh Illinois winter.

Alice didn't want another baby; Clare was all she ever wanted in a daughter—pretty, dutiful and loving. Alice was a plain woman who wanted desperately to be pretty, but knew she'd never be. What she did have that had attracted Harold, who was twenty years her senior, was a young, lithe body. It wasn't until after she married him and starved year after year that her one asset began to fade. Her pregnancy with Clare had been hardly a bother—her figure bounced back in less than a month. But with Alicia, she was sick from the moment of impregnation. Unable to afford the luxury of a doctor, she swelled to nearly twice her size, due to fluid retention, the pharmacist in Urbana had told her.

Alice never complained about her condition, but silently and in her prayers she cursed this unwanted baby who had refused to die during the first three months of pregnancy like her other four babies had.

When she'd had Clare, Alice had been young, stupid and very naive, believing Harold loved her. She had imagined their life would be idyllic living on the glorious farm of one hundred and fifty-seven acres of rich Illinois land. She believed the stories Harold told her about his grandfather and great-grandfather being frontiersmen dressed in buckskins and living with the Indians, even meeting Daniel Boone and Davy Crockett. She believed his tales of their spirit and courage to tame this land and plant the apple, pear, walnut, maple and oak trees that lined the long driveway to the farmhouse. She listened to the sound of the wind in the trees, hoping to hear Indian ghosts whispering to her on windy October nights. But she never heard them.

What she *did* hear was the sound of the sputtering old Ford truck they owned that needed constant repairs. She heard the sound of her own stomach as it growled with hunger and she heard Clare's screams of pain from winter colds, ear infections and influenza when there was no money to pay for heat or medicine. She heard the sound of her own voice as she screamed at her husband that his laziness was to blame for their starvation and for her unhappiness.

Harold's answer to everything was that "God would take care of them."

Alice tried to tell Harold that she and Clare, and now Alicia, were not lilies in a field; they were people stuck on a farm in Illinois. Their neighbors were doing well with their crops, even buying equipment, planning for the future now that the war was over. Why couldn't they?

When they went to Urbana once a month for the few supplies they could afford, Alice read the newspaper and discovered that postwar Americans were buying beef. She asked the pharmacist, Snoot Jansen—so named because of his long hooked nose—who dabbled in the commodities market, what he knew about cattle.

Snoot smiled broadly, exposing his crooked teeth, and hooked his thumbs into his suspenders, assuming the know-it-all attitude he enjoyed most. "Unequivocally, you *must* get into cattle. Beef's the thing. Folks been without pork and beef for so long, they think they died and gone to heav'n just chompin' a hamburger. Yep. Beef's gonna change the landscape of America. Sure will. Everbody at the grange says so. At the co-op, too."

"That's good enough for me," Alice said. She went home and told Harold just what Snoot had said.

But Harold refused to raise cattle. He didn't know anything about cows. And it cost money: he'd have to repair the barn, and he'd need to build barbed-wire fences; he'd have to turn over the pretty pastureland that sat next to the Sangamon River to a bunch of cows. That land was sacred—it was where his grandfather talked with the Indians. It was where he went to fish in the river, sit under a three-hundred-year-old oak tree and contemplate life, his favorite pastime. Harold would stick to wheat and corn.

Alice believed he didn't know much about them, either. If he had, he would realize that the demand for those crops could drop, just as cattle had during the war. Alice anxiously twisted her hands and, teary-eyed, she angrily returned to her kitchen to make yet another pot of vegetable soup taste like more than it was.

But the crops didn't fail, no one starved and the children grew up, despite Alice's dire thoughts and gloomy projections.

As a child, Alicia rode with her parents into the surrounding towns and villages to visit neighbors, to buy supplies and, twice a year, to go to the only social gatherings Harold would agree to: Easter and Christmas services at the Methodist church. As the years passed, Alicia learned to walk and talk, then she learned that the rest of the world was progressing and the Carrels were not. When she entered grade school, Alicia's father still drove the same old rickety Ford truck, while the neighboring Palmer family drove a brand-new red Chevrolet convertible. Mr. Palmer had bought the car in Chicago.

"Where's Chicago?" six-year-old Alicia asked Donna Palmer, the pretty blond eight-year-old, who wore a red gingham dress with black buttons down the back, shiny black patent-leather Mary Jane's and a red grogram ribbon in her braided pigtails.

"Up north. By the lake, silly. Haven't you been to Chicago?"

"No." Alicia shook her shiny cap of dark chestnut hair and wrinkled her freckled button-nose.

Donna sighed dramatically, pulling her shoulders up very high and letting them fall quickly with the expulsion of breath. She slapped her pudgy palm against her round rosy cheek. "Geesh! I thought everybody went there. I thought I was the last one of all my friends to go. I'm so glad I'm not the last."

Alicia had often contemplated the fact that she was last. She was last in her family, last to get the small portions of food her mother rationed out at the end of the winter, last to wear her sister's hand-me-down clothes, which were usually made from her mother's worn-out dresses and blouses. Alicia was last to learn any kind of family news, since her mother so clearly favored Clare. Most of all, she was last to receive any attention or affection from her father, who seemed to give what little praise he had to Clare, who was older and had figured out how to please him.

"Last?" Alicia said. "I bet there's lots of people who never went there. I'm not last."

"I didn't mean of everybody in the whole state. Just last of my friends. I don't care about everybody." Donna's young eyes became rounded. "You should just see it, Alicia. The lake is as big as an ocean and there's all kinds of boats there. We went to State Street and went shopping in this store where you walked on marble floors and you could look up all the way to a roof made of colored glass. It was like being in a temple, like in my storybook about the thousand and one Arabian nights. We bought caramel corn and then walked in Grant Park.

You should see these huge buildings . . . tall ones. Sky-scrapers. Bigger than anything in Springfield."

Alicia frowned.

"You haven't been to Springfield, either?"

Alicia shook her pretty head again. She felt a hint of envy.

"Next time my daddy takes us to Chicago for the weekend, I'll ask him if you can go with us."

Alicia's eyes nearly popped out of her head. "You can do that? You would? You'd ask him?"

"Sure," Donna smiled. "You're my friend."

Alicia smiled back then impetuously threw her arms around Donna, hugging her tight. Then Donna did the strangest thing—she said, "I love you, Alicia."

Alicia pulled back and stared at Donna. "No one has ever said that to me before."

Donna was aghast. "Your daddy and mommy don't tell you that they love you?"

"No. Should they?"

"Of course. My parents always do. Every night before I go to bed."

"Every night?" Alicia was stunned. "Maybe it's because you are an only child."

Donna's pigtails slapped the sides of her face as she vehemently shook her head back and forth. "That's not the reason. My aunts, uncles and grandparents tell me they love me whenever we see them. I've got lots of cousins. They tell each other they love them."

Alicia started to cry. She cried long and hard for a long time, and she put her face in her little hands. She knew she didn't like living the way her parents did. Their life was so meager compared to the Palmers', who had pretty furniture and a new Sylvania television set. Alicia hated the house she lived in with the leaking roof, the cold rooms, the rotted wooden back steps and the splintered wooden porch rails. Harold Carrel refused to make the necessary repairs to the house, always claiming to be overworked in the fields. He was too tired at night and too tired on the weekends when it was his time to go to the river and "contemplate." She hated the clothes she wore, though she appreciated the effort Alice took to make them on the foot-peddle-driven Singer sewing machine.

Donna patted Alicia's head. "It's okay, Alicia. I'll make my daddy take you to Chicago so you can see the city. He'll do it. Really, he will."

Donna did just as she said she would.

In October 1953, during Alicia's first fall semester in kindergarten, Zack Palmer, his wife, Doris, Donna and Alicia drove in the sporty new Chevrolet convertible to Chicago.

With the top down and the radio playing "Diamonds Are a Girl's Best Friend," they cruised up Illinois Highway 45 with the October sun warming their faces. Donna taught Alicia all the words to "Itsy Bitsy Spider," while the Palmers discussed things that Alicia had never heard of. Dr. Salk had found a vaccine for polio but so far it hadn't been tested enough to use on children, Doris said. Her nephew, Stevie, had been stricken with polio just last summer, and the crippling disease had taken a toll on the whole family. She told Zack she hoped that polio could be wiped out in her lifetime. That would be all the miracle she could ever ask.

They talked about Queen Elizabeth, who was crowned in London because the king died while Elizabeth was on safari in Kenya. The Koreans were being brought to task, Zack said, which would help the economy at home. The Rosenbergs were executed, and since the Palmers nodded sadly, Alicia thought they must have been relatives or friends. Alicia wanted to ask how the Palmers of Illinois could possibly know someone who was being executed. Somebody named George Jorgenson changed his sex, whatever that meant, and his name to Christine.

Alicia had never heard such talk. At their house, mealtime was silent. So was any time spent in the rattly Ford truck, because nobody could be heard over the noise. Alicia's parents didn't talk about the world, science, miracles or plans for vacations. Harold and Alice either argued about what Harold had not accomplished that day or what Alice thought he should have fixed, finished or repaired. Looking away, Harold would stuff his mouth with another spoonful of stew. Once dinner was over, he went to the living room, sat in the sagging, overstuffed chair and fell asleep.

Alicia was fascinated by the Palmers and the world they inhabited. She thought they were smart and very, very different from anybody she knew.

In Chicago they stayed at the Palmer House on Wabash Avenue—not because Zack was related to the owners with whom he shared the same last name, but because it was within walking distance of Marshall Field's for Doris and Donna.

They ate dinner in the Empire Room on the main floor where Alicia ordered her first meal in a restaurant from the first menu she'd ever seen. Not once did she feel badly that her dress was not as nice as Donna's, nor her shoes new and gleaming. She absorbed every smell, sound, taste and ritual associated with "fine dining," as Donna called it.

Alicia kept her hands in her lap as the waiter, dressed in a black suit called a tuxedo, took the fan-shaped folded napkin from her gold-edged white china plate, snapped it in the air making a popping sound, then placed it on her lap. She put her hand to her mouth and giggled, wrinkling her nose when she smiled approvingly at the waiter.

"What a pretty little girl you are, miss. Would you care for a Shirley Temple?"

Alicia stared at him as if he'd just landed from Mars. She was pretty? Why was he saying that about her? Nobody had ever said she was pretty before. Clare was the one who was pretty. And what the heck was a Shirley Temple?

Donna nudged Alicia with her elbow. "It's like a soda pop. But fancy." Donna nodded her head to the waiter. "We'll both have a Shirley Temple." Then she quickly looked at her father and smiled. "It's okay if we have one, isn't it, Daddy?"

"Sure, sweetheart," Zack replied with his own loving smile.

Alicia couldn't read the menu—she was only six and had learned just a few words, like the brand names of foods on the sugar bags and cracker boxes. Her mother never read anything but the newspaper she bought once or twice a month when they went to town. Alice always told her daughters that reading, except for the newspaper, was a waste of time. Clare had taught Alicia a few words from the reader she brought home from school, but in the Carrel house, books were a luxury they could not afford.

"What would you like to have, Alicia?" Doris asked her sweetly. "There's roast turkey with gravy, filet mignon, broiled red snapper."

Alicia looked at the sea of words on the enormous menu and thought everything sounded exotic. She had no idea what a filet mignon was and why anyone would want to eat a red snapping thing was beyond her. "I think . . . the turkey." She closed the menu, handed it to the waiter and sipped the ice water with the mint sprig floating on top.

Zack told the waiter they were expecting three more to join them in an hour or so for coffee and cognac, but the waiter explained that the restaurant was booked for the evening.

"Don't worry, dear," Doris said. "When the senator arrives, I'll take the girls upstairs and get them ready for bed while you finish your business. They can take our seats."

"Very well," Zack replied.

While the Palmers discussed the prospect of buying up surrounding farmland in their area before the proposed interstate highway was to begin construction, Alicia's eyes took in the elegant clothes the ladies wore and the attention the men paid to these beautiful and sophisticated women. She watched as the man at the table next to them seemed to hang on every word the dark-eyed brunette with the black suit and black hat was saying. Her ruby-red lips parted in a smile, and he smiled back taking her hand and kissing it.

At another table, a man was lighting a cigarette for a strikingly beautiful blonde wearing a silver-colored wool dress. Alicia noticed she still wore her matching gloves as she sipped a glass of something fizzy. When she asked Donna about her, she told Alicia the woman was drinking champagne.

The dinner was "divine," Donna said, telling Alicia that was the proper word to tell the waiter when he inquired about their selections.

Alicia didn't think "divine" quite described what she was experiencing. The turkey was so different from the dried thin slips of tasteless meat her mother made on Christmas and Thanksgiving. She'd never tasted oyster dressing before and had no idea what oysters were, but she knew she couldn't live without them again. She liked the orange cranberry relish that was served in a carved-out orange rind, and the rolls and rose-shaped pieces of butter the younger waiter placed on the little plate above her knife. Alicia knew that somehow her life had changed with this introduction to city life.

But it was when the three men dressed in expensive suits arrived and introduced themselves to Doris, Donna and Alicia that she knew deep down in the pit of her stomach that something was terribly, terribly wrong with her life.

These men exuded power. They laughed and joked with Zack Palmer, and they shook Doris's hand. Then the one they called "Senator" leaned down and took Alicia's hand.

"What an exquisitely beautiful child. I didn't know you had two daughters, Zack."

"I don't. This is Donna's little friend, Alicia Carrel. Her parents' land borders ours. She's never been to Chicago and Donna wanted to bring Alicia along this time."

"How wonderful!" the handsome, blond and blue eyed senator with the barrel chest and firm handshake said. He leaned his face closer to Alicia.

As she looked into his crystal blue eyes, his kind mouth parted over perfectly straight white teeth. She smiled back. She could feel an energy about him that she'd never experienced with any other person in her life. Certainly not her father or mother, or even Zack

Palmer, who was a compelling man, active and always talking about things that fascinated her. But this man was something else—she could almost feel vibrations eddy and swirl around him.

"Welcome to Chicago, Alicia. I hope you like our city." His words were simple but sincere.

She could feel strength in his voice and the kind of caring in his tone that Doris and Zack used when they addressed her. "I like it fine." I think it's heaven, she wanted to say. I think this is as close to paradise as anybody could ever know. I wish I never had to leave Chicago. I wish I could spend more time with the Palmers and sleep every day of my life in the soft bed upstairs with the smooth white sheets.

His eyes only lingered on her for a brief second longer, but in that expanse of time, a hundred years passed for Alicia. She knew she would never forget this man, the way he looked, the sound of his voice, the touch of his strong and purposeful hand. He was the kind of man that other men, important men like Zack Palmer, looked up to. Something told her that even if he wasn't a senator, he would have been just as powerful.

Later that night, after watching the city lights go out one by one and Donna and Alicia slipped between the immaculate white sheets, Alicia crossed her arms underneath her head and stared at the ceiling. Her mind was going a mile a minute committing the day's events to memory. She never wanted to forget a single detail. She wished for a lot of things that night. She wished Harold could be like the senator, that her mother would treat her with love and caring, the way Doris treated Donna, and that her parents would tell her they loved her at night before she went to sleep the way the Palmers did.

But those were all just silly dreams.

There were other things, though, she could make happen. That night, Alicia made up her mind that, no matter what, she would work hard and go to school and do whatever it took, but someday she would live in Chicago. She would live in a place that was as beautiful as the Palmer House, with a soft bed and expensive sheets and lots of white towels in a tiled bathroom. She would have a television set and beautiful clothes, like the elegant women she saw in the Empire Room that night.

She would make herself as beautiful as she could and someday men would look into her eyes, light her cigarette and drink champagne with her. They would tell her she was beautiful, just like the senator had that night.

And someday, if she was very, very lucky, she would find a man who was powerful and had the kind of magic the senator had. He would be handsome like him. And they would sit at night and talk about science, politics and business. And then, someday, Alicia would be happy.

20

Throughout her grade-school years, Alicia remained friends with Donna and continued to watch Zack Palmer as he carefully and methodically maneuvered his farm into prominence in Illinois. She joined Donna and her parents when they went to grange meetings, to the farmers' co-op, and to Republican political rallies, picnics and pancake breakfasts where she met state senators and representatives.

Alicia observed the world of commerce and power, which was, as the years passed, glaringly removed from the fallow lives of her parents.

She would often have dinner in the Palmers' sunny dining room, where Zack would challenge the young girls' minds with games and questions about current affairs. Alicia and Donna were equally matched, and the best part about her friend was that she didn't mind that Alicia stole some of her father's affection. Donna had observed Alicia's family and Alicia knew she felt sorry for her.

Once, when Alicia was ten and Donna was twelve, and they were sleeping over at the Palmers', Donna asked, "Do you ever think you were adopted?"

Alicia chuckled. "All the time."

"Do you really? I was afraid to ask. Your parents are so different from you, there's nothing of them in you. They're not bad people, it's just that . . ."

"It's okay, Donna. You can say it. They're white trash. I've heard the kids at school say that. My father is taking welfare now—he doesn't even work the fields anymore. All he does is sit by the river and fish. He's so lazy and it drives my mother crazy, but she never does anything about her situation, either. She's trying to get him to sell the land to your father. At least they'd have the money."

Donna looked aghast. "I hope they don't!"

"What? But I thought that would make your father happy."

"Sure it would. But think about it, Alicia. If they sold out, where would you go? You'd have to move away. Your father can't take welfare *all* his life . . . or can he?"

Alicia shook her head. "It makes me sick. He has no desire for anything. I just don't understand him. I have so many desires. Sometimes, I think I've made too many dreams for myself. How will I accomplish all of them?" She stared at the ceiling. "I don't care how much work it takes, I'm going to get out of this place. I heard there are money prizes for winning the spelling bee in Urbana."

"That's true."

"I asked Mrs. Jamison if there were other contests kids could get into and win. She told me there are state and national contests for just about everything. And you know what, Donna? They all give United States Savings Bonds. She told me the Jaycees in Champaign give out savings bonds, so do the Lions and the Rotary Club. Know what I'm going to do, Donna? I'm going to get so good at my studies that I win all those contests."

"You're already number one in your class. It won't be that hard for you," her friend said encouragingly.

Alicia crossed her arms behind her head. She could feel a thrilling heat course through her body. It was like she was on fire, and the best part was that *she* was the one creating that feeling inside herself. She almost felt powerful. "Naw. It won't be hard. It'll just take work. I'm going to keep making myself smarter and smarter. And I'm gonna enter as many contests as Mrs. Jamison can find. She told me she'd help."

"That was nice of her."

"Yeah, she's the best teacher I ever had. I got really lucky, there."

Donna nodded. "My mother agrees with you. She said she wishes I'd had Mrs. Jamison. Maybe she could have helped me with my reading."

Alicia looked at Donna. "But you're really smart. When your father asks us all his questions, you know a lot more answers than I do."

There was a pause before Donna spoke again. "If I tell you a secret, promise not to tell?"

Alicia tried to see Donna in the darkness. "Sure. You're my best friend. I'll never tell a soul unless you say it's all right."

"I cheat on those questions."

Alicia couldn't believe what she was hearing. "Cheat?"

"Yeah. I don't look up stuff in the encyclopedia the way my dad wants me to. I...I have a terrible time reading. The words seem to swim in front of my eyes and sometimes they're all backward."

"But maybe you just need glasses," Alicia offered.

"I went to the eye doctor. He said my eyes were perfect." Donna's voice held misery, but she continued. "I memorize everything he tells me. If I miss a question, I always, always ask the answer and then when he tells, I memorize it. He doesn't know how often he asks the same questions, but I do. Then I listen to the radio and I memorize all the countries and where they are and what's happening there. That's why I don't spell too well. I couldn't spell Dag Hammarskjöld if my life depended on it."

"I think it's amazing you can do that, Donna."

"You do?" Donna's voice sounded brighter.

"I have to see things written down to learn them. I almost never remember things I just hear."

"You don't think I'm weird?"

Alicia could see Donna in the twin bed next to hers now that the clouds no longer shadowed the moon. Light streamed into the room through the filmy white sheer curtains Doris Palmer had bought through the Sears catalog. She could see huge tears running down Donna's cheeks, making silver streaks as the moonlight struck them. "I think you're my special friend. Always were. Always will be." Then Alicia got out of her bed and padded across the wooden floor to Donna's and put her arms around her. She hugged her tightly. "I'll keep your secret safe."

When Alicia went to high school, she had to ride the bus for nearly forty minutes with Donna to get to Urbana. By the time Alicia was fifteen, she was a legend along the Sangamon River counties.

She'd won the state spelling bee three years in a row before losing out to Wilbur McKeechum. She won a fifty-dollar United States Savings Bond when she won the Champaign County Jaycees math contest. She won a hundred-dollar bond for a history contest sponsored by the Daughters of the American Revolution. She entered every scholastic contest that came across Mrs. Jamison's desk, and usually placed first or second. In all, Alicia had won over eight hundred dollars in savings bonds before she started high school. She told her parents she intended to use the money to go to college.

"College? What in the hell do you need that for?" her father asked one night as they ate meat loaf off the set of chipped yellow flowered dishes her mother had bought at a church junk sale in Savoy. "Girls just go and get theyselves married off, anyways."

Alice rolled her eyes. "She wants to better herself, don'tcha, honey?"

"Yes." Alicia swallowed hard. She couldn't imagine her mother being on her side; maybe she'd misjudged her.

Alice passed the flat of her hand over an errant hunk of gray hair that perpetually hung in her eyes. "I don't want her to have to settle for anything but the best. Clare, neither." Alice put her finger under Alicia's chin and lifted her face. "She's got a chance to find a *real* husband if'n she goes to college." She removed her hand. "That's right, honey. You keep workin'. You get one of them scholarships. Don't you marry some fool like I did."

Harold didn't even bother to defend himself, and Alicia realized that what little respect she'd had for her father vanished at that moment. Now, he was nothing to her.

"Don't worry, Mom. I *will* get a scholarship. Mrs. Jamison says that if I keep up my grades, and especially if I'm valedictorian in high school, I can get all expenses paid."

Alice's weary eyes widened. "Did you hear that, Harold? All expenses paid! Wouldn't that be somethin'?"

Clare flipped her brunette pageboy over her shoulder and cast a withering look at her sister. "Well, Miss Smarty-Pants, that's all fine and good, but you just remember, I was on the homecoming queen court. And I was snow princess at the Christmas dance."

Alicia glared right back at her twenty-year-old sister, who was working for fifty cents an hour at the Dairy Queen and, judging by the fifteen pounds she'd gained that summer, eating as much as she served. "I'll be homecoming queen *and* the prom queen. You just wait and see."

"Yeah? I dare you. I double-dare you!" Clare said angrily.

Before Alicia could toss her own barbs back, the sound of a car horn honking slipped through the late-summer-evening shadows.

"That Rodney?" Harold asked, running a piece of bread through the catsup and grease on his plate, then sticking the bread in his mouth.

"Yeah." Sticking her tongue out at Alicia, Clare pushed herself away from the table. As she got up, Alicia noticed for the first time that most of Clare's new bulk was centered in her abdomen. Alicia's eyes went to her mother's face.

Alice was trying not to stare at Clare's stomach, but it was impossible. Alicia glanced at her father and wondered if he knew. He looked at his plate, sighed, then left the table without a word.

Once Clare and her father were gone, Alicia turned to her mother. "Is Rodney going to marry her?"

Alice's eyes were vacant as she stared at the heavy wooden door that hadn't been varnished in twenty years. "Who the hell knows."

"But she can't wait much longer."

Alice merely nodded. After a moment, she said, "Clare don't seem too worried about time. Guess I won't be neither." She pushed herself up from the table.

Alicia looked away from her mother's vacant eyes and wondered what she or Clare had to do in their lives to get a reaction from their mother.

21

Alicia made straight As in her freshman year of high school, but by the middle of her sophomore year, she realized it took a whole lot more than smarts to make it in the world. Even the counselors told Alicia that in order to get the scholarships she wanted, she'd have to join clubs to show a well-rounded personality. If she were elected to an office, that would be better. But to do that she had to become popular. Alicia had spent so much time at her studies, she'd only cultivated one friend— Donna.

Though Donna's popularity was something to envy, Alicia wasn't jealous of her best friend. However, she would have given *anything* for the thin-soled Papagallo flats that matched the Bobbie Brooks mint green cardigan with white pearl buttons and the mint green wool skirt, or the yellow Papagallos that matched the Villager plaid wool jumper with the yellow turtleneck. Donna owned luscious pink angora sweaters that she mixed and matched with pink, black and beige plaid kilts, and baby blue sweaters that brought out the blue of her eyes and made her nearly platinum-colored hair seem angelic.

Donna's childhood pudginess had moved into the proper places, giving her a voluptuous figure that all the girls in school envied. Donna had more dates than anyone.

Alicia was still thin from undernourishment, but the healthy meals and snacks she'd routinely enjoyed at Donna's house had produced a vibrant complexion free of acne, thick, glorious chestnut hair with deep auburn undertones and long, lean legs that accounted for her five-foot-nine-inch height.

Alicia knew she could never compete with Donna for popularity—she would have to be inventive. The first thing she did was make friends with her school counselor, Mrs. Kennedy. She told her she was willing to baby-sit, work in an office, run the school switchboard—anything to make some money. Telling her she admired Alicia's tenacity and assertiveness, Mrs. Kennedy found Alicia a job after school at a local manufacturer's office.

Alicia knew very little about office work, but she had taken typing and shorthand her freshman year. Mrs. Graves, the personal secretary to the owner of DFEP, Inc., Jim Doyle, was authorized to hire a young girl to help her with filing and errands for a few hours each day. The job only paid a dollar an hour, she told Alicia.

Alicia never hesitated.

DFEP was short for Doyle Farm Equipment Parts. In less than a month, Alicia had memorized not only most of the parts the company made, but the names of all the department heads and clients, sales reps and advertising men who came to call on Mr. Doyle at the main office. Since she was responsible for filing every piece of mail, every outgoing letter and all invoices and orders, Alicia learned who ordered what at what price and where it went.

Every other Friday she stayed until quarter to six to receive her paycheck. She loved the feel of the perforated numbers that were impressed on her check by the machine Mrs. Graves used to issue it. She relished the process of going to the bank, endorsing her check and putting half her money in a savings account she'd not told her parents about, then receiving the rest of the money in cash.

Once she'd saved fifty dollars, she went to the local fabric store, sat on an ugly orange metal chair and began poring through the Butterick pattern books.

Alicia had never sewn a stitch in her life, but she knew Alice was a magician with cloth and the old pedal-operated Singer machine. Her mother had purchased a few patterns over the years, but usually she ripped old clothes apart and used them as her patterns when she was remaking housedresses and blouses into shorts and tops for Clare and Alicia. She was looking forward to taking her mother into a new world of experience. They were going to learn to sew together, making clothes that would rival any of Donna's.

Alicia bought a frightfully expensive piece of Pendleton wool plaid in gray, black and taupe to make a copy of the Villager jumper Donna wore. According to the yardage requirements, she would have enough left over to make an unpleated plaid kilt. She also bought a plain taupe wool to make a second jumper and a skirt—she already had a black sweater at home that she could wear under the jumper and with the kilt and the skirt. Proudly, she paid the cashier and carried her bundles on the city bus down the state highway to the end of the county road that took her past Donna's house to her own farm.

Sitting in an old chair with a lace doily on the headrest, Alice looked up when Alicia walked in the door. "What on earth have you got there?"

"Patterns, zippers, buttons. Wools that look like heaven, Mom. I want you to teach me how to sew."

Alice started laughing. "You? Sew?"

"Mom, I'm serious." Alicia had learned long ago not to pay attention to her mother's reactions to anything she did. At that moment, Alicia would have asked the devil himself to show her how to sew. She didn't care if Alice laughed at her for the next week and a half; she was going to have the kind of clothes she wanted, the kind of clothes that would help her become popular like Donna. Alicia was only sixteen, but she'd realized that popularity got a person elected to class office. Class office and club presidencies went a long way to getting scholarships. And scholarships would get Alicia on the road to her final destination of a job . . . in Chicago.

Pulling the Pendleton plaid from the brown paper bag, she held it up.

Alice quit laughing. She reached out her hand, then snapped it back, not daring to touch the fine wool. "Where'd you get this?"

"At Hanover's."

"I never seen anythin' so beautiful," Alice said with awe.

"Well, I have," Alicia replied, pulling the rest of the material out of the sack. "This is only the beginning. I'm going to make some beautiful things before I'm finished. You just wait and see."

Alice looked at her daughter. "I never worked with anythin' so fine."

"Look, Mom. Here's the pattern. I want to make this jumper. The lady told me we had to be very careful to match the plaids. Do you know how to do that?"

"Of course I do! I been matching plaids and putting petals on the right flowers for twenty years for Clare...and for you."

Alicia frowned, but she didn't remind her mother that, except for an Easter or Christmas dress, all clothes sewn in the Carrel house were always for Clare. "Good."

Alicia watched as her mother took out the patterns, handling them delicately. "My God, they give all kind of instructions here. They make it so easy, a baby could sew these clothes."

"So, you'll teach me?"

Alice's eyes were filled with wonderment and a child's appreciation. "I'd be happy to make them for you, Alicia. Real happy."

Alicia smiled at her mother. It was the first time she'd ever felt as if she'd given her mother something. She'd thought this project would just be more work for her mother, but by the way Alice looked at her, it was as if she were giving her the keys to the kingdom.

Alicia shrugged her shoulders. "Okay. I've got a mountain of homework, and then work tomorrow. Maybe even some extra hours on Saturday, Mrs. Graves says, because they're taking inventory."

Alice passed her hand over the taupe wool. "I never would have bought these colors. They sure look nice together, don't they? How'd you know which ones would be the best?"

Alicia shrugged her shoulders again. "I'm not sure." It was odd, now that she thought about it. Such things came easily to her. She and Donna had read *Glamour*, *Mademoiselle* and *Seventeen* magazines together. Donna only knew what she liked when it was all put together for her. But Alicia could take the purse from one page, put it with the dress from another, then find shoes in another magazine and give the entire ensemble a new twist and some character.

Alicia didn't know where this knack came from, but as she watched her mother place the fabrics over each other and the patterns with the materials, she realized that, strange as it was, perhaps this was her mother's deeply hidden talent. All those years of making scraps and oddities into garments for her and Clare had made an unconscious impression on Alicia.

Smiling, she unfolded the pattern instructions and showed them to her mother. Perhaps she'd been wrong to judge her, perhaps they were closer than she'd thought.

As she continued with her job at DFEP, she got more raises and earned a lot in overtime pay. She and her mother created a wardrobe that even Donna envied.

Alicia ran for president of the art club and won. She learned to sculpt and make pottery, as well as drawing and sketching, and she found she was creative and happiest when left alone in front of an easel. She decided she was passable in standard drawing and her still-life charcoals were the worst in the class. But when it came to colors and shapes, she excelled. She understood balance better than anyone. She didn't know what she could do with her creative gifts, but she knew that sooner or later she would think of something.

She ran for student council representative and won, and was nominated for homecoming queen in her junior year, finishing runner-up to Donna. All the senior girls were jealous because a junior had taken the title, but it was hard not to vote for sweet, beautiful Donna. Even Alicia had voted for her.

In her senior year, Alicia was nominated for homecoming queen, but Donna won again. And in the spring, when both girls were nominated for prom queen, Alicia was certain her pretty blond friend would win. But she didn't. She dropped out of school instead.

Donna was sick.

The Palmers took her to St. Luke's Hospital in Chicago, where the doctors told her she had infectious mononucleosis. She had to stay home and rest.

After Alicia attended the prom with Alan Templeton, who was more a friend than a real boyfriend, she and Alan went straight from the dance to Donna's house. Alicia wanted to share her crown with her best friend.

When she walked up to the front door, she could see the Palmers through the oval etched-glass door, sitting in the living room. She rang the bell excitedly. She couldn't wait to show them her crown. Alicia was wearing a confection of a gown with a deep royal blue silk bodice and a royal blue silk straight skirt covered in five layers of white organza. Alicia had designed the dress herself and her mother had executed every detail to perfection. She was proud of her mother's work and wanted to show it off to Donna and her mother.

Mr. Palmer seemed to be taking an inordinately long time to come to the door. She watched as he lumbered along, even stopping at the banister as if thinking about his decision to open the door.

"Mr. Palmer! It's me! Alicia... I'm with Alan Templeton... Mr. Palmer?"

A sickening sensation from the deepest wells of her being rang an alert. When Zack Palmer finally opened the door, she saw that his eyes were swollen and terribly bloodshot. Alicia peered past him into the living room and saw Mrs. Palmer sitting in an Italian-style chair, crying. Something was wrong, horribly and unalterably wrong, and she knew in an instant it was Donna.

A wall of tears prevented her from seeing past the door. Her mind screamed that this was not true and that as long as she could convince herself that she was dreaming these painful feelings, imagining these chilling thoughts, then nothing bad could happen to her friend.

"Alicia," Mr. Palmer said with a sob.

Alicia's eyes were filled with terror. "I want to see her..."

"You c-can't." His body jerked with a sob and he put his fingers to his eyes as if he were going to gouge them out so he wouldn't cry anymore. He dropped his hand. "You see...she..."

"Oh, God..." Fear clutched her heart and dug its fingers deep into the interior where her love for Donna lay.

Suddenly, it was as if Mr. Palmer's body turned to rubber and he leaned against the door for support. He put his face against the etched-glass pane in the door, his shoulders heaving.

"This can't be!" Alicia screamed. "She isn't dead! I know she isn't! She promised me she'd wait!"

Mr. Palmer let out a wail that pierced the night. He pounded his fist against the wooden doorjamb.

Alicia went to him and put her arms around his neck. "Oh, Mr. Palmer, I loved her so ..." Her cries caught in her throat. "Please, God...don't let this be true."

"I know," he said as he clutched Alicia close. "It doesn't seem fair. I can't accept that...Donna is dead."

Until that moment, Alicia had kept a faint flame of hope burning that Donna was alive and that this was some kind of sick nightmare. But now he'd said it, he'd made it real by saying the words. "How did it happen?"

"She was so weak. Always so tired. She just went to sleep and didn't wake up."

Alicia heard only the sound of her own grief and when she opened her eyes and looked up, Mrs. Palmer was standing in the doorway. Alicia's face crumbled as she held out her arms for Mrs. Palmer to fill.

Her friend's mother pulled her to her heart. "Alicia, dear. My dearest girl." She passed her hand over Alicia's hair the way she used to do with Donna, rubbing her back with her other hand in soft circling caresses, as if Alicia were the one in pain and she was not.

Mrs. Palmer kissed her forehead, gently pressing her head to her shoulder. Alicia felt as if the world had ended, but even in their unthinkable grief, the Palmers were still counting her as one of their own, still giving to her, the poor farm girl who cherished them and their love more than they could ever know.

She suddenly remembered Alan Templeton when he coughed uncomfortably. "Excuse me, Mr. Palmer," he said. "I'm really sorry about Donna. I liked her a lot. Everybody did."

Wiping his eyes, Mr. Palmer stepped over to take Alan's handshake. "Thank you. You're Alan, aren't you?"

"Yes, sir," Alan replied, then continued offering his condolences.

While Alan talked, Alicia glanced around at the familiar porch. She saw the white painted wooden porch swing where she and Donna had sat on summer afternoons, painting their toenails with Revlon's Fire and Ice red nail polish. They'd shared ice Pepsis and talked about the lives they would lead. Donna had promised Alicia she could be godmother to her first baby. She'd told Alicia she would take her to Paris and London when they graduated from college. She'd promised she would always be Alicia's best friend.

This house held more of Alicia's youth than her own home, she realized. It was here she'd learned love could be given *and* received. Here where she'd learned practically everything she knew about life that didn't come from books. She'd often pretended that she was really a Palmer and not a Carrel, dreaming she was some kind of modern-day Cinderella with a mix-up at the hospital nursery. She loved the Palmers. Turning her face again to Mrs. Palmer's shoulder, she felt a deeper wave of sorrow overtake her.

Alan excused himself to Mr. Palmer. "You'll give Alicia a ride home then?" he asked.

"Of course." Mr. Palmer stepped back and put his arm around Alicia's shoulder. "Don't worry."

"Great. Well, I'll be seeing you, Alicia," Alan said, walking backward to the porch steps. When he turned around and walked toward his car, he nearly broke into a run.

Alicia couldn't help thinking how death affected different people. Perhaps Alan thought he could run away from it.

Mrs. Palmer lifted Alicia's chin with her finger, her weeping eyes sweeping her face. "Come inside, Alicia. I'll make some tea for us."

Alicia tried to dry her eyes, but her tears were still mercilessly abundant. "I love you, Mrs. Palmer," she said, her voice choked, putting her arms around her friend's mother again.

"We love you, Alicia. Please, please don't ever forget that."

"I'm afraid it will never be the same again."

Mrs. Palmer's arms tightened around her. "No, dear, it never will."

They linked arms and walked into the house together. Mr. Palmer silently closed the door behind them.

Alicia graduated valedictorian of her class. After everyone had applauded her commencement speech, she walked back to her seat knowing she'd won her full scholarship to the University of Illinois, but there was no joy in her accomplishments, because sweet Donna was not there to share them with her.

As she watched the rest of her classmates receive their diplomas, she thought that she was right: nothing would ever be the same again.

22

In the fall of 1967, Flower Power hit the campus of the University of Illinois. The eggheads were now "blowing their minds" with LSD, the jocks had learned how to "tune in, turn on and drop out," and the nerds were quoting Jonathan Livingston Seagull and exploring transcendental meditation. Everyone was protesting the war more vehemently than ever before, and the peace symbol could be seen spray-painted on road signs, tree trunks and concrete railroad underpasses. Free love was everywhere.

Alicia was nineteen when she met Joe Smythe. His buddies on the football team called him "regular," meaning that he was a "regular Joe," but, to her he was anything but ordinary. Alicia believed her love for Joe was so deep, so pure, so incredibly earth-moving that there was nothing light or free about it.

Joe was only an inch taller than she with the same thick brown chestnut hair and green eyes so bright she felt she was looking into tropical waters every time she stared into them. He had a long face, small nose, sharp angles to his chin and full, sensuous lips she wanted to kiss the first time she saw him at the coffee machine in the student union when he had tried to grab her cup of coffee.

"Hey! I paid for that!" she said tersely as he lifted the cup to his lips and inserted a dime into the machine.

"I know," he said audaciously. "But I need it more than you do." He waited while the machine filled a paper cup with steaming fresh coffee, then he handed it to her. "There, now I don't owe you anything."

That was when he looked at her.

Joe stopped sipping his coffee and just stared at her. "You're beautiful," he said.

"Thank you," she said with a pleased smile. Then she felt herself blush. She put her hand to her cheek.

He grinned. "You're blushing! I can't believe it. Hasn't anyone ever told you you were beautiful?"

"Of course," she replied, thinking of the senator in the Empire Room when she was six. Some of the girls in high school had told her they envied her because she was pretty. And Alan Templeton had once said she was "gooood-lookin'." But *beautiful* was not a word she'd heard to describe her.

His grin was both sensual and mischievous, and she liked how his eyes twinkled with merriment.

"I haven't seen you around before," he said, taking a deep gulp of the coffee.

"I'm a sophomore. I've been here."

"The hell you have. You, I would never forget." He stuck out his hand. "Joe Smythe. Junior. Business."

"Are you kidding me? That's not really your name."

"Afraid so. It's English, with a '*y*' and an '*e*.' It's supposed to be very genteel, my mother says, but I never thought any of us were."

"How many of you are there?"

"Four. A brother and two sisters. We're all in the business."

"And what business is that?" she asked, noticing a group of students walking toward the coffee machine. She and Joe headed toward the outer door.

"Cars. My father is a car dealer on the north side of Chicago. We sell Fords right now, but my dad thinks it's time to branch out, get into GM cars with another dealership. That's the one I'll head up. I even bought a Firebird to see if it's better than my '65 Mustang."

Alicia liked how he held the door for her, and she graced him with a smile as they entered the autumn sunlight. "Is it better?"

"Not really. The 'Stang is a classic, or *will* be, given enough time. I put it up on blocks in the garage next to the black '67 'Vette I bought this summer."

"You have a Corvette?"

He flashed that entrancing smile and rocked back on his heels proudly. "Yeah. It was a good investment."

"I'm impressed."

He laughed. "Me, too. I don't know how I'm gonna make the payments with my all-night job at the pizza parlor."

Finishing her coffee, Alicia tossed the paper cup into a metal waste container. "You're working your way through school?"

"Sort of. And it's a bitch. My dad is paying for my tuition and room and board, but everything else, I'm paying for. I suppose it wouldn't be so bad if I didn't have two car payments."

Alicia couldn't help thinking Joe was foolhardy— none of this made any financial sense. "Why not make it easy on yourself and get rid of the cars?"

"No way! I told you, that 'Vette will be a classic. The 'Stang, too. I'll drive the shit out of the Firebird till after graduation, then I'll get something else. Besides, I'd rather work my tail off for something I know deep in here—" he pressed his fingers into his abdomen "—than spend my money on weekend keggers. I've got future vision. That takes guts and persistence."

"Future vision?"

Joe chuckled. "I always tell myself that when I really don't know what the fuck I'm doing, but I want to believe I do. That way, I *make* myself believe it. And when you believe in something, you'll go to the ends of the earth for it."

Alicia watched his face as he spoke. She could see determination in the set of his jaw and the fire in his eyes. He *did* believe in what he said and in making his beliefs a reality. Joe Smythe was the kind of person she'd read about in literature. He had passion and desire. He knew what he wanted and he didn't care what he had to do to get it. He was the kind of man who, once he believed he was right, would change the world to make it go along with his mind-set.

Joe exuded not only strength but power from every pore of his body. His well-developed muscles tensed underneath the tie-dyed T-shirt he wore. He had powerful forearms, large biceps and a well-defined chest that told her he lifted weights. His stomach was hard, his hips narrow and his thigh muscles bulged underneath the tight blue jeans he had on.

He seemed unaware of his clenched jaw or his balled fists, his eyes blazed with emerald fire when he told her about his dreams. His eyes alone seemed to pull her into his sphere, suddenly making her want to be a part of his dreams. It was the oddest sensation because she'd only felt that sort of magnetism once before in her life, when she was six. She'd always known she wanted to have that kind of power herself, and she wondered if Joe could show her how to get it.

Beneath a canopy of golden leaves with the autumn sun shifting over their faces, Joe and Alicia knew they were blessed.

"You never told me your name," he said softly, moving a step closer to her.

"Alicia Carrel."

"Two first names. I like that." His eyes burned his thoughts into her head. I want you, they said. I want you like I've never wanted anything or anyone in my life. And I intend to get you and keep you. Forever. Joe made his mark on Alicia with his will. "Would you like to go out with me, Alicia? Not Friday night because I have to work, but Saturday night."

She chuckled. "I would have thought a handsome guy like you would already have a date for Saturday night."

"I do. I'll break it," he said, smiling that wickedly sensual grin.

"So do I," she said truthfully. "I'll break mine."

Alicia and Joe were inseparable from their first night together. Joe told her all about his plans for his life. He wanted to be a businessman and make enough money so he could travel the entire world. He wanted to see the Grand Canyon and ski in Colorado. He wanted to visit the West Indies and learn how to scuba dive. He wanted to see London and Paris and the castles along the Rhine River in Germany. He wanted to go to the Orient and eat octopus. But best of all, he wanted to do these things with Alicia.

Alicia felt as if there had been a black hole in her life after Donna died. Now that she'd met Joe, she realized the feeling had been there long before Donna's death and that losing her best friend had only exacerbated the emptiness in her life.

Joe filled that hole and indeed her heart, giving her dreams beyond her own. In only a few short days, he'd expanded her life and her horizons.

She told him about Donna and the Palmers. She didn't tell him much about her own family because there wasn't much to tell. She told him about her dream to live and work in Chicago, and he told her they were destined by God to be together.

For the first time, Alicia felt that she was right with the world. Joe had brought her a gift she'd never opened before, he had awakened the joy within.

"I love you, Alicia," Joe said on their third date, taking her into his strong arms and kissing her. They'd known each other exactly nine days, but she felt as if she were flying out of her own body. His lips were full and possessive and very demanding, and even with his kiss, Joe showed her he knew what he wanted. His arms held her close to his rock-hard chest, and she felt her breasts being crushed against him—the feeling was intoxicating. It was as if he was trying to press her so close that in some mystical, mysterious way, he could push her inside him where she could stay next to his heart at all times.

That was what he'd said.

Joe wanted to see her for lunch, in between classes, in the evenings to study in the library and on the weekends. They spent the entire night sitting in his Firebird in the Steak and Shake parking lot, talking and kissing until dawn. When the sun came up, Joe kissed Alicia and asked her if she agreed that they were meant to be.

Looking into Joe's fiery green eyes, Alicia felt her life being swept into his. She felt the deep sea of emotion within her come to life, roaring and rolling as he threw her up and down at the slightest upturn of his smile. Not since Donna died had Alicia cared about another human being. She'd forced herself not to feel anything.

Smiling, she touched his kiss-swollen lips, gazed into his eyes and said, "Yes, Joe. We were meant to be."

Alicia was amazed at how different this sophomore year was than last year. To stem the tide of her grief over Donna's death, Alicia had plunged herself into her required courses. She hadn't dated and she didn't meet anyone except her roommate, Sandy, who was so consumed with her boyfriend that she nearly flunked out of school in the spring.

Alicia had spent her weekends studying and trying to forget the dreams she and Donna had made—it had seemed sacrilegious to think about having fun without her. She'd gotten straight As but she couldn't remember a thing about last year.

Now, she felt her heart open. Joe sent rippling waves of passion through her body. He had claimed her and she was glad. She felt love and lust, but she also felt joy for the first time in her life. Now she knew what songwriters meant when they spoke of wanting to climb the highest mountains and forge the deepest rivers to get to their one and only love. That's how it was for her. She knew she would never—could never—love anyone but Joe.

"I love you, Joe," Alicia said. "I'll always, always love you."

"Me, too," he said, kissing her again.

They made love in his Firebird, in an apple orchard, after Joe helped win the game against Kentucky State University. They made love whenever and wherever they could, which wasn't easy as both were living in the dorms.

"I'll get an apartment," he told her as he lowered his head to her breast and caressed her nipple with his tongue.

"How? You barely have enough money, as it is. Your father would never help you pay for an apartment."

"You got that right," he said, kneading her flesh and looking down at her. Slipping his hand around to the back of her neck, he kissed her deeply. As always, Alicia felt as if she'd lost her ability to process thought. She was nothing but a bundle of physical lust and a heart filled with bursting love for Joe.

He eased off her slowly. "I swear I could eat you alive." He grinned his mischievous grin. "Let's try that!"

"Joe, I'm trying to be serious here. Maybe we shouldn't see each other so often. I've barely had time to study. I know with your job, football practice and homework, seeing me isn't easy."

"Seeing you is real easy. It's the homework that takes a slide."

"Joe, you can't do that. You've got to keep your grades up."

His eyes were fiercely intense as he looked at her. "I'd risk anything to be with you, Alicia. You're everything to me. What difference does it make if I lie awake in my dorm room thinking about you or if I stare at my statistics textbook all afternoon? I'm still thinking about you." He took her hand between his and pressed her fingers to his sensuous lips. "God, I need you, Alicia. I come alive when I'm with you." His eyes were emerald fire as they probed deeply into her.

She felt as if he touched her soul when he looked at her like that. There was something deep in her unconscious that told her this was not only right and good, but that he was familiar to her. If she believed the mumbo jumbo of the kids who'd gone to California she would say they were soul mates. She would say they had known each other, loved and made love to each other in so many lifetimes over thousands of years that they had no choice but to return to be together again.

But Alicia didn't know much about soul mates. Maybe someday she'd read up on the subject, but right now she was too busy loving, touching and feeling to care about metaphysics. She only cared about their love and finding enough time to be together.

"You're obsessed," Sandy, her roommate, said one Friday night as Alicia was rolling mascara onto her long eyelashes.

"No, I'm not. It's just that I'd rather be with Joe . . ."

". . . than eat, sleep, study . . . live!" Sandy threw her hands up in the air. She wore an Indian-print calico skirt, a tight V-neck long-sleeved top that showed off her small but high, rounded breasts and a half-dozen strings of love beads.

"Look who's talking. Miss 'screw 'em all day' Sandy Moore."

"Hey! Love 'em and leave 'em. Guys are fun for that kind of thing, but they aren't my life."

"I can't be like that. I love Joe—I more than love Joe. It's like he's the other half of my heart. I feel sort of empty when I'm not around him."

"It'll never last."

"Why not?" Alicia demanded.

Sandy flopped onto her single bed, which was covered with the Mexican serape she'd bought in Tijuana last summer. "It's too, too intense. Don't you see? Like I said. You're obsessed."

Alicia frowned. "Is it a bad thing to want to be with somebody so badly you'd do anything for him?"

"Yeah, it is." Reaching over to the metal nightstand, Sandy picked up a roll of Lifesavers and popped a cherry one into her mouth. "Take me, for instance. I was really hung up on this guy, Mel. He was everything to me. I couldn't sleep or eat during my Mel period. Then I find out he's boffing Sue Lewis. I'm devastated. I cry and wail. I get pissed. I get even. I boff Jerry. Then I find out while I'm doing Jerry, that Jerry is much better at sex and a hell of a lot more fun than Mel." Sandy chomped on the red Lifesaver, then ate a green one. "The thing is, you may *think* you're in love with this Joe, but there could always be something better down the line."

Alicia considered this advice. "So, that's what you're doing? Moving on down the line?"

Sandy's face lit up. "Yeah. And don't it sound excitin'?"

Alicia finished applying blush to her cheeks and some clear lip gloss. She picked up her windbreaker from the edge of the bed. "Well, if you ask me, you're just in love with being in love. I'm in love with Joe. Only Joe. And he loves me."

"Before you met Joe, you were all hell-bent on getting your degree and making it big in Chicago. What happened to all that ambition?"

"I'm still going to live in Chicago. Joe's family lives there. It's perfect!"

Sandy nodded. "Nothin's perfect, honey. Don't forget that. Like I always say, 'There's flies in every ointment.'"

"You're a pessimist."

"I am not." She paused, considered Alicia's comment. "Well, then again, maybe I am. Nothing wrong with being a pessimist. At least we never get disappointed." Sandy laughed heartily and bit into another Lifesaver as Alicia rolled her eyes and left the room with a wave of her hand.

They never considered that his slipping grades could change the direction of their lives.

"I've been drafted," he told Alicia after he'd driven all night to her family's farm on the Sangamon River in late June 1968.

"No!" she nearly screamed.

"My grades were a lot lower than I'd thought."

"There's been a mistake," she replied frantically as visions from the nightly news about Vietnam swam across her brain. Suddenly, she felt as if she were back in time, standing on the Palmers' porch with death swirling around her like an icy winter shroud.

Joe's voice caught in his throat. Grabbing her forcefully, he held her close, as though she could save him. "I don't want to go. I'm not a soldier. I'm just a college guy. All I know how to do is sell cars. I don't know anything about killing, and I don't want to know."

Joe started to cry. Alicia cried along with him.

Joe held her face in his hands and kissed her ravenously, letting her swallow his baleful moans, his sadness. He was shaking as his tongue caressed hers, and his cheeks were slick with salty tears. He cradled his face in the crook of her neck and felt her pulse point with his tender lips. Joe moved his face to the valley between her breasts and lingered there.

"I never thought I would be any farther from you than this," he said. "Now I'll be halfway around the world."

Guilt riddled Alicia like a spray of bullets. "This is all my fault. If I hadn't taken so much of your time, your grades never would have fallen."

"Baby, it's not your fault. If it's anyone's fault, it's mine."

She tried to kiss away his tears, but just as quickly a new stream would begin. She held him closely as he made love to her. Alicia knew their lovemaking was different. It was just as intense as before, but gone was the illusion of utopia she'd conjured for them. There was a stinging poignancy, a desperation that it would be months before she saw Joe again. She couldn't imagine going back to school without him. But she would have to.

Joe went to boot camp at Fort Hood near Killeen, Texas, and Alicia wrote to him every day as she'd promised. He was terrible at letter writing, so he recorded tapes on a portable recorder his father had given him, taping a message to her every day. At the end of every week he had filled a tape and mailed it to her.

Sometimes Alicia laughed when she heard his teasing messages and sometimes she cried when he told her he wanted to take her in his arms and make love to her.

The days moved with excruciating languor. Alicia packed her clothes for the autumn semester and went back to school. The Palmers drove her to Springfield and promised they would come back for the homecoming game and, as they'd done the previous two years, they would return for Parents' Weekend in October.

If Alicia's parents had any interest in these activities, they never said as much. Alice was busy with Clare's daughter, Mindy, helping Clare find a new job as a manicurist in Urbana and still pushing Harold to get some work done on their dilapidated house.

"I've got my hands full with everthin' around here, Alicia. Besides, the old truck would never make a trip like that. It'd conk out for sure." Then Alice would sweep her gray hair away from her deeply lined face and go back to Mindy, who toddled across the yard faster than a roadrunner.

Joe came home on a week's leave before he was to be shipped out. They spent the whole week in a motel in Springfield, and Alicia cried as much as she made love to Joe. He tried to be brave for her, but couldn't.

"I don't want to do this," he said with tears in his eyes. "I want to marry you, Alicia. I want us to buy a little ranch house in the suburbs and raise kids. I want to take you to all my favorite places in the city. We'll go to plays and watch the yacht races. We'll go to Chinatown and eat wonton. We'll take our kids to the Field Museum and the Museum of Science and Industry and show them the mummies. We'll have a great life when I get back."

"We will, won't we?"

"Yes, baby, we will. And that's what we're going to do. We're going to plan for our future. They say I'll be back in fourteen months."

"I can double up on my hours at class and graduate early."

"You can?" His emerald eyes brightened.

"Sure. Since I'm on scholarship, I could even go this summer."

"But you still need your summer job to pay for books and stuff," he said, tracing his finger over the shell of her ear.

"I could ask the Palmers for help. They'd loan me some money."

Joe kissed her quickly and deeply, sending shivers through both of them. "Then we'll get married the second I'm back."

"Oh, yes, Joe. Yes. We'll be married that very second."

When Joe left from the Springfield Airport, Alicia waved to his plane long after it was out of sight. She didn't want to miss a second's time being with Joe.

Alicia's grades soared now that Joe was gone, but her heart wasn't in it anymore. Homecoming came and went, then Christmas, then Easter. Alicia signed up for summer classes. She planned to graduate in December, a semester early.

She followed the war with a passion, just as all the kids on campus. Antiwar demonstrations hit their zenith in 1969. In May, Governor Ronald Reagan called out the National Guard to Berkeley when the students renamed a patch of university land People's Park, then physically fought authorities to keep it. Senator Edward Kennedy triggered Alicia's fear when he called American war tactics "senseless and irresponsible."

Worst of all were Joe's own letters to her. He told her everything he saw—the atrocities, the deaths of four of his buddies, the maiming of guys in his platoon. And how he'd caught a bullet in his arm, but after three weeks in a field hospital, they sent him back to the rice paddies.

His letters were so gruesome that Alicia felt sickened when she read them. She could tell the horrors of war were changing her sensitive and passionate Joe.

I hate this war where half the time we sit around and smoke dope sold to us by our commanding officers and the other half I want to take my gun and blow my own brains out. The only thing that keeps me going is you, baby. I listen to the songs that are popular back in the States and, as I crawl through the jungle fighting the Cong praying I kill him before he kills me, I think I'm on another planet. This can't be happening to me. All I ever wanted was to hold you and feel myself inside you. I can't wait to come home. I'll always love you.

Joe

But Joe never came back to Alicia; he went home to Chicago in a casket. Joe's mother called her at the farm when they received the telegram about his death. Even though Alicia had never met Theresa and Paul Smythe, they were gracious enough to invite her to stay with them for the funeral.

Alicia's mother tried to be empathetic, but it wasn't in her to feel for anyone but herself. She was tactless and self-absorbed.

"Don't you get all in a fret, Alicia. You'll be graduatin' and goin' to Chicago where there's all kinds of young people. You'll meet somebody else."

Alicia knew she should have known better than to seek sympathy from her mother. She didn't bother telling her father about Joe's death but left the house and went to the Palmers.

Doris held Alicia's hands and cried with her. Together they let their tears flow for both Donna and Joe. Zack Palmer told Alicia they would not only drive her to Chicago for the funeral, they would go with her. He would make reservations at the Palmer House. Doris smoothed Alicia's hair the way she'd done when Alicia was a little girl.

"We'll go window-shopping on State Street, Alicia. Maybe buy some caramel corn."

"We could scout out the area for a suitable apartment for you," Zack offered with a faint crack in his voice.

Alicia blew her nose on a tissue and thanked him. "First I have to find a job," she said with a painful smile.

"Yes, well. I was meaning to talk to you about that," Zack said. "I've spoken to a friend of mine who owns Taylor Advertising. He's located on Michigan Avenue. I told him all about you and he wanted to interview you over the Christmas holiday. Maybe we could move that interview up a smidge."

Alicia shook her head. "I . . . I don't think now is the time. I . . . I'm not too . . ." Alicia's eyes filled with tears.

"We won't do that, then. But we can go take a look around the place. See if you like it," Zack replied.

Doris rubbed Alicia's back. "You must think about what Joe would want you to do now, dearest. He was so full of life. Zack and I admired him a great deal. Joe would want you to build your dreams like you've always talked about. You're going to miss him all your life, Alicia. And that's okay. It's not wrong, it just is. Like we miss Donna. But you know, you can talk to him. He's not really gone. He's with you in spirit. That, you must always remember. Joe still loves you, and you will always love him. But your life here must continue."

Alicia felt that horrific black hole inside her yawn and threaten to suck her in, just as it had when Donna died. But she listened intently to Mrs. Palmer's words. She took each word and forced her heart and mind to memorize them. Once again, Alicia knew her life would never be the same. It seemed to her that every time she loved someone, fate took them away from her. She didn't know why she was being forced to walk this torturous path. Perhaps Mrs. Palmer was right: she had no choice but to go on with her life.

From the most remote channels of her heart, Alicia knew that no one would ever replace Joe. He was the love of her life. He was her Joe and she would love him always and forever.

23

Alicia was thirty-eight years old and had been in business for herself for over ten years, after learning all she could from Taylor Advertising. She lived in a co-op apartment north of the Chicago River on East Ontario, just a few blocks west of the Museum of Contemporary Art, and decorated the rooms with English and French antiques she'd found on her many business trips to Europe. She tried to re-create the romantic look of English gardens inside her home with patterns of English cabbage roses in peach, pink and dark hunter-green chintz on the windows, bed and comfortable upholstered chairs. It was a woman's home with few masculine trappings, except for a profusion of television, video and stereo equipment. Alicia was a high-tech junkie.

She bought one of the first home PC computers, an IBM clone, which cost a small fortune at the time. She took night classes to learn how to maximize its use, starting out with a simple word-processing program, then graduating to a small-business accounting program, to desktop publishing and finally to computer graphics, which she used for her advertising business.

Alicia was fascinated with each new invention that came on the market. She often joked that she was addicted to electronic gadgets—and the smaller, the better. When AIWA came out with the first hand-held stereo system with an automatic reverse tape player, she gladly paid the four-hundred-dollar price. She bought one of the first credit card–size calculators when they cost two hundred dollars and one of the first cellular "flip" phones for a whopping eight hundred dollars.

For many years, Alicia was never lonely, though she was alone. She had a large network of business associates, clients and friends across the country whom she visited on her jaunts between New York, Los Angeles and Chicago. She'd met many powerful women in business, and once they realized Alicia wasn't in contention for their job or their husband/boyfriend/lover, they befriended her, inviting her to sailing regattas, picnics on the lake, plays at the Shubert and Cubs' games at Wrigley Field.

It didn't bother Alicia that she had no children, she left the mothering to women who were more inclined that way. She believed her babies had died with Joe. She dated many different men over the years, but was never serious with any of them. The men enjoyed her company, her intelligence and her ideas, but she wouldn't let anyone—man, woman or child—get close.

Alicia told herself she was having a blast with life. She traveled where she wanted and when she wanted. She met interesting people and tried many different things, depending on the man at the time and the place; downhill skiing in Colorado, scuba diving in the Caymans, mountain biking in Arizona, hang gliding in California and sailing on Lake Michigan. She told herself it didn't bother her that there was no one waiting for her at home when she crawled into bed exhausted, and pretended not to notice the tuggings at her heartstrings when sentimental songs played on the radio. She ignored the lack of roses on Valentine's Day and the absence of a special man on Christmas Eve and worse, New Year's Eve. She reminded herself she was living out her childhood dream of being in the big city and building a business.

Alicia didn't listen to her friends when they told her that she couldn't, and shouldn't, carry a torch for a dead man *all* her life. They knew she had built her memories of Joe into such mystical and mythical proportions that no man could take his place.

Then Alicia's world changed, once again—the stock market crashed and she met Richard Bartlow.

"We're ruined!" Sally Cramer wailed, throwing her hands on top of her head as the television blared the news about the plummeting stock market.

Sally was twenty-nine years old, with carrot orange hair that spiraled around her round white face like fat bedsprings. She had enormous blue eyes with long, pale lashes and a smile so warm and inviting that not a single client could resist Sally's requests for payment. Sally was pudgy, though not fat, and quite short. She was the only person Alicia had ever met who had as much energy as Alicia did.

Despite her rounded shape, Sally was a vegetarian and holistic-health fiend. She read every label on every food item she purchased, and memorized the chemical contents of nearly every one of her favorite staples. She read reports in medical journals about MSG and struck the culprit that caused water retention and high blood pressure from every food item going through the Carrel and Company doors. When she read an exposé that a popular sweetener caused severe headaches, she banned all diet drinks from the office and substituted herb tea.

Sally believed it was her duty as Alicia's assistant, secretary, receptionist and friend to protect her from the horrors of pollution, food chemicals and all upsets coming from the world outside the Carrel and Company offices.

"We are not ruined," Alicia argued, though she was already feeling her stomach begin to lurch. In her push to bring in new business, Alicia had been pounding on a great many doors this past summer and had gotten more rejections in a three-month period than in all her years in business. She'd known for a while that something dire was brewing. She'd heard grumblings about the new changes in the tax-shelter laws and about the volatile Japanese bond market and its collapse. Oil had recently plummeted in West Texas, setting off a chain reaction of bank losses, real-estate bankruptcies and business closings. She braced herself for some bad times to come; however, she hadn't prepared Sally.

She placed her hand comfortingly on Sally's shoulder. "We'll make it through this. I've just been to see a new client and he may hire us."

"Oh, yeah? Who?"

"Richard Bartlow."

Sally propped her chin in her hand glumly. "Great! I just saw an item in the business section that his company is going down the tubes, too."

Alicia's jaw fell. "I don't believe it."

Sally pulled open a deep desk drawer and withdrew the newspaper. She pointed to the column headline that read: Bartlow Building…Isn't. The story stated that the hardest hit of all the secondary home builders in the Chicagoland area was Richard Bartlow's company. His success at targeting his market in the early- to mid-eighties was now causing his company to falter with the passing of the new tax-shelter law, which forbade companies and individuals from deducting the maintenance costs and interest paid on mortgages for second and third homes.

Alicia had heard many such stories. Condos in Miami Beach were being abandoned in midconstruction and skyscraping luxury apartment buildings in New York City were being rented free for one, even two years. Across the country the story was the same. Richard Bartlow wasn't the only victim.

Alicia handed the paper back to Sally. "The way I see it, if I can come up with an idea to save Richard Bartlow's business, I could market the same concept to every one of these retirement- and resort-area homes."

Sally rolled her blue eyes. "It's gonna take more than a thinking cap to help you out with that one!"

Alicia laughed. "I'll just have to save the world."

"Oh, God," Sally moaned, rummaging around the top of her desk. "This is stressing me out. Where's my chamomile?"

Turning away from Sally, Alicia went to her office, which had a small window that looked out over the lake. She paid an extra hundred and fifty dollars a month for that little view, but Alicia felt it was worth it. The lake always inspired her.

She sat down at the burled-wood desk she'd bought in Staffordshire, England, from a country estate. The drawers were perpetually stuck and there were burn marks on the top from one of several previous owners who must have smoked a pipe. She looked at the lake and watched the long shadows of the tall buildings begin to creep out to the water's edge as the day drew to a close. Turning back to her desk, she switched on her computer. Then the telephone rang.

A month ago, Alicia had purchased her newest electronic toy: a photo telefax machine. The fax line picked up the call and slowly, from the back of the machine, a letter from a client in San Jose, California, rolled out.

Alicia smiled. She knew she'd been right to put out the nearly fifteen hundred dollars for the fax machine. She'd had three clients tell her that faxes were the wave of the future. Contracts and negotiations that usually took a week to mail back and forth, even with the advent of overnight mail, were instantaneously concluded with the fax machine. Russ Johnson in San Jose said he believed the world of business had just gone into warp speed.

Alicia received a second call from another client in New York, who wanted to send her the revisions to an ad she was going to run for him in the *Wall Street Journal.* She pulled up the ad on her computer and had the client modem the changes directly to her computer, then she quickly made her own corrections and sent them back to the client.

Alicia could still hear Sally banging her desk drawers. "Vitamin B, that's what I need." She shuffled past Alicia's door as she went to a cupboard where they kept their personal belongings. Sally opened and shut another door, still mumbling to herself. "Maybe a little aromatherapy. . . Where the heck is my vanilla-scented candle? I knew I shoulda ordered more of those things from that lady in Des Moines."

Alicia remembered the day the crude flyer for the homemade scented candles came through the fax machine. While Sally criticized the artwork and layout of the flyer, Alicia was impressed this homemaker in Iowa had the good sense to use a fax machine to market her aromatherapy candles.

Suddenly, the idea burst into Alicia's mind like a clap of thunder. "Sally!" she shouted. "I've got it!"

Her assistant stuck her head in the door, a quizzical look puckering her round face. "I don't remember giving you my scented candle."

"I'm not talking about the candles, though that was the inspiration."

Sally smiled. "It was? For what?"

Alicia got up from her desk and walked toward Sally. She put her hands on her friend's shoulders. "With this ad idea, I *will* save the world."

"Oh. I was hoping you found my candle."

RENT YOUR OFFICE AT THE BEACH.

Alicia's ad for Richard Bartlow showed an executive in a Brooks Brothers' suit without shoes or socks, sitting on a canvas cabana chair under an umbrella, a PC computer in the sand next to him and a fax machine in his lap. He was smiling at the faxed memo. Long electrical cords snaked over the sand and up to a condo building behind him.

Since Richard's largest current project was at Lake Geneva, a vacation spot loved by many Chicagoans, the home-office idea came across clearly.

Alicia made a call to Richard's office and set up a meeting, finding it a bit odd when he suggested they go to lunch rather than meet in the office. In the meantime, she began scanning the *Wall Street Journal* for the names of faltering commercial real-estate companies, from Florida to Maine to California. She made inquiry phone calls first, and once she established a level of interest, she set appointments, then called the airlines. This idea deserved a formal presentation. It was a costly gamble, but she was hoping to use the money from the account she was going to land with Richard Bartlow to pay her expenses.

Alicia met Richard at a small Italian restaurant off Wacker Drive. It was one of those blustery days that gave Chicago the name of the Windy City. Alicia could barely get the door open, juggling her purse, her huge ad/art zippered folder and her daytimer. She was early, but Richard was earlier. He smiled as he watched her come in the door.

The hostess showed Alicia to Richard's table. He stood, shook her hand and helped her with her chair. "I hope you like Italian food."

"One of my favorites," she said.

"You're so slim, I thought for a minute maybe one of those health-food places would have been more to your liking."

Alicia fumbled with the art folder, which refused to stay propped against her chair. She was so intent on her presentation she barely caught what he was saying. "Huh? Oh, no. My secretary, Sally, is forever shoving alfalfa sprouts down my throat. She's sort of a mother hen type. But I suppose they are good for me."

Richard smiled a blazingly charming smile. "Do you need that?"

"The sprouts?" Alicia lifted her water glass to wet her nervous, dry mouth. God, she thought, I need this account.

"Mothering," he said, propping his elbows on the table and resting his chin on his laced fingers.

"Don't we all?" Alicia asked, realizing suddenly that Richard was looking at her intently. Intensely. Intimately. Uh-oh, she thought. She glanced around the restaurant. Every table was filled with couples talking happily or mooning over each other. There wasn't a single business conversation going on that she could see.

"I know I do," he said. "Though I don't get much."

"Sorry," she replied, leaning over to pick up her day-timer. "I thought I'd give you the pitch first and then show you the artwork."

"I'm getting a divorce," Richard said flatly.

Alicia stopped cold, her hands in midmotion of un-zipping her daytimer. She shifted gears, zipping up the daytimer and replacing it on the floor. It was going to be a long lunch.

Richard's handsome face was filled with pain, and his eyes held a faraway look. Alicia knew that the last thing on his mind was her presentation. "Perhaps we should talk another time. Maybe next week, when you're in better spirits."

Her words seemed to shock him back to the present. He took his elbows off the table, placing his hands on the edges of his silverware. She could tell he was fight-ing tears. There was an emotional strain to his voice. "Yes, perhaps you're right. I shouldn't have said any-thing. I don't know you. You're a stranger, really. But then it seems that everyone in my life is a stranger."

Alicia was shocked, his words hitting home like a thunderbolt. She knew *exactly* what he was talking about. She had people around her all the time—Sally, the clients she saw or spoke to every day, her friends. But what were they, really? Just strangers. They didn't live her life. They weren't there when she got the flu or when she wanted to celebrate a special deal she'd cut. There was no one special she could call her own. She'd spent her life living with a ghost.

"I know what it's like to live with people all around you and feel alone." She was surprised she'd spoken.

He looked up at her. His blue eyes were so clear, so filled with loneliness. Alicia hadn't realized until then that she was looking at the reflection of herself.

"I thought I was the only one," he said.

"No." For the second time, she felt a magnetism between them.

Richard expelled a deep breath. "I wonder if it's because I'm forty that all this is happening to me. I read that in one of my self-help books—"

"You read self-help books?"

"All the time." His smile was fleeting as he laughed at himself.

"Me, too. I'm addicted to them. Tapes, too. I have dozens. Hundreds."

"My wife laughs at me for reading that stuff. She says none of it is working. Anyway, I read that part of the middle-age crisis is that we reevaluate our lives and, in particular, our childhoods. What happened to us. The pain and agony. And that now we must assimilate those difficult times into more balanced behaviors and outlooks."

"I think that's true," she replied.

"I guess that's what I'm doing. I'm not really sure."

Alicia looked at him thoughtfully. Ordinarily, she'd be anxious to get the hell out of here; she didn't like taking on other people's problems. She'd never been the Ann Landers type, too afraid that the advice she would give might be wrong. Who was *she* to say how someone should or shouldn't live? It was hard enough for her to make her own decisions, much less help someone else. Sally was much better at this sort of thing.

But there was something about Richard's vulnerability that spoke to her and made her stay. He looked like a lost little boy hoping someone could direct him. She knew all too well that his business was failing, and that in itself would be enough to make her half-nuts. But to have his marriage crumbling at the same time must be hell.

Alicia believed she wasn't the person with the right answers for Richard, but she did know she was a good listener. She did not believe in coincidences; she believed there was a reason for everything. Putting aside her thoughts about ad pitches and account closings, she asked, "Did you have a lot of difficult times in your childhood, Richard?"

Richard told Alicia about his visionless, emotionless father whom he never respected, his father's death and his selfish, avaricious mother who still demanded money from him on a monthly basis. He told her he'd made a mistake getting married so young and having children so quickly. But there was nothing he could do about that. He told her how difficult it had been working for his father-in-law for so many years before striking out on his own. He felt as if he were constantly battling the world, he said, and always, his best was never good enough for his wife.

He painted a picture of a spoiled, unambitious woman who, pampered by her parents all her life, expected Richard to continue to provide her with everything she wanted. He'd found himself sinking deeper into personal debt every year, he said. And now with a daughter in college and a wife wanting to play in the rich social circuit of her parents' crowd, Richard felt overburdened with her expectations and the hard reality of losing his business.

"I don't even have the energy to explode anymore. I feel flattened, if anything "

"You're burned-out," Alicia offered.

"Yes, I suppose I am. I feel I have to get out before I have a heart attack or something. Things like that happen to guys like me."

She nodded.

"I moved my things out of the house a few nights ago. I'm subletting a one-bedroom apartment from a young stockbroker who lost his job during a downsizing at his company last month."

"I see." Alicia knew she should let him continue to vent.

"My wife demanded she keep all the furniture, the house, the car, the savings. Everything. I told her we're going to have to sell the house to break even. She went ballistic, screaming, hitting me. It was terrible." Richard looked away from her, and she could see a swell of tears in his eyes.

Clearing his throat, he looked back at her. "I'm really sorry."

"For what?"

"Dragging you into my story. This must be very awkward for you."

"It's okay."

Richard shook his head. "No, it's not. You want my account and so you figure you've got to listen to my sob story, hoping I'll still sign with you."

She started to protest, but he put up his hands. "I know I'm right. I planned it that way."

Alicia tried not to let her surprise show. "You what?"

His smile faded quickly as a forlorn look creased his forehead. "I picked you as my victim. I don't have anyone else to talk to."

Alicia couldn't imagine her life without Sally or any one of a number of her friends. No matter what time of day or night, Alicia had people all over the world who would listen to her problems. Still, she did know what he was saying. There was no one special for him, either.

"I've been told I'm a good listener," Alicia said.

"I appreciate that," he said. "And a beautiful one, too."

Just then, the waiter came to the table to take their order. Richard ordered them vegetable lasagna made with phyllo dough and stuffed eggplant as an appetizer. Alicia agreed to a glass of Merlot, but only one, she told him, since she made a practice of never drinking wine at lunch.

When the wine was served, Richard asked to hear Alicia's pitch. Once he saw the ad drawing, he burst into laughter.

"This is terrific!"

"Do you really like it?" she asked.

"You bet I do. I never thought of this angle. My God! You've given me the first ray of hope I've had in weeks . . . months maybe. Thank God I decided to take this meeting."

Alicia felt exhilarated—there was nothing more thrilling than knowing she'd hit the mark with her work. "I have a strong feeling about this concept, too."

"There's only one thing that upsets me about all this."

"Upsets you?"

"Yeah. Why didn't *I* think of it?" Again, Richard laughed heartily, raising his wineglass to hers. "Let's drink to our new partnership."

Alicia didn't miss his double entendre as she took in Richard's penetrating crystal blue gaze over the rim of her glass. She liked the fact that her ideas brought back the color to his cheeks and a powerful sparkle to his eyes. He was even sitting up straighter in his chair. She'd given him hope. Maybe she'd even found some for herself.

24

—▶ ◀—

Alicia's ad campaign saved no less than eight major real-estate developers from going bankrupt. Richard Bartlow was not one of them—but Richard was the only one of the group going through a divorce at the same time.

His judgment was clouded by the emotional battle Mary Grace waged against him. Not once in his weeks of calculations prior to filing for divorce had he believed Mary Grace would turn into such a wildcat. She fought him at every turn, making demands on his financial resources he couldn't or wouldn't concede to at the time. He paid his attorney double what he'd thought it would cost for his divorce.

He spent so much time arguing with Mary Grace that any chance he'd had to save his real estate ventures slipped through his fingers. Richard had assumed Mary Grace would take solace and financial support from her parents. He'd never counted on her pride.

"Mary Grace refuses to live with her parents," he ranted one night to Alice. "She's so bitter and angry, she even threatened to go on welfare! My wife!"

Alicia frowned as she stirred chopped green, red and yellow peppers in a wok. "Ex-wife," she corrected, wondering why Richard was still possessive seven months after the divorce was final. "Mary Grace may not like having to grovel to her parents, but she's not stupid. She's not going to make those children suffer because of her pride or anything else. Now that the house is sold, doesn't she have to move out next month?"

"Yes."

"You wait and see. She'll move in with her parents. They'll take care of her."

Richard looked at her thoughtfully. "Just like you're taking care of me?"

Alicia's smile was a halfhearted effort. "Sorta."

Richard sat on a bar stool at the kitchen counter, watching as Alicia prepared their dinner. "She won't let me see the kids until I give her the child support I owe her."

"Then pay her. Take the kids to the ball game and have a good time."

"With what? I'm busted—really busted. I'm down to my last credit card and I have no cash in the bank. The money I got from the sale of the office equipment went to pay one of the creditors." He passed his hand over his face. "I don't know what to do."

"Surely one of your friends has some work for you. Consulting. An office manager..." Alicia stirred in a cupful of mushrooms and added a bit of olive oil and more chopped garlic.

"Are you crazy? I'm a builder. I build palaces, luxury apartments. I'm not a glorified secretary!"

Alicia shook her head. "When the going gets tough... the tough get going. That's always been my motto. Sometimes you just have to do what you can until the right opportunity comes along."

"That's easy for you to say," he replied glumly. "You're a woman."

Alicia put her hand on her hip. "What the hell does that crack mean?"

He chuckled. "Actually, it was my way of complimenting you. Women always seem to rise to the occasion better than men. I've noticed that about many women I've met. You'll clean toilets, take out the garbage . . . waitress . . . anything to keep it all going somehow. I don't think I can do that." He turned away from her.

"Why not?"

He continued looking at the floor. "I don't know how."

It's the male ego, Alicia thought, then started laughing. Turning off the gas burner under the stir-fry vegetables, she walked around the counter and put her hands on Richard's shoulders.

He looked up at her, longing in his eyes. On days like this when he got so down on himself, he looked like a beaten puppy. "I wish I was more like you," he said. "Nothing gets you down. You always think of something . . . a way to turn everything around for yourself. Like that ad . . . you're doing quite well with it, aren't you?"

"Yes, I am," she replied, continuing to look at him. He was hesitant to continue. "Do you want a loan, Richard?"

"Hmmh. Got ten million?" Then he laughed loudly. "Christ! I never thought I'd see the day I'd be asking a woman for money."

"Is that what you're doing?"

"No." He stood up and went to the window. "I need more than a loan, Alicia. I need a new life."

"Thanks a lot. I thought I was part of that new life."

He turned and went to her, gathering her in his arms. "I didn't mean it the way it sounded. I meant a new career. You're all the woman I've ever dreamed about. I didn't know it was possible to find someone so smart and beautiful and dedicated to pulling this old boy up out of the muck like you do. You're one special lady. I love you."

"I love you, too, Richard."

Alicia put her lips against his, feeling Richard's strong kiss become aggressive and hot. She could never resist him. He held her so close that she felt as if she were a part of his body. When he was like this, he was the old Richard, powerful and ready to take on the world. Even his personal demons of besting his father-in-law. *Ex*-father-in-law, Alicia reminded herself.

She had dated two men who were going through a divorce, and she remembered how immersed they'd been in their own worlds at the time. She realized that was part of the pain and part of the healing process. She loved Richard enough to allow him that time. However, it was over eighteen months since she and Richard met, and he was still acting as if it had happened just yesterday.

Sally had told her that a divorce was grieving similar to death, only worse because there was always a great deal of self-accusation that went with it. The feelings of failure were killing Richard—he couldn't concentrate on business of any kind, flitting from deal to deal, thinking with each one he was going to "hit it big" and he'd be back on top.

Alicia didn't see it that way. She believed that business was like life: one had to advance a step at a time, always hoping each step was in forward motion. Unfortunately, many times they weren't.

His tongue probed her mouth, and she felt the familiar tingle of excitement begin at the roof of her mouth traveling across the top of her skull and cascading over her entire body like a waterfall. She put her arms around his neck, drawing him deeper into her. With her eyes closed, she could already feel passion lifting her body, then her spirit, out of the world. She was no longer on the earth plane, but caught someplace where her love for Richard was unconditional and sublime.

His hand cupped her breast and she felt licks of heat sear a path to her loins, barely aware her legs had spread. A hot, moist liquid slipped down the walls of her vagina as she already imagined him inside her.

"God ... Alicia ... how can you do this to me? I have no control when it comes to you." He was breathing heavily.

He slipped his hand inside the black leggings she wore. At night, after her long days at work, Alicia wore no underwear, loose baggy shirts and leggings and never, ever any shoes. It was as bohemian as she ever got. His fingers probed her, teasing her hardening bud. She felt as if every muscle in her legs and thighs had turned to water. She began to sink.

He yanked off her leggings with one quick, very impatient movement. Effortlessly, Richard hoisted her legs around his waist, settling her onto his thighs as he unzipped his slacks and placed her atop his engorged penis.

Alicia nearly screamed with pleasure as he filled her. Putting his hands on her waist, he moved her up and down while she pulled off her sweatshirt, exposing her naked breasts to his hungry lips. He suckled and lightly pinched her tight nipples with his lips and tongue.

She moaned his name. "Richard ..."

He moved his hips in double time with his hands, still lifting her by her waist. He pumped and stroked her sweet slick walls until she could feel herself pulsing around his shaft. She was climbing to the heights of desire, the edge of the galaxy before she climaxed at the same time as he. She could feel her soul as it left her body, spinning around him, engulfing him in the cocoon of her love. She could feel his spirit unite with hers in the most sensual, mystical experience of her life.

It was always like this with Richard. There was some kind of union they shared that went beyond the physical, beyond time and earth. She hadn't thought about soul mates or destiny since Joe, but she did now. Because so much about him was familiar to her, she was convinced she had known Richard in many lifetimes. They were comfortable together, moving through their days and nights as if in perfect flow, like waves on the sea.

He buried his face between her breasts, still not satisfied. He rolled to the floor, taking Alicia with him. Pulling her under him, he nearly buried her frame with his huge chest. He nuzzled his face in the crook of her neck and began kissing her ear, ringing the edge with his tongue, breathing her name. Talking erotically and turning her on all over again.

"You want me to do it to you, again, don't you, baby?" He asked. "And you want it just the way I do it . . ." He took off his shirt and kicked off his pants. He pushed his penis inside her.

"Yes. Oh, yes." She barely breathed the words as his slick stroking, eased now by his own semen, made his lovemaking even more delicious.

She raised her hips, grinding herself into him, feeling as if she could never get enough. He massaged her breasts with his strong fingers and tweaked the nipples, sending shock waves through her body. Her second orgasm sent her body into jerklike fits. Clamping her hands on his buttocks, she pulled him closer into herself. She screamed his name. "Richard!"

Quickly, he rolled her over and onto her knees as he entered her from behind. Her vagina never felt so full, she thought. He played and toyed with her hard bud until she could barely breathe. They were both sweating. His chest slipped over her back as he lay himself on her, still pressing and pushing deeply into her.

Juggernauts of ecstasy rocked Alicia's body as she climaxed over and over again. She felt as if she were being washed out to sea on a tumultuous tidal wave. Her elbows gave way at the same moment as he climaxed with a groan. They collapsed together on the floor.

Alicia snuggled next to Richard, who was so spent he couldn't lift his arm to hold her. She could smell the scent of their sweat and sex, blended to create an erotic perfume.

Slowly, he opened his eyes. "I don't know what comes over me with you. It's never been like this for me. I think I lose my mind . . . I cross some kind of barrier and become almost an animal." He pulled her onto his chest. "You make me wild!"

He kissed her and she responded playfully. "I hope it's always like this for us."

He rolled his eyes. "I don't! I'll never live through it." Laughing he spanked her bottom.

They giggled and talked for hours as they sat on the floor naked, sharing the stir-fried vegetables and angelhair pasta she'd made.

"You make me feel so special, Alicia," he said sincerely.

"That's mutual, darling."

He leaned over and kissed her. "I wish I was in a position to buy you jewels and furs and cars . . . what else? A trip to Capri."

Tenderly, she put her hand on his cheek. "I don't want all those things. I'm perfectly happy right where I am. I just want you to be happy, too, Richard. Get past this pain and anger you keep feeling. I like it when you're able to forget the outside world and it's just the two of us."

"Yes," he said as a dark shadow passed over his face. "The outside world is pretty fucked up, isn't it?"

Alicia looked deeply into his eyes. "Ever hear the saying that our outside world is a reflection of our inside world?"

He shook his head. "I was never into philosophy."

She chuckled lightly. "Don't be so afraid. It doesn't hurt all that much."

"Oh, yeah? I'm not so sure about that."

Alicia decided that the best way to help Richard come around was to give him truths and nurturing in alternating doses. His ego and self-confidence were badly bruised, even damaged, from his business failure alone. The ongoing battle with Mary Grace only seemed to get more bitter every day. Alicia could only hope that both of them would grow up and learn to act like adults instead of bickering children.

Richard kept his life with Alicia separate from his old life. She had not met his former business associates, other than his attorney, Jack Billingsly, and he especially kept her away from his children. For a long time, Richard was afraid that if Mary Grace knew about Alicia, she would make life even more difficult for him.

Now that the divorce had been final for over a year, he felt it was time for Penelope and Lawrence to meet her.

Richard asked Alicia to meet them at NikeTown on North Michigan Avenue. He'd told Penelope and Lawrence he was going to buy them shoes for school, leaving out the fact that Alicia would be picking up the tab.

Lawrence, seventeen and a junior in high school, was wearing baggy pants, an oversize long-sleeved T-shirt that looked as if it hadn't been washed in weeks, a Chicago Bulls baseball cap over his dirty shoulder-length hair and very old, worn-out Nikes. Penelope was wearing tight faded blue jeans that revealed every curve of her rounded twenty-two-year-old hips. Her breasts strained under a knit bandeau top. Alicia couldn't tell whether her breasts would finally career over the top of the bandeau or spill through the bottom. Fortunately, Penelope had the good taste to wear a hooded, long-sleeved shocking-pink nylon parka so that if there was a mishap she could cover herself.

Alicia could tell Penelope's affected, bored behavior rankled Richard and that Penelope knew it.

His broad smile was tense as he greeted them. "Gee. I hope you kids weren't waiting too long. We had to park on the top level of the parking garage."

Penelope munched on a hard candy as she scoured Alicia from head to toe with a scowling look. "She the new bitch?"

"Penelope! What the devil has gotten into you? Where are your manners?"

"You call all women bitches . . . behind our backs." Turning around, she slammed her palms against the glass door and went inside.

Alicia was filled with shock as she turned to Lawrence. Richard introduced his son, but Lawrence refused to look at her. "Mom says she needs more money. When are you gonna take care of us, huh?"

"I'm doing the best I can. Lots of guys are out of work right now."

Lawrence dropped his head. "Fuckin' asshole." He marched inside behind his sister.

"Charming," Alicia said, thinking this was her cue to leave. Then she saw Richard's embarrassment. She saw that his hands were shaking and she empathized.

"This is all their mother's fault," he said. "She's poisoned them against me."

Alicia nodded and went inside after him.

While Lawrence and Richard went to the third floor to inspect the hundred-and-thirty-five-dollar basketball shoes that the Chicago Bulls presumably all wore, Alicia found Penelope looking at the aerobics shoes.

Alicia thought that perhaps if she went slowly she could try to be friends with the girl. "Do you take aerobics at school?"

Penelope slammed the lavender and pink shoe back down on the pedestal. "I don't go to school anymore. Haven't you heard? We're fuckin' broke."

"Sorry."

Penelope didn't move away, and Alicia got the feeling she needed someone to listen to her problems, her side of the story. "I had to drop out this fall."

"Does your father know this? He told me your grandparents were paying for your education until he could repay them when he gets back on his feet."

"And you fuckin' believed him?" Penelope snapped.

Alicia realized she was getting nowhere with this brat. "I fuckin' did."

Penelope dropped her acidic stare. "Oh, well. That's true. But see, I flunked out. I gotta take night classes here in Chicago and get my grades back up."

"And why did you flunk out?"

Penelope laughed. "Boyfriend problems."

"Oh." Alicia nodded. "I understand."

Penelope waved her off. "The hell you do. The hell you understand anything about me or Lawrence or Mom. Why don't you get the fuck out of Dad's life so he can go back to Mom and we can be a family again?" She ran out of the store.

Alicia hadn't even closed her gaping jaw when Richard went running past her, quickly followed by Lawrence.

She watched through the glass doors while Richard spoke to his children on the sidewalk. She saw arms slinging the air and hatred and guilt in their eyes. She saw Lawrence hit his father in the chest and Penelope burst into angry tears. She saw Richard return their accusations volley for volley. She saw the children wrap their arms around themselves and stomp away. She saw Richard call after them but they never turned around.

Alicia saw Richard look back to her as if she had some magical answer for his broken family. But she didn't.

Richard told Alicia he had fallen deeply in love with her, claiming this was the one time in his life when he felt he needed somebody. But Alicia realized that Richard had turned love and need into narcissism.

Mired in severe depression, Richard was using up Alicia mentally and spiritually, and as the weeks became months, she realized Richard wasn't giving her what she needed. She wanted to feel her emotions returned on an unconditional basis. But she knew that he could not give love when he didn't love himself.

Alicia wanted things to change. Hanging around Chicago where he couldn't seem to get anything going and living off her income was not good for his self-esteem. They both needed a break.

Stepping out of the shower, Richard wrapped a thick, fluffy towel around his middle. He ran a stiff brush through his blond hair, slicking it back from his strong face. "What did you say, sweetheart?"

"I said I've got a surprise for you. Come see."

He walked out of the bathroom and looked at the hand she was holding up to him. "What is it?"

"Two tickets to Phoenix." She smiled broadly.

It had been days since Richard had smiled, and he wasn't smiling now. "They must have cost you a bundle. Why are you going there?"

"I'm taking you on a vacation."

Shaking his head, he stomped across the white carpeted bedroom to the chest of drawers and pulled out a pair of briefs. "No woman is gonna pay for *my* vacation. Jesus Christ! You make me sound like a gigolo."

"I wasn't trying to, darling. Think about it. Let's get out of town. A change of scenery will do you good, a lot of good. There's a client down there I have to see and I got the extra ticket for no charge. I used my frequent-flier miles."

"Really?"

"Yeah. We can go to Scottsdale, play some golf. Go up to Sedona and check out the Indian art. Maybe I'll get a painting for the bedroom. We could go watch the sunrise at the Grand Canyon. Just bum around for a few days, a week even. What do you say?"

Frowning, he dropped his shoulders and looked at his briefs, which were gray from too many washings. "It isn't Capri."

She rushed to him and threw her arms around him. "We'll do Capri next year, darling. Let's get the hell out of Chicago."

She kissed him passionately. Richard put his arms around her and pulled her into his chest. "You're too wonderful to be with a bum like me."

"Don't talk like that. You'll get back on top. I just know you will."

Alicia's client, Jay Bradstone, a residential developer in Scottsdale, arranged for a room at the Arizona Biltmore Hotel at a corporate rate that Alicia could easily afford.

The hotel, designed by Frank Lloyd Wright and built in the late 1920s, had been a popular playground for a multitude of Hollywood movie stars before the war. Alicia was in awe as she strolled through the lobby still filled with the original furniture designed by Frank Lloyd Wright. Their room was magnificent, with a king-size bed and long sleek contemporary lines in all the furniture. Though the hotel had been refurbished with new carpets, paint, phone system and modern amenities, things like the original tile work in the bathrooms pleased Alicia's sense of good taste and quality.

Since they didn't have to meet Alicia's client until the following day, they played a round of tennis, then went for a swim in the pool. There were still 1930s-style cabana rooms along the east side of the Olympic-size swimming pool where many of the hotel guests gave private cocktail parties. They rested in the sun, each reading a new novel, and at dusk they went back to their room and made love for over an hour before showering together and dressing for dinner.

Alicia had rented a car at the airport so they wouldn't have to take a cab into town. Driving up and down Camelback Road, they discussed the pros and cons of which restaurant they would try. They compromised her craving for seafood with his desire for a mesquite-grilled steak and went to the Famous Pacific Fish Company and ate mesquite-broiled shark steaks.

On their ride back to the hotel, Richard turned to Alicia. "I've never felt so much at home as I do here. I don't know what it is about this place—it's peaceful and beautiful and yet, there's something else . . ."

"I know what you mean. I've always liked Scottsdale. I get rejuvenated here and find some peace."

"Yeah, that's it."

"Good. Maybe we'll make a new beginning here," she said hopefully.

The next day, Alicia and Richard met Jay Bradstone at the construction sight of the luxury condominiums he was building. Jay was a likable man in his late fifties, with graying black hair and a facial bone structure so strong and sharp he looked as if he were Indian. But his family had come from Nova Scotia, he said, where the people resembled the rocky coastline. Jay showed them the three-thousand-foot villas he was building and selling for a hundred and fifty thousand dollars.

Alicia fell in love with the open-concept room arrangements and triple dining areas all overlooking patios or terraces facing the desert.

Richard was stunned at the prices. "My God, man! In Chicago, similar houses would cost twice that much.

Even more, with some of the amenities you've got in them. How can you do it?"

Jay shrugged. "I don't believe in raping the public the way you fellas do up north. 'Course, we don't have basements, but I still put the same amount of insulation in the walls and roof. Air-conditioning gets expensive when it's a hundred and ten in the shade."

Alicia held her hand over her eyes to shield them from the sun. "I don't see any shade."

"My point exactly," Jay said. "I have to say that I thought I'd lost my ass until Alicia contacted me. I followed her ideas right down the line and I've sold three condos this past spring. I made enough to buy the materials to finish off the other four I've started and we just got a bid on one of them the other day. I'm not a millionaire, but my bills are paid, I'm squeaking by and I'm still in the game."

Richard didn't respond, but Alicia could tell he was taking in Jay's every word.

She went over the details of her next contract with Jay while Richard poked around the condominium site. When he came back, he started asking Jay more questions. Had Jay tried the new steel-frame construction rather than wood? How much of the cost did the saltillo tile floors cut out of the expense? Did the pavestone walkways and driveways really hold up? Did he use zoned heat and air? How much did he save by using off-brand windows?

Then he asked a question that shocked Alicia. "Would you be interested in a partner, Jay?"

Jay was taken as much by surprise as Alicia. "Never thought about a partner."

She could tell Richard's mind was spinning with ideas. As he started outlining them to Jay, she shivered as if death had come to visit. She had brought Richard to Scottsdale to give him hope. He had not only found that hope, but he was already planning a life that would cause him to move to Arizona and away from her.

She swallowed hard and hoped the acid in her stomach would quickly abate. Somehow, she knew it wouldn't.

25

━━━ ◄━━

Cynthia Folsum pulled a reluctant Mary Grace through the cortiles and the quaint European-style streets of the fashionable Borgata in Scottsdale.

"This is the best shopping in the country and you look like you just ate rancid guacamole. Come on! Get into the spirit here. We're having fun. You remember fun, don't you?"

Mary Grace pursed her lips into a firm pout. "I wish you'd shut up. Why on earth would you bring me to this incredibly expensive place when you know I can't afford Kleenex!"

"I told you. The trip is on me. The food is on me. I want to buy you one of these cute southwestern outfits. Boots, hat and all. God knows I can afford it."

"Why? Why are you doing this?"

"Because, goddamn it, I'm your friend. And for once, I want you to realize that there is life beyond Richard. It's okay for a girlfriend to buy you an outfit. It's okay for you to laugh, have a margarita and smile. We could go out dancing. Meet some nice fellas by the hotel pool. Talk to them instead of treating every man who walks the earth like dirt."

"I don't care."

"That is obvious," Cynthia said as they walked out of the cool air-conditioning into the Arizona autumn sunshine.

Mary Grace squinted as she looked at Cynthia. She was amazed at what money could buy. Cynthia didn't look a day older than when they'd all come back from Europe in 1966. Cynthia had not only kept her figure, she'd improved it with exercise and all her organically grown foods and herb pills. She had not a trace of gray in her hair, but then Mary Grace wouldn't have known since Cynthia said she spent a fortune getting it high-lighted and low-lighted and in-between lighted. Mary Grace hadn't stepped foot in the hairdressers since the divorce had been final.

She'd moved to a small ranch house off Cicero Avenue, which she paid for with an allowance from her father. Mary Grace had discovered that pride had no place in her life—except when it came to motivating herself to get her degree. Rather than take charity from her father, Mary Grace had wisely bargained with him to give her a loan over the next four years that would pay for both her education and maintenance for herself and the children.

James had agreed. Then he'd bargained further that he pay for his grandchildren's education, not as a loan or a gift, but as their "early inheritance." Mary Grace had to agree with him that spending his money on their educations at this point in their lives was much more valuable than a trust fund twenty or thirty years in the future.

In his own way, James loved her very much. The only problem was that both her parents were just as con-trolling as she'd always thought them to be. They were too old to change. They thought they had only Mary Grace's best interests at heart, but the reality was that they still wanted her to do only as *they* thought proper.

She could have agreed to live in more flamboyant surroundings, but she always believed there would be paybacks in the end. Living with Richard had taught her that nothing in life was free, and she'd had to pay for those loans by eating crow. Her mother must have stayed up nights thinking of different ways to say I told you so. It made Mary Grace sick. But she'd gotten through the worst of it.

She had five more semesters of school before she graduated—two and a half years, to be exact. It might as well have been centuries, she grumbled to herself.

Many times she thought she'd never see the light at the end of the tunnel. But then she envisioned how gratifying it would be when she could walk up to Richard, shove her diploma in his face and tell him to go screw himself.

Anger was an intense motivator, she'd learned.

"Look, doll, you aren't the first woman who was dumped on by a man. I've been dumped by plenty. I understand you're pissed, but it's been two years. Enough already. You know what you're doing now?"

"No, but I gotta feeling you're going to tell me," Mary Grace said sarcastically.

"Damn straight I am. You're letting Richard control you."

"What? Are you crazy? I do everything myself these days."

Cynthia walked to the Lincoln Town Car she'd rented. "I'm not talking about taking out the garbage. You're letting what Richard did to you keep you from having a good time here in Scottsdale. You're still so hung up on what he did or didn't do or the money he shoulda, coulda given you that you won't even let me buy you a concho belt!" Cynthia slammed her fist down on the roof of the car.

Mary Grace wasn't sure if she'd stood in the hot sun so long that the cobwebs had melted from her brain or if Cynthia was truly making sense for the first time, but suddenly, Mary Grace felt her life turning a corner.

"He *is* still dictating my life, isn't he?"

Cynthia shook her head. "You're letting him do that. You're giving him that kind of power."

"So, what do I do now?"

Cynthia smiled broadly, tossed her keys back in her purse and spread her arms out wide. "Like I always say, when the going gets tough . . ."

Mary Grace laughed. "The tough . . . go shopping!"

"You got it!"

They turned and went back to the Borgata. "This time, we'll hit all fifty stores!" Mary Grace said confidently.

Cynthia was exhausted and had tense shoulders by the time they got back to the Sheridan where they were staying.

"I'm calling for a massage," Cynthia said, picking up the hotel phone. "Should I book one for you, too?"

Mary Grace flopped onto the bed. "I feel great. I might go for a swim while you're gone."

Cynthia told the concierge that she wanted a massage and if possible, she'd like the masseur to come to the hotel.

The concierge called back, he told Cynthia every masseur in town was booked, but he'd found a new girl who was willing to come to the hotel in half an hour. Cynthia agreed.

"Darn. I was hoping for one of those young pumped-up guys who can really dig into the muscles. All I could get was some young girl who's just starting out." Cynthia rose from the bed to change her clothes.

"I'm sure it will be fine," Mary Grace assured her as she looked at the new electric blue western suede skirt and silk blouse with blue fringe to match.

"I suppose. But she sounds more like a topless dancer. Who ever heard of a name like Michelle Windsong, for God's sake?"

Mary Grace shrugged. "Cyn." She looked up, eyes filled with emotion. "I'll never forget what you've done for me. No one has ever been as good to me as you've been."

Cynthia squeezed her hand. "Look, doll. One bad apple doesn't spoil the bunch. Your life isn't over because Richard is gone. You're entering a new phase, that's all. You may not think so, but you're young. There's lots of guys out there. And there is one who will treat you with all the love and affection you want and deserve. It doesn't take a genius to figure out that if Richard had given you some affection, a lot of affection, you'd still be happily married. You'll find someone else someday."

Mary Grace sniffed. "It's not that easy. Look at you. You've never been married. And you're perfect."

Cynthia laughed. "Mary Grace, sometimes I think you're still back in high school. I could have been married a million times and it's not because the guy wasn't right or any of that crap. I'm not married because I don't want to be."

Mary Grace's eyes went round. "You're kidding?"

Cynthia shook her head. "Sorry, but that shit cramps my style," she said with a far-away look Mary Grace knew. When she looked like that Mary Grace always wondered what Cynthia was really thinking.

Cynthia eased off the bed. "I've got to hurry."

"Yeah," Mary Grace said. "Me, too."

It was a beautiful balmy night, ideal for dining outside.

"Let's go to Rick's Café Americana," Cynthia said. "It's won a ton of awards and the food is divine."

"You know this town better than I do," Mary Grace said as they got into the Lincoln.

Located in the Mercado del Lago, walking into Rick's was like walking onto the movie set of *Casablanca*. Mary Grace could feel romance and intrigue oozing from behind every palm and orchid.

"This place is heaven," she said later, biting into a sautéed scampi shrimp. "It would be rather wonderful to think about coming here with another man. One I didn't know. I've never been to bed with anyone but Richard. Is it very different with different men?"

"Why, little Mary Grace, you're getting rather personal here."

"I really want to know."

Cynthia smiled. "It's different as night and day with each one. You'll never find two alike. Men tell me it's different with women. We pretty much feel the same. But men are all different. That's what makes them so delicious."

"Geez, Cyn! The way you talk!" Mary Grace blushed.

"You asked," Cynthia said. "You should try a couple out. See what you think."

"God, you talk like I was test-driving a car."

"What's wrong with that? We're not kids anymore. It's not like you gotta get married to have children—

you've done that. Now you've got to think about Mary Grace and what she wants and needs. Maybe you'll find you just want a lover. Maybe you won't want anybody."

Mary Grace shook her head. "For so long I just thought about getting Richard back and getting my life to be the way it was before the crash. Before he left. Before I was poor."

"This poor shit is stupid. Go to your folks and get some real goddamn money and ease up on yourself."

"I can't do it. I know this may sound stupid but I want to do this for myself. The kids hate me for it, but I want something I can call my own. I have to do this my way."

Cynthia nodded. "That's very noble. I understand you a lot better now." She peered intently at Mary Grace. "I think it's stupid, but it's your deal." She patted her hand. "If you change your mind and need my help, just let me know."

Mary Grace smiled back at her friend. "Thanks."

Cynthia's eyes moved away from Mary Grace's face, then suddenly her jaw fell open. Pulling her mouth closed, she swallowed hard.

"This isn't happening," she said aloud.

"What?" Mary Grace didn't wait for an answer. Instead, she turned around and followed Cynthia's gaze. What Mary Grace saw horrified her. It was Richard with his arms around a woman.

Alicia was more beautiful than she'd imagined—and thinner. She was nothing like the "pointy-nosed witch" Penelope had described, nor the "stuck-up bitch" Lawrence had called her. This pretty woman with the peach-blushed cheeks, perfect skin, luminous eyes and chic black dinner dress and high heels was not only commanding attention from half the men in the restaurant, the women were giving her the once-over, as well. But the worst, the very worst for Mary Grace, was that Alicia wore a look of love.

She wasn't sure if it was love she read in Richard's face, but he was certainly enraptured.

Mary Grace wasn't aware of rising from her chair, and she didn't hear Cynthia's pleas to stop and return to her seat. Mary Grace heard nothing but the pounding in her brain, like the sound of the mallet that pounded the foreclosure sign into her unwatered front yard. She heard the slamming sound of the back door to the Ryder truck when she'd moved the kids and herself to the South Side. She heard the sound of her attorney's phone when he hung up on her the day she realized she couldn't hang on to Richard any longer.

Mary Grace heard everything painful she could remember, the noise drowning out the sound of reason.

For the first time in years, Richard felt like himself again. He and Jay had talked for the past two days about doing a coventure project. Richard believed he had an angle that no one in the construction industry had thought of: he wanted to build houses that would sell at near cost to homeowners, a whole city of beautiful, well-made, well-designed houses at next to nothing. He'd blow the industry away.

Richard felt reborn that week, his depression was gone. He was back in the game and he was never, *ever* going to let anyone get in his way again.

Richard leaned over and whispered into Alicia's ear that he loved her. "You're the most beautiful woman—" He looked up and saw Mary Grace marching toward him like the gestapo. "Holy hell! What's she doing here?"

"She?" Alicia looked around innocently. Then she spotted Mary Grace. "Your wife?"

"Ex," he said, holding his breath.

Mary Grace walked right up to him and punched him in the stomach. "You have so goddamn much money you can bring your mistress to a fancy restaurant like this when your children are practically starving to death?"

Richard clutched his stomach, though the blow didn't hurt. "My children are not starving."

"No thanks to you!"

Richard saw Cynthia making her way toward Mary Grace.

"Mary Grace, calm down," he said. "You're making a scene."

Mary Grace's eyes were filling with angry, bitter tears. "Who gives a damn? I don't know these people."

"Well, I know some," he said, looking at Alicia.

"You asshole! You're worried about her sensibilities? Screw her!" Mary Grace shouted. "All I care is that you send me a check next week."

"Shit, that's all you've ever cared about. What do you need this time? Another ball gown?" he taunted her.

"Grow up, Richard! I've got dentists' bills, contacts for Penelope. Lawrence needs clothes. He's growing so fast I can't keep him in blue jeans, though I don't know how, he hardly eats anything. But a lot you care!"

Just then, Cynthia reached Mary Grace's side. "Hi, Richard." She took Mary Grace's arm. "C'mon, Mary Grace. It's time we were leaving."

Mary Grace yanked her arm away from her friend. "The hell I will. I was here first." She turned back to Richard. "Don't you and your lover think you should find another restaurant?" Mary Grace glared at him.

Richard glared back. "I don't think so."

Alicia stepped forward. "I think she's absolutely right, Richard. We can find something much better." She placed her hand on Richard's sleeve.

"I don't—"

Alicia tugged a bit more forcefully. "Leave her be, Richard. This isn't the time or the place."

Richard glanced at Alicia, then back at Mary Grace. "I see your point."

Putting his arm on Alicia's waist he escorted her out of the restaurant.

When they reached the car, Richard got into the passenger's seat. "You drive. My hands are shaking."

"All right." Alicia got in, turned on the ignition and backed out of the parking lot. They drove toward Camelback Mountain.

Taking deep breaths, Richard tried to calm himself. "My God, that woman is a bitch. Did you see her eyes? She looked half-crazed."

Alicia didn't respond.

"She's got her attorney breathing down my throat morning, noon and night and she's not satisfied. Shit!" He passed his hand through his thick blond hair. "Who the hell would ever think she'd be in Scottsdale?"

"Why is she here? I thought she was broke."

"Cynthia Folsum is loaded. They've been pals since high school. My guess is Cynthia is paying for the trip."

Alicia nodded. "I've done that for friends when they were really down."

"Fuck, Mary Grace isn't down. She's just waiting to strike . . . like a snake."

I wonder, Alicia thought. She thought about what Mary Grace had said about the kids—dentists', doctors' bills did have a way of mounting up. And she re-

membered thinking Lawrence was *awfully* thin for a boy
his age.

"Richard."

"Hmm?"

"Was that true what she said? About the bills and all."

"Who the hell knows? Her parents can buy half of
Chicago. They should be giving her money. They've got
more than I've got."

"I understand," Alicia said. "But you could at least
have some compassion for her." Alicia couldn't help
putting herself in Mary Grace's position.

As proud as she was of Richard for all he'd accomplished on this trip, she realized this encounter with
Mary Grace had caused his stature to drop a notch in her
eyes.

It was the first time Alicia had difficulty separating the
good guys from the bad guys.

26

Two months later, Richard made plans to move to Scottsdale. Once he'd formulated his idea, drawn up a business plan and an investor package, he contacted Jay Bradstone and offered him a partnership. Jay was a methodical man and Richard's idea seemed too risky for him. Jay declined to invest. Undaunted, Richard then spoke with his old private-investment banker he'd used when Bartlow Building was in its heyday. Together they raised the money he needed for his project.

Richard was so absorbed in his new venture, he barely realized Alicia's qualms about his leaving. She sat on the bed, watching him as he packed his tennis shorts next to his dress shirts.

"I'm going to miss you terribly," she said. "I've gotten used to having you around. Sharing our nightly talks."

He didn't look at her while he picked his favorite books from the book stacks along the bedroom wall. "But you don't understand, Alicia. We always talked about your business, your triumphs, your successes. Do you know what that was doing to me? Now I've got a chance to be on my own again."

"I didn't know it was that difficult."

He turned to her. "Don't take it that way. It wasn't. It's just that I've been dying inside. To live off you like Mary Grace lives off her parents was demeaning, but I felt I had no choice."

"Are you saying I was your meal ticket, Richard?" Alicia's anger rose to the top of her head.

Dropping to his knees next to her, he took her hands. "No, baby, it's not like that at all. I'm a man—I'm used to being the breadwinner. I never knew it before, but being out of work is the worst thing that can ever happen to anyone. Even the divorce wasn't this bad. I've felt worthless. And it's not your fault. It's no one's fault. It just was. Now I have a chance to make it again." He lowered his head and kissed her hands, her abdomen, her lips. "Honest to God, sweetheart, I really meant what I said when I told you that I wanted to buy you jewels. I want to give the world. You deserve it for putting up with me all this time."

Smiling, she touched his hair tenderly. "The only jewelry I want is a gold band."

He looked away from her quickly. "I'll marry you, Alicia. But not until the time is right. When I'm back on my feet."

"I can understand that. You want to feel good about yourself again."

"Yes, I do."

"I want that, too," she said, kissing him tenderly, soulfully. But he broke off the kiss.

"Hey, hey. No time for that now. I've got a lot to get done if I'm going to meet with the kids and get to that plane in the morning."

Alicia felt deeply hurt; she was surprised his attentions had come to mean so much to her. "Sure."

Just then, the doorbell rang.

Richard looked at his watch. "Where did the time go?"

Alicia went to the door and opened it. "Hello," she said. "I see you found the apartment without any trouble."

Lawrence walked through the doorway without acknowledging her presence, but Penelope glanced inside at the beautiful decor and smiled at Alicia. "You gave great directions and the doorman said we were supposed to come right up. That was okay, wasn't it?"

"Yes, fine." Alicia closed the door behind her. "Would you like a soda? I was going to make hot cocoa."

Lawrence looked up from the array of remote controls he was inspecting. "Cocoa is good. Say, do all these work?"

"Yes," Alicia said.

Lawrence whistled. "I've never seen so much shit in my life."

At that moment, Richard walked into the living room from the bedroom. "Kids! It's great to see ya!"

Penelope went running to her father's outstretched arms and hugged him. Lawrence didn't look up from the gadgets. He pushed a button and the television turned on. He picked up another and switched on the power to the VCR. The movie *Die Hard* began playing. "Far fuckin' out!"

"Watch your language, Lawrence," Richard barked.

Lawrence didn't pay any attention to his father as he picked up another remote control.

"Daddy," Penelope said, "I can't believe you're moving to Arizona. We'll never see you."

"Like we see him so fuckin' much now," Lawrence grumbled.

Richard frowned. Alicia moved into the kitchen area to start making cocoa.

"When can I come visit? I've never been to Arizona," Penelope asked excitedly.

"We've never been anywhere," Lawrence said, watching Alicia as she pulled out a copper-bottom pan to heat the milk.

She measured out a cup of sugar and a fourth cup of cocoa and sifted them through a strainer into the pan.

Lawrence shook his head. "Man, she doesn't know what she's doin'," he said to himself, but loud enough to be heard.

Penelope was still babbling a thousand questions at Richard. "Where are you staying? What's the phone number? Will you be back for Christmas?"

"No, I won't be home for the holidays."

"I don't see why you just couldn't wait till after Christmas and then go to Arizona." Penelope folded her arms across her chest.

Lawrence punched another button and turned on the CD player. "Because he ain't got no money for presents, fool," he said under his breath.

The sound from the television and the CD player was too loud, and Richard tried to speak over it. "There are papers that have to be signed before the end of the year. Frankly, Penelope, I'll be working day and night to get everything done. There's another developer who wants the same tract of land that I do. It's like we're in a race."

"I was hoping we could all be together for Christmas," Penelope said.

"What?" Alicia saw Lawrence finally look up at his father and sister. "And all sing damn carols together? Get real, sis."

"Oh, shut up!" Penelope leaned against Richard, holding his hand as if she were his girlfriend.

Richard moved away from her, pointing toward the kitchen. "Alicia made some Christmas cookies. Would you like some with your cocoa?"

Penelope shrugged and flopped down on the rose chintz sofa. She touched the fabric, then leaned back into the soft down cushions. "This is a really nice place you have here, Alicia. You buy all this stuff yourself?"

"Or did some dumb fuck like my father buy it for you?" Lawrence snickered.

Penelope kicked him with her Nike.

Ignoring his comment, Alicia put fat marshmallows into four matching porcelain mugs, then filled them with the hot steaming cocoa. "How's it going?" she asked Richard.

"Fine."

Alicia handed him two mugs, which he carried to the living room. She shook her head. As far as she could see, both these kids were case studies for a psychologist. There was enough anger in the room to blow up the building.

She rinsed out the pan and put it in the dishwasher. Then, picking up the last two mugs, she started toward the living room. Richard was at the television, turning down the volume, Penelope was helping herself to a cookie and no one was watching Lawrence except her as he deliberately poured half his cup of cocoa on the white carpet.

"Oh, dear," Lawrence said with fake dread. "I've spilled my cocoa."

Alicia rushed back to the kitchen area and grabbed sponges, cleaner and wet two dish towels. She wanted to ram the sponges down Lawrence's throat. She couldn't help wondering if Mary Grace had put him up to his little act of vandalism or if he'd concocted the idea himself.

She cleaned up the spill as best she could while Richard took Lawrence by the scruff of the neck to the dining room table and reprimanded him as if he were still a child.

Alicia noticed that none of this turmoil seemed to faze Penelope. She was wandering around the apartment, looking at every piece of artwork, every candle, every silk flower. It looked as if she was taking some kind of inventory.

Richard leaned close to his son. "What's the matter with you? You're acting like a surly brat."

Lawrence ground his teeth. "What the fuck do you care?"

"And since when did that become your favorite word?"

Lawrence looked his father in the eye. "You didn't answer my question."

Richard sighed. "You didn't answer mine."

"When are you going to quit screwing this bitch and get back with Mom?" His words were loud enough for Alicia to hear.

"I'm moving on with my life, Lawrence. I suggest you do the same," his father said with restrained anger.

"Mom says you been boffin' her since day one. Is she right?"

"I didn't meet Alicia until after I filed for divorce."

Lawrence snarled at his father. "I don't believe you."

"It's the truth. I can't help what you do or don't believe. It's the truth. I didn't get divorced because of another woman. I got divorced because—"

"Because Mom was a bitch?"

"Yes."

Alicia couldn't believe what she'd heard.

Lawrence shot out of the chair. "I'm outta here, man!" He headed for the front door. "You comin', sis?"

"No. And you're not leaving. I have the keys, remember?"

Lawrence crossed his arms over his chest as Penelope walked up to her father. "I want to leave," he repeated.

Penelope glared at him. "I said, I'm not ready yet." Turning to her father, she said, "Listen, Daddy, now that you're going to Arizona and you won't be living with her—" she jerked her head sideways indicating Alicia "—I was thinking how great it would be if I came to live with you."

Richard's jaw dropped. "What? Are you out of your mind?"

Alicia could see Penelope was taken aback. "Out of my... No. I just wanted to live with you. Be with you. Spend some time together."

"Forget it."

Penelope's eyes filled with tears. "Daddy...I just..."

"Look, ordinarily it would take three men and five lifetimes to accomplish what I want to do in two months. I can't have some kid following me around."

"I'm not a little kid! I could get a job during the day. Receptionist work or learn computers or something. Jesus, Daddy! I just want you to love me!"

Before Richard could answer, Lawrence stepped in. "Forget it. He won't take you. Let's go."

Richard looked at Penelope. "I do love you."

"But not enough to live with me," she said flatly. Turning on her heel, she walked out the door with Lawrence.

Visibly stunned, Richard stood stock-still. "Holy shit. What was that all about?"

Alicia couldn't believe her ears. "It was about a young girl begging for attention from her father. Take my advice, Richard, as soon as you get to Scottsdale, pick out a weekend in January and fly that girl down to visit you."

"But that could cost—"

"I don't care if you don't eat for a week, she needs help. And Lawrence needs it even more." Alicia frowned as she looked at the stained carpet. Odd, the spilled cocoa looked like dried blood. Well, why not? Alicia thought. There had been some bloodletting here tonight.

Her face was stern when she looked back at him. "You're so self-absorbed sometimes, Richard. Just remember, these are people you're dealing with. Lives, hearts, heads. They need time and attention. You were lucky with me because I'm pretty self-sufficient and have had an enormous amount of work."

"Yeah, I was lucky." His tone was cynical.

Suddenly, something in Alicia's brain clicked. "Lucky or smart?"

Avoiding her eyes, he started to walk away. She grabbed his arm and forced him to look at her. "What's the matter with you?" he asked.

"Tell me I've got this all wrong, Richard. Tell me that you really did love me. Tell me you weren't using me as some kind of crutch until things turned around for you. Tell me that my suspicions are crazy."

Richard's expression hardened. "I'll tell you anything you want to hear. It's always worked in the past."

Alicia thought for an instant the world had come to an end. *Her* world, anyway. Shock bolted through her body. "You planned this."

He laughed derisively. "Come now, Alicia. You aren't that naive. You were with me in Scottsdale when this happened. It was a fluke. My lucky break."

"But all along you planned to leave me when things went your way. You never intended to marry me, did you?"

Richard shook his head. "I was married to Mary Grace. Once was enough. That's a mistake I'll never make again."

"Get out!" She began pushing him. "Get your shit and get out!" She shoved him so hard the second time, he nearly fell.

"Take it easy!"

"I *am* taking it easy! I'd like to kill you! Now get out of here! Get out of my life and *never* come back!"

Richard went to the bedroom, grabbed his suitcase and walked to the front door. "Don't worry. I wouldn't dream of it," he said and was gone.

Alicia locked the dead bolt and slid the chain in place. Sinking into the sofa, she hugged a pillow against her chest. "Bastard! How could I not have seen it coming? How could he be that good an actor? How could I be so foolish?"

Alicia laid her head back and began to cry. She cried till long past midnight when she finally took a hot bath, drank a long strong brandy and went to bed. She didn't sleep.

The next morning, she told Sally what had happened. "Richard's an asshole," Sally said. "Don't ever give him so much as the time of day."

Alicia never did.

THE MISTRESS

27

Michelle Windsong realized she'd been as naive as a newborn babe before coming to Chicago for Richard Bartlow's funeral, but seeing her name and face plastered across the front pages of the tabloids in O'Hare airport forced her to grow faster than Alice eating the magic mushroom. Michelle knew that half the world believed her to be an immoral gold digger, while the other half believed she had a father fixation. Nothing could have been further from the truth.

Michelle was neither a wanton nor a teenager. In a week, she would be twenty-six years old, with a growing massage-therapy business in Scottsdale. She prided herself on her training, her skills and most of all, her God-given talent for healing the sick. Even though Richard had made the cover of *Time* magazine, none of the reporters had bothered with her. She wasn't news and had Richard lived, no one would have ever paid any attention to her affair with the only man she was destined to love.

Michelle believed her love for Richard was spiritual, pure and born of accumulated centuries of past lives, in which they had loved and lost each other. She believed Richard was her soul mate. And as the other half of herself, she knew he wouldn't intentionally hurt anyone, though his stories about his ex-wife, children and ex-lover were fraught with pain and anger.

She remembered the first day she met Richard at the sports-massage clinic in Phoenix where she worked as a masseuse. Richard had thrown out his lower back playing golf. His friend, Dennis Maitland, a young attorney, had rushed him from the eighth hole at Camelback Golf Club to the clinic, which Dennis often frequented.

Richard was naked when Michelle first met him—naked and facedown on the massage table. He groaned as she walked into the room.

"Hello, Mr. Bartlow. My name is Michelle and I will be working with you today to clear your body and ease your pain. My assistant tells me you've pulled a muscle."

"Goddamn right! I don't have time or patience for bullshitting around. Just get to work."

Michelle stepped back from the table. "So much negativity isn't good for either of us, Mr. Bartlow."

"Call me Richard. Just please make the pain stop."

Regular massage would take too long, Michelle decided. Besides, he needed something stronger. Rubbing her palms together, she closed her eyes. She mentally focused her own body's energy into her hands in order to take the pain out of Richard's body. She placed her hands on Richard's back just above his waist. She slowly ran them down to the lumbar region where she felt the hot spot. She kept her eyes closed during the entire procedure.

"I want you to breathe in through your nose, Richard, to the count of ten, hold for four seconds, then expel through your mouth to the count of seven. With your eyes closed, I want you to focus on the pain in your back. With your mind, surround the pain with golden light."

"I don't want any cockamamy bullshit about lights," he said angrily. "I want a massage. And when you do it, dig deep. I can take it."

Michelle kept her eyes closed. She envisioned white light around herself, then used the same process to put

white light around Richard, breaking down his wall of
negativity. In her mind's eye she was absorbing his pain
into her hands; she could see her hands going past the
pain in his back to the true origin of the tight muscle. She
was traveling inside him now. Moving past the tight ball
of muscle, she became one with the flow of blood in his
body. She could see herself moving swiftly up his spine,
easing out the tightness, the rigidity, the burdens of fear
he carried on his shoulders. She splayed her hands over
the terrain like magic wands and dispersed the pain. She
moved further inside him, cleansing his organs of fear
and hopelessness, melting his feelings of isolation. Then
she found him inside his heart; an uncharted and unused portion of his body.

She found a little boy there, nearly frozen with loneliness and crying. Telepathically, she spoke to him,
putting her arms around him and holding him close to
her breast. He clung to her as he wept. She told him she
loved him, that he had nothing to fear. She would protect him and care for him and teach him how to love. He
would grow in wisdom and one day, he would use his
heart as it was meant to be used. Michelle stayed with
the little boy until she was satisfied he had grown in
confidence. He smiled at her and told her that he trusted
her.

She left Richard's body, returning to her own. She
opened her eyes. Her hands pressed deeply into Richard's tanned flesh.

"What is this . . . acupressure?" Richard asked, his
voice softer now.

"You could call it that." She smiled to herself. "Keep
breathing, Richard."

"I won't—"

"You will," she interrupted with gentle command.
"You will do everything I tell you and more."

Richard breathed in. He breathed out. She could tell the pain had disappeared as he was able to breathe more deeply, filling his lungs to capacity.

"I want you to see yourself on a grassy hill filled with colorful field flowers," she said.

"Uh-huh," he barely whispered.

"It is the most perfect day," she said, closing her eyes and seeing it with him.

"I don't . . ."

"Breathe, Richard." He did as she ordered. "Start walking down the hill, and as you do, you will see a golden cup filled with an incredible liquid light. Take the cup and drink it. Drink. See all the lights flowing into the cup and drink until you cannot drink anymore."

"This is nuts."

"Drink and breathe." She pressed again on his back, breathing along with him. With her mind, she keyed into his thoughts and could see that he was doing as she told him. She could see him drinking the light and filling himself, filling the caves within his heart. He drank as if he'd never drink again. Finally, she saw him put the cup down on the grass again.

"The cup was filled with unconditional love, Richard. You have healed yourself. There is no more pain."

Michelle opened her eyes, shaking her hands to rid them of his pain. She went to the table in the corner and covered her hands and arms with eucalyptus oil. Then she rubbed off the oil with a terry-cloth towel. She turned back to Richard, who was sitting up with ease.

His face was devoid of lines or stress. He looked no more than thirty, though she knew from his chart that he was forty-eight. He smiled at her. "You're an angel."

Michelle suddenly dropped the towel. Those blue eyes were the same blue eyes she'd seen in countless dreams all her life. She would know that smile anywhere. The

sound of his voice, when not filled with anger and bitterness, was the sound she'd heard in her meditations.
She wanted to tell him that he was her soul mate, but she
didn't. He had a lot to learn still.

"Angels are better at this than I am," she said, shaking her head.

"I wouldn't be too sure about that. I can't believe what
you just did. How did you do that? Did you study in
China or something?"

"I've never been farther north than Sedona where I
was born, nor farther south than Phoenix. I did have a
Hopi friend or two, though."

"Oh." He nodded.

"I can give you a massage since we still have forty-five
minutes left."

Richard spun around to look at the clock. "You did
all that in only fifteen minutes?"

"Ten. We've been chatting." She poured rose oil on her
hands and rubbed them together. She noticed that he
could not take his eyes off her hands.

"If you're not an angel, you're a witch, then." He
looked up at her with a look of confusion and doubt.

"Some would say it's all the same—just a different
point of view. Lie down on your back, Richard. I want
to fix your face."

"What's the matter with my face?"

She passed her rose-scented fingers under his nose
then pressed firmly as she ran them down the slopes of
his nose and onto his cheekbones. She circled his eyes
and pressed her fingers into his temples, the hinge points
of his jaw and along his chin. Richard's tensions melted.
She erased the gnomes of confusion from his eyebrows.
"You have allergies, don't you, Richard?"

"Yes. How did you know?"

"Your eyelids are swollen and you have a discharge in the corners, usually from hay fever. The rose oil will ease the allergies. Rose is good for nervous dispositions like yours, too." She continued gently stroking his face.

"I'm not nervous," he tried to argue.

Michelle knew that rose scent was also an aphrodisiac for women, and when the urge to touch Richard's chest and solar plexus hit her, she fought it with a vengeance. She told herself she was reacting to the rose scent and not to Richard. She must go slowly with him—he wasn't used to her ways, her kind of knowledge. But he would see her again. And again. They would be lovers. She could see it in their futures.

Michelle was silent as she finished Richard's massage and he was nearly asleep when she was done. She lowered the lights and covered him with a blanket. "I'll be outside when you feel like getting up, Richard. Take your time dressing."

Richard felt brand-new as he got up from the table and dressed. He went to the receptionist and booked two more massages, requesting Michelle's services. Just as he was about to leave, she emerged from another massage room. She shook his hand.

"I was delighted to be of help to you, Richard," she said.

He looked into her shining blue eyes. She was beautiful and very strong for someone so young. He found himself drawn to her, an odd feeling since normally, when he met a woman, he was the one with power, with magnetism. Michelle was different from anyone he'd ever met. He couldn't imagine her ever falling under someone else's power. Instantly, he was both challenged and fascinated by her.

"Are you allowed to have dinner with a client?" he asked.

"Yes."

"How about tomorrow night? Thomaso's? Say, seven-thirty?"

"That would be great," she said, walking back toward the room she'd just left.

Thomaso's was romantic and elegant, the kind of restaurant Michelle had never frequented in Scottsdale or Phoenix. Working her way through massage-therapy school had left little time for dates, even if she'd been so inclined, which she hadn't. Ever since she was a little girl, Michelle knew she must wait for her soul mate to come along. She was overjoyed that Richard had appeared in her life—his presence was like an affirmation of all that she believed in.

The only problem was that her beliefs were poles apart from Richard's experiences and thoughts.

"You're nuts," he said as the waiter served Michelle a vegetable lasagna and him veal oscar. "There's no such thing as past lives."

"Of course there is. It's the only logical explanation for our existence, for the bad things that happen to good people and to the unusual twists and turns of fate. There's no such thing as coincidences, Richard. Only divine paths being followed. If you could skim the bitterness from your eyes, you'd see life more clearly."

"Look, I believe in bank accounts with a lot of money in them. I believe there are good restaurants as long as I have room on my Visa card. I believe in movie theaters with six screens and bookstores that serve cappuccino. Anything is possible in this life. It's this other life you talk about that has holes in it."

"Astral planes, Richard, higher planes. I have many gifts besides healing. I'm psychic. I've been able to talk to my spirit guides since I was a child. I see auras. I know how to use astrology to my advantage."

"Sounds like one big garbage dump to me." But by the way she looked at him, she could tell he was enchanted. "Jesus, you're beautiful," he said, putting down his fork and reaching across the table for her hand. "I don't know what it is about you . . . I'm old enough to be your father. I should have my head examined."

She smiled at him and squeezed his hand. "We're soul mates, Richard. It's so simple, if you'd just accept the truth."

He shook his head exasperatedly. "You're young. You have a lot to learn."

"You're the young soul. I'm a very old soul. I have much to teach you."

He caressed the palm of her hand with his thumb, then pulled it to his lips to kiss it. "We'll see about that."

Michelle told Richard she loved him that very same night, and when he laughed at her she wasn't hurt or wounded. She was wiser than he and knew that he was only guarding his feelings. She wanted him to know that what they were about to share was not an ordinary love.

Three nights later, they went to dinner at a Mexican restaurant off Camelback Road, then straight back to Richard's apartment afterward. His furnishings were meager and cheap: there was only a couch, one wing chair, a cardboard coffee table, a used dinette set and a used double bed outfitted with cheap sheets she'd seen at one of the discount retail stores. Still, it was clean and quite neat. "Taj Mahal it's not," he said apologetically.

He'd barely closed the door when he pulled Michelle into his arms and kissed her. His kiss was quick, hard and lacking passion. There was an urgency about him, as if he needed sexual release. Michelle believed he needed emotional release more but that he was too afraid to allow it.

Slowly, she encircled his neck with her arms. Putting her hand on his nape, she pulled him gently toward her. She suckled his mouth, forcing him to feel the sensations she was feeling. His body was rigid, his shoulders tense and his arms filled with caution. He would not abandon control.

She moved her body against his, molding her young curves into his hard chest. Pressing her slim hips into his pelvis, she found some parts of him that could not resist her for long. His erection was hard. Her lips curved into a smile beneath his kiss.

"You want me," she said seductively.

"Too much," he groaned, forcing his tongue between her lips.

His arms were incredibly well developed and they clamped around her like iron bands, locking her next to him. She could feel his strong heart slamming against his chest wall.

"Richard...you are mine and no one else's," she said, kissing him back with explosive passion.

Michelle believed she'd found the reason for her existence in Richard. All her work, her study, the miracles she performed for her clients meant nothing if she didn't have anyone to share her triumphs and heartaches with. Michelle had waited for Richard to come to her since she was a child. She didn't care if he were sixty...seventy. She would love him all the same. He was herself; she was him.

"I love you, Richard," she said as they sank to the floor.

Richard said nothing as his hand slid up underneath her T-shirt, along her slim rib cage to her small breast. He was amazed at how tight and firm her nipples were. He'd barely touched her, had only begun to kiss her, and she was ready for him. He'd never met such a willing partner before. The thought excited him beyond comprehension.

He slid his hand beneath the waistband of her shorts, over her flat belly to the furry mound between her legs. He deftly plied the warm lips apart, found her bud and it, too, was hard, swollen and aching for his touch. He teased her with knowing strokes, and her hips began to arch to his touch.

He was breathing heavily, panting as if he'd been running a marathon. He couldn't believe how excited her eagerness made him. Her heat stoked his heat. Slipping his fingers inside her, he found her incredibly wet and ready as she pushed herself down on him. She groaned when his fingers found her maidenhead.

She was a virgin, Richard told himself. A virgin! A twenty-six-year-old virgin! He couldn't decide if he felt like a lecher or her mentor.

He opted for the latter as he yanked off her shorts and T-shirt and stared at her young body. How different she was from Mary Grace and Alicia's womanly curves. But the look in her eyes was imploring and mesmerizing, it was if she were commanding him with her thoughts to take her. To show her what love was all about.

In one quick movement, he stripped off his clothes and straddled his very hard erection between her legs. "Open your legs, little one. Spread them far apart," he said as he moved his hands under her small rounded buttocks and lifted her to his penis. Slowly, he entered her. Her skin was flushed nearly crimson and her arms were trembling with need as she reached out to him, pulling him to her chest as he slipped himself into her tightness.

"I have to hurt you, Michelle. I don't want to, but I must."

"I know. I've been waiting so long for you . . . all my life."

Richard couldn't believe what she was saying, yet he knew it must be true. It amazed him that anyone would think he was the man of their dreams, but he was willing to go along with it, as long as it lasted.

He pushed his penis against her barrier and when she screamed he knew he'd broken through. Then he slid himself deeper into her and found a hot sweetness he never thought he find the equal to again.

Her arms held him possessively. Her lips curved around his clavicle and her tongue buried itself between his shoulder and throat. She kissed the pulse point on his neck and he thought he'd go through the ceiling with desire.

He stroked her torrid pulsing walls with his shaft again and again until he heard her breathing mount to a fever pitch. Her entire body tense, stilled and then exploded with a climactic cry.

"God! Oh, God!" he yelled as he ejaculated into her, spewing himself against her throbbing walls.

"Richard, I love you," she said sincerely.

Richard nearly collapsed on top of her. He'd never felt so connected to anyone in his life. He didn't understand it. He'd been in love with Alicia, or so he'd thought. He barely knew Michelle, but already he felt protective of her, even loving toward her. He'd nearly told her that he loved her, but how could that be? They were strangers. To him, she was practically a child, with a child's body—something that had never been appealing to him. And yet, he felt he knew her body better than his own.

It was as if he'd had an internal map of every pulse point and sensitive place on her body. He knew he could lift his finger and place it on the small of her back inside the dimples on either side of her spine and make her shiver. If he kissed the crook between her upper thigh and buttocks, her nipples would harden. The backs of her knees were sensitive to his stroking and the tip of her anklebone would respond to his kiss. He knew her, but he didn't know how.

Michelle was the strangest, most enigmatic woman he'd ever met. As he looked into her compelling eyes, he wanted to know more about her. He couldn't accept her explanation that they were soul mates, but he did know he found her fascinating.

She looked at him. "Someday, you will tell me that you love me, too."

"Maybe," he said hesitantly, not understanding why the word *yes* was nearly on the tip of his tongue.

28

Richard and Michelle sat poolside at the Paradise Valley Resort having lunch. Michelle knew Richard loved to lunch in elegant surroundings because it took his mind off the ugliness of his small and sparsely furnished apartment. He liked to think of himself as already having made it back on top. He was struggling with his housing project, but he was making long, sure strides.

Michelle, though, wasn't making the kind of progress she wanted with the enlightenment program she'd devised for her soul mate. She wanted him to rise to her level of wisdom, but instead he concentrated too much on her physical being. Today, he couldn't see much of it—she had on a gauzy crinkled cotton blouse over a matching broomstick skirt. She wore no makeup, only a light application of mascara and clear lip gloss. To protect her flawless white skin from the sun, she'd tied a floppy sun hat under her chin with a matching piece of gauze. She wore number forty-five sun block on every inch of exposed skin.

"Wouldn't you like to know about our past lives together?" she asked. "I've seen over a dozen of them in my regressions."

"Look, kid," he said, tearing his eyes from her breasts. "First you're born, then you live, then you die. That's it."

"That's not it," she replied patiently.

"I suppose my ex-wife and Alicia were in your dreams, too."

"Of course, we all have karma together. Before you were born, you chose to finish out your lessons with them. That's why I keep telling you that it's wrong to carry this bitterness and anger with you. You only hurt yourself and you make yourself sick."

"Mary Grace was a bitch—*is* a bitch. All she cares about is my money. She blames me for her... situation right now. When I went bankrupt, we lost the house. She and the kids had to move in with her parents, which to Mary Grace was eating crow since her mother always hated my guts. I would have liked to bail them out, but I was bust myself. Life hasn't been a bowl of cherries for me, you know." Richard looked off to the distance. "Then there was Alicia. She saved me during that whole bankruptcy scene. She fed me, bathed me, nurtured me like a mother. She was so confident. I felt like I'd been run over by a tank back then. I fed off her energy. I used her, I admit it. When this opportunity came along, I had to take it."

"So, you did just what you did to Mary Grace? You shut her out of your heart?"

"Yeah."

"How did you do it, exactly?" Michelle asked thoughtfully.

"When she was home, I would work at the computer. When she worked during the day, I slept by the pool so I could stay up all night. I made certain our paths didn't cross that much. In short, I made certain she didn't have a chance with me."

Richard balled his napkin and tossed it angrily onto his unfinished lunch. He put his elbow on the arm of the patio chair. "Look, I don't want to talk about this anymore."

Michelle was unaware there were tears in her eyes. "So many lives...so many broken hearts. I feel sorry for all of you."

Richard shook his head morosely, then passed his hand over the errant lock of hair that fell across his forehead. He looked back at her. "You're not jealous at all, are you?"

"Why should I be? You had karma with them. Now, your time is with me. The trouble with you, Richard, is that you only see the street under your feet. Your vision is narrow. To make the right decisions in the present which create your future, you must understand the past."

"None of this shit is logical," he said with exasperation.

"But logic limits your creative side. It's important to achieve balance."

A hot breeze lifted a lock of Michelle's hair. Richard smiled sensuously. "Are you finished? Can we go back to my apartment so that I can take off that blouse of yours that is driving me crazy and bury my face in your breasts?"

"If you weren't my soul mate, I'd say you only wanted me for sex."

"What's the matter with that?" He grinned seductively, rose and paid the bill.

Richard's heart was attacked while he was talking on the phone in the mobile home he'd converted into an office on the job site of the first phase of three hundred houses that were being constructed. Feeling a pain in his left arm, he passed the receiver to his right hand. He held his breath, willing the pain away. He was about to close a deal that would tie up enough land for him to build another fifteen hundred houses. Jack Billingsly, his attorney in Chicago, had helped raise the last two million dollars he needed.

"Jack—" Richard sucked in his breath "—you're . . . a wizard."

"Richard? What's the matter? You sound funny," Jack said.

"It's nothing. When will the money be transferred?" Another pain shot down Richard's arm. His eyes rolled in his head and he stifled a groan.

"In the morning. It's all set. I'll fly down over the weekend. We could play tennis . . ."

"I don't . . ." Suddenly, the room turned black and he realized he was having a heart attack. He couldn't . . . wouldn't let this happen.

"Richard? What's going on? Something *is* wrong." Jack's voice was filled with concern.

Another pain shot down Richard's arm and crossed his chest. He looked over at Heather, his secretary.

"Heather . . ." Richard dropped the receiver. He put his hand to his chest, feeling as if an elephant had sat on him. He couldn't breathe.

"Richard!" Jack's voice shouted from the dangling receiver. "Richard!"

The last thing Richard remembered was hearing Heather scream.

Michelle was by his side when Richard awoke in the hospital. He tried to speak, but his mouth was dry. "What are you doing here?"

"I love you, Richard," Michelle said, starting to cry.

Richard closed his eyes. "I don't . . . want to hear it."

Michelle placed her hand over Richard's heart, believing she could feel him healing. It didn't matter if he believed in her powers, only that she did.

Michelle visited Richard every morning before work and every night until the nurses asked her to leave. She stayed much longer than most visitors in ICU, but several of the nurses took private healing lessons from Michelle and so they bent the rules for her. They believed Richard would heal a hundred times faster with her than without her.

The day Richard was scheduled to leave, Michelle got off work early to drive him home. When she arrived, she found Dennis Maitland and Richard discussing something they obviously were uncomfortable about her hearing because the minute she walked into the room, they immediately quit talking and their serious faces were replaced with fake smiles.

The previous month, she and Richard had moved in together to a new three-bedroom condominium in the luxurious New Gainey Ranch development. Richard had fallen in love with the place at first sight. There were plenty of tennis courts, swimming pools and walking trails to keep him fit. They hadn't realized it at the time, but those amenities could mean the difference between life and death for Richard. He'd always been an athletic person, but lately his stress level had been as high as the stratosphere and the doctors had told Michelle that if Richard didn't do something to reduce his stress and improve his eating habits, the next heart attack could be fatal.

Michelle now worried that the beautiful condo—with the saltillo-tile terrace and adobe balcony walls that looked out onto the desert sunsets—might be too extravagant for them. She told him they didn't need a formal dining room, large kitchen with Sub-Zero appliances, dining nook, living room, family room and three and a half baths. But Richard assured her *he* did.

Comfortable surroundings made him feel secure. "Poverty makes me nuts," he'd told her.

"It was nice of Dennis to visit you," Michelle said as she flopped onto the king-size bed, clad only in her Jockey athletic bra and panties.

"Yeah, I just wish he had good news," Richard said, taking off his shirt and throwing it in the wicker clothes hamper.

"Oh, Richard, you don't need any bad news right now. The stress . . ."

"Look, kiddo, it's no big deal. Just my ex-wife making waves again. Nothing new. Same old song for her. I'll deal with it in my own way."

"And Dennis is helping you do that?" she asked as he crawled over to her.

He nuzzled his face in the crook of her neck. "He's a godsend. Let's not talk about attorneys or hospitals, okay? I want to remember how good it is to be alive."

Putting her arms around his neck, she pulled him down on top of her. She luxuriated in the weight of him, how his chest pressed into her. "And I'm just the person to help you, right?"

"Right." His blue eyes twinkled as he slanted his mouth over hers. "I've never told anyone this, Michelle, but I'm terrified of being alone. I need you," he said seductively.

But do you *want* me? Michelle thought as she kissed him back.

Richard called his new residential community Bart's Land and as construction started he told Michelle he wanted to learn how to eliminate the stress in his life. She taught him how to meditate, how to breath in prana and exhale negativity. She told him that forgiveness was the key to happiness but Richard didn't listen, choosing instead to make love.

Richard wrote to his children and told them that once his houses began selling, he would send his much-overdue child support. They did not write back.

In January, Richard was astounded that his lots were selling as soon as they were marked for sale. The model home was finished in time for the February showcase of homes, and by the time the week was out, every house and condominium was spoken for. Richard had money.

In March, the foundations were poured on the first three dozen houses. Richard scrambled for more construction crews. He called Jack in Chicago for advice and hired out-of-work carpenters and plumbers from Minnesota, Wisconsin and Illinois. The frames went up in days.

At night, Richard stood on the balcony of his own condominium at New Gainey Ranch looking to the south where he could see Bart's Land becoming a reality.

The builders' association touted Richard as a "man of vision." Since one of the local journalists was also a stringer for *Time* magazine, he sent the story to the magazine's managing editor at the magazine along with several dozen photographs of the man, his land and the artist's rendering of his dream to provide housing at near-wholesale costs to the public.

The *Time* editor, Alan O'Grady was stunned at Richard Bartlow's wacky and magnanimous project in Scottsdale. It didn't hurt that Richard had recently undergone a heart attack, a divorce and bankruptcy—his was the perfect underdog story that Americans loved. He dispatched his best journalists to Scottsdale to dig up the story on Bart's Land.

When the journalists told their editor Richard Bartlow's story was fine for *People* magazine but wasn't earth-shattering enough for *Time*, Alan O'Grady's Irish temper flared.

"No reporter is going to tell me what is news and what isn't!" he barked to his secretary. "You tell those guys to bring me the story of the decade or they're fired! When I get through with Richard Bartlow, the country will think he's the Second goddamn Coming!"

By October, Richard Bartlow was a national phenomenon. Alan O'Grady made certain Richard's story was picked up by CNN, the wires and even arranged for a "Today Show" interview with Richard. O'Grady knew that Richard's handsome face and charismatic smile were meant for television. And he was right. Richard won scores of fans after his interviews and thousands of requests for near-cost homes came pouring in to Richard's offices.

Richard could see that Scottsdale was only the beginning for him. He could build similar communities in Los Angeles, Kansas City, Seattle, Dallas, Chicago—anywhere in the country builders were taking advantage of the public. He realized he was changing the face of the nation.

Mary Grace realized Richard was going to be rich. Very rich. She met with her divorce attorney and arranged for a judgment to be filed against Richard. She wanted all his back-due child support immediately. The courts froze his bank accounts and he was denied access to his assets. Worst of all, she was filing criminal charges against him. If he didn't pay the back child support, he would go to jail.

Just the thought of incarceration made his blood run cold. It galled him to admit it, but Mary Grace had gotten her revenge: she had shut him down.

Then, one morning after playing golf with Dennis Maitland, Richard dropped dead of a heart attack in his New Gainey Ranch condominium while Michelle was at work.

Dennis called Michelle while the coroner's ambulance was carting away Richard's body on a gurney.

"Michelle, this is Dennis. I have some bad news. And I apologize for telling you this over the phone, but it can't be helped."

Michelle felt her blood turn to ice. She knew something was dreadfully wrong, but nothing in the world could have prepared her for what Dennis eventually told her. "What is it, Dennis?"

"I'm at your condo . . . Richard and I came back here after our game this morning. It was so hot...I guess that and the fact that he's been under a strain with all this publicity lately. . . ."

"Dennis, what's wrong?" Michelle nearly screamed as alarm bells sounded in her head.

"Richard's dead."

"What?" Michelle's hands were shaking so hard she had to use both of them to hold the receiver to her ear. "This is a mistake . . ." He's my soul mate, she wanted to say. We were supposed to spend the rest of our lives together. I've lived all my life just to be with Richard. He was beginning to understand me...beginning to love me. I just know it!

Tears streamed down Michelle's numb cheeks. She could still smell his scent on her—he'd made love to her before she left for work, and she'd been running late and she'd barely had time to put on clothes, much less wash her hair and shower.

How could this be? she asked herself, asked her angels and guides. Where in the universe could she find meaning for this? She was put on earth to love Richard. He was put on earth to love her!

How could her meditations, her visions be wrong? Had she misinterpreted her dreams? And if Richard was dead, why was she not being visited by his astral body?

"He's not dead," she said quietly.

Dennis hesitated before saying, "Michelle, I know this is a shock. But the coroner's assistant is here now. They're taking him down to the morgue. I have a signed death certificate."

Michelle clenched her teeth. The world was filled with idiots! "He's *not* dead. Richard would never die on me! Never. He can't die yet!"

"Why not?"

She burst into tears. She could hardly talk over the burning lump in her throat. "He hasn't . . . told me that he loves me yet."

Sam and Summer Windsong received the hysterical phone call from their daughter at two-thirty in the afternoon. They got in their car immediately and drove the hour and a half to Scottsdale from Sedona, where they had made their home since the mid-sixties.

Sam and Summer had always credited themselves with practically inventing the sixties' flower children. At one time, they'd been famous for it. Summer was the streaked blonde who sat topless on Sam's shoulders in the photographs taken at Woodstock which appeared in nearly every newspaper and magazine in America. It was at Woodstock that Mary Frances Ridwell changed her name to Summer and finally married Sam Wineberg. The ceremony was a civil barefoot one with mostly strangers in attendance. Earlier that same day, Sam had his name changed to Windsong to please Summer. Sam didn't care—he would do anything to please Summer.

In 1966, at the age of seventeen, both Sam and Mary Frances had felt misunderstood by parents and teachers. They wanted to expand their consciousness and see the world; they wanted to have sex.

They adopted the free love movement as their credo, dropped out of school and left home. They painted Mary Frances's baby blue Volkswagen Beetle with roses, tulips and daisies and left Kansas City to find themselves in the streets of Haight-Ashbury in San Francisco. While Sam begged for money, Summer handed out flowers she'd stolen from the city's parks. "Flower power" was their motto that first summer, but when autumn arrived, they realized they couldn't live outdoors any longer. They took odd jobs waiting tables and at a car wash. They were happy and carefree.

They marched for the end of the Vietnam War and protested for equal rights. Summer burned her bra and never put one on again. Sam smoked a little grass and Summer hand-painted blouses and vests that she sold on street corners. Sam learned to paint flames and racing stripes on cars and vans at an auto-body shop. Summer grew herbs in pots and blended her own teas. They made love incessantly because Summer had gotten the Pill at a free clinic. Life was grand.

By the end of 1968, hard drugs had moved into Haight-Ashbury and the fun had turned gruesome. Kids they knew overdosed on acid and wound up in psychiatric hospitals. Drug pushers and dealers stalked the streets at night and the flower children moved inside to snort cocaine. Martin Luther King, Jr., was assassinated, the cops beat kids on the streets of Chicago, Bobby Kennedy died in a hotel kitchen and Kent State put a lid on the whole shebang. Sam and Summer left California and moved to Sedona.

They realized many things about themselves in those few short years, including that they were both blessed with incredible artistic talent. Summer took up pottery and sculpture and Sam began to paint on canvas instead of cars. They sold their creations on the streets of Phoenix until a gallery owner, Marion Lyon, discovered them and put their works in her gallery. Sam and Summer drew a steady client following year after year.

When Michelle was born in 1970, Summer nearly lost her life struggling to give birth naturally. Fortunately for her, her doctor believed in cesarean sections. He did not believe Summer, however, when she told him she had left her body and had spoken to an angel. Summer tried to tell several others of her experience, but no one was listening.

Summer became fascinated with the world beyond. She read everything she could find on psychic abilities and how to hone these talents. She was living in the right place: Sedona, Phoenix and Scottsdale had become a mecca for those seeking answers to spiritual questions. From New Age escapists to guru con men, Sam and Summer met a lot of kooks. But they also found many truths.

Sam and Summer raised Michelle to explore the world within her own mind, heart and soul. Not wanting Michelle to be bound by the limits of state-ordained educational curriculums, Summer taught her daughter at home until it was time for her to go to high school.

Michelle struggled to make good grades in high school because she wanted to go on to college, and she managed to get accepted to the University of Arizona. But she dropped out after two years, knowing in her heart she'd been gifted with healing hands and wanting to use them. She went to massage-therapy school, studied acupressure and took classes in chiropractic. She obtained her state license when she was twenty-one.

Sam and Summer were proud of their daughter. Not for a single minute of any day had Michelle ever caused them to worry. Until she met Richard Bartlow.

As they raced to be with their daughter, Sam remembered the first time they met Richard Bartlow. He and Summer had come to Phoenix to deliver his new landscape collection to the gallery. Sam was discovering that fame, even the small measure he was accumulating, had its price. Long, intensive and challenging workdays were becoming the norm in his life, but oftentimes he would think back to their first days in Sedona when Michelle was a baby and life had been simple. Now, in order to keep up with the demand for his work, Sam found it necessary to seclude himself from the outside world for months at a time. He would work eighteen and twenty hours at a stretch, Summer the only contact he would allow. He couldn't afford to break his concentration.

This visit to Phoenix was important to Sam. He was truly looking forward to spending time with his daughter. He knew that Michelle was dating someone new— they didn't know much about him, but he and Summer were anxious to meet him.

When they arrived at Michelle's apartment, they were greeted by a tall blond man, who opened the door while still talking on the telephone. He stuck his index finger in the air to indicate that he would be finished momentarily, then ushered them into the apartment as if he owned the place. He cussed at the person on the other end of the line, then without missing a beat, flashed them an insincere smile and said, "Michelle is in the shower. I'll tell her you're here." Then he went back to cussing into the receiver.

"*I'll* tell Michelle we're here!" Summer nearly shrieked, racing into the bedroom.

Sam kept reminding himself that he was a pacifist, but it sure would have felt good to deck this guy who looked as old as himself.

Finally, Richard finished his call. "Sorry about that, old man." Laughing, Richard stuck out his hand. Before their hands connected, Richard snapped his fingers. "Shit! I forgot to call Jack. 'Scuze me."

And he went right back to the phone, punching out a long series of numbers. Sam wondered if Michelle knew this man was putting long-distance charges on her bill.

"Who the hell are you?" Sam finally asked Richard, interrupting his conversation.

Richard's head jerked up and he stared at Sam. Suddenly, he finished his conversation and hung up.

"Jesus! I'm sorry. Michelle tells me I get in a zone as she calls it. And I guess she's right. I get really carried away with my work and I just shut everything out. You ever do that?"

Sam cleared his throat. "Yes."

"Good! Then you know what I'm talking about." Richard slapped Sam on the back.

Sam *knew* he was going to have to reverse his personal code never to strike another human. This guy was going to get it, but good.

"How about a drink?" Richard asked, looking around the kitchen cabinets.

"I don't drink," Sam replied coldly.

"Right!" Richard snapped his fingers. "Michelle told me that. She doesn't, either, just in case you were worrying."

"You seem to know a lot about my daughter," Sam said.

Richard's broad smile suddenly disappeared. "She didn't tell you I was old enough to be her father?"

"No, she didn't."

"How old are you?" Richard asked Sam.

"Forty-five."

Richard swallowed hard. "I'm forty-eight."

"You want to tell me what the fuck you're doing in my daughter's life?" Sam could actually feel his hands levitating toward Richard's throat. Maybe he wouldn't kill the bastard—just scare the shit out of him so he would leave Michelle alone.

Richard actually took a step backward. "I . . . know this is going to sound strange. Very strange and believe me, if I were in your shoes, I'd be upset, too."

"You're not in my shoes."

Richard's smile was a strain. "I think the world of your daughter. She's a very special person."

Sam was aware Richard was saying everything except that he loved Michelle. "This is bullshit!" Sam nearly yelled.

Just then, Michelle came running into the room. Putting herself between the two men, she pleaded with her father.

"Daddy! Please! I was going to tell you...in my way. I had it all planned. Except . . . Daddy, you're two hours early. Richard was on his way out. Really." She turned to Richard and glared at him. "I thought you'd finished your calls."

"I thought so, too. It just took a bit longer. I'm sorry, darling."

Sam thought he'd erupt. "Don't call her 'darling.' I . . . call her that."

"Sorry." Richard looked completely deflated.

Michelle turned to her father. "Daddy. I don't want it to be this way. I want you and Mom to understand. Richard is my soul mate."

"Oh, for God's sake," Sam moaned. He felt every one of his once New Age ideas backlash on him.

"It's true, Daddy. I've seen him in my meditations and my dreams for years. I knew it was him the minute we met. Please, Daddy. If you could just look beyond this tiny little thing about Richard's age."

"Tiny! He's three years older than I am!" Sam spouted angrily.

"Couldn't we all go to dinner and talk about this? This is *my* life, Daddy. I'm not going to cut out and run away with Richard, if that's what you think. I'm not going to leave home forever like you and Mom did."

Summer glared at Sam. It was Sam's turn to deflate. Christ! How was it that one's own flesh and blood could deliver death blows so accurately? Michelle was making the whole situation look as if it were his fault.

He looked Richard directly in the eye. "Get this straight. I think you're a dirty old man of the worst kind because you've duped my daughter into thinking that you love her. But I'll give you the chance to prove me wrong."

Sam and Richard had many false starts and dead ends over the following months, but once Richard became used to Sam and Summer's life-style and their protectiveness of their daughter, the animosity began to wane. Richard made a concerted effort to win Sam's friendship, and Sam respected that.

Sam never made a secret of the fact that he wished Michelle would have fallen in love with a man her age, gotten married and had children, but he loved his daughter. And as time passed, Sam and Summer both could see that Michelle was truly in love with Richard and, to them at least, Richard acted lovingly toward Michelle. Eventually, Sam came to believe that his daughter had in fact found her soul mate.

When they arrived at the New Gainey Ranch condominium where Michelle was waiting for them, Summer wished almost anything had happened to her daughter instead of this. Michelle was naive and vulnerable almost to a fault, and Summer blamed herself for that. She'd never prepared Michelle for tragedies, always teaching her to be positive, to create her happiness with her mind. However, she'd never prepared Michelle for death—even Summer believed death was something that happened to other people.

Summer took one look at her hysterical daughter and threw her arms around her. "Baby, baby. It's going to be all right. We're here. Sam will take care of everything."

"Daddy can't make Richard come back to me," Michelle said, sobbing. "He's really gone, Mom."

"I know, baby. I know," Summer said, pulling her daughter closer. "You loved him so much." Summer choked back her own emotions. She wanted to be strong for Michelle, but she'd never dealt well with death.

"He was my soul mate, wasn't he, Mom?" Michelle asked.

"Yes, he was. I saw it the first time we met."

"He was...only three years older than me." Sam's face paled as he looked around the apartment where Richard had told them about his plans for Bart's Land. Summer looked at him worriedly as he folded into the white silk sofa, still half-dazed.

Michelle's sobbing was becoming uncontrollable and she could barely catch her breath. Walking her to the sofa, Summer said to Sam, "Get her some blankets, Sam. She's freezing. I'm afraid she's in shock."

Summer's words had the desired effect, jolting him out of his thoughts. He bolted off the sofa, his concern clearly now for their daughter and her health. He went to the linen closet and found two blankets and an afghan Summer had made Michelle years ago. He rushed back to them.

Summer held Michelle in her arms while Sam covered them. She rocked Michelle back and forth in her arms, knowing that when she was a little girl, her daughter had always loved to be rocked.

"Calm down, baby. Everything will be all right," Summer said as she looked at Sam pleadingly.

"Quit saying that!" Michelle screamed. "Richard is gone. I'll have to live my whole life without him!"

Summer never missed a beat. "Why on earth would you think such a thing?" She began humming softly as she continued to rock Michelle.

"Because he's dead."

"Only his body is dead. You can't have children by him and you can't introduce him to your friends at work, but you can talk to him whenever you want . . . with your heart."

"I can?"

"Why, yes, baby. You've been doing it all your life with other spirit guides," Summer said, hoping that by recalling Michelle's childhood for her, she could give her comfort.

Michelle threw her arms around her mother's neck. "I love you."

And Summer knew she hadn't failed her daughter.

THE THREE
WOMEN

29

The priest threw a handful of cold Chicago dirt on Richard's casket, folded his hands over his prayer book and was stunned to watch the entire crowd quickly turn from the grave and march off to the waiting limousines and cars, chatting animatedly among themselves about the luncheon that was being held in the church hall for the mourners.

Minicameras zoomed in for close-ups, looking for tears and grief-stricken faces, but they found none. In less than ten minutes, Richard Bartlow was buried and forgotten.

Mary Grace entered the limousine and quickly whisked off her mourning veil. Her Jackie Kennedy role was over for the time being. "God! I thought this charade would never end."

Penelope crossed her legs, frowning as her skirt rose, nearly exposing her crotch. Mary Grace looked disapprovingly as she yanked at the spandex, only managing to cover another inch of flesh. Propping her elbow on the armrest, her daughter stared out the window at the reporter who was still ogling her. She smiled broadly and waved at him.

"Damn, he's cute," she said. "I should get his card."

Lawrence's top lip curled into a sneer. "You mean, you haven't fucked him yet?"

Penelope ignored her brother. But Mary Grace grimaced. "Must you always be so vulgar, Lawrence?"

"It's my nature," he said sardonically.

Fury spiraled like a hot wind through Mary Grace. "No, it's not. Your nature is nothing of the sort, but you have chosen to become a rude, crude, angry young man. You children and I have had some bad breaks and some of it was due to your father, but not all of it. Perhaps I did you a disservice not asking my parents for more money when Richard left us." She eyed him narrowly. "Maybe not. Perhaps this is a test of your mettle, Lawrence. And you know what? You're failing miserably. You are becoming the kind of person I don't like—that no one likes. And unfortunately, life is about learning how to get along with people. I suggest if you want to adopt this kind of behavior, do us all a favor and leave. Go to the mountains or a valley in Mexico, but don't inflict yourself on the rest of the human race."

Lawrence was clearly shocked at his mother's words. "You don't mean that."

Mary Grace folded her arms across her chest. "Don't bet on it."

His expression was aghast and he fumbled for words. "You . . . you would miss me."

"No, I don't think so. I would never choose a friend who acts like you. Why would I choose to be around a relative like you?"

"But I'm your son!"

"And that gives you the right to treat me like dirt under your feet? You deliberately say these things to make me angry. Why?"

Penelope couldn't keep her mouth shut any longer. "Because you made Daddy leave us!"

"What?"

"If you'd been more loving toward him, acted like a real wife instead of a nun, he'd still be with us!"

"Is that what you think?" Mary Grace's shock froze her breath—she felt as though she'd had the wind knocked out of her.

"It's the truth!" Penelope protested.

Mary Grace wouldn't let her daughter off the hook that easily. "You have developed this scenario in order to validate your whorish behavior. You believe you can get and keep a man with sex. It doesn't work that way."

"How the hell would *you* know? You haven't the slightest idea what the joys of sex can bring. You cut Daddy off years ago. I heard him telling Jack when I was a little girl."

The wound Penelope inflicted upon her was quick, deep and devastatingly painful. Penelope was right. Mary Grace had been so frightened of pregnancy she *had* cut Richard off. She'd put an end to her marriage before she'd turned twenty-five. God! If she looked at it like that, perhaps it explained in part why Richard had not given her the affection she needed—though she knew that he had been essentially incapable of loving anybody. What a mess they'd made of their lives! And in the end, what did it matter? Richard was dead. She was left with two bitter and angry children who, she was scared, were beyond her influence. The only thing she could do was get her career up and going so that she could help them. If she helped her children to change, to better themselves and learn to be positive, then they might have a chance at a relationship.

Mary Grace was glad that Kathryn and Cynthia had come to give her moral support. It was as if their lives had come full circle. She needed their support and acceptance now more than ever. She needed their nurturing, and this time, she was not too proud to accept it.

* * *

When Mary Grace and her children arrived, the church hall was filled with the smells of good food and the sound of lively chatter. Richard's wake was like a celebration of his leaving, she thought. Three bartenders served mixed drinks, the liquor provided by Mary Grace's parents, who had refused to attend the funeral or graveside services but who had no qualms about arranging for and coming to the party afterward.

Caroline greeted her daughter with a hug and a kiss. "Thank God the bastard is dead," she whispered in Mary Grace's ear. "Maybe now you can have some peace of mind. Hopefully, he left you something in his will."

"Mother, please."

James walked up to them. "Your mother is right. It's time you accepted our help, as well. We want you to look at a house we've found in Evanston. It's old and needs some fixing up, but a friend of ours recently passed away and the estate is willing to let it go for a song. With your talent and vision for design, you could make it into a showplace. Give yourself a chance to display your real talent. Maybe we could get some pictures published in *Chicago* magazine or even one of the national decorating magazines. Please accept our help this time, Mary Grace. You've been hard-assed about this for too long."

Mary Grace looked at her father. He really meant what he said, but old habits died hard. "I'll look at the house, but I'm not making any promises."

"That's all I can ask for at this point," James replied, hugging her warmly.

Mary Grace couldn't digest all that was happening to her and her life. But good feelings of self-esteem washed over her. She felt reborn. And maybe she was.

Cynthia was talking to Kathryn and Mary Grace, catching up on their news. Kathryn was now married and happier than she'd ever been. The years had been kind to Kathryn; she'd aged very little and had not succumbed to plastic surgery. She was living proof that love kept a woman and a man young and vibrant.

Cynthia glanced across the room and saw Alicia in a very close huddle with Jack Billingsly. There was no mistaking the love light in Jack's eyes. Cynthia thought it odd that as sophisticated as Alicia seemed to be, she was totally unaware that Jack was falling in love with her.

Then she noticed Lawrence sitting at a long table, toying with a plate of uneaten food. His head was bent over his plate, and she had a feeling he was crying.

Mary Grace had told Cynthia about the lambasting she'd given both her children that morning in the limousine, and she thought maybe Lawrence needed an outsider with an objective opinion at this point.

Cynthia excused herself to her friends and went over to him and sat down. "You can tell me to leave if you want, Lawrence."

"Naw, it's okay," he sniffed, wiping his nose on his jacket sleeve. With the palm of his hand, he mashed his tears into his cheeks rather than wiping them off. To Cynthia, it was a gesture of anger.

"Where's your sister?" Cynthia thought she'd keep the conversation light and let him be the guide.

"Talking to some reporter she has a crush on who snuck in."

"Oh," Cynthia answered simply. She decided to press on. "Are you upset over what your mother said to you this morning?"

"No, yeah. I don't know. I guess I've been pretty mixed up since my dad died. I can't figure it out."

"Figure out what?" she asked.

"Why he never liked me. I was just a kid. He ignored me half the time and the rest of the time, it didn't matter what I did, I always managed to make him mad. I felt like he was always blaming me for something."

Cynthia nodded. "He was."

Lawrence's head shot up and he looked at her. "Really?"

"Of course. I'm going to be very frank, Lawrence. I'm going to tell you things your mother can't or won't say. Your father was an asshole. We all knew it. Your mother was in love with him and she didn't see it. She still doesn't, not really. Richard was so damn self-absorbed, there was no room in his life for your mother, you or your sister. Richard never needed anyone but Richard. It was always what *he* wanted that counted. He abused you, his employees and he used his friends. I was there when he met your mother. It's my opinion he married your mother for her money but when he didn't get any of the Whittaker fortune, he felt like he'd been cheated. From that day on, he decided his role in life was to take. He never gave anything to anybody. . . why would he have been any different with you?"

Lawrence's eyes were was big as saucers. "I've never had anyone tell me this."

"Don't you think it's about time?"

He smiled. "Yes, I do."

She smiled back and put her hands on his shoulders. Pulling him toward her, she rested her forehead against his so that their faces were very close. She peered deeply into his eyes. "You are a fine young man, Lawrence. You had the bad fortune to have a shit for a father. I believe you take those drugs you've got stashed in your pocket to get attention, to make your mother mad, to piss off your father, as you say. But, you know what? The only person you have to be accountable to anymore is Lawrence. It no longer matters what your mother thinks. She's got her own life to live now. Your father is dead, so he's out of the picture. I think your drugs have outlived their usefulness."

Lawrence pondered her advice. "Maybe."

"If you need medical assistance to kick them, let me know. I've worked for several privately funded agencies in town who have helped a lot of people like you."

"Why are you doing this? Why are you taking time with me?"

"I like you, Lawrence."

"But why?"

She smiled again. "When *you* answer that question, you'll know everything you need to know about yourself, life and where you're going."

He rolled his eyes. "I think you're weird."

She laughed. "I think you're terrific," she said. And very much worth saving, she thought.

30

Jack Billingsly drove Alicia home less than an hour after the reception began.

"I know you probably feel obligated to stay with Mary Grace and the children. I appreciate your taking me home," she said.

"Mary Grace can take care of herself, believe me. She's learned a lot since she divorced Richard. Actually, I think it's the best thing that ever happened to her. In time, I hope she agrees with me. As a person, I like her more now than I ever have."

"I'm glad to hear that, Jack. I've always thought that crises happen to make us look around and take another road. Not to stop us, but to make us think."

Jack's smile was thoughtful. "That's wise of you. Not many people view life like that."

"Too bad. We'd all be better off if they did."

"Amen."

Jack turned off Lake Shore Drive and headed toward the tall apartment building Alicia called home. The early-afternoon sun sparkled on the lake, christening the bare autumn trees with its last warm rays.

"I hate this time of year," Alicia said, looking at the riot of rust, gold and burgundy chrysanthemums that filled huge flowerpots and planters at the doorways to the fashionable apartment houses, restaurants and retail stores. They were the only spots of living color left. "Winter is so cold and long and . . ."

"Lonely?" Jack asked, thinking out loud.

Turning, Alicia gave him a considering and thoughtful look. "Is winter lonely for you, Jack?"

"It didn't used to be. When I was younger and full of ambitious fire, weekends were a time to work, burn the midnight oil and try to leap ahead of the pack. Now, I've made a reputation for myself, my client base is solid and I seem to have a great deal of time on my hands. Racquetball and tennis don't have the appeal for me they once did."

"What does appeal to you, exactly?"

"I dunno," he mused. "Winters in the south of France. A Pernod on the Left Bank in Paris. Sightseeing in Italy. I'd like to go to China before the end of this century."

"So, why don't you go? Is your work load too heavy?"

He gave her a sidelong glance and tightened his grip on the steering wheel. He felt he was stepping across the border to unfamiliar territory. He'd never been married, but he'd been infatuated with Alicia for over eight years. He'd never wanted to admit to himself that he'd been yearning for his best friend's mistress, but that was the truth of it. He'd tried to forget her many times, always telling himself that she would never be interested in him after falling under Richard's charismatic spell. Jack was just an ordinary guy down deep. He didn't think a beautiful, classic and ambitious woman like Alicia would find him attractive. His nonassertive behavior had gotten him nowhere. Perhaps it was time for him to change some things about himself. "I don't have anyone to go with me," he said, taking the risk.

Alicia chuckled. "You can't be serious!"

Jack's face was inflexible. "I'm most serious."

"I would have thought a handsome man like you, an accomplished man, at that, would have women falling all over you."

Jack wasn't sure he was hearing right—it had been awhile since he'd heard such honest flattery. "I don't," he said simply, then pressed on. "I don't suppose you'd be interested in anything like that?"

"Are you kidding? I love Europe. I spent most of my twenties in Europe. Granted, I was scouting fashion locations and baby-sitting models half the time working for an ad agency, but I love it there. If I could just get my company solidly on its feet, then I could take a vacation."

"I see."

"Jack, are you trying to ask me out?"

"Yes." He pulled the car up the curb at Alicia's apartment building. Wouldn't you just know it, he thought, my timing is always for the shits. Now she can slip out of this car and my chances will be gone forever.

Jack stared straight ahead. "I know a little coffeehouse around the corner. How about a cappuccino?"

"Sounds great."

They sat at a round granite-topped table at a small cappuccino bar a block and a half from Alicia's apartment. Alicia encircled the huge white porcelain cappuccino cup with both hands so that Jack wouldn't see them shaking. Suddenly, she was very nervous and she knew why. She liked Jack. She liked the way he protected her and watched over young Michelle. She liked the way he handled himself with aplomb and grace when faced with Mary Grace's anger and pain, not to mention Penelope's and Lawrence's outrageous behavior. Jack was the kind of man she'd dreamed about as a lifetime mate.

She didn't want to play games with him—those days were over long ago. She wanted a mature relationship, not only companionship, but passion and deep caring.

She'd made the mistake of pitching her hopes too high once before.

She realized that she had grown a great deal since her days with Richard. Even if he were alive now, she would never go back to him. She and Richard had shared something special for a time, but she'd always felt as if she was fighting his children, fighting his depression, giving him encouragement and trying to keep her company afloat—all at the same time. If she'd been frank with herself, she'd have admitted it had been exhausting.

Jack reached out and took her hand. "I know you loved Richard a great deal—"

She stopped him with a shake of her head. "Yes, but he didn't love me back. That's the lesson I learned. Love has to be a two-way street, otherwise it goes nowhere. Richard didn't have the capacity to love anyone but himself. I also learned that I deserve better than that for myself."

"Good for you."

"Next time I want something better. I want a real helpmate. A companion and someone who . . ."

"Loves you?" Jack asked, squeezing her fingers.

"Y-yes." She looked into his eyes and what she saw nearly took her breath away. His face was naked, vulnerable and filled with a thousand times more love than she'd ever seen in Richard. There was no mistaking Jack's feelings for her. This time she knew she wasn't just looking at her own reflection; this time she was seeing a deep well of emotion that had been kept hidden for a long time.

Alicia remembered the old saying that love always comes when you least expect it. Never in a million years had she expected to find love at Richard's funeral.

"That's what I want, too, Alicia," he said.

"You do?"

"I know, I've never said anything before. For a while, you were Richard's lover; and then you seemed to carry a torch for him for a long time." He looked down at his hand, which was holding hers quite possessively.

"Sometimes it's possible that when you've loved someone else a great deal, you learn how to love deeper and deeper each time," she said.

"I think you're right." He lifted her hand to his lips, kissing each finger seductively.

Alicia trembled as a light sprinkling of shivers blanketed her skin and then burrowed down deep. She watched as he looked up at her, a mischievous, sexy gleam in his eye. He did not release her hand. Instead, he placed his full lips over the rim of her knuckles and with his tongue probed each crevice where her finger met her palm. Carefully, expertly, he licked and caressed her skin, letting her know that his lovemaking would be as painstakingly slow and tormentingly pleasurable.

"You're holding your breath, Alicia." His voice was thick.

"I...I didn't realize..." She couldn't tear her eyes from his.

"Realize what, Alicia?" he asked, raising his head from her hand and putting his face very near hers. He encircled her nape with his hand and sank his fingers into her thick silky hair.

Alicia had never wanted to be kissed so badly in all her life, but she resisted. She knew if she let his inviting lips touch hers, she would be lost. "I didn't realize I was holding so much back."

"We both have. For far, far too long." His unrelenting eyes pulled her further into him, as if he were allowing her to hear his thoughts and see his soul.

She swallowed hard, thinking it might not be such a good thing to keep holding herself back. She hadn't let her feelings pour forth for a long time. Perhaps that was why her business was drying up—she was dried up. Maybe it was time to take a chance on life again.

"Tomorrow, after the reading of Richard's will, I'd like to take you to lunch," he said. "Then I thought we could drive up to Lake Geneva, kind of bum around for the afternoon, maybe pick up a couple pumpkins and some squash at one of those farmers' markets up there."

"It's beautiful there, even in winter. I'd like that . . . a lot." She smiled at him, unlocking the place in her heart where she'd kept her trust imprisoned. Suddenly, she felt incredibly free.

Jack stood up and held both her hands as she rose from her chair. Putting his arm around her waist, he walked her out the door. Neither of them mentioned it to the other, but they were both thinking how comfortably they fit together. It was the best of all feelings.

31

Jack Billingsly's law office was located in a glittering tower overlooking Lake Michigan. The day after Richard Bartlow's funeral, the entrance to the building was crammed with even more reporters than had been at the church and the cemetery. The story of the dynamic builder who had lost everything, then made history with his unprecedented building project was nothing compared to Richard's private life. The juxtaposition of three diametrically opposed women involved with the same man was too juicy, too intriguing not to exploit.

Michelle Windsong had not slept in the uncomfortable hotel bed the night before. She'd stayed awake reading every article about herself and Richard. She was shocked at the distorted view the journalists had of her. The conservative local papers depicted her as a conniving cultist who'd had designs on Richard's rising fame and, had he lived, his fortune. The national tabloids treated her dismissively, as they did most unaccomplished young people, stating she was an "out-of-work, live-in lover." They made it sound as if she had no education, no work and only wanted Richard for a meal ticket. Other papers hinted she was a paid whore. A streetwalker.

It pained her that her love for Richard had been so vulgarly decimated. It wasn't fair. For the first time in her life, Michelle was angry.

The next day, she marched up to one of the reporters, ready to state her case. She had to make them understand. She chose to tell her story to Barry Allen, the nice guy who had helped her at the church. He was holding a microphone and his cameraman stood in front of him, testing for lighting.

Barry Allen had spent the better part of yesterday afternoon with Penelope Bartlow. After sneaking into the reception, they had talked, meeting later for a walk along the lake. She had talked and he had listened. They'd sat on a park bench, and he held her hand while she cried, anger and pain about her parents had poured out of her until she was spent. When she finally had nothing more to say, Barry took her to dinner at a family-owned home-cooking–style Italian restaurant, where they shared pasta, wine and bread. Barry drove Penelope home, but rather than leave her, they'd sat in his compact car and talked until nearly five in the morning.

Barry told her about himself, about his dreams and his goals. Penelope seemed fascinated by him and told him she wanted to see him again. They had made a date for after the reading of the will.

Barry's mind was so concentrated on thoughts of Penelope that he hadn't noticed Michelle Windsong approaching him. It was the red light on the Minicamera that alerted him to the fact that he was being taped. He quickly slid into his anchorman role.

"Michelle Windsong is with us now," Barry said. "Tell me, Michelle—"

Barry never finished his question. Taking the microphone from Barry, Michelle looked directly into the camera's eye.

"I've read the lies the press has printed about my relationship with Richard. It's not their fault they don't understand—most reporters are shallow people working for people who don't care about the truth. News is not truth. It is something that exists in order to validate commercial time and support the advertisers. No one seems to care about truth anymore. But I do. Richard Bartlow was not lecherous, nor going through a midlife crisis. He was and is my soul mate. Richard and I have been together in many, many lifetimes over thousands of years. We had come together in this lifetime to create something positive for the world. Richard built beautiful homes in Scottsdale that even a very young, struggling family could afford. Before his death, he was looking for even more ways to cut costs so that a single person on a limited income could afford to live comfortably.

"Richard believed, as I do, that there is abundance in the universe. He believed that all of us are entitled to a better way of life. When Richard lost all his money, he realized that poverty does not breed contentment." She turned to Barry. "I resent the press's dark portrait of my beloved soul mate." She handed the microphone back to Barry and, before he could comment, she stalked off to the opening elevator door.

Barry turned his practiced on-camera expression to the camera. "That was Michelle Windsong in her first interview. It's my opinion we haven't heard the last from this young lady. Do I see a kiss-and-tell book here?"

Just then, Alicia Carrel walked into the lobby of the building, dressed to kill in a knock-off black-and-white Chanel suit. She carried herself with the same confidence and quiet assertiveness that the press corps admired. But Barry Allen noticed there was something different about her today. Today, she glowed.

"Miss Carrel, any idea what's in store in the will? I noticed you and Jack Billingsly were pretty tight at the funeral—"

"Oh, Barry," Alicia interrupted cordially, "don't be making up stories now." She flashed a radiant smile at the camera. "I have no idea what's going to happen. To be honest, it doesn't matter much to me, anyway. With or without Richard Bartlow, I'm just fine." She walked away.

"Class," Barry said to himself, his face glazed over with admiration.

"There you have it," Barry continued into the microphone. "Unfortunately, we've learned that Mrs. Bartlow, her son and daughter arrived much earlier this morning to avoid the press. Therefore, we won't have any comments from them."

Barry switched back to the anchor at the studio and the cameraman shut off his Minicam.

Jack greeted Alicia at the door to his office with a very warm handshake. "You look wonderful," he whispered.

Alicia smiled. "Thanks." Then she walked over to the empty green leather wing chair next to Michelle Windsong. She nodded to Michelle and smiled at Mary Grace, who was holding herself with stiff control. Alicia was surprised to see Penelope wearing a conservative skirt and sweater, loafers and a black velvet headband. Her blond hair streamed down her back, straight, clean and unpretentious. More important, Penelope's face had lost its customary defiance. Instead, Alicia saw acceptance.

Penelope turned to look at her, her mouth curved gently into a peaceful smile. Alicia smiled back, though she couldn't imagine the cause of Penelope's transformation. Something had happened last night—to both of them. Alicia wondered who or what had helped Penelope turn such an important corner in her life, but turn it, she had.

"I'd like to get this over with as quickly as possible," Jack said. "There is a statement from Richard, which he sent to me at the time of his first heart attack, nearly a year ago. There is no doubt in my mind that Richard was already going through a catharsis at the time. I feel that I must mention to everyone here that it is *my* belief, though not necessarily Richard's, that Michelle had a great deal to do with helping Richard to look inward. His heart attack simply drove home to him the reality of the precariousness of his life . . . of all our lives."

Jack picked up a piece of stationery and began reading. "'Dear Jack, I am only a week away from nearly dying from a heart attack. I suppose I'm as guilty as the next guy that I always believed I was immune to attack of any kind. I thought I was invincible. Losing my building company and the respect of my friends in Chicago proved to me how vulnerable I was. But I'd always prided myself on my healthy body. I thought of myself as twenty-five years old, not fifty. Time catches up with all of us. I don't know how much time I have left. I know that Bart's Land is just getting up and rolling right now. It will take decades to really bring in any great amount of money. Therefore, the will and bequests that I send now will change two and three years from now. I want Mary Grace, Alicia, Michelle, Penelope and Lawrence to know that I tried to provide what I could for them at this time. In the end, I'm just an ordinary guy doing the best I can.'"

Mary Grace's head was filled with flashes of Richard when they were young and in love. She remembered Rome and making love to him for the first time. Her eyes filled with tears. "God," she said, lifting a tissue to her eyes, "I wish now I hadn't been so hard on him. I wish I hadn't started that lawsuit."

Jack's eyes darted to her face. "What lawsuit?"

"Richard didn't tell you?" she asked.

"No."

Alicia and Michelle both looked at Mary Grace. So did Penelope and Lawrence.

Mary Grace shrugged. "I needed money to get my design business off the ground . . . or starve. I owed my parents so much money and I had no income to report, so no bank would loan me anything. Investors laughed at me. I began a lawsuit against Richard about two months ago. He owes me over a hundred thousand in back child support. I wanted my money. I had his bank accounts frozen. Through the state family-services department I found an attorney, Martha Bateman, who does not charge me for her time. She told me that I could even stop Richard from building any more houses if I wanted to. I thought that was rather stupid, but I called him and threatened him, anyway. I told him if he didn't pay me, I'd shut him down."

"Mother! You did that?" Lawrence looked shocked.

"Yes, I did. Martha recommended that I file criminal charges against Richard. She told me there was no doubt in her mind that he, and men like him, would be faced with prison for not paying child support."

Penelope clenched her jaw. "It wouldn't have killed you to ask Grandpa for another loan. Why must you always punish Daddy? Why do you do this to us and to yourself? You make us suffer for your pride! I'm sick of it."

"Listen, Penelope. I've learned a lot in the last few days. I've realized that I've been caught in a battle with him that, had he lived, I'd still be waging. It was tit for tat. Each time I hurt him, he'd hurt me back. It was sick and never-ending." She breathed a sigh of relief. "I'm so glad it's over."

Jack looked at Mary Grace. "For the past five months of Richard's life, he and I had been working on a building project here in Chicago. Just off North Michigan Avenue on Ontario Street there was a seven-story building that needed refurbishing. I found a half-dozen of Richard's old colleagues who were willing to invest in the venture with me. That area is so hot now, and they all agreed that the old building could be converted into condos. Richard did all the work in exchange for a lease of the ground-floor rooms for a period of five years, rent free. Richard gutted the largest sections that face the street and remodeled them into a showroom for you, Mary Grace."

Her hands flew to her face. "I don't believe it." Suddenly, her dream of being a designer, garnering the kinds of clients she needed to make a name for herself, was reborn. "He's given me the time I need to build a business. With the design award I just won and this leg up that Richard has given me, there's no limit to what I could do. If I do very well, I could continue—pay the rent to you and the owners and keep my showroom!" Her eyes were wide with the possibilities. "I could go back to Europe, hunt for some of those fabulous antiques I saw back in the sixties when I went with Cynthia and Kathryn. They would both help me. I know they would! Kathryn knows so many people over there."

Mary Grace's mind was spinning with plans, dreams and ideas for her future. She had never felt so alive in all her life. Excitedly, she looked to her children and saw wonder in their eyes. She was startled to see Lawrence's face brighten with a smile.

"You can do it, Mom!" he said encouragingly.

"I know I can, Lawrence. Think about it. I could go to China and buy—".

"Those hand-painted screens I like. And those rich silks like Grandma bought when she was there."

Mary Grace blinked her eyes twice. "I can't believe you remember that. I didn't know that had made any impression on you."

"Are you kidding? Ask Grandma. I make her talk about that trip all the time. That's one of my dreams. To see China and India. Maybe," he began hesitantly, "maybe I could go with you . . ." His eyes were tentative.

Mary Grace realized how little she knew about her own son. This chance to make *her* dreams come true could be Lawrence's opportunity to put the past behind him, as well. Maybe if he had something exciting to occupy his time, even if it was just a trip to Hong Kong, she could bring him back to her. Maybe he would find redemption. "You'll have to learn about antiques and Chinese porcelains. It'll be a lot of reading and studying."

"I don't care," he replied cautiously but firmly. "I can learn fast if I want to."

She smiled at him. "Yes, you can. You can do anything you want if you put your mind to it."

Opening his desk drawer, Jack pulled out a set of keys with a long white tag. "This is yours, Mary Grace. The address is written on the tag."

She took the keys and held them gently in her hands. Her eyes were filled with tears. "I wish . . . Richard were alive so that I could thank him."

"Richard specifically stated that Alicia was next to be mentioned." Jack continued reading the bequest. "'To Alicia, I leave the equivalent of two years' worth of office rent, payroll to employ three staff members, office furnishings, computers, graphic software, faxes, phones and enough money to pay all utilities and phone bills for that length of time. Through a trade bargain with a friend of mine, who shall remain anonymous, this office space was made available to me. The equipment is also his and is to be considered on loan. However, after the two-year period, if Alicia's advertising business is profitable enough, she may purchase all the furnishings and computers at cost from my friend. My attorney, Jack Billingsly, will arrange the purchase so that my friend remains anonymous.'"

Alicia was smiling at Jack. "Hallelujah!" She clapped her hands together. "This is all I need, Jack. Just this little boost is all I need. I *know* I can do the rest by myself! I can't believe it. If Richard had given me a million dollars, I couldn't be happier."

Silence filled the room until Jack turned to Michelle and told her about the massage-therapy clinic Richard had left to her back in Scottsdale.

"I know right where it is," Michelle said. "It's small but very posh and close to the best hotels. I'm not worried about clients—I will always be sent the people I am destined to heal. Unfortunately, I may have too many clients. There is so much disease in the world."

Finally, Jack read the part of the will that mentioned Penelope and Lawrence.

"'To each of my children, I leave a twenty-five-thousand-dollar trust fund, the interest from which will be reinvested for them every year by my counsel until they reach the age of thirty-five, at which time they may elect to take the profits and spend each year. After the age of thirty, if gainfully employed, they may borrow against the trust fund, but only for the purposes of education or the purchase of a home."

Penelope looked at Lawrence who shrugged his shoulders good-naturedly. "I guess it's not so bad."

Penelope smiled at her brother. "I guess not. Could have been worse, huh?"

Lawrence nodded, smiling at his mother and taking Mary Grace's hand. "I say we go check out that showroom, Mom."

"Good idea." Mary Grace looked at Jack. "Are we finished?"

"Yes. I'll be sending copies to each of you for your files," he said as he stood up.

Mary Grace opened the door to the reception area and found Kathryn and Cynthia waiting for her. They embraced one another as Michelle walked out of the office behind Penelope and Lawrence.

Alicia remained behind to talk with Jack.

Cynthia looked at Michelle. "I still can't get over the fact that we've met."

"You did?" Mary Grace's eyes filled with surprise.

"Remember when I took you to Scottsdale several years ago when you saw Richard with Alicia? I got that massage from the young girl and I raved about how good she was?"

"You're kidding! That was Michelle?"

Michelle smiled happily. "I reminded Cynthia about it yesterday at the church hall. She had forgotten, too. But I never forget a face." She paused for a long moment as she looked from Kathryn to Cynthia to Mary Grace, Penelope and Lawrence. "I know you all think I'm some kind of New Age kook, just like the papers say I am. But in time, I can only hope that you will find the wisdom to remember what I've told you. We are all connected in this life, each of us part of the other. That's why it's so silly to hate and fill ourselves with resentments. When we forgive, we're only forgiving ourselves. I think Alicia knows that now. I think you do, too, Mary Grace."

Michelle shook hands with each of them. "I have a plane to catch." She started toward the door.

Cynthia stopped her. "Let me give you a ride, Michelle."

Michelle smiled. "That would be nice."

They walked out together.

Kathryn looked at Mary Grace, Lawrence and Penelope. "I'm free for lunch. Where would you like to go?"

"Ever been to Hong Kong?" Mary Grace asked as she winked at her children.

Kathryn's eyes narrowed suspiciously. "What are you talking about?"

Lawrence slipped his arm through Kathryn's. "Mom has a business proposition for you. Don't you, Mom?"

"I certainly do. I can't wait to tell you all about it." She chuckled as she took Penelope's hand and they all walked out of Jack's office together.

Circling his desk, Jack stood next to Alicia. He slipped his arms around her waist. She could see a tender fire burning in his eyes, and she smiled, pulling him to her. She reveled in the warm strength she found in his arms.

"It's over," she said.

"Yes, it is," he replied. He pulled away and lifted his hand to her face. He held her chin between his finger and thumb. "I've waited an eternity to do this," he said, covering her mouth with his eager lips.

It was the most thrilling kiss Alicia had ever experienced. She hoped it never ended.

EPILOGUE

Like the stricken face of Michelangelo's fallen Adam, Richard Bartlow stared back at his reflection in the black monitor screen. He was alone in an empty office across the hall from the room where Jack Billingsly had just read his will.

Faking his own death had seemed like the idea of a lifetime two months ago when he'd first approached Dennis Maitland—the perfect way to circumvent Mary Grace and her continued legal revenge against him.

Richard thought back to their pivotal conversation before a game of tennis. He had never trusted Dennis the way he had Jack. But Dennis was nefarious and greedy—the perfect accomplice for his plan.

"Dennis, as you know, I had a heart attack several months back and that incident has caused me to re-evaluate my life."

Dennis's face was barren of response or emotion. Richard had noticed that little seemed to ever move him, dispassionate to the degree that Richard had often wondered if the man had any blood in his veins. However, Richard had hired him as his corporate attorney to make certain his land contracts were airtight, that even the most minute aspects of the property negotiations were solidly in Richard's favor.

Richard realized early on that Dennis's previous failure as a successful lawyer was not that he was inept, but that he lacked the charm and salesmanship necessary to garner clients. Dennis's robotic manners made him appear jaded. Most people wanted sympathy from their attorney as well as legal advice. Dennis didn't have an empathetic nerve in his body, and that was why Richard hired him.

"That seems to be a common occurrence these days. So, are you born again or simply philosophic now?"

Richard laughed. "That's the first humorous thing I've heard from you, Dennis."

"Really? I'm not known for my humor," he replied dryly.

Richard inserted his key into the trunk of the car, lifted the rear hood and retrieved their tennis rackets, balls and tote bags from the interior. "That's what I like about you, Dennis. You have no humor. No heart, either."

"Thanks a lot."

"Hearts cause trouble, believe me. No one has learned that lesson as well as I have."

They walked side by side to the tennis court. "Is Mary Grace giving you problems again?"

"To say the least." Richard opened the chain-link gate and walked onto the court. "This time I think she's figured out a way to nail my ass."

Dennis stood next to the net, the noonday sun beating down on his sandy hair. "And you want me to bail you out."

"I've thought this through to the nth degree, Dennis. Everything I'm about to tell you I consider confidential and that, as my legal counsel, you cannot testify against me. Correct?"

"Yes."

"I want to make it perfectly clear that I chose you because I believe you are a great deal like me. You're concerned about your financial security as much, perhaps even more so than I am. I also believe you would take unprecedented risks to ensure that future. How am I doing so far?"

"I'm listening."

"I am willing to cut you in for a great deal of money— I don't have all of it right now, but I will with your help. You will have a substantial income for decades to come if you agree to be my partner. And that is what I'm proposing here, Dennis, a partnership. This would be more than simply being my attorney. But I also believe that with this business venture you would never need another client again for the rest of your life. From what I've seen, you have a problem getting and keeping clients. With my business and the revenues we could generate together, you'll have plenty of work and money, but you'll also have enough free time to play tennis whenever you goddamn well feel like it. In other words, Dennis, the rat race of life will be over for you."

"Just how illegal is this venture?"

"It is illegal," Richard confirmed.

"Are you going to kill someone?"

"In a manner of speaking."

Dennis started to walk away. "Count me out."

Richard grabbed his arm. "What if I were going to ask you to wash money for some drug deals?"

"That's different," Dennis assured him.

"Then hear me out," Richard pleaded.

"Start talking."

"Mary Grace is my problem. I don't want to kill her, just shut her up," Richard began. "When I left her, she was convinced I'd stashed some money in an offshore account."

"And had you?"

"Yes. No one knew about that money, not even Jack. But somehow, she found out about it. She told me she'd had a dream that I had plenty of money and was letting my company go down the tubes on purpose. She accused me of sticking it to my investors, the banks, the mortgage holders and the government while I danced on their financial graves. Those were her words exactly."

"How much truth was there to that accusation?"

"Some. But what money I had wouldn't have made a dent in the tens of millions I lost. Hundreds of guys like me got wiped out by the crash. I tried to tell myself there was some comfort in the fact that I wasn't alone, but you know what? Failure like that is devastating. I don't know which is worse—the actual loss or not having a place to go every day. That was the part that made me nuts. Just not having a place to go." Richard paused for a moment, sucking in his breath.

"Mary Grace was incredibly unreasonable during the divorce. She was demanding maintenance of over four thousand a month, and I had nothing coming in and everything going out. I suppose I could have given her some of the money from my hidden account, but I was damned if I was going to give that bitch a penny. She'd just blow it all on clothes or shit for the house that we didn't need. You wouldn't believe all the crap she had stored in the attic. She was obsessed with redecorating. Christ! I never knew what my house was going to look like when I came home at night. I told her once to quit changing everything on the outside of her life and work on the inside."

"That was insightful of you."

"I'm not known for that kind of thing," Richard admitted.

"I know." Dennis chuckled. "Go on."

"Anyway, she did nothing of the kind. I closed my offices and her demands got louder and more extravagant. She went out and bought a goddamn mink coat and charged it to my business. When the store called to verify the purchase, the phones had been disconnected. She was living in a dreamworld."

Richard ran his hand angrily through his hair. "The courts ruled in her favor, demanding I pay her five grand a month for child support. Shit! I had no job, nothing. I couldn't support myself, much less her and the kids. Who, by the way, had turned into spoiled brats, just like their mother. I couldn't stand to be with them more than an afternoon, but I took my scheduled time with them just to piss her off. I cash-advanced my credit cards to take them to movies, plays, buy them stuff I knew she couldn't afford. Mary Grace kept hauling my butt into court and I always managed to come up with some money, not much, but enough to keep her off my ass. But it never lasted long. God! But that woman was full of venom.

"In the meantime, I was living with Alicia. She was terrific. She had *her* shit together, supporting me, putting up with crap from my kids. I needed that time to get myself back on top again. I don't think she ever realized how much I was using her. She was in love with me, or so she said. Until I left. I told myself it was okay, because I was out of there. I was doing my own thing. But the truth was, I found out I had actually loved her. I missed her. Can you believe that?

"Fortunately, Michelle came along and replaced Alicia. Sort of. The sex is incredible with Michelle. She's so young and full of energy, she nearly wears me out. I haven't told anyone this, but I'm sure my heart attack was brought on by the all-night sex Michelle and I were having. She nearly killed me!"

"What's all this got to do with me and our coventure project, Richard?"

"That's what I like about you, Dennis. You are just as self-centered as I am."

Dennis frowned slightly. "Self-preservation, I call it. Please continue."

"My ex-wife is suing me for a hundred thousand dollars in back child support. She's threatened to freeze my bank accounts, and she says she'll file criminal charges against me for nonpayment. I don't doubt she'll do it. I can stand a lot of things, Dennis, but jail is *not* one of them. I've got a bit of time to fend her off, but I know now, she'll never give up. I have to protect myself."

"And how do you intend to do that?"

"I have come to realize that with this interview I've given to *Time* magazine, I could be getting quite a bit of national publicity. That will bring me the buyers I need. I'm telling you, this idea of mine is the greatest thing I've ever come up with. Scottsdale is just the beginning. I can see us building communities all over the country. In ten years, I should be making hundreds of millions of dollars. Ordinarily, I'd look at this like manna from heaven, but I don't. Mary Grace will figure out a way to either take half my money or she'll put me in jail. Frankly, I think she'd rather see me rot in jail than take the money, she's that vindictive. If we move fast, I can set myself up so that she never gets a chance to do either."

"By doing what?"

"I'm going to kill myself."

Dennis's eyes opened wide. "Are you fucking nuts?"

"Do you think it would work? Would she leave me alone?" Richard teased.

"Hell, yes!"

"Good. Because I'm only going to pretend to be dead. I'm going to fake my own death."

"Aw, shit. This is nuts." Dennis tried to walk away again.

Jumping ahead of him, Richard grabbed his shoulders. "Listen to me. This plan is airtight."

Dennis nodded with resignation and Richard continued.

"I'll give you power of attorney to acquire future lands for the corporation as sole executor of the corporate estate. All my assets will be under your control and you will have the swing vote on the board of directors for Bart's Land Corporation. I'll have Jack Billingsly be my personal executor and he'll oversee everything, except for my corporate assets. Jack is so dead honest, so trustworthy and has known me for over twenty-five years. No one, not even the IRS, will question his integrity. If I play this right, it will just look like you are carrying on with my company. You and I will split all the profits I make. I've already bought a condominium under an assumed name in Puerto Vallarta. Mark Spencer. I have bank accounts set up, my driver's license, fake passports and visas."

Dennis was shaking his head. "This will never work. Somebody will get wise to you. It can't work."

"It can and it will," Richard said adamantly. "Listen, I've had a real heart attack. My medical records will show how volatile my health is. I have purposefully kept on with my relationship with Michelle for one reason and one reason only. She's so damn naive, believing in all this spiritual, self-healing horseshit. I've told her I've had a change of heart since my attack. I've got her teaching me everything from yoga to meditation to deep breathing. As far as she knows, I've had a complete spiritual transformation, and she can't wait to tell everyone she meets about it. When I arrange for my own funeral, I'll make sure she's there to convince everyone I had a conversion at the time of my heart attack."

Richard could see Dennis was beginning to sway to his side. "She is adamant about your spiritual progress. I must say I've seen that for myself."

"Didn't you tell me you have a buddy at the coroner's office? An assistant who is easily corruptible? Someone who would sign a death certificate for us for a sizable sum of money? Say, ten thousand dollars?"

"For ten thousand Jeff Holgren would declare his own mother dead."

"That's all I needed to hear," Richard said, rocking back on his heels. "Are you with me or not?"

Dennis stuck out his hand. "I'm your man."

Richard continued to explain how they would pick a particularly hot day on which to plan a tennis match or a very long golf game, depending upon whether they could get open courts at the club or not. Richard would make certain Michelle was at work. Dennis would make a call to Jeff Holgren, who would personally drive the ambulance to the condo, declare Richard dead and move him on a gurney to the ambulance. He would arrange for an empty casket to be sent to Chicago and buried. Part of Richard's will would stipulate that the casket would never be opened for viewing. Dennis would make the phone calls to Michelle and to Jack Billingsly, who would then call Mary Grace, Alicia, Penelope and Lawrence, informing them of Richard's death and the will in which they would each be mentioned.

"So why leave them anything, Richard?"

"I want to see their faces when they finally realize how little I'm giving them. I'm convinced they all think I'm made of money. Even Michelle. You can't tell me a young chick like that hangs out with me because of my dynamic personality. She's waiting for me to hit it big like they all did. I can just see them dancing on my grave.

They'll probably tear each other apart trying to see who gets the most. Especially Mary Grace. She'll kill anyone who comes within five inches of a single dollar she thinks is hers. She's the greediest of the bitches. You'll see."

Putting his hands in his pockets, Dennis looked off to Camelback Mountain. "Well, you know them better than I do."

"Damn straight. And don't forget it." Richard rubbed his hands together. "I'm going to fly to Chicago and have an old buddy of mine wire Jack's office so I can watch the reading of that will. This is one show I wouldn't want to miss."

"Why should you? You produced it."

Richard splayed his fingers over the blank video screen on the closed-circuit monitor. "It wasn't supposed to be like this," he said to his reflection. He'd never looked so old.

"Why weren't they all fighting?" he asked aloud. For weeks he'd envisioned this day, and in his dreams he'd seen Mary Grace digging her nails into Alicia and Alicia wanting to annihilate Michelle. Where was the bickering? Where was the screaming and wailing? Why was there no gnashing of teeth?

Even Penelope hadn't put up much of a fight.

What had gone wrong with the world? With *his* world?

His wife and mistresses acted as if they actually *liked* one another! It was ludicrous, but it was true. If he didn't know better, he would say they supported each other.

The craziest thing was that he'd set up his will and the bequests as a joke. He'd intentionally given each one something that was supposed to piss them off. Make them hate him even more. And they acted as if he'd given them the goddamn moon!

What had happened to them?

"They've lost their minds, that's what's happened!"

Richard replayed the scene over and over, and each time he came up with one incredible truth. They didn't need him.

If they needed so little from him now, they probably would have all gotten along without his bequests. Eventually, they each would have made it. Without him.

With the same surety of time passing, the events of that morning clicked off in Richard's mind, forming a tapestry of his life, drawing him a picture of what could have been and what his reality actually was.

He realized that he could have stopped his life at any point and formed a loving relationship with any one of the three women in his life. But he had thought of himself first, last and always, choosing the path to the most dangerous love, selfish love.

The face in the screen stared back at him, promising him a life without his family, without Alicia, without Michelle's naive wisdom, and a world in which he could no longer play with his own company.

Gone was the opportunity to reach even greater heights of fame, the chance to build something meaningful and worthwhile for his community. He could no longer try to win his son's friendship or his daughter's love. Good or bad, they were lost to him forever.

Richard had proven he could do anything with his life, even end it, but he could not resurrect it. The press would annihilate him, and the law would incarcerate him.

Richard could no longer stand the soul-penetrating gaze of his own reflection. He rose and began disassembling the equipment. He'd arranged for two cameras to be placed in Jack's office and one in his outer office. Tonight, when the cleaning crew came in, Richard's accomplice would slip into the office and remove all traces of the surveillance.

Locking the room behind him, he went to the elevators and left the building. He took the back door out of the office building to the alley behind, where a rental car was parked around the corner.

After driving away from the curb, he checked his jacket pocket for his AeroMexico ticket issued to Mark Spencer. Richard Bartlow was dead.

Today, he was a new man. He had no past, but as he looked at his life, Richard realized that his plan had gone awry.

He was worse than dead. He was alive, but he had no future.

Dear Reader,

Dangerous Love was a particularly challenging book to write because the hero was just the kind of man we all love to hate! I know many of you are wondering *why* would Alicia waste her best recipes on him!

Well, those of you who have followed my stories over the years know that I sneak some very good recipes into the writing. Fortunately, for me and you, my wonderful new editors, Dianne Moggy and Amy Moore, think that is a great tradition for us to continue.

So, for those who like to cook, I have copies of "Alicia's Stir Fry" just waiting for you. Please send me a stamped, self-addressed envelope to P.O. Box #110, 5644 West Heimer, Houston, Texas 77056-4002 and I will send it on.

Fondly, Catherine Lanigan

MIRA Books

Proudly presents
the newest novel from

CATHERINE LANIGAN

Elusive Love

For a sneak preview
of this elusive love story
please read on. . . .

Look for *Elusive Love*
in the summer of 1997,
wherever books are sold.

Prologue

The dream was always the same.

It began with Susannah looking out over a charcoal-colored ocean. A thick fog crawled over its surfaced belly making her feel suspended between heaven and earth. As if both pushing and pulling her to this place, a supernatural force supplanted her will with its own. Then, an eerie foreboding emanating from the sea, fog and sand covered her like an invisible cocoon. Flooded with anxiety, she desperately began searching for something—she just didn't know what.

Susannah was six years old when the dream first appeared. That first night she had awakened screaming for her mother. Her mother had reassured her there was nothing to fear and that dreams were not real.

The dream usually reoccurred two or three times a year. Frightened and a bit embarrassed, Susannah never mentioned it again to anyone. She carefully locked the image away in her subconscious and went on with her life.

Not until the week before spring break her freshman year at Indiana University did Susannah Parker allow the dream to alter her plans.

That night the dream changed drastically.

The first part of the dream followed its usual sequence. Frantically she paced the shoreline. Anxiety riddled her mind as she mumbled to herself. "Have I missed the appointment? What will I do if I'm not on time?"

Then she stopped and wondered what exactly it was she was missing.

In all these years she'd never understood the importance of this particular place. Even as a child she'd struggled to unscramble the meaning. It made no sense that she should be standing by an ocean: there was no ocean in Indiana, though Lake Michigan, at the very northern tip of the state, was quite vast. Powerful white-capped waves and strong currents told her this was surely an ocean. But which one?

The same questions she'd asked herself since she was six always plagued her mind. And just as she was at her wits' end, *he* would appear.

He rose from the sea wearing ink blue robes adorned with translucent sapphire and amethyst translucent jewels, seemingly made of water and not fabric. He was majestic and possessed an overwhelming presence. When she was young King Neptune from the fairy tales her mother read to her. But by the time she was seven, she realized he did not carry Neptune's forked scepter or wear a crown.

The fog always masked his face, making it impossible for her to discern his features. She wanted to ask him his name, but she was too awestruck to speak. He did not smile at her, but would beckon her to join him. Terrified that if she walked into the midnight blue sea she would die, Susannah always shook her head in refusal.

Sometimes he would give up his plea, become transformed into seawater and blend into a wave that crashed at her feet. As she grew older, the only change in the dream was that his visits with her lasted longer and longer. Though he never spoke, she could feel his pleas with her heart. As time passed, his urgings became more sincere and were riddled with profound sadness.

In her young mind, Susannah empathized with the sea king. Though he appeared to be made of seawater, shells and golden sand, she believed he was out of place somehow. They were alike that way, she'd realized because she'd always felt she was a misfit.

Susannah's mother, Kate, was from Atlanta and had carried her Southern accent, manners and generosity with her to Indiana when she married Stu Parker, a pharmacist.

Susannah adored her mother's stories about the Old South and the life of gentility that existed before the Civil War. When the family took short trips in the summer, Susannah always begged to go anywhere south of the Mason Dixon line. Walking through antebellum mansions on the banks of the Mississippi transported her back to a time in which she wished she'd been born. More than an affinity for the architecture and the furnishings, she felt a strange familiarity with these homes. The fragrance of night-blooming jasmine, tea roses and camellias blended with hundred-year-old leather-bound books left too long in the humid climate sparked Susannah's imagination. She envisioned herself walking among early spring dogwoods and enormous magnolias, dressed in hooped skirts and straw bonnets. The deeper into the South the family traveled, the more Susannah felt at home. Humid Gulf breezes along the coastline of Alabama and Mississippi filled her mind with visions of turn-of-the-century resort hotels and fabulous carriages. The only way she could bring the South with her back to Indianapolis was by collecting pocketfuls of Gulf Coast sand and seashells. Every time she rearranged her crowded bedroom shelves to add a new sand dollar or dried sea horse, her curiosity about the dream grew.

By the time Susannah was twelve and the dream came to her again, she mustered the courage to ask the sea king which ocean they were standing by. Again, he didn't speak, but when she looked at her feet, drawn in the sand was the word *Atlantic*. In the dream she placed her hand in an oncoming wave and found it was cold as the Atlantic should be. She'd hoped it would be warm like the water long the Gulf Coast of Alabama and Mississippi.

The week before spring break her freshman year at Indiana University, Susannah had planned to stay on campus to get caught up on her research papers. Putting in a few extra hours waiting tables at the Steak Shack would help pay off her Ayers department store bill and her gasoline charge card. Her Alpha Phi sorority sisters had offered a variety of invitations, ranging from a week at Alyson Baker's parents' horse farm in Kentucky, to Charisse Claybourne's vacant Fifth Avenue penthouse while her parents were in Paris, to joining a group of the girls in Daytona Beach and Fort Lauderdale.

Susannah was too practical to blow what little savings she had on what she considered a frivolous trip. She steadfastly refused every lure they cast her way.

Such as her thinking until the Thursday night before everyone left for break. She dreamed about the sea king again.

From the beginning, Susannah knew something was odd. The fog was not as thick as in previous visits. The sea itself was a radiant crystal blue marbled with streaks of the most incredible turquoise green. This time she was not a little girl but nineteen, as she was now. Rising out of the water, the sea king dispelled the remaining fog. A clear-cut royal blue line separated the earth from the sky bringing the landscape into focus.

His straight hair was light sandy brown, which he wore back from his face, revealing a high forehead. His cheeks and jawline were sharply defined, making him seem vulnerable at one moment, yet determined and purposeful the next. He was tall and slender, though his shoulders were wide and his arms were strong. His hips were narrow and the muscles in his lean thighs and calves reminded her of an athlete. To her, he looked as if he could bear the weight of the world while swimming across its oceans.

She waited for him to beckon to her, but this time he did not. Instead, he walked toward her, the waves lapping against his calves. She was surprised that he would leave the sea and venture onto earth with her. For years she'd wondered if he were half man and half fish. Standing next to him, she knew he was all man.

Suddenly fearing him to be a sea monster, she expected his eyes to be fathomless pits, reflecting eternity abyss, and refused to look into them. He waited patiently as she drew up her courage. She was stunned to discover that his eyes were a soft honey brown with golden flecks.

The sea king's eyes were warm and glowing like candlelight, offering refuge. She felt like a wayward child who had been lost for a long time, only to return home and find all the lights in the house burning just for her.

He put out his hand, and she took it. She was amazed to feel real flesh and the rhythmic heartbeat of the pulse point at his wrist.

"I expected you to vanish, like smoke," she said marveling as she smiled at him.

"Never again," he replied with a thick Southern drawl.

She gasped when she realized he *was* the embodiment of her childhood musings about the South, its customs and people.

This is impossible! she thought to herself. *Silly fool, this is only a dream. He's not real. I'm not here, and when I wake up I'll be in my room at school and everything will be normal.*

"You are a silly girl," he said. "Dreams are meant to become real."

He'd read her thought! She wondered if she could read his mind, as well. Just as she was about to ask him another question, he moved closer, putting himself only a breath away. He gazed at her.

"Your eyes are the color of the Caribbean where the blue swirls with green," he said as he placed a very strong arm around her back and pulled her body to his. "Look in my eyes when I take you. Then you will be mine."

Chills blanketed her. *What if his kiss changes me somehow? What if I die from his kiss?* As a child she'd feared he would transform her into a mermaid and she'd never see her family again.

As an adult she was aware of her curiosity urging her to put an end to her questions. She was suddenly willing to throw caution aside.

Maybe he's my guardian angel come to take me to heaven.

"I assure you, I am no angel." He pulled her closer to him. "You must kiss me so that you will know me when we meet."

"When we meet? You're not just a dream?"

"Only for now," he said, moving his lips over hers.

Tenuously, Susannah gave in to the kiss. Had she known that kiss would alter her life, she never would have consented.

Shivers trickled down Susannah's back as he explored her lips. She could feel his passion building as he slanted his mouth over hers again and again. Her skin tingled with millions of tiny electric shocks. Slumbering emotions awakened her heart. Tears burst through creases of her closed eyelids, while joy rang through her soul.

The sea king was breathing life and love into her.

She put her arms around his neck and pressed her breasts into his hard chest. A rush of warmth annihilated the last of her goose bumps, and she felt as if she were melting into him. They were becoming one person, she thought.

"We have always been one," he whispered lovingly.

Slowly, his flesh transmuted to a ghostly persona and Susannah was no longer human, but spirit.

An awe-inspiring love filled Susannah's mind, heart and soul, banishing all her fears. Like the rushing tides of the sea, she was washed clean by a power so strong, yet deeply caring, she felt as if every atom in her body, every cell in her brain had been nourished by his love. She felt an ecstasy she'd never known existed. Her heart overflowed with such deep emotions she realized she could never describe this feeling, this experience to another human being for the rest of her life.

More incredible was that Susannah found the same unconditional love in her own heart for him. Never had she known a human could give love like this.

But Susannah did.

I want this kiss to last for eternity.

Those words had no more than skittered through her head when she realized that the closer she held him, the less she felt the press of his body. She opened her eyes to see him slowly vanishing while still in her embrace.

"Don't leave me!" she pleaded, not fully understanding her frantic sense of urgency.

Susannah had not yet lost anyone close to her. She knew her parents would die someday, hopefully long into the future. She had so much of her life ahead of her, her only thoughts had been focused on her goals and accomplishments. Not once had she ever considered what she could lose.

She tried to touch him, but he was almost vapor. She wanted to tell him that she loved him, but he couldn't hear her.

"I'll leave the earth! I'll stay with you here . . . in the dream. Just don't go!"

Standing alone on the seashore, she felt sadness rise inside her leaving her hollow. She almost hated him for showing her how empty her heart could be. Loneliness clung to her skin as she scanned the horizon one last time.

The fog rolled in, erasing all clarity to the landscape. Enormous tears filled her eyes, making it more difficult to see.

"Why have you done this? Why are you torturing me? All these years you have haunted me, only to abandon me! Come back! Please, come back!"

Susannah awoke to find herself staring at the ceiling. She was holding her breath as hot tears rolled down her cheeks and wet her pillow. She touched the hair at her temple and found it soaking wet. She'd been crying for quite some time.

The light from the full moon illuminated the glistening tear on the pad of her finger. *I don't understand any of this.*

She heard the echoes of her roommate Marilou's voice as she urged her to go with all of their friends to Fort Lauderdale.

"We'll have a blast, Susannah. You can't stay stuck behind a book all your life. That's not living! You've gotta go!"

Suddenly Susannah knew. The sea king was there. She had to go with Marilou and the others.

It was a crazy notion, but her parents had always told her that nothing in the world was impossible, if only she believed.

If dreams were meant to come true, then maybe, just maybe, the sea king would come back to her.

National Bestselling Author

JOANN ROSS

Welcomes you to Raintree, Georgia—
steamy capital of sin, scandal and murder.

Southern Comforts

Chelsea Cassidy is the official biographer of
Roxanne Scarbrough—the Southern Queen of good
taste who's built an empire around the how-to's of
gracious living. It's clear to Chelsea that somebody
wants her employer dead.

As Chelsea explores the dark secrets of Roxanne's
life, the search leads Chelsea into the arms of
Cash Beaudine. And now her investigating becomes
personal with potentially fatal consequences.

Available this September wherever books are sold.

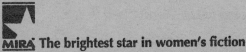

A woman with a shocking secret.
A man without a past.
Together, their love could be nothing less than

Scandalous

The latest romantic adventure from

CANDACE CAMP

When a stranger suffering a loss of memory lands on
Priscilla Hamilton's doorstep, her carefully guarded secret
is threatened. Always a model of propriety, she knows that
no one would believe the deep, dark desire that burns
inside her at this stranger's touch.

As scandal and intrigue slowly close in on the lovers, will
their attraction be strong enough to survive?

Find out this September at your favorite retail outlet.

MIRA The brightest star in women's fiction   MCCSC

Look us up on-line at:http://www.romance.net